THE DEVIL IS A SOUTHPAW

ALSO BY BRANDON HOBSON

The Storyteller

The Removed

Where the Dead Sit Talking

Desolation Avenues Untold

Deep Ellum

THE DEVIL IS A SOUTH PAW

A NOVEL

BRANDON HOBSON

ecco
An Imprint of HarperCollins*Publishers*

Without limiting the exclusive rights of any author, contributor or the publisher of this publication, any unauthorized use of this publication to train generative artificial intelligence (AI) technologies is expressly prohibited. HarperCollins also exercise their rights under Article 4(3) of the Digital Single Market Directive 2019/790 and expressly reserve this publication from the text and data mining exception.

This is a work of fiction. Names, characters, places, and incidents are products of the author's imagination or are used fictitiously and are not to be construed as real. Any resemblance to actual events, locales, organizations, or persons, living or dead, is entirely coincidental.

THE DEVIL IS A SOUTHPAW. Copyright © 2025 by Brandon Hobson. All rights reserved. Printed in the United States of America. No part of this book may be used or reproduced in any manner whatsoever without written permission except in the case of brief quotations embodied in critical articles and reviews. For information, address HarperCollins Publishers, 195 Broadway, New York, NY 10007. In Europe, HarperCollins Publishers, Macken House, 39/40 Mayor Street Upper, Dublin 1, D01 C9W8, Ireland.

HarperCollins books may be purchased for educational, business, or sales promotional use. For information, please email the Special Markets Department at SPsales@harpercollins.com. hc.com

Excerpts from this novel appeared in *McSweeney's*, *Conjunctions*, and *Southwest Review*.

Ecco® and HarperCollins® are trademarks of HarperCollins Publishers.

FIRST EDITION

Designed by Alison Bloomer
Art by Brandon Hobson

Library of Congress Cataloging-in-Publication Data has been applied for.

ISBN 978-0-06-325965-2

25 26 27 28 29 LBC 5 4 3 2 1

> Envy is insatiable. The more you concede to it the more it will demand.
> —C. S. LEWIS

> Perhaps to lose a sense of where you are implies the danger of losing a sense of who you are.
> —RALPH ELLISON, *INVISIBLE MAN*

CONTENTS

FOREWORD	1
I	3
1. THE TRAGIC DEATH OF MATTHEW ECHOTA	5
2. SHADOW OF A GREAT ROCK	22
3. OLD DUBLAN	31
4. TOPHET COUNTY DETENTION	38
5. SOLITUDE AND CONFINEMENT	56
6. CASSIE MAGDAL SEES THE DEVIL	68
7. ACROSTIC FOR CASSIE	75
8. SUFFERING	76
9. A PLAGUE OF FROGS	85
10. STRANGELOVE	100
11. LETTER TO RESIDENTS	108
12. WOULD I YES TO SAY YES MY MOUNTAIN FLOWER	114
13. ACROSTIC OF A SCHOOL SHOOTING	131
14. LETTER TO PARENTS	136
15. LETTER FROM MOTHER	142
16. S.O.Y.C.D.	145
17. WHERE WOUNDS OF DEADLY HATE HAVE PIERCED	151
18. PRIDE, THE DEVIL'S SIN: AN INTERLUDE	168
19. THE SICKNESS	174
20. A DIZZYING DESCENT INTO THE HYPOGEUM	183
21. ESCAPE	193

II	231
1. THE LAST INTERVIEW	233
III	239
1. THE CONFESSIONS: AGAINST A SEA OF TROUBLES	241
2. SAINT MATTHEW AND THE FOOL	251

　　1. (In Which My Twin Brother and I, Longing for Attention, Pretend to Be Conjoined Twins from the Underground City)
　　2. (In Which the Fool Describes Hallucinations, Gets Bullied, and Suffers Horrific Nightmares)
　　3. (In Which the Fool Has a Snowball Fight with Matthew and Visits His House)
　　4. (In Which the Fool Reads Shakespeare and Matthew Runs Away)
　　5. (In Which the Fool and Matthew Get Locked in the Basement)
　　6. (In Which We Begin Writing Poems and Contemplate the Value of Art)
　　7. (In Which I See the Imitations)
　　8. (In Which the Fool Struggles to Understand the Meaning of Love)
　　9. (In Which Walt's Suicide Reveals a Secret)
　　　　(a) Leeches and the Wolf
　　　　(b) Fear
　　　　(c) Aftermath
　　10. (Humility)

3. THE VISION	326
ACKNOWLEDGMENTS	341

FOREWORD

Recently I received, via air mail, a manuscript titled *The Devil Is a Southpaw*, written by someone who was institutionalized with me in the Tophet County juvenile facility in 1988. I still have nightmares about our experience being locked up, even after all these years. The last time I heard from Milton Muleborn, he was living in a yurt in the woods to research and write, he claimed, a book about a blind saint surviving a bleak midwinter. It's been a long time since I heard from him. Every so often he would send a postcard or email, telling me about his travels and his writings and asking whether I'm writing reviews of marijuana dispensaries under the pseudonym Sanbo Hornbond and still keeping to myself out here in the desert with the birds and the spirits and the donkeys.

I'll say this: Milton was always super perfervid about his subject, Matthew Echota. Better known by his initials, M.E., a childhood rival, fellow artist. A boy whose artistic talent tortured Muleborn and riddled him with pride and envy throughout his life. The manuscript that follows is a bit of a detective story. Milton refers to himself as a fool, but a fool he is not. Acute readers may notice the title of Part 3 is aptly named to mirror Saint Augustine's famous *Confessions*, a book Muleborn quoted from, even as a kid. In Tophet County so many years ago, when he wasn't being physically restrained due to making hateful attacks against other residents or staff, the damn fool forced me to talk about his obsession with Pink Floyd. After reading his book, I see now that this book eerily follows the structure of "Shine on You Crazy Diamond."

What I remember most about Milton is that he always scribbled in a notebook like a maniac, as evidenced by his wild and bullyish prose, but he also took time to teach me a prayer in Latin and another in Aramaic. I find it necessary—even crucial—to mention that he talked often about the importance of forgiveness.

Peace be with him.

—BRANDON H.

PART I
THE DEVIL IS A SOUTHPAW
A NOVEL BY MILTON MULEBORN

"Do not be fooled by Dublan's shackles,
Or else be eaten by pigs and grackles."
—AGATHA KLEMM, *SUFFERING AND THE SOUL* (1962)

1. THE TRAGIC DEATH OF MATTHEW ECHOTA

I n the spring of 1988, on a Sunday night in our last days at Tophet County Juvenile Correctional Facility, the dogs escaped out of the courtyard by chewing apart the bottom of the fence's rotted wood and then crawling underneath it, and at sunrise on Monday morning when the alarm rang throughout the buildings, the guards discovered that Matthew had disappeared, too.

Only then were the rest of us allowed to search deep into the woods without using butcher knives to cut through the thick brush and twigs, as the drill sergeants had proposed, and without a Thermos of water or fruit to keep us hydrated, as the cooks had suggested, because all we really needed was one another. The guards and staff and drill sergeants, who weren't concerned with finding the dogs, claimed they would call the police and began searching in the more open areas down the hill from the grounds, but they sent us, for whatever reason, into the dark woods. We weren't afraid of finding snakes or even murderers, not after all the physical labor and punishments we had endured over the past year, and going into the trees was like entering the thin, cool atmosphere of a land we had heard only from fairy tales read aloud to us, because the air was calm with a brooding tranquility, and the susurration and sighing of the trees gave us an immediate sense of repose, and certainly we were silent, not even clearing our throats or gasping in all our anxieties and fear as we trudged slowly through the boggy wet leaves, past dimbles, scrogs, and shrubbery, and into the slanted streams of morning sunlight. All across the narrow paths that curved around trees, where the worms and insects crawled in the dirt that held the tracks of deer and snakes, we heard the sound of footsteps from the little people we assumed were spirits running away from us, those little tricksters, and though we never caught a glimpse of them, we did manage to descry a deranged vulture ahead of us pecking at the ground, eating the last gobbet of a dead carcass. Nora, Matthew's sister, worried the vulture was chewing on her brother's body; however, we saw fur and a snout and realized the vulture was, in fact, eating a dead animal, not a human being. Nonetheless, we turned and headed down a different path in an abyss of silence to a berth where we could get a grip of our surroundings and try to keep all the stress and rigors of the deep country, those primeval boondocks, intact.

Matthew had run away once before. The first time the guards found him had been at the beginning of the winter, when frost covered the grass and icicles hung from tree branches after a recent ice storm, and still he walked away without even trying to hide as if he knew he was predestined to be caught and punished, which was inevitable in that dull, sleepy town called Old Dublan, where most of us were born and raised. When they brought him back, he told them that he simply needed to go for a walk to clear the bad thoughts from his head and adjust to the new thinking of the everyday people, that's what he told them, that his mind was an enervating dissolution of severe anxiety and vulnerability prime for brainwashing. We were always a little uncertain as to whether Matthew was brilliant or a smidge eccentric, possibly even crazy, but we admired his courage. In his earlier punishments, for instance, he had avoided so many food restrictions, beatings, and deprivations, that it seemed almost sententious of him to prefer the long confinement of the Columbus House basement. Yet, as the days passed and the rest of us continued chopping wood and pulling weeds and loading piles of damn dirt in wheelbarrows, even the most impervious among us waited until we were back in the facility at night to share our predictions, such as that Matthew would emerge from confinement unable to speak, that his mind would become so disoriented from the isolation that he would no longer be able to recognize us, and that he would die down there by suicide. Only minutes after he was set free from the basement, the look on his face told us he was fine, that he had, in fact, preferred the confinement because he was able to find the books he had hidden behind a pile of wooden shelves when he was supposed to be sweeping and cleaning in there some time before. Confinement became a spiritual awakening for him as well because he grew closer to God, and soon he was listening to the laughter of angels and the distant laments of his ancestors that encouraged him to be strong in faith and not project his anger onto the everyday men whose foolish words and actions were cruel, and also that he speak very little and listen closely, which was why it was so difficult to get him to talk about those nights of punishment and solitude. Even the most incredulous of us listened to him describe the visions of fleeting stars that were enchanting enough to swoon the most beautiful people on this poor Earth.

Previously, during the extra free time on certain Christian holidays or on weekends, Matthew would shut himself in his room and read, write, and draw as much as he could, later telling us he actually missed that about our public school, reading and writing stories and taking art class, so certainly he devoured an immoderate number of books, reading them as often as he could and staying up late thinking about them, knowing he would be so tired the next day that his muscles would ache, yet he still stayed up late sketching faces and bodies and writing stories and poems in his journal with a pencil he had stolen and kept hidden. No one paid much attention to his journal until Nora told us he was writing about his own death in the future, and that he had, at the age of seven, predicted the exact date and manner of death of their paternal grandfather, whose throat was slashed by an intruder. His grandfather died face down with his left arm under his head as a pillow, three years after Matthew's documented prediction. Matthew made other predictions listing the specific dates of world events that included bombings, mass shootings in the U.S., and a horrific deluge that killed over ten thousand people and wiped out an entire town—all proof, Nora told us, that Matthew held the crucial and compulsory predictions for what was to come for the facility, for the guards and drill sergeants who made our lives miserable, and for all of us. Yet, when we asked Matthew about these predictions, he had only written a story and all the events that passed were coincidental, but those of us who knew him understood he wasn't being truthful, he invariably displayed peculiar behavior after the lights were out, some would see him with his ear placed to a window in the hall as if he were listening for something outside, others would say he wrote stories in his sleep, but nobody was ever certain who was lying and who was telling the truth despite how much we trusted one another and everything we had been through together, all the daily work and harsh punishment we had endured. Some said he preferred rewriting the fairy tales we had all heard as children.

We felt like we were in some flexuous jungle from one of the Indiana Jones films. Certainly, our journey could've been deadly, we feared, yet there was something alluring about existing in the fantasy that we were on the search for a stolen, priceless artifact. (I believe the best movies involve a search in the face of death, as in many of the James Bond films.) The path we took in the woods twisted around trees until we got lost, and for three hours we continued aprowl, calling his name, listening for anything we could, and despite the frustrations we pushed on until we noticed ahead a shadowy figure. The woods were filled with the little people who lived there who captured children and ate them, so we turned down a different path. Back in the courtyard, behind the hedges where Matthew had passed out from anxiety on the same day some of us were beaten for stealing the green apples from the apple tree, were hidden the dead baby rats we kept for future revenge on our perpetrators once we figured out how to make the stench most effective. Maybe Matthew was out here dead, too, we thought. The air was now asphyxiating as we stared at the figure before us, unafraid, before heading down a different path among the pale brush where cobwebs stretched from branch to branch and where moths fluttered around our feet. Insects buzzed around us.

In recent months, when Sergeant Cash fell absent to visit a sick family member three counties away, we were told to take a break from our shoveling duties and instead spend the days sweeping, cleaning, and checking the facility greenhouse for the yellow jacket nest the drill sergeants said was in there somewhere due to the sudden appearance of yellow jackets, and those who dared to crawl on their knees to check around the bottoms of the polycarbonate panels among so much shrubbery were stung more than once; just imagine crawling in such a space and getting attacked by yellow jackets, which then buzzed around us because yellow jackets are so aggressive. We had endured enough misery and threat not to be afraid of the little people in the woods. We took the path without looking back to see whether the little person was following us, arriving soon enough at a gigantic black velvet curtain hanging nearly twenty feet high. We all wondered why: What was a black curtain doing hanging in the middle of the woods out here in rural Oklahoma? Then we heard frightened cries from people on the other side of the curtain, and we stood still for a few minutes contemplating whether we should turn and run back or else stay and look behind the curtain, and finally when we peeked around the corner of it we noticed the naked bodies of lepers whose faces were indistinguishable from their disease, those poor, suffering people, begging to lick the salt from our hands and necks, pleading for the salt to bring them healing and life everlasting, but we didn't fall for their tricks because there were so many grim stories about the evil in the woods out there that we all knew and recognized, so we backed away from the lepers. "My brother used to talk about his nightmares of the moaning lepers," Nora told us. "I remember the mourning souls of the dead who cried out to him. There was a forest filled with poisoned fruit and blood-sucking ticks, remember, you remember he had seen and described them. Isn't that weird how he knew we would see them?"

We told her, Yes, yes, yes, Nora, we remember his nightmare, of course we do, he told us all his nightmares and dreams and everything else, Nora. Those unprecedented decisions to speak out loud about what was going to happen to us, and how he remained so serene telling those of us, indifferent, with the slow inflection his father had infused in him due to his speech impediment, a stutter, so that he would blur the linear identity those people assumed we all possessed, because speaking costively and with such inflexible decorum was significantly different than the rest of us spoke, which was to say we rarely talked and whenever we did we tended to mumble or talk as little as possible, but the hope was that Matthew could communicate better with them and could drive the furious curse out of the everyday men who bore the insults and hatred and contemplated the beatings and punishments with the sick ardor of their ancestors, these men not even blinking, spitting tobacco, thinking they could rip away any culture, thought, and beliefs in order to brainwash us, so yes, Nora, we remembered the nightmare Matthew had because we had them, too. There were nightmares we hoped we never encountered such as the killings and stabbings by these men wearing masks to hide their identity and the protection they received from the police and government to keep us against our will and torture us until we either were eradicated from our identities or else we died, so we all shared the same nightmares, Nora, the difference is that Little Matthew's has already happened and ours are still out there waiting to unfold.

Other than Nora, the people who commented on Matthew's extraordinary profundity were two hydrocephalic male guards with crew cuts who resembled inbred peccaries (think of the two terrifying men from *Deliverance*, a movie that remains in my top ten comedic films). The guards noticed Matthew sitting in a wicker chair in the first floor's living room enduring the drowsiness of a postlabor afternoon, after he had removed the worn shoes they had given him that were at least one size too small for his feet, his pants rolled up and his socks stained with dark red blood from scabs, when the girls were standing outside the window waving at him for his attention (Nora said they thought him the most handsome of us, which was absolutely not true, at least from this fool's perspective), and with great celerity he would flutter his hand like a bird, and the girls outside were all smiling while the guards took mental notes of everything miraculous, including, for instance, how the church bells in the cathedral would start ringing whenever he stuttered, "ch-ch-church bells," which gave sheer pleasure to those of us toiling away, especially during hot days when Cash and the other damn towsers yammered on about how slowly we were working.

THE DEVIL IS A SOUTHPAW

Sometimes Matthew blinked quickly when someone spoke directly to him, which gave the impression that he had the manner of someone deep in social anxiety, but truthfully, he was tormented by the idea that people talked about him at all. Copious attempts made to settle the rumors that he would be taken away from us and used for the benefit of the drill sergeants were useless; they discussed using him for financial and personal gain among themselves, which some of the girls overheard when they were mopping the administration building's third-floor hallway and were caught listening and later subjected to punishments denying them meals for an entire day, but the tendentious guards and drill sergeants who were in that meeting claimed it wasn't even discussed, that instead of talking about Matthew's prodigious abilities they deliberated for three or four hours over how some of us would have to dig three separate graves all the way out at the cemetery due to the recent deaths of the three brothers who passed away from malnutrition; all three brothers died within hours of one another, and they were also some of the angriest and most rebellious of us, Spider and Brandon and Edgar, and as a result of their anger they were also the most severely punished, of course, how sad to think back on this, how we could hear their cries at night coming from their rooms, how we saw the broomsticks and all the bruises and blood in the toilet, and how the guards and pigs were faced with the debilitating problem of who was going to dig the three graves, and furthermore, how were they going to transport us out to the cemetery when we were all such flight risks, hell yes this was what they said they discussed for so long in the meeting, not Matthew, and they had the minutes in writing to prove it. Although he didn't know of the rumors, Matthew told us he was certain something significant was about to happen in his life and that he would not be locked up for much longer, that sitting for long periods of time in the wicker chair helped him visualize this fatidic thought, which he described as looking like the slow development of a chess game, and he needed to understand how each decision affected the next, a game he had learned to play from his grandfather only months before his grandfather passed away, and even then, at the age of seven, he understood there was an implication the game held him acutely susceptible to comprehending how much each decision affected the next, and how after he checkmated his grandfather he rushed into the bathroom and vomited, the crisis of a potential blame developing that his grandfather's loss contributed to his death six months later and so rendered his glory bitter, and for the next seven years he took advantage of his solitude to reflect on that game and how each move represented a step leading toward death.

Following a winding path against a sea of troubles, we managed to see through the slanted stream of sunlight the three brothers, Spider and Brandon and Edgar, sleeping in the branches with their arms hanging down, and when we called out to them, they opened their eyes and glared down at us, shaking the tree limbs so that leaves and twigs fell, laughing like devils, and then they climbed down and said, "Do not follow the path because it leads to evil things."

Waving away the flying ants, Nora asked, "How do you know?"

They told us to sit and listen, so we sat down in the dirt and they told us about the children who ran away from home and were mutilated to pieces and eaten by the little people who roamed the woods; they tore into the children and ate them alive, each prowling out from behind the trees and pouncing on the children before any of them even had a chance to run or help one another, and the three brothers said, "Listen to us, we speak the truth to you, beware of these little people and the moaning lepers begging to lick the salt from your hands, and instead follow us because you know us, look at us, you recognize our faces," and then all three brothers lowered their heads to avoid looking directly at us. We abandoned ourselves to their story, trembling with the rage of knowing how the others before us had died, but we were wiser and more solicitous than they suspected because we quickly realized these three were actually tricksters veiled in the illusory cloak of Spider and Brandon and Edgar, and Nora was the first to lash out at them and call them liars, we won't fall for your tricks; she told them, "If you think you can fool us you're wrong—we can find him without any help."

We decided to keep walking and not talk to anyone else. The distractions were meant to throw us off course, but the bigger question that still loomed was whether Matthew was even alive, and if so, was he hiding in those woods? It was all a mystery to us, and we could see that the sunlight had shifted in the trees and was now jagged all around us, and Nora was staring into the shards of light when she told us that Matthew believed the less people understood about him the less afraid they would be, which was why he remained so elusive, quiet, and removed from everyone, and why he wrote in his journal about staring out the foggy window of his room where one night he swore he saw arrive in front of the detention building a horse and carriage with the hooded image of Death driving, which he'd read about from the famous Emily Dickinson poem, something that frightened him particularly when he spotted the figure of Death leaning forward from the carriage to look up at the building, as if looking directly at him sitting by the window, but the night was cold with a light mist falling, and the gray horses shook their manes, and Death stepped out of the carriage and started walking—Matthew had described the figure to Nora as a "shadowy thing with a limp"—but at that moment Matthew pulled the window curtain closed and spent the remainder of the night sitting cross-legged on his bed with the light on and the door locked. He wrote in his journal then, describing what he had seen, worried for not only his own life but for the lives of everyone at the detention center, because children had already died (the three brothers, for example) and now Death was back for more.

Nora told us this very matter-of-factly, noting that she had read the journal entry, unlike the rest of us, on one of the days he was serving his punishment in the Columbus House basement, and that he also spotted gorged vultures and ghosts hanging in the moonlit sky, dogs spooring around in the garbage bins behind the cafeteria where the stench of dead animals hung in the air, the shadows of the sergeants in the windows of their building, where they cast evil spells in the middle of the night, and the nimbuses of the dead moving from one building to the next and smelling like their rotting bodies which lay in putrefaction down in the graves we all had dug. "Is he alive?" Nora asked us, in hysterics, as if the thought suddenly hit her, "what if he's dead like the others?" Maybe we were all dying slowly, one by one, our minds corrupted and brainwashed, our bodies poisoned. Whole nations are disappearing, we thought, they're slowly killing us, driving us into extinction and torturing us before we die. Nora was breathing with difficulty in the thin air, feeling herself lean into her friend, until she was able to calm down as we all comforted her, telling her we understood how frightened she must be because we were frightened, too, that we were all in this together no matter what happened, and soon enough Nora was able to continue with us as we walked down the path for a ways, though too quickly a figure up ahead of us appeared who was standing beside a tree. We recognized the figure was Sergeant Ambrose, broad-shouldered and hands authoritatively on his hips, shouting for us to "keep looking for Matthew," and when we told him we *were* looking, he stomped his foot and rattled on about the importance of the will to live, "Strength is mental and physical," he said, citing examples from names we'd never heard of and didn't care about anyway, and then he spewed on and on about how little we'd learned and changed from the months we'd been there.

 Sergeant Ambrose was as iniquitous as Sergeants Jackson and Lee, talking so much they often lost track of what they were saying, staring cataleptically into the distance, the type of ascendancies who liked to hear their own bombastic voices and orders, like the U.S. Marine sergeant from the movie *Full Metal Jacket* (a film I saw only once, enough to keep me from signing up for the military). Those fools demanded that for us to eschew any punishments we speak more fluently than we did when we had first arrived—by nature most of us were way more introverted than they ever suspected—and they required that the boys speak in full complete sentences, speak the hell up, spit it out, they'd say this among other things, such as look a man in the eye and shake his hand like this, firmer grip, say yessir, stand up straight without slouching like you're a defeated knucklehead so that people won't think you're a withered churl, tie your boots so that the laces are nice and tight like this, no like this, look at me, fools, and here's the proper way to grip a shovel and dig so that your back muscles don't strain or injure, do it right or else, hold a knife and fork like this, cut your meat like this, chew with your mouth closed, try not to look savage and maintain eye contact in a way that's acerbic but not overly threatening, you dogs, look at people in the eye when you talk to them without having to fiddle with your hands when you're talking to any doyen in dominance and control, runts, because your sanction means giving respect, and you'll need to learn to give it and show it to higher ranks in control here, you sons of bitches. Besides all that, those haughty bastards drank whiskey from flasks when they thought we weren't paying attention, you could smell it on their breath, you could catch them stopping in the stairwells to take a swig or stepping into a bathroom stall and locking the door, meanwhile the rest of us suffered from the nauseating heat and were permitted to drink only warm water from a garden hose until lunch. We knew the only reason they let us take our time and eat and replenish fluids to hydrate was an imprecation so that we could march right back out there into the sweltering sun and keep toiling throughout the afternoon.

The rules were strict. Boys weren't allowed to be too close to the women staff, who were way friendlier than the drill sergeants. Part of their agenda was to try to integrate us into everyday society by informing us on trades in mechanics, plumbing, or custodial skills so that we could earn a living wage, this was what they told us, because they said we wouldn't afford college or be able to make it in an academic environment, and that we should consider a career in the military once we turned eighteen. Some of us craved writing, painting and drawing, learning music and history, and reading books and talking about them, which was one of the reasons Matthew once told the sergeants that he would rather be a teacher than an artisan of manual labor, and Sergeant Lee grimaced, so we read and wrote by ourselves.

Sergeant Ambrose stomped his foot and yammered at us to keep moving and looking, telling us his face and neck were flushed as pink as the time he discovered the news of the hurricane that brought so much rain it swallowed the land and drowned the army base where he was stationed during the energy crisis back when the Iranian revolution raised the price of oil, damnit, and hearing such execrable news straight from the president's mouth had flushed Ambrose's face so pink it brought tears to his eyes, which Nora said was sad for about six seconds until he turned and told her that no one would ever understand the circumstances of his suffering and that the savages surrounding him were like an invasion of some strange cloud of pestilential vapor slowly destroying him, he called us "wild" directly to Nora's face, and she stepped into the shadows of the Columbus House hallway full of so much sorrow and rage that she wanted to sneak up on him the next time he was lying on that hammock behind their quarters and strangle him while he napped, that's how angry Nora said she was—and who could blame her? We sensed his presence along with the other sergeants anytime we were outside by the apple tree in the courtyard, where we would sometimes congregate after sneaking out to compare blisters on our hands or bruises so that we could make sure to have the details correct for any proper authorities if we ever made it out of that place. Beside that apple tree was also where we were standing when we first noticed the large Doberman with bloodshot eyes staring at us from across the road at the edge of the woods, and none of us moved or breathed, but then we heard Sergeant Ambrose step out of the barracks and yell, "YONDER SHINES THE BIG RED MOON OVER THE DEVIL'S LOST PLAYGROUND!" with his arms raised as he stood barefoot and without a shirt looking up to the sky, and the black dog turned and ran into the woods; we knelt down as Sergeant Ambrose stretched and smoked a cigarette before he went back inside. Whether he knew the black dog was there or not wasn't as important as what he yelled, "YONDER SHINES THE BIG RED MOON OVER THE DEVIL'S LOST PLAYGROUND!" and why he shouted it, whether it meant anything or whether those shouts reflected his own bout of insanity.

We wondered how so much dominance and power delegated to each of the sergeants might not have been the cause of their misfortune, if it wasn't Sergeant Ambrose who would go crazy first, then it would be Jackson, or Lee, because at night they each had their own eccentric rituals: Cole often stepped outside between two and four in the morning, heavily sedated on pain pills, wearing camouflage shorts and black military boots and practiced marching with a limp, which was peculiar because he never walked with a limp, but there he was every night, limping back and forth in front of the barracks; Sergeant Jackson woke before the morning bell, usually at sunrise, and ran up and down the stairs in front of the building, then did fifty push-ups, twenty-five jumping jacks, ten knee bends, and several shoulder rotations before heading back inside; Sergeant Lee sat on the steps at night and played the fiddle until the songs he sang brought him to tears and crying out various prayers of hope for a woman named Cleva; and we learned Sergeant Ambrose stepped outside to shout, "YONDER SHINES THE BIG RED MOON OVER THE DEVIL'S LOST PLAYGROUND!" any time there was a full moon, even if it wasn't red.

What had the strongest impact on us regarding Sergeant Ambrose in the woods was realizing after we walked away that it might not have been Sergeant Ambrose at all, but another trickster trying to lure us into some unknown hole in the ground, a thought that terrified us until Nora reminded us we were there to find Matthew, "Remember, he's missing and we have to find him, forget the tricksters," so we squelched down a path in the woods until we heard the rushing water of the tributary that flowed into the Gudgekin River miles away.

We followed the trail toward the sound of water, a walk that took forever, and we could see the clearing at the end of the woods, which none of us even whispered about because we knew we were about to emerge into new territory. Birds scattered as we moved slowly out of the woods and edged down a declivity into the sleech where we regarded everything we had feared from Matthew's prophetic stories: the devil's lost playground full of the bones of dead children, a bubbling stream, and beside it, Matthew's body face down, one arm spread out and the other by his side, silent as the dead, and Nora screamed as Matthew's life passed directly in front of us, steam coming off the water like braids of smoke, birds flying all around.

2. SHADOW OF A GREAT ROCK

His full name was Matthew Echota, a cripplingly shy, talented, smart, and handsome boy, although many poked fun at him for being short, the poor soul, trailing along like a rabbit trying to keep up—little Matthew dodging around, chasing squirrels and groundhogs, confirming everything we'd heard throughout those elementary-school years: that he and his family captured rabbits and birds and ate them with their bare hands. We heard lots of things: that his grandfather developed trachoma and became blind, which led to his suicide; that his (brief) girlfriend, Cassie Magdal, had so dazzled both an Episcopalian priest and a Baptist minister with her genius knowledge of theology, biblical passages and interpretations, as well as her talent for playing the piano like a prodigy since the age of six, that each one of them fell into an irrepressible obsession with trying to be as smart and talented as her, and that they scourged each other and gouged their eyes out and became blind, too. We also heard rumors that the house that Matthew lived in near the train tracks held the ghosts of diseased men with afflicted faces and animals deadened by the heat from the family's bonfires; that fireflies batted violently against their windows and worms crawled along the windows' corners so that even the slightest wisp of clean country air would not creep into the cracks, and the chickens pecked around in the yard, and the mangy dogs slept on the porch, and the ridiculous goats gnawed on the wire fence like the town's sinful drunks; and that, for a few years, Matthew's mother's hair was so long that she wasn't able to leave her house because her hair dragged along the floor and mice had built nests there. Call them rumors, inscrutabilities, whatever, but our Matthew's lack of response to such stories only made him more irreproachable.

Some of us were artists, too, even though our teachers had a special affinity for his work ethic and gentle demeanor, I mean, of course they labeled him highly intelligent and creative as opposed to the way they viewed the rest of us, sinners that we were, 99.5 percent of the time showing Matthew favoritism by using his work as an example in class of how to draw a tree with crooked branches, or how to paint a sunset, or, most frustrating, how to write a good, compound-complex sentence (we already knew how, of course). Because he kept to himself and avoided eye contact, whenever Matthew looked at you, he had the desolate eyes of a sleepwalker in the shadows deciding the fate of the world, with an aura of premonitory silence and antagonism and a stare, as if controlled by the cycles of the universe, that made the room feel darker; or maybe it was the way he hesitated in broad daylight whenever he contemplated your motives, listening as if startled by something you said, focused on some unmistakable act of vivacity that was unique to you. Look at his drawings, mostly charcoal portraits of the less fortunate—beggars, addicts, the homeless, etc.—and his writing was composed with the intensity of an eclipse, as his younger sister, Nora, put it—breathing through his mouth, squinting in his glasses, writing under the fleeting stars at night, or scribbling poetry on his arm or on the palm of his hand, and we were so very jealous because of his inexplicable artistic talent and the favoritism he'd received in school from teachers who loved his poems and stories (despite their laconic, annoying, grotesque giddiness), because he loved Leslie Marmon Silko and Toni Morrison as opposed to, say, James Joyce or Ernest Hemingway (some of us challenged one another as to who could write the longest, most complicated but clear sentence, full of beauty, risk, and vigor, or who could draw the best eagle or rabid dog, but Matthew was never interested in such competitions). He dressed less eccentrically than any of the Indians no matter what their tribe was, I mean, his style was neither anachronistic nor modern, adhering strictly to a dress code like the poor, unfortunate, because most of the time he wore black jeans and a T-shirt, nothing special whatsoever, I mean, he was never interested in things like fashion and especially general grooming because his habits were atrocious, of course, since his hair was long and unmoussed or gelled, often unkempt, and those who knew him best said he was disinterested in belt buckles or leather vests, turtleneck sweaters, designer sunglasses, cowboy boots, or listening to metal rock or goth New Wave that made the rest of us feel tormented and uneasy, even angry, serious as we were about our choice of music on the school bus or outside on the boom box during lunch. One could never notice the oxycephalic skull due to his roundish face, but rather the way his eyes squinted whenever he smiled as he talked with his friends at school was delightful, because he was beautiful, and we often wondered what he was laughing about, and the rest of us found ourselves made miserable by his abstruse demeanor around others at school; we rarely heard him speak. Many thought he was complicated and tricky because he would be in the hallway one minute and outside the next, interrupting a game of kickball or Red Rover, as if he'd walked right through the walls. He was indeed a handsome devil who told people he needed a legitimate meditation partner. He kept his jeans rolled up at a time when nobody else did. He was condemned, he said, to die of love.

Of course, boys and young ladies found him adorable. (Of course, Cassie Magdal did.)

Lots of boys wanted to be like him, to be accepted, given attention, admired and loved by teachers, but the rest of us were looked down upon. We lifted him up to icon status, a type of worship, wishing he was not among us in the classroom with his beauty and gifts, wishing he was somewhere else, invisible, because he was entirely himself with a confidence unlike anyone else, although we thought that this was a sign that he would burn out too early, that the teachers had imposed upon him a penance of success for Old Dublan that would lose all its appanage, his prowess had peaked and that he would be left as a struggling prodigy with nothing but bread to eat and tap water to drink, and some of us thought, Isn't God incontrovertibly clever to allow the rest of us to thrive after Matthew floundered so that our own fame would come? O' Father, fame would arrive so that smart readers and literary critics recognized our boy was not to be taken too seriously in his youth and that we would be read in the most intimate libraries and universities like true gifted mature novelists, that the inclemency of power remained in the consciousness of critics who took photographs of us reclined in easy chairs and beside swimming pools, while our texts were bound in human skin and enclosed in glass cases.

We knew early on that he possessed what we wanted, even if his mother put his glasses on him first thing in the morning, or read him Anacreontic verse while she trained him in adages written in modern English as they relaxed in the sultriness of low clouds on warm afternoons, or when she sat with him upstairs at the public library longer than any son had ever dreamed of on the face of the Earth, training him with the apodictic determination of a mother whose love for her son was inexhaustible, a fierce and immortal influence, an irresolvable love none of the rest of us had received or could even comprehend. It wasn't fair. While he received this attention, we brought him mercilessly closer to us by looking at him as if he were like the Old Dublan hunters, ruthlessly shooting quail and hungry deer with frightened eyes, the instantaneous signs of someone whose expressions were ungraspable and filled with terror; our boy was facing the impassive horrors of listening to his girlfriend, who wore a promise bracelet and accused him of loving his art more than he loved her, an immature and immoderate romance, wasn't it, our boy afraid of the beautiful Cassie Magdal, who brought him homemade beef jerky in his backyard despite the fact that we had dumped piles of mud and slime back there, and yet he told her (I spied on them whenever possible since I figured he might start lies, and I wanted to be there to defend myself) that he could hear the sparrows and cardinals and other birds singing on starry nights in that exact spot, that's what he told her, and that he had written a poem in which a pretty girl brought a popsicle to a boy in a garden somewhere far away among the fragrance of lilies where souls wandered without rule or law, a beautiful spirit world, where everyone recovered the strength to live and where nobody urinated or bled or shat, where houses were made of glass, colors were as blue as the deepest sky, and windows opened to the endless sea.

He knew he was needed, of course, he really understood that Cassie, his mother and family, and the teachers whose admiration for him was like the anxious barking of unneutered stray dogs—they all needed him. Insensitive to the attention of anyone else besides Matthew, they never gave equal attention to us or listened to the timid requests of those of us who had no opportunities or contact with the rest of the world, more solicitous than ever, we whose guardians and foster parents inculcated us with a criminal perceptiveness those dreadful teachers would never understand. The rest of us were the ones the Dublaners despised, of course, we were the sinners they hated, who never had a chance, who did whatever we wanted, and whose teachers and parents gave up on us a long time ago when the shouting and cursing and beatings all dissipated like smoke somewhere in the diaphanous sky. We were the ones who never had the privilege of choosing punishment and whose hope therefore grew as empty as forgotten rooms, whose ingratitude and insolence taught us that even the toughest people never wasted bullets on deer or birds but instead considered the austerity of death with a light of fire in our eyes and without the ignominy of fierce morality or religious orders; call it sadistic or obstreperous, whatever, but we lived in accordance with nothing, too wounded and angry, too weak and depressed to listen to any delusive truths our hearts needed to hear, resolved to mandatory counseling, grieved by our own injustices.

O' Father: You knew Matthew possessed every bit of artistry we wanted, and we were jealous of him, disheartened, lonely and morbid and plagued by the deadly sin envy, shadows in nightmarish school hallways, irredeemable in our vast manipulations and appalling destructive behavior. We stole and cheated and stole more. We belied our identities as wild and filled our lungs and bellies with poison, yes sir, we smoked anything to try to see You, dear Father, as if we weren't also skipping school, fighting barefisted, firing guns, dear Lord, but our crimes were necessary. We were bullied, after all, by the older teenagers who beat us on a regular basis, bloodied our mouths with one punch. Those who predicted a doomed future for all of humanity called us addicts and criminals, leeches and slime (and way worse things) because we were detested, shouted at, dragged by our arms across bedrooms and public sporting events. Timorous thieves and runaways, addicts and truants, twerps and punks leading an uproar of younger siblings and suburban middle-class gangster-wannabes to wear their clothes with primary colors the way we did, never even threatening anyone in our way, especially not the ones who never complained about our behavior or wallowed in our paths with a gloomy aura, too dismayed to try to talk to us and realize we didn't commit any flagitious acts, no Lord, we were children envious of those other children whose gifts were greater than ours, whose parents made more money than ours, and whose lives felt more important than ours.

All we wanted was to create art, to paint and draw and write, and develop a strong and positive value of ourselves; while at school we watched a ton of films and television shows to learn because our teachers were Dublaners whose communication skills were below par, I mean, they were these really terrible, shlubby teachers who wheeled in the squeaking cart with a TV and VCR and then played programs like *Electric Company, Sesame Street,* and (my personal favorite) *Let's Draw!* We watched Captain Kangaroo finger his sideburns and talk neighborly to Mr. Green Jeans about growing corn and cabbage and then, per instruction, we wrote our own stories about farms and vegetables, drew pictures of talking cornstalks and the pork-bellied cockeyed farmers who ate them, and afterward our teachers asked us to share. Indeed, art and writing were our favorite subjects, though Matthew was clearly the "most gifted" student, as the teachers referred to him, winning all the awards, earning the most praise.

Forgive us, Father. Forgive us, Matthew.

Forgive us for our vile and felonious behavior, for everything that we said about you, Matthew, in our fearful state and in all the manner of mortifications we imposed on our conscience, with nothing to show for ourselves but our envy and admiration and a realm of gloom; after all, we were as petrified as your own timid and indulgent eyes, boy, and later that night we awakened in our beds from short and unpleasant dreams with an increasing and torturous sense of guilt, trying to grasp why we allowed ourselves to do such a thing to you. Yes sir, the act of vandalism and holding you down and punching you in the face and ribs were fatal experiments, of course, because we understood that we were the real victims, as we realized in our insomnia, staring into the murk and holding our breath in horror, cringing with pain until one of us had the mercy to confess what we had done to you and how we had taken great pleasure in such a cruel, careless, and selfish act. We needed anyone's empathy while we sat at the police station, oppressed by the heavy humidity and faded colorless walls the hands of inmates had touched after they had wiped themselves, while you, our dear and innocent boy, upon waking, recited the poignant and percipient verses of saints.

3. OLD DUBLAN

magine van Gogh's 1890 painting, *Wheatfield with Crows*, for a glimpse of what O.D. resembles—an aberrant and desolate town with pale, open fields, and birds flying overhead, deep in the middle of nowhere, a somber place full of bad omens and airborne viruses, politically conservative, rife with self-anointed evangelists shouting prognostications in front of the town's only diner whose owner openly praised both God and carnival animals. O.D.: a town in Tophet County, reeking of trailers and feed lots, swirling with dust and trash and dead leaves from squally windstorms, full of suffering, poverty, and loneliness.

O.D., in all its agrarian eccentricities, possesses a primordial homogeneity with a simple and rank candor and a population of four digits, with nothing to see these days except old houses and yards full of weeds, because drought and wildfires killed crops and people moved away without having to bear the humiliation of their town becoming a cemetery full of dead Old Dublaners in the burning sun and dust, with most businesses going under, leaving downtown buildings vacant. No more local fabric shop or Food Mart or bowling alley, no more auctions or Saturday-night suppers or our beloved baseball diamonds. Downtown's Absalom Street, once filled with fallen demons that flew among the haze and volute smoke, with its hazy sky and low buildings and children playing Find the Killer in alleys, with its painstaking boredom and indolent and silent melancholy and townspeople muttering about with clenched teeth, closing their eyes to protect themselves from the sudden and intense gusts of wind and dust that were harmless but annoying, a street where ambition was rarely discussed and drunkenness prospered, especially on nights in summer when it was too hot to do anything except swim in the river and then sit in the dusty tavern called Absalom's on Absalom, which was once owned by Ward Byron who electrocuted himself in the bathtub with his wrists wrapped in electric cords plugged into an outlet—Absalom, which became the kind of street people avoided despite that Wicked Plains Food Market, J.R.'s Liquor, Leopold's Shoes, and Exley's Pawn Shop were lined along the south end with easy access from neighborhoods. Absalom Street became spookily hypnotic, absorbed in visions and fear: at night people noticed birds falling dead and possums and rats the size of cats creeping around the river and in abandoned buildings.

The 1971 low-budget film *The Devil Is a Southpaw* includes a scene that was filmed in downtown Old Dublan, when the main character, Charlie Roth, played by actor Andrew Miles Harper, finds himself in a dusty town, running from a gambling debt. The scene filmed in O.D. takes place at a party late in the night in a decaying apartment building when Charlie takes a psychedelic drug and stumbles downstairs to an alley where actor John Wayne, wearing a leather vest and cowboy hat, is supposed to be the devil, and asks in typical John Wayne drawl: "Do you prefer fame, or do you prefer friendship?" Charlie sees John Wayne reach for the gun in his holster, at which point he runs into the street, only to get hit by a junky 1970s Volkswagen driven by a man named Don, played by newcomer C. E. Briggs, who takes Charlie home and cares for him until he gets better. Charlie becomes disturbingly, dangerously obsessed with Don. (Though the film did poorly and received negative reviews, it soon developed a cult following after actor Briggs disappeared in real life. The mystery of his disappearance was never solved.)

Around the time of the film's release, a sudden case of facial blindness and temporary confusion infected so many O.D.ers that a typical conversation between two coworkers, in this case brothers-in-law in an office break room, went like this:

GUILDEN: Awfully humid out today, Jim. How are things in accounting?
ROSEN: I'm Ron.
GUILDEN: You're not Jim in accounting?
ROSEN: I'm Ron in sales. Is there a Jim in accounting?
GUILDEN: Aren't there two Jims in accounting?
ROSEN: What department are you in?
GUILDEN: I'm Jim in accounting.

The town was dull. In the early 1980s, some of us played youth baseball for the O.D. Demons in the summers when the humidity was so bad that sitting under the ballpark lights among the bugs and mosquitos was absolute torture, even in the clouds of citronella-heavy insect repellent. What was once a quaint town disparaged into a place for incertitude and abhorrent behavior, especially toward the last of the heifers and mules, but also toward the ballparks. The overbearing, callous Give-'em-Hell folks terrorized and vandalized many public places. Our ball diamond especially, once a place of tradition and fellowship, became the platform for drug addicts, needles and spoons, waste, exanimate sex in dugouts, the homeless, and those autochthonous dudes who carried tools for weapons and sheltered their vagabonds there. Our youth baseball leagues were finished. If there was one thing all Dublaners loved, it was America's game, because that's all they had.

Back when the juvenile detention facility was built in the spring of 1987, visitors often remarked how Dublaners were either unwilling or simply unable to have any sort of constructive conversation, often mumbling, avoiding eye contact, giving stock responses, or, in some cases, never even responding to outsiders, and Dublaners were never even fond of traveling anywhere either, except to the lake thirty miles on the outskirts of town, where they went camping and fishing and held cookouts (what else was there to do?), storing sacks of catfish they caught in freezers and having community suppers at the park, which was the favorable alternative after the town was devasted by an atrocious outbreak of food poisoning from bad beef sold at the local supermarket which temporarily resulted in some of the townspeople resorting to hippophagy when they were tired of eating catfish. An ample number of hapless children with timid and doleful eyes fell ill, and elderly people with sunken faces, all angular and bony, petrified with the threat of a looming death from malnutrition or disease; all this in a time when a quarter cent sales tax was voted on by Tophet County to construct the detention center on the north side of O.D. These days, the dried-up Gudgekin River snakes past that old juvenile detention facility, which is now an abandoned building full of cobwebs and rats that once housed twenty-seven of us residents awaiting placement in group homes, rehabilitation centers, or long-term lockup.

The rock house that overlooked the river, on Highway 6 and a mile east from the facility, is now an empty piece of land after the 1969 tornado, known as the Big 69er, tore through the area and ripped the shingles and part of the siding off the house (I later discovered it was demolished). The owner of that house was the Tophet County Juvenile Facility director, Mr. Lanius Shrike Strangelove, who lived alone and survived that storm, having taken shelter in his closet. Lanius Shrike Strangelove was disabled and confined to a wheelchair from a previous suicide attempt when he had put a .38 caliber into his mouth and pulled the trigger (the bullet only pierced part of his brain and left him paralyzed from the waist down). After the juvenile facility closed in 1990, many of us remember driving past that rock house and seeing the curtains in the window and the spilled flowerpots on the wheelchair-accessible ramp leading to the porch, wondering whether Strangelove had succumbed to a fearful state of paranoia and confusion and become a forlorn dotard, or whether he had imposed upon himself the misery and complications of a nervous breakdown since he was fired, locked up and out on bail, awaiting trial for allowing the abuse of residents in the facility, and probably fooled by the illusion that Dublaners still liked or admired him. Whenever he communicated, which was rare, he either talked openly of his ischemic colitis or, more often, discountenanced all kinds of angry and racist bullshit based on some ipsedixitism or his venal personality; like the drill sergeants and a few staff at that facility, he attempted to deceive anyone he thought might take advantage of him, gambling in late-night card games and having an objurgatory manner about him that made people dislike him even more, clueless as he was to the unforeseeable future, tormented by defeat. Before his trial, one foggy night, Strangelove drank half a bottle of Wild Turkey and wheeled himself in his wheelchair onto Interstate 40, where a semitruck crashed into him and killed him instantly. His body was thrown a hundred yards into a ditch alongside the highway. Broken parts of the wheelchair were everywhere.

If it's worth mentioning, despite these tragedies and failures, O.D. is proud of its two famous residents. The first was a man named George Echota, a Cherokee southpaw pitcher who was drafted by the Cincinnati Reds during the Bench/Rose Big Red Machine era before disappearing into obscurity. George broke all kinds of unimpressive records in high school tournaments for most strikeouts, fastest pitch, and even beaning batters in the helmet, earning him headlines in the weekly *O.D. Tribune* like:

"Echota Pitches Sixth Consecutive No-Hitter" and "Old Dublan Demon Pitcher Gives Another Pounding." A wild thing with a hard slider, George Echota was drafted to the Reds straight out of O.D. before Seaver arrived in 1977; his career ended too early when a lover stabbed him in his left hand, his pitching hand, claiming infidelity and that he had impregnated another woman (so tragic and a disgrace, isn't it?). After that, George Echota fell into obscurity and became homeless, wandering around town, drunk. (George always reminded me of Harry Dean Stanton's character from the Wim Wenders film, *Paris, Texas*, always a wild rover, as the song goes, not unlike myself.) The beautiful woman who carried his child gave birth to a boy she named Matthew.

Matthew Echota, little bird, a distant shadow to his father, became the next famous Dublaner, briefly, but not for baseball. His prose poem, "Child Choking in Boarding School," appeared in the *O.D. Tribune*, won the National Youth Writing Award when he was twelve, and earned him a prize (only fifteen dollars), although the poem held imagery of a gibbous moon too analogous to that in his classmate Milton Foolborn's poem, "Cacodemons Flying Through the School." (The latter of which holds a deliciously creepy iambic pentameter verse that Matthew's spare style frankly lacked.) The English teachers favored Matthew's behavior in the classroom because, sadly, Foolborn was perfidious and challenging, whereas Matthew was obedient and meek. No poem had appeared in the *Tribune* since Agatha Klemm published her poem, "Dublan's Dying Grackles" in 1948. Milton the Fool, as usual, was placed in after-school detention.

It didn't end well. Despite the early success and attention, Matthew Echota, stutterer and silent saint, died too young, broke and broken, without a successful career.

4.
TOPHET COUNTY DETENTION

We arrived in the middle of the night, handcuffed and shackled by the ankles, sick with stomach pain, bleary with fatigue, and restless with anger. The police officer driving the car had turned sharply off the highway and followed a rocky, downhill road, jarring us in our seats. Outside the window, we could see the dead trees absent of leaves, branches twisting into the moonlit sky, and there was a sense of gloom and heaviness in the air, which already made the oppressive humidity more miserable; it was like entering a whole other time period, because once the car pulled into the facility's garage and the heavy garage door roared shut behind us, we felt a kind of sempiternal stillness (which was creepy, from what I recall), then sure enough we noticed security cameras on the walls around us as we stepped into the intake room with its cinder block walls and concrete floors. We were told to remove our shoes and sit on our hands after the police officer uncuffed us, and one by one, we were led into a shower area where we emptied our pockets, removed all our clothes, and put everything into a large plastic bin, so that we then stood naked in front of two male guards who wore rubber gloves and checked our heads for lice, told us to squat and cough, and watched us shower.

Everyone was given the same clothes, a white T-shirt, gray sweatpants, and Velcro sneakers (shoestrings could be wrapped around the neck), then they asked a bunch of questions like, did we have any food allergies or were we on any medications, did we have any known diseases or hepatitis, and what drugs did we take? When was the last time we used drugs? We urinated in clear plastic cups while they observed. They read us the facility rules and our rights from a policy and procedure manual while we stared at the floor because we were so exhausted that all we wanted was to lie down and sleep, to be unconscious, and to not have to think or talk. Finally they assigned us our rooms and led us down a long corridor, past the dayroom with the Ping-Pong table and window overlooking the dark night, and into a wing with metal doors, like a prison, which was how the facility felt, a large, dead place with a total of five wings with ten rooms in each wing; the sound of heavy doors shutting reverberated through the wing every few minutes.

Stripped of our identities, we hung on our feverish restlessness and public condemnation like suffocating prisoners with our mouths full of earthworms, too afraid and wounded to speak against the clones they were turning us into and shell-shocked into fear among the droves of our contemporaries whose insides burned with the inescapable torment of victimhood and trauma. We were stripped of our rights as well, to walk freely or speak about our cases unless our court-appointed attorneys or caseworkers were present, which led us to lie in bed at night and wonder whether the judicial system was fair or morally concerned with the well-being of youth the way staff claimed. We were stripped of free will or any measureless power built inside us and left with only the hope that our suffering would draw us closer to God and memories of unforgettable mornings in the rain when we stared out windows and saw visions of saints, like Saint Paul of Thebes, who ate the bread the raven dropped for him every day as a gift from God, or images of Christ's suffering on the cross, or dreams of pillars of light hovering over our beds that formed into angelic beings who watched us in our sleepy state and urged us to consider that our frightened, tormented lives were temporary, and the kingdom of heaven meant eternal joy.

The first night we were too afraid to fall asleep. All around the facility, where floodlights stood high over the parking lots and basketball court, shadows from the trees spread across the lawn, and a stream of hazy light slanted in from the narrow and soulless windows high on our walls, and how we imagined such a light as a symbol of hope, an apparition streaming its way into our rooms to examine us, abandoned as we were in our solitary rooms. We thought of the train outside as it roared by from across the stream and wondered where it was headed. We thought of the moon outside and its trailing glow in the dark, dropping a steady drizzle of astral dust overflowing the plains with terror to signal the end of our lives as we knew them, and even the most skeptical of us could not deny the suppositions of nature's fury, never taking refuge in prayer under our scratchy blankets, too collapsed from exhaustion and malaise while at the mercy of the guards walking around the morguelike shadows of the wings, too tight-fisted and as helpless as a drowned man, some of us even trying to sleep on the floor as if resigned forever to the conviction that the universe had it in for us.

Our thoughts turned to dying late that first night, they really did, because we allowed ourselves to succumb to the weaknesses of evil and impurity, and some of us were afraid of being beaten to death by other residents or staff, growing more jittery and tense by the minute, captured in our bedclothes and dragged out into the woods, whipped and left for the bobcats to find us. We feared, too, vomiting in the middle of the night from stress or anxiety as we lay in our beds staring at the round shadows from the deciduous trees spread across the floor, shadows that played tricks on us in the dim room, worse than the miserable slums where most of us came from. From outside we could hear the furious wind because this was O.D., in the middle of nowhere, where the wind howls in the night like the torrential seas, swirling dust around. We heard other things, like a man's voice rise out of the darkness saying, "YONDER SHINES THE BIG RED MOON OVER THE DEVIL'S LOST PLAYGROUND," in a cryptically hillbilly voice, as if it were an announcement to frighten us, which it was, followed by the echo of a heavy door shutting somewhere in our wing.

Our first night was like that, full of panic and incongruity, sitting in those rooms of putrefaction with their single toilets and their flame-resistant, three-ply vinyl, polyester mattresses that felt like sleeping on the hood of a car, the walls left without a trace of slogans and cries of pain once traced with a bloody finger of the past. We sat up in bed in the darkness, wondering how long we would be there, or what time it was, or how long we had slept, if at all. Staff peeked in the windows on our doors every fifteen minutes to make sure we weren't dead. When we did manage to sleep, if only for a few minutes at a time, we dreamed of the birds outside, carrying us away into the sky like angels. There were no cardinals, sparrows, or blue jays. No finches or orioles, only screeching grackles, too angry to sleep, too wounded to fly away.

The first night we heard someone's voice in our wing, and when we peeked out the windows in our doors, a woman, a staff member, was sitting cross-legged on the floor, painting designs on skulls. They must've been animal skulls (or were they the small skulls of children?). She dipped her brush in various jars and painted tiny patterns in bright colors, reds and yellows and blues, while humming in a high, soft voice as she worked. (She must've been an angel, beautiful as she was, with her long dark hair back in a ponytail, paint splattered on her jeans and hands. I leaned against the door as she painted until my eyes grew too heavy and I dragged myself back to bed.)

Hour by hour, throughout the night, we continued to hear disturbing sounds: the woman's humming, pipes knocking, heavy doors closing. Somebody, a young boy, crying out for help.

◂

Before juvenile detention centers, teenagers were thrown into dirty jail cells alone, or worse, with adults, forced into nullity and surrounded by fulvous walls and insensate criminals who stared at them with their mouths open, creepy and incorrigible and disinterested in their terror and pleas for help. Youthful offenders were abused verbally, raped, beaten up, and like some random Golyadkin were left on the dirty floor to stare victimized into the darkness and wishing for death. At some point social services stepped in due to the inhumane treatment and recognition that these were essentially kids who deserved better facilities and treatment, so juvenile centers were built with the idea that youth could be reformed, rehabilitated, and ultimately given a second chance. (I later discovered in a public library that the frontal lobe of the brain, which is the part that recognizes consequences, takes years to develop, especially in boys, and that juveniles will repeatedly make bad decisions for reasons they can't explain; think, for instance, when a child throws a rock or breaks something and can't give a logical, concrete reason why). Everyone at Tophet County Juvenile Correctional Facility entered on level three. There were five total levels, one through five, with one being the best. The staff scored us every shift on a ten-point scale based on our behavior, how well we followed rules, etc., and by the end of the week a resident could go up or down in levels based on their weekly score. The higher levels, one and two, got more privileges than lower-level residents, such as getting to stay up until ten at night, receiving an extra snack, longer phone time, and getting to wear their own shoes instead of the Velcro sneakers the facility provided. The lowest level had an 8:30 p.m. bedtime and no extra snack.

Our days began with the pain of waking early after a night of little sleep, with guards opening our doors and telling us to hurry and get dressed. We lined up in our wing, ten of us, and were led into the dayroom for breakfast with the other residents. Breakfast, like all meals, was quiet; the only talking allowed was asking permission for condiments, like salt or pepper, so most of us ate with our heads down. The cooks, all male and pale-skinned with sagging jowls and enormous bellies, simian, grotesque, with vague criminal histories, were even more terrifying than the guards with their bulging eyes and hairy arms, while we ate like dogs. Some of us didn't even know how to chew with our mouths closed or how to hold utensils properly. Some of us gripped our forks and stabbed at our sausage while others preferred to eat with their hands. The least pitied of us ate as if there was no one around, thinking of the dead hours of work, classroom, and exercise to come, wondering whether we had the spirit and strength to survive however many weeks or months it would take to complete the program. We drank from our plastic cups and wished to disappear into the morning fog outside, amusing ourselves with the fantasy of wandering into a whole other land somewhere far away, picking fruit from trees and peeling their skins away under the warm sun, fanning ourselves with our hats as we followed narrow trails down to a remote beach, only to realize we were on a remote island, a secret place full of bamboo huts and lychee and papaya growing in the gardens. What else could we do during meals but dream?

After breakfast we lined up and entered classrooms. We were given the instructions for the day, which meant attending school, counseling, and large-muscle exercise over at the Columbus House with the drill sergeants. We could then return to our wings and rest before dinner and showers. A teacher on staff handed out worksheets for us to do. He was a short man with a beard and razor buzz haircut who sat at his desk doing stuff on his computer. He (claimed he) was a certified teacher but rarely spoke, never really taught anything all day, and gave us easy worksheets to keep us busy. Some of us did them quickly and were able to read or draw or write in our notebooks. (I was smart enough to finish quickly, despite my nerves, so I sketched geese and trees full of fruit. I drew angels with bulging eyes and portly children with red jam smeared on their faces. I would begin writing stories inspired by my drawings.) Others struggled with their assignment, asking staff to help them with basic math or labeling maps. One or two staff members sat in the classroom with us, occasionally talking into their radios to other staff members or looking at the tattoos on their forearms.

We were there to complete the program, learn life skills, follow orders, and practice restraint and appropriate behavior while living in a secure facility. Many of the residents were Indians from tribes around the area. (I wasn't.) A few of us like Rosemary, Brandon, Trusty John, and Ace knew one another from school, but many were from other counties around the state.

The first day, a drug and alcohol counselor took us into a room before lunch to talk about the dangers of substance abuse. "I know the slang terms for everything," he told us. "I know pot. I know blow. There are people in this world who smoke scorpions and see things dance for ten hours afterward. Let's talk about life. Let's talk about choices." His name was Vlad Siren, and he was well groomed and slender and spoke as energetically as George Bailey. "Let's talk about forgiveness," he told us. "It means everything to learn compassion and forgive yourself, doesn't it? Feel passionate about rehabilitation. Keep hope. Keep living."

Some of us listened to him, but most wished him dead. He taught us the serenity prayer: *God, grant me the serenity to accept the things I cannot change, the courage to change the things I can, and the wisdom to know the difference.*

"Can't you see it's a beautiful prayer?" Siren said, perspiring. "You have to learn what you can and cannot change. What do you think this place is all about, anyway?"

Some of us had never even used anodynes, or recreational drugs, or had never committed any serious crime. Some of us were guilty by association, caught with the wrong crowd; it didn't matter, we sat there with our hands in our laps and careful not to move our hands because doing so might resemble a gang sign. We listened as Siren flailed his arms around and talked with such passion that he suffered a nosebleed and had to dig into his pocket for a used Kleenex to stuff inside his nose. "You need to find your own happiness inside of yourselves. Memorize the serenity prayer and say it to yourself often. We'll say it together every day because, for Pete's sake, you gotta live by it."

He stuffed his Kleenex into his pocket. "Some of you are Indians. Some of you are whatever. Addiction doesn't care. You say you're not addicted? Let's talk about control and making smart choices."

Siren looked like the type of guy who danced alone with his hands in his pockets. He had a way of making us feel sorry for ourselves, pitiful as we were. We raised our hands to ask questions. Some of us fell into confession, revealing truths and pain. Our pain came from guardians and parents, from beatings and assaults, feeling alienated from peers, family, community, and anyone else who left us alone among our cryptic and shadowy dreams. Our pain came from poverty and hunger, from being locked in rooms and attics and subsisting in the drowsiness of goodbyes, feeling around in the dark and muddy atmosphere for a lamp or lighter while the smell of stew lingered from the kitchen, giving up and wondering whether we could breathe our last breaths. We held back our emotional state. Such pain never brought on an understanding why our sheets or pillows were taken away, of course, because we were not suicidal, not really, not even after they told us stories about lepers and the blind and children from other countries who had it way worse, now didn't they, and how lucky we were to have a roof over our heads in the land of the free, the good old U.S. of fugging A., able to wear our civilian clothes and shoes, and able to obtain a free education none of us cared about while ridding ourselves of the larger issues inside of us, all the rage, lust, and egotism we never realized were strangling us way worse than spending nights locked in a darkened room.

"Keep me here," Ace said. "Keep me here so that I don't have to return to the people who hate me."

"Let's talk about self-actualization," Siren said.

"Keep me here. I don't want to go home."

"I understand." Siren's empathy, no matter how forced, was always evident. "We're all products of our environment, son. Look around. We make mistakes and should deserve another chance."

"Can we put our heads down?" Brandon asked. "Nap?"

"Good idea," Ace said. "We're all tired, sir. Can I use the restroom?"

"What the heck do you mean take a nap?" Siren said, then rambled on about making smart choices and setting goals. The longer we listened to him, the more we noticed his mannerisms, the way he gestured or snorted his nasal inhaler, the way he suffered his nosebleed. "Look," he said, "we have to learn to understand what we cannot change about ourselves." The tinted window behind him reflected his body with a soft and clear glow as he stood before us. Some of us said we had overdosed and spent time in the hospital, while the rest of us spoke nonchalantly of smoking weed or crack cocaine on occasion, or smoking joints laced with embalming fluid, which was neither a fiction nor an embellishment because the ones who had used described seeing God in heavy rain coming down on the river, or bananas dancing while hanging from trees, or having a strong and unusual desire to remove one's intestines, then cook and eat them.

We ended with the serenity prayer.

After our session, we settled into our seats on the couches in the dayroom in front of the TV, where staff made sure nobody was flashing gang signs with their hands. Some of us had to sit on our hands. Others were allowed to sit with their hands in their lap.

General rules: Keep your hands still. Don't move your fingers. Ask permission first. Raise your hand and ask.

Rosemary asked: "Can I scratch my head? Or my nose? Can I rub my eye?"

"Quickly," they said.

The more we thought about having to ask to scratch a part of our body, the more we itched. You could sense it in the room, the way people stirred in their chairs. There was no whispering, no unusual hand movements, no throwing gang signs. No looking around at other residents, no long eye contact, no talking to staff about our court cases or our crimes. Our crimes weren't to be discussed at all except during phone calls with our social workers, probation officers, or lawyers, and while such privacy was supposed to eschew any sort of exploitation, we talked about them anyway during recreation time or outside in the courtyard, which was the ideal space to occupy in lockup because the staff barely paid attention out there, too concerned with looking at their forearms or talking among themselves. Our crimes were rumors with nobody showing any sufficient shame, yet we could hear these crimes announced through the wild bushes in the courtyard. (Almost as if everyone took turns waiting to confess their crime, like the diseased waiting for the salt of the Earth, and still, at least for the first few days, as I recall, it wasn't too bad there.)

We learned the work shifts: 7:00 a.m.–3:00 p.m.; 3:00 p.m.–11:00 p.m.; and 11:00 p.m.–7:00 a.m. After we had gone to bed, the staff gazed in the little window in our door every fifteen minutes like they had done the first night, and while the graveyard-shift staff spent their shift doing laundry and walking around the different wings, checking on us, some of us were more emotional during these late hours at night, especially if we couldn't sleep, which we knew would've created problems for staff because of occasional suicide threats, panic attacks, or deep sorrow, requiring employees to practice de-escalation techniques and calm reassurance that we were safe and everything was going to be fine. They didn't give us bedsheets, only blankets, because it's way harder to hang yourself with a blanket, and anyway there was nothing on the walls to tie the blanket to. Some residents were smart enough to ask about the threat of suicide, which meant they could leave and be transported to a hospital for a mental evaluation, though the staff assured us that when someone had tried to threaten suicide in the past, they usually returned.

That afternoon when they released us from the classrooms,

we were led around the courtyard to the Columbus House, where Sergeants Cole, Jackson, Lee, and Ambrose told us they could smell our weakness and trepidation the whole way across the lot. All four drill sergeants wore army-green service uniforms and campaign hats with a forward tilt. They told us they would break us down and build us up again, that's right, if they had it their way they would've cut all our umbilical cords with a rusty knife and toasted our future failures over beers right there in the delivery room—or was it, they asked, that we were born in the back of pickup trucks, on dirt roads too far from our trailer homes, or beside the amber tributaries flowing with piss and garbage our families were too lazy to dispense into trash cans? Were we born on kitchen floors, carpet, or outside on blankets laid over the dirt and rock? Did angular, half-drunk buzzards drop us on our doorsteps, or were our mothers taken to a real hospital that cost taxpayers extra to pay the doctors so that we could be born into this world only to take it all for granted? Were we all, they continued, offspring of the sixties' hippy generation with our hair and disjointed bones caused by a lack of proper nutrition and exercise and medical care? Were we distressed from lack of discipline and dental care, poor us, offspring of whorehouse soubrettes who ate crickets and withered fruit before rehearsing for their pointless community artsy stage plays, whose bad judgment was never questioned, whose early childhood consisted of urinating in our pants due to disillusionment from poor parenting and an atavistic fear of control? Or was it, they asked, that we were incapable of learning personal courage and conviction, products of abiogenesis birthed and formed out of nothing, engaged without duress and lust for pleasure?

"This is the end of the eighties as we know it," they said. "Things are tough as we edge toward the nineties. How do you cope? Look at us in the eyes, every one of you, as we stand here before your sorry selves and ask: How do you stand there and wonder all pug-eyed and foolish like hippies? The answer is simple, runts. You'll need to learn strict discipline to succeed in life. You poor, spoiled, selfish runts without discipline."

Some of us called them pigs. Others called them evil. They removed their aviator sunglasses and glared at us with bloodshot eyes from brutal hangovers, knowing well we were suffering all kinds of emotional pain, awed by their indefatigable manner and incapable of dragging any truth out of ourselves, they told us, embittered and selfish, lacking a soldier's obedience under the fierce vigilance of an authoritarian, without a clue or care and living in a bleeding-hearted world losing its capitalist values, our voices never to be heard on the street despite our affiliation with community or culture, that's what they said, we were destined for a life of shoveling cow shit or carrying severed chicken heads in sacks, too focused on the sad glow of TV screens and VCR movies with fuzzy tracking, too distracted by the satanic lure of Ozzy or Iron Maiden and arcade games in malls, too amused by fantasy and the devil's music that Jim and Tammy Faye Bakker were weeping about in terms of its rotten influence on youth today, prisoners in our own gruesome dungeons that would ultimately leave us with no military protection, screwed.

"Y'all are screwed," Sergeant Cole told us, slurring from his pain pills.

Poor Ace was smaller than even Matthew, and prepuberty, with a constant look of fear and timidity in his eyes, knowing he was smaller than all the other residents and quickly garnering a reputation for taking the fastest shit in the history of shitting, and walking catatonic and entranced in his own thoughts and Romero-like anywhere he went, poor little Ace. He was obsessed with Wall of Voodoo's song "Mexican Radio," and did a below-average but humorous impersonation of the singer's facial expressions whenever he was in a good enough mood to sing, but those moments were rare. Most of the time Ace sat quietly making hirrient sounds, like a cat getting a belly rub. The drill sergeants told us never in a million years would we survive anything—not school or work or the adversity of a dying nation, unless we get Reaganomics back and understood the whole nation was suffering from the threat of implementing socialist values and a rash of protests to the campaign that we all needed to adhere to "Just Say No," because we weren't paying attention to the crack cocaine epidemic that was rising, too nescient to the war on drugs that Nixon had begun in the seventies, too indurated in our obtuseness to attend the Drug Abuse Resistance Education program, DARE, which was blasphemy, so numb and dumb we were that we'd probably end up drinking carbolic acid at our hippy parties without realizing how lethal it was.

"Blasphemy," they said.

Those lecherous scrotes ordered us to do insane calisthenics, push-ups, squats, and sit-ups, along with stretches, ordering us to look at them directly in the eye because no eye contact meant weakness and failure, but looking at them in the eye for too long was detestable, too, they informed us, and weird. Don't be weird, don't stare—a strong, virile man knows how long to give eye contact without the fear of conveying weirdness. We were ordered to line up and then spread out for exercise, to do our best, to give everything we had no matter how little sleep we'd had or how full our bellies were with breakfast, quite often even they ordered us to refrain from obtuse breathing or coughing or hacking up phlegm, which was inappropriate behavior and unnecessary for rehabilitation. No whining or crying or gnashing of teeth. No slinging snot or looking around at others. Good soreness was a blessing, they told us, to be so sore we wouldn't be able to lift our forks to our mouths at the dinner table, and sure enough their manner became more intense with each exercise as we struggled, believe it or not, they laughed and said they'd seen more action in armpit polyps.

"Better get in shape, runts," they said. "Better do a thorough examination of your bodies and muscles before the older hippies brainwash you into thinking it's all about the mind and spirit."

Nobody there wanted to hear any whining about missing our families, or disillusioned thoughts and fantasies of reunification with loved ones, or touching the concealed body parts of former lovers or classmates in the oblivion as it left a trail of hope for more, giving an eternal glory to the useless hands that kept appearing in our thoughts more than the naked bodies did, and how pitiful to imagine such things in our loneliness, wondering what our little dogs were doing without us as they curled up in the dog beds back at home, or how our siblings passed through rooms after dinner without a thought of us in their heads, so appalling, isn't it, and pitiful, during our insomnia, how we avoided thinking about slaving away with chores outside in the heat, or building a strong spine for our drudgery so that fatigue would never make us drop to our knees and fall unconscious, instead dreaming of hotels in Mexico with our loved ones under a tense protection from all things evil or the threat of being locked up in such a desolate and grim area in Tophet. They didn't want us to think or speak of such things so that we focused on a narrow and linear thought: entrapment. Isolation. Being locked up, punished. Being surrounded by the fence the dogs gnawed on occasionally, though we'd heard rumors of electric wires to be installed around the fence and around all exit doors inside the buildings. Where were our saviors? Where were our heroes, our angels, our social workers and lawyers and court-appointed advocates?

Whenever we tried to ask questions or respond to anything the sergeants said, they cupped their ears dramatically as if they couldn't believe we had the nerve to say anything at all. We might as well scream into the pillow, that's what those hypocrites told us, their faces twisted in a stupor, taking turns walking behind the Columbus House building to smoke cigarettes while calling over to the detention staff who were also smoking on their break to get back to work. "Stop wasting our tax dollars," they called out.

Slowly, we felt ourselves on the edge of misery and death whenever we were around the drill sergeants, clinging to any kind of hope that they would let up and stop making us do pushups or duckwalks across the yard. By the end of the hour we were so exhausted that it seemed better to be dead than subjected to their rigorous humiliation, surfeited with soreness and pain, soaked in sweat and moaning with unbearable despair in time to hear Sergeant Ambrose's deep and intentional long belch, such a strange eructation, followed by an announcement that the next months would be the most difficult of our lives because none of us, especially the Indians, were going anywhere.

By the end of the day someone got released. She was a thin girl with short dark hair, likely an Indian most of us didn't recognize from school, so we expected she was from some other county. She never spoke a word that any of us heard and kept her head down whenever she walked. The staff called her back to the intake room, so we knew she was leaving. Outside in the courtyard, she was escorted away by a staff member, and we wondered whether our names would be called next. Because she left, our anticipation and anxiety only grew worse. We waited, but nothing happened, nobody followed her. We remained, showered, and then retired to our rooms.

At breakfast the next morning, a new resident arrived.

It was Matthew.

5.
SOLITUDE AND CONFINEMENT

Matthew arrived for mysterious reasons. Some said he traduced the police officer who courted his sad and lonely mother, that his contempt of the officer led to a scuffle that resulted in Matthew lunging at him and being restrained and arrested for assault. Others said he had contrived a plan in his journal to attack the officer with a broken glass bottle while the officer slept naked in his mother's bedroom. Whatever it was, the poor boy's face was swollen from what looked like a blow to the jaw.

He sat at the far end of the table next to a female staff member and spoke about how the distant light of fires in his dreams represented God, while the rest of us never made a sound, eating with our heads down and wondering why the staff weren't telling him to stop talking the way they told the rest of us whenever we started talking at the table. Here he was, a favorite even among each of these indifferent staff members, passive, holding a certain dignity attributed to possessing the gift of soft-spoken speech, with the fortune of a beauteous face and body, seen by those of us who studied him closely as a gentle figure with an elegance beyond any other boy, and plenty of boys in the summer swam in the river on the outskirts of O.D. anyway, we all splashed and swam naked, swung on tire swings, and lay on the riverbank in the sun with them.

In the classroom, out of nowhere, he told the teacher about a phosphorous glow of a shooting star and its trail of sparkling light as if the weight of time was pressing down on him, separating constellations into groups of eight different families, which he said he'd memorized after reading Menzel's *A Field Guide to the Stars and Planets* during a sad and formidable winter when his mother battled seasonal depression, leaving Matthew to help out around the house more than usual. On another unpleasant night when the house was melancholy and full of loneliness, he had seen the galactic quadrant that formed Pavo, Indus, and Grus, he had seen Taurus, he had seen a new light and then fell into a panic attack, alone, right there outside in the backyard, with gall froth foaming in his mouth and a blue jay entangled in the wild bushes by the shed. (We calculated that during his life he had had at least seventy panic attacks, each one as difficult and dizzy as the last.)

Other than the lure of his beauty, we scrutinized him in the classroom his first day because he knew very well what he was talking about whenever he spoke, looking at the teacher as if wallowing in a fen of disillusionment, speaking of stars and constellations like a bitter madman, stumbling over his words and questioning the concept of reality versus fata morgana, were we really locked up in the confined space or was it all in our minds, he asked, in solitary tears and sputtering at his desk while he lamented his father's absence, his mother's sadness, and his sister's failure to acknowledge his crippling anxiety, poor thing, worried demons were possessing his body and he would fall dead any minute.

"They th-th-think I'm dying," he stuttered. His breathing was quick and heavy.

"You're not dying," the guard told him, then glanced at the teacher, who agreed.

"Right," the teacher said, "remember last time? Your mom brought your books from home. She understands what's going on."

"B-but my mom," Matthew said.

"B-but my mom," the guard mocked.

The guard, the teacher, and the rest of us held the same dead expression on our faces, wondering whether he was mentally fit to withstand being locked up or whether he needed to be transported to the hospital to have a psychological evaluation, which had evidently happened a few times with former residents' failed suicide attempts, and we knew from staff that those residents regularly returned, frauds that they were, ashamed of their iniquities and failure to manipulate everyone no matter how crazy they pretended to be.

Still, the rest of us dreamed of leaving, breaking free like blood brothers and sisters, running into the woods while songs spun around inside our souls, our heads dizzy with the continuous buzz of hope and free will, running and hiding until finally retiring in a cool pool hall full of food and drink. (In the film *One Flew over the Cuckoo's Nest*, the residents of the mental hospital escape, led by Jack Nicholson's character, and take a boat out on the water, something I remember suggesting to the other residents that we try; sadly, nobody else had seen that movie and eventually resisted.) At first, the only ones who dared to ask us whether we thought seriously of leaving were some of the girls because they were thinking about it, too, naturally; one girl had even written one of us a note while outside in the courtyard. The note became a topic of conversation among those of us in our building. It detailed the times each night the drill sergeants played dominoes in the Columbus House and then retired to sleep, and how the graveyard-shift staff couldn't see the western side of the grounds, past the Columbus House, because no cameras were out there. When the graveyard-shift staff weren't in the control room, monitoring the cameras or watching TV, they were doing laundry and bed checks every fifteen minutes, which meant they kept busy enough that they didn't need to stare at the monitors or TV every night, and anyway, the dogs would start barking if anyone took off on foot toward the fence.

Still, we talked through the small open windows in our doors when they weren't in our wing. We discussed whom we would invite to a party if we could invite any three people alive in the world, and while most of us chose actors and rock stars, Matthew said his three would be American Indian activist Russell Means, Saint Teresa of Ávila, and Jesus Christ. (It was I who first suggested we band together to form an escape):

"The guards will figure it out," Brandon said.

"He's right," Ace said. "They'll work the crap out of us so that we'll be too tired to even think about it. I'm scared of dying, guys."

"I'm this close to going apeshit."

"Me, too. We'll die, going apeshit."

"Shut up. Nobody's dying. Meet outside tomorrow by the basketball goal."

"It won't work," Matthew said.

"Why not?"

"You can't get away with talking in a group here without a guard getting suspicious. Better to write something down in the classroom. Someone make a plan."

"You make a plan."

"I'm gonna start tripping if you guys don't figure this out."

"Someone ask one of the girls to do it tomorrow. Staff like them better and they're smarter than you guys."

"No shit."

"Ya'll like homemade pie?"

"Shut up."

"Guys? It's not too bad here when you think about it."

"Who said that? Farmer, was that you, you inbred cooze?"

"Shut up."

"Room checks any minute, losers."

This sort of thing went on nearly every night. Matthew wasn't interested in planning an escape with us, not at all, which we found annoying, this dismissive behavior toward us, never engaging in conversations in the courtyard or during any recreational activity, focusing instead on scribbling in his notebook like an officious runt taking notes on everyone he observed throughout the day at the facility, notably the following:

a girl named Jessie who played soccer better than anyone in O.D. and who could cut twine with her teeth;

a boy named Spider who defecated on the floor of his room, and constantly talked about how unfiltered water causes cancer, and who sometimes irritated staff with his childish, doggish whine at night in bed;

and a girl named Charlotte who had screamed any time she tried to express herself with an unequivocal urge to consider the will of her enemies, the men who hurt her, and who obsessed over the history of cults.

Matthew was basing his characters off them, he told us, for his novel, which he never spoke about. (I asked him repeatedly, but he never uttered a word except to say his novel had "prolix sentences" and "profoundly keen descriptions," which irritated me.) He was to live for his art, that's what he told everyone, even skipping lunch to write in his notebook so that everyone could see he put aside his shame and had something with meaning to concentrate on, leaving some of us to burn inside with raging envy, too jealous to conceive the infallible system he was employing in public, and we wondered whether he travailed as hard at night and then slept with his eyes open, mumbling goodbyes in the drowsiness of his dreams, sleeping better than anyone else, never worried, never participating in our basketball games or board games before bed, meanwhile the rest of us were shrieking into our pillows every night like raging madmen.

Outside, rules were different than indoors in the dayroom, and the staff didn't care about enforcing them. What else could we do but try to pass time as quickly as possible? In the courtyard, or on the basketball court, we talked about our neighborhoods while the staff stood at a distance. Those of us who couldn't play hoops didn't join in on three-on-three basketball with the others, so we sat alone reading a book or drawing, and still others sat in the grass looking up at the sky as if deep in prayer, their lips moving silently. Nobody wanted to talk sports. Most of the athletes weren't in the kind of trouble the rest of us were. Girls who kept their hair in ponytails talked among themselves in serious meetings, less interested in talking to the boys and more focused on their own conversations, and many of us wondered whether they were planning their escape, and if so, how could we be included in their plans. At night we played Ping-Pong and chess and had discussions with staff about making the right choices and, more importantly, appreciating the value of self-worth instead of being diffident, meek, weak, timid, afraid, shy, dumb, and thinking like a hippy. *What did we want to do with our lives? What were our dreams and aspirations? Our future?* We watched TV and old war movies in black-and-white, but some grew bored and anxious. "If you don't want to sit in front of the TV," they told us, "you can go to a wing and stare at a book." (I was particularly drawn to the TV even though I loved to read; TV was like an anodyne to me.) Guards harassed Matthew more than the rest of us because he was the smallest Indian, and also he had admitted (so naively) that he possessed an unusual phobia of frogs, which caused laughter from everyone.

"Who's afraid of frogs?" Rosemary asked. "*You* are? You're scared of *frogs*?"

Matthew didn't respond.

"There are plenty of frogs down by the river," one of the guards told him. "Hope they don't make their way up here. Sometimes we find them around here in the middle of the night."

"They'll suck blood from your neck," another guard said.

"They cling to your neck and hump."

"Fornicating frogs. Bloodsuckers."

Matthew wanted to spend time alone to read, he said, and honestly he found nothing helpful in being around the guards, who we assumed had high school diplomas or G.E.D.s but no further education, which must have made him feel prideful because he thought he was smarter than all of them put together, he really did. He announced to the rest of us that he was lying on his bed trying to read, and that he wanted to go to sleep out of boredom, so we imagined him lying with his arm folded to serve as a pillow, ignoring any comments the staff made to him to try to get him to come into the commons room to watch a war movie with everyone else. We wondered whether Matthew was writing another poem about children hiding or whether he was writing scenes about us in his novel, and would he write about us being locked up here, too afraid to tell us? Would he find comfort in doing such things?

Some of us chose to remain in our rooms during the day and play sick so that we would miss schoolwork in the classroom, miss the exercises outside, and miss being able to walk around and try to keep our sanity intact with the other residents, because it felt safer to remain in that confined space. We had a toilet. We had a bed and a pillow and blanket. What else besides food and drink did we need? Protecting ourselves came first.

Even during evening game time, if we played dominoes or checkers, we chose safe, conservative strategies, never caring about winning so much as wanting the game to provide a sense of relief and fantasy so that we could forget about what time it was or where we were.

Most of us feared solitude, and unlike Matthew, we couldn't bring ourselves to sit in our rooms and stare at the eerie shadows on the wall in dead silence, worried no emergency forces at hand could save us in case one of the drill sergeants lost it and left us like animals to rot or else beat us with our shovels and buried us alive out in the woods. They told us they would make us scream in anguish by putting us in solitary confinement in the basement, in low lighting, subjected to the eternal condemnation of our own minds unless we completed all our exercises, poor us, too simple and undisciplined to be thankful that someone was taking the time to train us in our misfortune, someone who could drink from the garden hose and then tell us our domestic disasters were nothing compared to the physical pain we were about to endure outside in the heat of the day, so we worked hard digging in the flower beds and pulling weeds and then followed the trail of our own sweat back to the Columbus House.

We decided being alone in a room was like someone pointing a gun at our heads and telling us to shut our eyes, disturbed by an unalleviated sadness whose visible face of enforcement we did not want to access, repeatedly asking ourselves: Where in God's name have you put yourself, and what have you done to deserve this? We lay there afraid and worrying about the rhythm of our pulse in the ominous moonlight streaming in through our windows, unable to sleep, questioning our own confusion and paranoia and scarcely even noticing when the staff peeked in our little door windows to check on us every fifteen minutes, sometimes feeling the stomach bile come up the back of our throats with a burn, wondering whether we would die in our sleep.

We told the counselor, Vlad Siren, that solitude felt like disordered terror, that's how one of us described it, too inscrutable. Siren's eyes narrowed as he nodded in contemplation, telling us to consider self-actualization and appreciating the gift of life, his answer for everything. "Appreciate life," he told us. "Think of other countries. The poverty, the suffering. All the pain and neglect. All the sickness and death."

A spell was cast on us that swelled our breathing and turned our dreams violent: snakes slithered across the river where we swam, raising up and trying to bite us; we were blindfolded and forced into sinking ground, worried we would suffocate—all nightmares we shared, too specific and peculiar to be a coincidence, too absorbed in our imaginations. Our worst days were spent writing long letters to our parents and guardians. Our worst nights we whispered for help from God and our mothers because they understood the unprotected state we were in: help us not to fear the enemy that they told us was inside of us, stirring into something bigger than we can handle, unraveled by our chores and suppressed anger, yet so far removed from the world that we struggled to describe the places we dreamed of; the more we tried talking about the dreams, the less real they felt, even if we casually brought them up during a game of dominoes or chess, or during a snack before bed when the room was still and the guards were so exhausted their eyes were heavy with dark circles underneath them. We talked, instead, of what it meant to stand without shoes on the sunbaked concrete outside in a heat that shook our sudoriferous glands wild, and whether the weather was an omen or a reaction of trauma from the way people mistreat the Earth, because Matthew brought up that the

Earth reacts to trauma in the same way people do, that's what he usually said, in fact, even when nobody was talking about the clime.

The most treacherous kind of solitude was the time spent without access to a clock, never knowing the time or how long until the sun came up, shaken by the continuous, fearsome interrogators of our dreams, who dragged our bodies over the frozen ground and dumped us into deep rivers. Some of us lost it, crying out in the night. Our fists and hands went bruised and bloodied from the times we beat them on the concrete wall, hollering for them to free us, to let us talk on the phone, and to stop hiding the brutal truth of our final destinations. Our blood spewed from our hands and flooded our rooms while we prayed for the facility to be leveled by a tornado the way one rolled through up north and destroyed houses and buildings a few years before, yes, we put our bloody hands on our hearts and begged to be released, relieved, and forgiven of all we had done, wondering whether this was the end or the beginning, the start or finish, confused by our own cries and the angst of hopelessness surrounding us in this brothel of rules. (Amid one vicious anxiety attack late in the night, while witnessing a beautiful woman paint designs on skulls, I bloodied my fist on the wall trying to get her attention. She never saw me. She must've been my own hallucination. I suffered from an inguinal ache and lay supine on my bed, sleepless, in misery.)

Meanwhile, Matthew kept quiet and wrote (or as teachers put it, "He wrote like the truly gifted, a born writer"), probably scribbling the modern fairy tales we wanted to write. Was he writing poems or stories? Letters to his new girlfriend, Cassie Magdal, confessing his love for her? But ultimately, we were worried he was writing about us.

THE DEVIL IS A SOUTHPAW

In *The Devil Is a Southpaw*, Charlie spies on Don, who writes prayers at his typewriter. When Don falls asleep later, Charlie sneaks into his room and reads what Don has typed: "This man is dangerous, and I have to find a way to get rid of him before he kills me."

6.
CASSIE MAGDAL SEES THE DEVIL

A month before Matthew arrived at the juvenile facility, Cassie Magdal and her boyfriend, Milton Foolborn, were sitting in Milton's 1984 Oldsmobile in the parking lot of O.D. High School, waiting on Milton's cousin Trusty John to pull up next to them. They were parked near the back of the lot, far enough away from Highland Street and the school for them not to be noticed, and Cassie was shaken by the certainty that someone had seen them looking suspicious before school, even though the two rifles were in the trunk.

"It's not like people go around shooting up schools every day," Cassie kept telling Milton the Fool. "It's too small here, they'll know it's you."

"Do what Trusty John said," he told her. "That's all you have to do."

All morning, Foolborn had contemplated not going along with the plan, but once they pulled into the parking lot, he had made up his mind, of course, and Cassie's job was simply to stagger into the English 2 classroom on the first floor down the hall from the administrative offices and tell the English teacher, Mrs. K., that she was having a panic attack until Mrs. K. left the room to get the nurse and she could follow her but then slip away out the door and give Foolborn and Trusty John the signal to enter the classroom. Foolborn and Trusty John didn't want to shoot Mrs. K. after all, of course not, they even liked Mrs. K., especially on Fridays when they had a free period to catch up on their work from all week while Mrs. K. graded papers and played the radio at a low volume as long as everyone was quiet. Trusty John, who was antisocial and known for getting caught crawling out of the window in the boys' bathroom after huffing paint during P.E., knew in his heart that, unlike Foolborn, he was a pathetic mess, as Cassie had told him many times. She was surprised at her own behavior, the way she supported anything Foolborn said or wanted to do no matter how puerile or irreverent, given the bewildering nature of her circumstance in realizing he was no longer the boy she once thought him to be, and somehow along the way he had lost his good looks and charm due to his persistent chatter about going to the arcade and the gun range with his cousin. Well, that and the fact that Grandley, Lister, and Fayle were in the English 2 classroom and needed to die there because they had bullied the hell out of Trusty John since elementary school, calling him a greaser and skank and taping "Kick Me" signs to his back. Foolborn and Trusty John had lists, both of them, along with a page from a journal assignment on writing about their emotions that Mrs. K. had assigned in English class:

MILTON ON GRANDLEY: He grazed alone on the playground in third grade and made bovine sounds. Hillbilly.

TRUSTY JOHN ON GRANDLEY: The guy is a huge asshole and always has been and I wish someone would gouge his eyeballs out with a sword.

MILTON ON LISTER: Listening to him talk is always a disappointment.

TRUSTY JOHN ON LISTER: He shish kebabbed a mouse with a pencil.

MILTON ON FAYLE: He dawdles around school like a lascivious mouth-breather. Can the guy even speak fluent English? Absent of any sapience or wit, a deipnosophist he is not.

TRUSTY JOHN ON FAYLE: Fayle plays frisbee golf with a bunch of nerds.

Milton the Fool had recently noticed a worsening condition on his skin, which was that he was becoming more hirsute, especially on his feet and hands, and sometimes he felt like an animal trapped inside a human's body, as if he were undergoing some metamorphosis into a werewolf or some other beast. His eczema was worse, probably from the stress of wanting to shoot up the school, but he also held a deep animosity toward his father, a nondenominational pastor who worried Milton was following the devil, having gotten into trouble for car vandalism in the past, and concerned, too, that if Milton didn't repent of his sins with a pure heart, he would later regret it, poor Milton the Fool. His father pushed him away and made him feel like he was a disgusting thing, the poor fucker, and now Milton felt it was impossible to rid himself of that knowledge.

In the car, Cassie was shocked to realize that she wasn't as nervous or afraid of helping the two Fools as she thought she would be because she still wasn't fully convinced that they would go through with it. She kept thinking they would back out; they weren't ready for this because they weren't that risky. Milton adored Cassie and never talked back to her whenever she told them their behavior was inexplicable and dumb.

Milton Foolborn stared straight ahead, clicking his tongue.

"Come off it," Cassie told him. "You guys can't to do this. Trusty

John's making you. He's the one who really gets treated like garbage, like Matthew. They bully Matthew because he stutters."

"Stop talking about Matthew," he told her. "I know you like him."

"You get caught shooting up the school, your life is over," Cassie replied. "You realize that, right?"

"You like Matthew," Milton said, staring straight ahead. "He's not as smart as everyone thinks he is. He's in class right now with Grandley and Lister."

Through the passenger's-side window, Cassie caught sight of a figure crossing the street, an old man who walked stooped over with a cane. When she turned to tell Milton, he was biting on a thumbnail so hard it was bleeding. "That's gross," she told him.

He wiped his bloody thumb on his shirt.

"There's an old man over there," she said. "I think it's the enemy. The devil. He's here."

"Where the hell is Trusty John."

Cassie, raised in an evangelist church and by philoprogenitive parents whose love of children resulted in Cassie's seven younger siblings, couldn't find the old man now, but she knew it had to be the devil, that devious pest, messenger, the enemy, taking the form of an old man at times, an apparition only a few people could see. Cassie believed she was one of them. In church, she was overtaken by the Holy Spirit, that's what she so often said, seeing people fall over, but more importantly, when she was little she witnessed the devil disguised as the old man with the cane. She was outside playing with her sister when she noticed him standing beside the house next door, stooped over with his cane, but when Cassie's sister turned to look, he disappeared. *Oh, stop, don't be dumb, you're scared of everything* . . . but only the devil could play those kinds of tricks, right? "I'm scared it means something terrible is going to happen," Cassie's sister told her, and that night their father was sitting in his recliner when he fell over dead from a brain aneurysm.

Milton had heard all these stories from her, that throughout Cassie's childhood she saw the devil other times, like once when Cassie was walking home from school one day when the old man was sitting in a rocking chair on her porch, and as Cassie walked by the man tapped his cane to try to get her attention, which of course frightened her, and she began to run inside. But her mother told her not to be afraid. "God protects us," she told her, and yet, the next morning her grandmother had a stroke, collapsed in the kitchen, and was taken by ambulance to the hospital. There were other stories like these, usually tragedies that followed seeing the old man with the cane, all of which appeared to be moments of paranoia in Cassie, or hysteria, but most likely coincidences.

In Milton's car, looking out the passenger's-side window, Cassie saw the low, darkening clouds and the grainy land below them, the trees with bare branches and the roofs of buildings past the school. The old devil was nowhere to be found, but there was a storm approaching for sure, as if confirming the impending doom of the last days of the Earth; the end was near, they said. Scripture points to it. Fires and earthquakes. People killing each other.

When Trusty John pulled up next to them in his battered Geo Metro blasting Guns N' Roses with the windows down, he was wearing a shaggy wig. Cassie said she espied horns growing on Milton's head, with a bird crawling out to mock Matthew because he was Native, which made her begin to cry.

"Don't move," Milton told her, and stepped out of the car and got into the passenger's seat of Trusty John's car, where the two discussed their plan of entering through the south doors of the school, near the administration offices; that way they could get to the principal, vice principal, and dean of boys first. Whoever they saw first would be the first to get shot.

They quickly got out and opened the trunk. She thought Milton looked as evil as he felt. He was constantly telling her about his dreams of metamorphosis into some type of animal, and now she could almost see it in his face. Trusty John had the expression of someone in such a state of panic that she wasn't sure whether he would pass out right there in the parking lot; or maybe she felt dizzy herself from panic. Without any hesitation, they armed themselves with their weapons, and then she felt the heavy slam of the trunk. She thought of the distractive rivalries and enemies and wondered about any indications that confirmed public suspicion of their violence, trying to free herself from the evil thoughts that had also taken shape in Milton and Trusty John's minds, and what about anyone who bore public witness to all this, what of the survivors, the teachers and staff and innocent students still drowsy from the smell of floor cleaner and the early morning's lull? What about them?

Milton the Fool motioned for her to go, so she got out of the car and ran toward the school, her anxiety and adrenaline pumping, and what of those poor victims? What did all this mean anyway, six hundred students about to be released for the day in chaos, policemen and ambulances ready to speed down Second Avenue with screaming sirens, and she was too far beyond the space of rational thought as she opened the door of the school and hurried down to the end of the hallway before turning a corner to find, to her surprise, her new love interest, poor Matthew, fresh from a beating, leaning against his locker with a bloody mouth.

7.
ACROSTIC FOR CASSIE

Capricorn, whose star is Deneb Algedi,
As a goat with horns (or horned goat)
Swims like Pan, sick with love,
So do I.
I do not know how he captured you.
Envy is never gentle on Holy ground.

8. SUFFERING

We tried to remain positive in all our suffering, strong in faith that working through the torment on torrential waters would bring us closer to our healing and salvation, but how was this possible? Outside in the courtyard, we collected pebbles and rocks and hid them in our shoes, hoping they would aid in our escape at some point even though we didn't know how we would do it yet, and some of us played possum to try to get released to the hospital, but it always failed, the guards were on to us. They allowed us to throw breadcrumbs to the birds like mentally ill patients, but only grackles gathered and then flew away, making noises. The guards told us, so methodical in their cruelty and phlegmatic mannerisms, that there were missing children somewhere out in the woods who were bloodthirsty demons living like animals; that's what they said in their attempts to get us to believe everything they told us, that we could possibly contract syphilis by mosquitoes, and that the full red moon shining in the sky meant the cocks were crowing in warning of the parasites slithering out of the Gudgekin River to crawl into our ears and anuses while we slept and could only leave our bodies through waste, otherwise they grew inside our bellies and would eat our intestines and major organs. Parasites could destroy us slowly and leave us suffering with an intense pain worse than the cruelties of a long life living on government support, full of food vouchers and reputations for living in poverty.

We tried to stay healthy. Some of us worried we would rot away alive there and have our bodies dumped in the woods among the beasts and critters, while others thought of malnutrition and disease. How could we trust the guards or drill sergeants after the way they treated us and talked to us like vermin? How could we flush our stew down the toilet and survive without collapsing from weakness? We were hopeless insomniacs, dragging our feet around our rooms, worried about getting sick, contemplating the vast and inscrutable sky, the fleeting sunsets, the sterile illusions that we would somehow survive all that agony. Some of us fell to pieces and were led away to our rooms, and those of us who tried to remain strong felt like street dogs or feral animals who refrained from shrieking or losing it, blinking rapidly in the shock of disaster and succumbing to the crisis of terror, struggling to remain calm, unperturbed in the circumstance of the guards' power, hiding our emotions as we worried about the coming days and weeks. Others felt it wasn't that bad, not really, because the guards and drill sergeants often argued among themselves and forgot about harassing us for a little while, and the state workers wouldn't allow any real harm to us, otherwise they would all go to jail and the place would shut down.

One afternoon, the local recluse, Agatha Klemm, made a rare appearance to read her poetry to us. She arrived escorted by one of the guards, who explained that she requested to read a few poems to us, something she apparently did every so often. She was wearing a long black dress with sleeves, black shoes, and a black hat that made her look like she'd just attended a funeral, but that was the way she dressed all the time, evidently, and in town people would see her walking downtown carrying her groceries and wearing all black. The guards brought her a chair to sit with us in the dayroom. Now that we saw her up close, we could see her pale skin and sunken, light eyes, and her frail hands, all bone and veins; perhaps she wore the long sleeves and hat to protect her skin from the sun—that's what one of the guards later told us.

"I understand loneliness," she told us. "I know what it's like to hurt, to be alone and feel like nobody cares whether you live or die."

She read us her poems about coiled branches of trees, about wind chimes, roosters, and loneliness. She read about losing people close to her. "*I had a constant longing to explain,*" she read, "*and to see the world's complexities unwind. I loved the rain, collecting insects, and seeing God in the eyes of a giraffe.*" She told us she burned rosemary in her house so that the aroma would help her sleep. Once, as she was trying to close her window during a windstorm, the leaves from her yard blew inside and swirled into the form of a colorful bird. We leaned forward and listened to her, the only person we felt showed us any empathy. She understood the passage of time as an investment in learning and changing. She knew our fears, our nightmares, and told us that life was unfair and brutal and that understanding would come when we needed to find the beauty in others and in the world. When she got up to leave, we wanted to embrace her, implore her to stay with us, talk to us, help us feel alive again. She encouraged us to write down our feelings and to persist in writing. (That night I felt inspired and wrote a fragment of a poem, which I revised over the next few days. I've kept that poem fragment and have copied it here.)

> Desiring something new, I took up art,
> photography, and writing Cassie Magdal,
> A girl I loved from school who would begin
> her letters, "I Love You!" Then, one July,
> she wrote, "I have a boyfriend—so goodbye."
> My Matthew hid his letters in a vase,
> while others were discovered in the den
> (by me, of course), inside a camera case.
> Inside his desk: a necklace, ring, a pen,

a garment made from satin, trimmed with lace.
Why did he steal the girl I loved?
One day I'll know and leave this place by train,
And hope to find Matthew dead in the rain.

(Pitiful. This fool, so tumid with dramatic asperity.)

Our evenings were rough. After dinner as we sat in the dayroom and watched *The Fresh Prince of Bel-Air* or *Cheers* with the guards, nobody was allowed to even talk about the shows or anything else. Those of us who grew bored with Ping-Pong or chess or checkers watched TV as a way to pass time until bed. Many of us grew up watching TV when we were home alone, especially after school or while skipping school. At home some of us didn't have video games or weren't allowed to play them. If we had cable TV, we could watch *I Dream of Jeannie* with Barbara Eden, whose beauty, according to Trusty John, was comparable to Dawn Wells, who played Mary Ann on *Gilligan's Island*, another show that played in syndication on afternoon cable TV. The detention staff had many of those old shows on VHS. As we watched an episode of *Gilligan's Island*, Trusty John mused aloud the question as to why the character The Professor was busy building washing machines and playing with bamboo sticks instead of having threesomes 24/7 with Mary Ann and Ginger, an outburst that landed him in the wing facing the wall for twenty minutes as punishment. Most nights we watched *Sanford and Son*, *What's Happening!!*, and *Welcome Back, Kotter*, because the staff seemed to like those shows more than we did, but we could relate to the poverty even though the shows were set in faraway places. The Sweathogs in *Welcome Back, Kotter*, for example, lived in Brooklyn, a place many of us couldn't even point to on a map, yet we rooted for them like they were in our O.D. classrooms, the same way we rooted for Raj, Dwayne, and Rerun in *What's Happening!!* We rarely watched movies, and when we did it was usually something terribly depressing and G-rated on the weekends. (The only movie I recall us watching was *The Outsiders*, directed by Francis Ford Coppola, taken from the book which, not shockingly, none of the guards had read.)

From where we sat in the dayroom, we could see the western doors with bulletproof glass that led outside to the courtyard. The floodlights lit up the courtyard enough to cast shadows across the tall fence, which tended to tremble if you looked at them long enough, shadows that tormented us like strange noises in the night. The shadows under the luminous stars brought us mercilessly closer to thoughts of despair, death, and suffering, conjuring all kinds of different shapes that ranged from giant axes to deformed figures who might leap out at any moment and break through the bulletproof glass to kill everyone, or at least that's the way they appeared most nights, and we could see the dogs roaming around out there every so often like ferocious beasts, at times even hearing their soulful howl or incessant barking, and we wondered whether they were eating the small animals or fighting coyotes. The two dogs were black Dobermans who, according to the staff, were temperamental and could turn on a human at any moment due to their skulls being too small and creating a pressure against their brains that made them, essentially, insane. "Not much different than you people" is how one of the guards with a crew cut put it. The guard's name was Mr. Elden, and he was the most bullyish of all the guards, always standing with his arms crossed over his big belly and using a Coke can to spit tobacco into. When he wasn't harassing us about fidgeting our hands or telling us about his high school wrestling career, he would step outside and smoke a cigarette in what appeared to be record time. One of the other guards said

Elden could smoke in his sleep with Skoal in his mouth. Like many of the other guards, Elden picked on Matthew the most, often pointing out his stutter and calling him "Chief." He tried to get him angry, which never worked, unlike some of the other Indian residents, who lost it and began yelling and then were sent to room confinement.

We watched things like this unfold in the dayroom, especially at night when people got anxious or irritable more often. The control booth was also visible from the dayroom, though due to the two-way glass we couldn't see inside even though we imagined the staff sitting in there observing the empty suspense and the illusion that they were giving us orders, more absorbed in themselves than in us. The four wings were also visible from the dayroom, and depending on where you were sitting you could see either wings A and B together or wings C and D, which didn't matter unless someone was forced to sit facing the wall in punishment, like what usually happened to Trusty John from opening his mouth and saying something inappropriate. Nobody liked to sit facing the wall for thirty minutes. Trusty John was on level five, the lowest level, due to his behavior and getting low scores from the guards. He had to go to bed at 8:30 p.m. with the others on levels four and five. At night we thought of our loves, our friends, and our pets. We lay in our beds until the staff in the control booth turned off the lights in our room. We knew the moment the lights went out that they would remain off until morning when they unlocked our doors and opened them to wake us. The silence in our rooms gave us time to long for the people we loved, to reflect on what we had done to land us there, and to consider how our misfortunes would be resolved in onus. Time fell over us like a stuffy blanket while the long deliriums of sleep left us feeling alone and diminished in solitude, in suspicion and doubt, even during the days as we sat doing simple handouts in the classroom, restless as a wild horse, worried.

"Do the handouts," they told us. "Draw a square. Make a pie chart. It's simple math."

"Make a pie chart?"

"Follow the instructions," they told us. "Study the examples and read them. Simple. We're not getting paid to do your schoolwork."

We scribbled and erased. We worked through as much as we could. When we were done, we put our heads on our desks.

What did it mean to forgive ourselves, as so many people instructed us to do, and how was that supposed to make us feel better, heal us, like they said it would do, as we managed to accumulate all the guilt that led us to this horrible place, lost in the anechoic tunnel of incarceration and bitterness and instruction as drill sergeants, teachers, and staff controlled our every step like we were a group of cattle awaiting slaughter, sitting in small rooms, mute, still, unsure whether our actions would worsen our inevitable fate because the staff informed us they would report everything we said and did to the court, which only worsened our anxieties and terror.

What did it mean to forgive ourselves for hurting our families or teachers or the people we stole from or attacked or left feeling no remorse for us in our mistakes after second, third, and even fourth chances, and why in the terrible grief of the world were we supposed to forgive others who hurt us first? The ones who thrust themselves on us, abused us with their bodies or words or objects that left scars and terror way worse than any fear and pain we had felt before?

What did it mean to forgive anyone for that matter, hanging on to the interminable pain and restlessness of trauma? We tried to relax and keep our minds focused on anything except our own troubles. We played Ping-Pong, chess, and read kids' adventure books. We watched TV any chance we could. We tried talking to the staff and guards to pass the time, but they wouldn't let us talk much about personal issues, especially in front of everyone. All we could really do was survive and hope for nice dreams.

We tried to bide our time outdoors. Waiting against the despotism of days so that we could have our chance to go to court and be released, we doubted the legitimacy of the juvenile justice system and wandered around the courtyard, walking in circles when we weren't reading or playing basketball, walking through the paths of infamy where no happy person ever walked, or slept, or read books while sitting alone beside the shrubbery, this place where detention staff exulted at the rancid stench of cattle from the feed lot a mile down the road or the heavy clouds of grackles that muddied the afternoon sky, their voices filled with a deep jauntiness and cruelty, "Look, they're free! They're free!"

What else could we do but keep our heads down and walk around the path in wide circles, wishing vengeance on them until the world became saturated with their corpses, sighing in the gloomy auras of their merciless rancor until we could no longer alleviate such gibber and nonsense and shut them out? So we entered and existed in the space of our own imaginations, drawing comics and writing stories that filled up pages and pages. Some said blessings and chanted, "I am in control," and some said they would rather be dead than forced to live in these conditions, while others said this place was better than any place they had lived, with three meals every day, a snack at night, a clean shower, and a place to sleep. But most of us waited embittered in the custody of the state, under their surveillance, feeling as if we were drowning like rats, thinking of the people we loved, avenged in the agony of incarceration.

9. A PLAGUE OF FROGS

Despite all his pleading that it would be inconceivable he would cause any friction among residents who disliked him, or that he would say or do anything to make the guards believe he was a physical threat to anyone else in the facility, or even that he would fixate on his bitterness about being held against his will like everyone else, Matthew could not stop the guards from waking him in the middle of the night to lead him down to the Columbus House basement. We wondered whether he documented anything we said in the courtyard or while we persevered in our labor that would be used against us in court, because we were paranoid, but he also told us his most gratifying writing was done in that basement (which was why we believed he actually didn't mind being sent down there), sunken into the boue of his punishment and accepting his insomnia with an illusory vertigo sparked by outpourings of insane thoughts and images, describing everything from the imagined curve of a shooting star to the stench of the dead slime in the corners of the damp basement, convincing himself (and us) that the most feared enemy was not the punishment from the drill sergeants or the guards, but rather ourselves, and that the very men who came against us, despite inflicting their panic in us, were actually sighing a grief and pain of their own that was way worse than anything we were experiencing, that was for certain he said, that's what he told us in the courtyard, and once we understood it, we would appreciate and honor the disconsolate sludge he was pulling from our lives.

What sludge, we wondered, and what specific details about each of us were unraveling in his mind down there in that damp hellhole, which none of us had seen? What sludge? What inspired him to write about us down there, under the affliction of the drill sergeants' harsh punishment, muttering to himself and trying to tame the bitter rage in the dim light as he scribbled while the rest of us were asleep, while the world around us slept, what names did he refer to us by if he didn't use our real names, was it fiction or real events, did he punish us in his imagination by lashing us with the hard rain and lightning, did he whip us until our backs bled, did he confine us to adult prisons and basements where rats scattered about, did he take breaks and feel a joy in knowing we would read his stories one day and recognize ourselves (because he was the *gifted* artist after all), pissing in the corner into empty paint cans and cardboard boxes, checking the lock and repeatedly knocking on the door to ask one of the drill sergeants for a drink of water, hiding his notebook and pencils, and falling asleep as easily down there as he did back in his room?

By morning he emerged well rested, healthy and alert as before, though we imagined him suffocating down there, breathing in the same air that would asphyxiate him, under the menace of the drill sergeants' dominion, confusing their shadows with the ghosts of past residents who drowned in the Gudgekin River, at the mercy of an inescapable fate unless it meant an exchange of sexual favors first, a licentious and painful affair between drill sergeant and Matthew while he pounded the concrete floor with his fist. "Don't speak a word about this," they would tell him, "never say anything about how we will force you into uncomfortable poses in the presence of only our shadows on the walls," because he would not have the strength or will to resist the ravages of their power, or their charge on him, which was better for him because he could hold it against them, unaware it was happening to us, too. That's how we imagined it all playing out, sighing in the volcanic heat in our rooms and wondering whether he was writing the novel that would make him famous and well loved, adored, praised, and becoming the insanely sententious advent of a certain type of fiction to arrive and blast everyone away with his genius. That's what we feared would happen when we talked in the courtyard about him or during the long hours spent outside.

Most days we worked for hours in the worst drought in O.D. history, the absolute worst, trying not to die, wounded and feeble from so much work. Every day Brandon pretended to faint from heat exhaustion, and each time he fainted was more dramatic than the previous time, staggering around like a drunkard before collapsing and mumbling to himself, but the guards caught on after a few days when they found his journal in the classroom containing prolix passages he'd written about how dumb they were for believing his shenanigans. Even drenched in sweat, they quit dickering with him whenever he complained of the heat or confessed that he was suffering from hallucinations; I mean, he and Ace had such an affinity for marijuana that they claimed they would respectfully take a military kick to the groin in exchange for one measly joint, and that they were better off buried alive than having to enter rehab because nothing could ever save them, not any former hippy drug counselor or propitious rehab facility or being locked up among drill sergeants with foul breath and cirrhotic livers. The drought had lasted several months, with cold, breezy days clouding the air with blowing dust while we moiled outside the facility in the oppressive gusts of dirt, tearing fish apart with our fingers and pulling weeds along the perimeter of the barbed-wire fence, every day worse than the last, every day a more frightening hell full of blizzards of gnats and headless roosters hanging by their feet, dripping blood on our hands, haunting us like the ghosts of lepers rising up out of the brackish water whose bodies looked like burned flesh, every day holding our breath in horror while suffering withdrawals and debility, constipated from codeine and dragging our feet through tepid animal guts, our judgment and actions irremediable in the views of all staff, drill sergeants, and especially the facility director, whose name was Strangelove, which really was his name, Mr. Strangelove who said we were too weak-minded to do anything correctly, even as addicts and criminals, and that we all might as well burn.

The wind picked up. The sun went pale behind a cloud, casting a shadow across the grounds in what felt like a moment of dolorous doom. In his wheelchair, Strangelove raised his arms and cursed while the guards and drill sergeants yelled at us to work harder and stop complaining that our knees and backs ached. The longer they monitored us, the more they noticed our asthenia and mannerisms, but we ignored them, we really did, and allowed the afternoons to disappear from our minds so that, rather than succumbing to their abuse, we celebrated in our imaginations, pretending we were somewhere else and weren't juvenile addicts and criminals; we pretended we had discovered a secret island that needed to be cleared for construction of a future destination for tourists, a multimillion-dollar, three-hundred-room resort with swimming pools, restaurants, marbled floors and entryways, coffered ceilings, and a sculptured garden with fountains all overlooking an ocean where one could see whales and dolphins in the distance and the sunset on the horizon. We needed to do this to survive, creating maps and drawings, focusing on our artwork and talking about it in the courtyard when nobody wanted to do anything except stand around and talk, because that was all we could really do when we worked, exist in the fantasy. In this space of our imaginations, Strangelove and other contemptuous sergeants and guards slowly morphed into beasts with pig snouts and bulging eyes and an excrescence of facial warts, which was why we began to think of them as island pigs, freakish beings who lifted their arms and hollered while the rest of us ignored them, kept our heads down, and persisted in our drudgery.

They yelled at us to work harder. They called us selfish, impudent grues. Strangelove was as abstruse and sordid as his mannerisms. Hard of hearing, he motioned for us to lean in to him in his wheelchair whenever he spoke, like an elderly man, and as we did so he grabbed our shoulder with a firm and unnecessary grip, sometimes refusing to let go until he was done talking. He talked openly of his interests in those of us who liked to draw or paint, claiming he was once an art student in Chicago in the early seventies, and a darn fine one he said, favoring nudes and surrealism, and challenging us to draw inordinate-sized body parts, he really did—though more often his conversations turned grim, to his declining health and epilepsy, his ischemic colitis, or, even more often, he sputtered all kinds of angry ipsedixitisms based on his venal personality, and like the drill sergeants and a few staff at that facility, he attempted to deceive anyone he thought might take advantage of him, gambling in late-night card games and having an objurgatory manner about him that only made people dislike him even more, clueless as he was to the unforeseeable future, tormented by defeat. He was a sad man. The agency he and the staff imposed on themselves to enforce in us a state of trepidation became less effective for them and less threatening for us. The drill sergeants inculcated no decorum with their haughty manner of walking around the grounds while we toiled, grinding the ground, digging and pulling and sweating, stinking of fish guts and dirt, and watching them was like observing a senile crisis happening before our eyes because the more we ignored them, the more they began to rebel against one another in what appeared to be a shouting match filled with humiliation. As in the classroom earlier, most of us remained quiet as we worked and, of course, daydreamed. Our minds (or at least my mind) was able to fill long periods of time with narrative fantasies loaded with nightmarish details, like the drill sergeants as anthropomorphic characters sprouting horns on their heads or girding each other during some military circle jerk, or the way their eyes bulged from their heads like those of a pug. Fantasies as such involved whole scenes that fleshed out in our minds like cartoons, as in the way the chimp in *Speed Racer* hopped up and down whenever he got excited and followed Speed Racer's dad around in the garage, or how when the drill sergeants walked together toward the Columbus House we considered them as Fleegle and Drooper and Snorky from *The Banana Splits*, running around and bumping into one another and falling down. We were able to maintain such fantasies and play these films in our minds to help pass the time (something I still do all these years later, any time I find myself in a shelter, without a TV, or sleeping outside).

We heard thunder rumble in the distance. There was so much disorder that the drill sergeants began arguing with their own shadows stretching across the grass while the rest of us felt exhausted in midafternoon dust and wind, gripping our shovels and trying not to interrupt their insanity as they stomped their feet in the dirt and yammered about the need for discipline and respect, pureness and conservative values, the foolish wastefulness of our lives, sin, welfare, food stamps for the lazy, unnecessary social services, bloodthirsty advocates for socialism and raising taxes, a disregard for military compliance and honor of the Constitution—they asked themselves questions and then answered them, showing their fists to their own shadows, their shiny black boots well oiled and buffed by us with a fine chamois, each of those lubricious bastards gritting their teeth behind their aviator sunglasses and telling us to get back to work, all of us, because we wouldn't be able to sleep peacefully without an understanding that we were developing a work ethic, even if we didn't fully accept it at this point in our lives, we wouldn't be capable of mopping some old drooler's ordure in a nursing home, which was where we'd be employed someday if we didn't get our priorities in order and realize the values they were trying to teach us; and when one of us spoke up and said, "Sir, I'd actually like to be a nurse someday," a mighty anti-favonian wind lifted the dust around the drill sergeants' feet while they shat their pants and waved their arms in alarm and disbelief.

The weather turned worse. Overhead, as if a sudden and interrupted kismet from God, we heard a loud crash of thunder as crows circled above us, in warning of the coming storm. Someone screamed. Under dark clouds the crows took equivocal positions, croaking and circling, *cacaw*, the chant of the ever-circling crows, a noise we would hear in the grip of our insomnia each night whenever we reflected back on that day, *cacaw*, although in the moment we could only follow the bulbous clouds as the wind blew harder and wonder whether the crows were an augural sign of a coming plague or cozening us by making their angry noises, *cacaw, cacaw*. Sergeant Jackson, possibly the most diseased of the drill sergeants, called forth that his liver poured upon the Earth for the destruction of life in his own mocking chant of the ever-circling crows: "*Cacaw, cacaw!*" (Coincidentally, in *The Devil Is a Southpaw*, a group of crows attack Don outside as Charlie watches with delight from the window.)

The others told us to get in line, so caught up in their own vociferations that even they were unaware of any stormy coruscations in the sky, focused as they were on our bodies maintaining a straight, firm line, reminding us to keep our hands at our side and our faces looking forward, but then the thunder clapped and the rain started, and they remained unaffected while the rest of us covered our heads because the rain was coming down harder by the second with an incredulous fury, growing more voracious and horrifying the longer we stood there in the downpour, yet they remained firm in their persistence to maintain order and told us we would walk in a straight line into the Columbus House basement for our own safety and well-being until the storm passed through. Sure enough, Sergeants Ambrose, Lee, and Cash were already jogging toward the building while Jackson remained with us and told us to stay in line.

Then the torrential storm hit. We had never felt such a pluvial storm where the sky turned a pale shade of yellow and gray, the wind circled in gusts, and rain beat down on us so hard that we could barely see or hear anything, such a miserable, cold drastic change from twenty minutes earlier, and now the rain splattered the sidewalks and formed puddles at our feet, and still Jackson told us not to move, threatening to tackle anyone who made a run for it—he seriously said that—and we called out for help, of course, who wouldn't? I mean, we were all pleading for him to let us run inside to protect us from the torrential storm, but that fool Jackson remained silent, without any sense of empathy or fear of losing his life, and certainly not worried that any of us would die, that soulless, square, rigid, unsympathetic lout whom we all could've taken down right then had we been in agreement to charge him and wrestle him, because it would've been twelve against one, but nobody moved; we all obeyed and got soaked, struggling to stand still in the furious weather. Across the grounds, the high winds bent tree branches and sucked frogs out of the river, sweeping them into the air before they rained down on us. Jackson told us to run, so we ran after him toward the Columbus House while frogs fell on us like large hail described in Ezekiel, Exodus, Joshua, and Isaiah; I mean, it was crazy how the frogs landed on the ground and bounced, guts exploding and soaked in the rain as if we were the victims of a bad augury, numerous and turbulent in our measureless nightmare, frogs like hail falling from the sky in the storm that demolished us as we ran covering our heads, our steps splashing in rainwater and blood. Once we made it inside the building and let out moans of relief, we heard the tornado sirens going off in the distance while the drill sergeants crouched in fetal position, covering their own heads, and telling us to crouch, too, unless we wanted to die. The panic in their voices was nothing like we had heard from them before, rattled and hoarse, and seeing them in the fetal position and so unhinged was satisfying. None of us crouched down beside the sergeants; we ignored them and wandered down the halls and rushed up the stairs to the windows, the most dangerous area during such a storm, and yet it did not feel terrifying to be standing in front of a window; the anguish and humiliation we succumbed to every day at the Columbus House was worse as we were held captive and confined to our island of buildings and concrete beds. The windows before us were too foggy to see anything in the storm, but we imagined what was out there: tree limbs and power lines down all around in Tophet, the frogs covering the grounds the whole way to the woods, the tire swing still swaying outside, and the nearby Gudgekin River overflowing and bubbling with the stench of dead catfish. This was a storm that made you wonder what was real and what was deceptive, because through the foggy window we heard the cries of the dogs and the screeching of the birds. We heard a bobcat screaming from somewhere deep in the woods.

The storm didn't last long. Once things settled down and the tornado warning lifted, the sun broke through the clouds, the forces of disorder calmed, and the sergeants sat on metal chairs under the cool shadows of the Columbus House's roof; therefore, we walked around the grounds inspecting the frog remains. They were everywhere, shriveled and torn apart, splattered on the sidewalk and fence. Their bodies were already hard despite so much moisture on the ground.

The frogs were gifts to spare our suffering, like flowers on mirrors or angels fallen from the sky, overflowing our fate with the possibilities of time and space for our future where a person would have to squelch through the moss and swamplands of a flooded Earth, stepping over dead bodies and animal carcasses with the exposed bones and open flesh where their spirits broke free and rose to the heavens. We recognized the blood of Christ that covered our hands like the blood that splattered the walls in our nightmares, filling the swamps and ponds we trudged through during our imagined escape, blood that covered our clothing and stained no matter how hard we scrubbed or wrung them out, our moans ringing through the night in the blue-gray world, our miserable, gloomy moans that shook the trees around us like an explosion while we remained seized in a spell of dizzy horror and anguish, but of course, there was no blood. Yet we picked up the guts and innards, we were a nation of heroes aroused by the smell of war and dead things, wrapped in our own salvation and courage, refusing to embrace any weakness despite being under the surveillance of a brutal regime. We continued to walk, half-asleep into the evening, picking up the frogs while that sadistic grobian Sergeant Cash and the others piled together in their barracks in a private Columbus House room where they got drunk on gin and whiskey, roughed-up and pink-faced under drab-colored paintings on the wall of generals in wigs and military men in uniform.

What else were we supposed to do under such circumstances, anyway, except acknowledge a purpose to our suffering? What else but feed our own enthusiasm for freedom? We lingered for hours in the voracious swarm of insects among the dead frogs. We raced around a blazing fire, we walked across London Bridge before it collapsed, and we parted the Red Sea in front of the children of Israel. The helicopters overhead arrived to rescue us from that hellish prison and then transmogrified into giant noisy birds whose heavy wings shed skin and bits of ash as they all went up in flames and burned on their way into the otherworld, or underworld, chasing some bizarre evil that surrounded us like a thick fog.

After fishing the roaches out of our stew that night, we sat in the dayroom drawing frogs and blood and destruction. We sketched underground tunnels where we escaped in our imaginations, through meandering paths into a caliginous underworld full of swarms of mosquitoes and rats, a place where the dead crawled on their bellies as they cried out for help, where the misfortunate suffered from their sins, and where people with burned skin and goat heads and long tails lamented to one another about their pain, because there had to exist a place worse than where we were; surely our punishment was nothing compared to those with rotting souls tormented by some evil presence that slithered through the underground tunnels in the world to seek the unruly who were never held accountable for their actions, where justice was never served. In whatever way possible, we tried to cling to the hope that we wouldn't find ourselves trapped there, too, and that we would find our way out and back to freedom; justice would be served, lessons learned, sins forgiven. Some of us grew up in households with fathers as preachers and wondered whether the storm was an act of God or whether it was an act of nature's free will.

Across the grounds outside and under the moon, where the Columbus House's shadow sloped down the grass to the woods, the possums and snakes came out and ate the remaining carcasses of frogs we weren't able to gather in our trash bags earlier in the day, or at least that's what the guards told us that night, and how we tell it whenever we tell the story today, that the courtyard was as bright and verdant as the countryside, and then gators crawled out of the woods from the swamps and attacked the drill sergeants then carried them alive back into the swamps, in the drizzle, and as we celebrated their deaths under the moonlight, the cobwebs were hanging from the trees, everywhere, holding the deadly spiders we feared, because we were never absent of terror; even when the possums and snakes came to rescue us by eating the dead frogs and the drill sergeants were eaten alive by the alligators, our fears were never completely obliterated from our minds. When we tell the story that way, it is more pleasing to have the drill sergeants suffer like us and die.

None of them wanted us to talk about our worries, though, or anything batrachian, or how harrowing the storm felt. It didn't matter, they told us, never explaining why they didn't want to talk about it, and yet the frogs filled our minds in the delirium of our incredulity, falling and wafting in the air in our imaginations and dreams, flooding the land as we had seen, yet so far removed from the world that we tried to describe the places we dreamed of; the more we tried talking about the dreams, the less real they felt, even if casually bringing them up during a game of dominoes or chess, or during a snack before bed when the room was still and the guards were so exhausted their eyes were heavy with dark circles underneath them. We talked, instead, of what it meant to stand without shoes on the sunbaked concrete outside in a record heat wave, and whether the weather was an omen or a reaction of trauma from the way people mistreat the Earth, because Matthew brought up that the Earth reacts to trauma in the same way people do; that's what he said, in fact, even when nobody was talking about the weather.

We were awakened by the frogs that night as they ran down our walls and doors like the excrement we smeared in retaliation, and when the guards opened our doors and noticed the frogs we had smashed and smeared across the walls, they brought us mops and buckets and rolls of brown paper towels to clean it all up. All night frogs kept coming through the cracks in our rooms, and the more we wiped the walls the worse they appeared, smearing their skin and blood everywhere, returning to their folly as a dog returns to its vomit.

10.
STRANGELOVE

We woke twisted in terror from disturbing dreams and restless sleep, wondering whether things would feel any different after such a catastrophic storm, especially one as abnormal as frogs falling from the sky and plaguing our rooms. Many of us, too, were concerned about Matthew's emotional state, we really were, because the poor stuttering boy was terrified, especially at breakfast when we noticed how he viewed the conversation about the storm as an opportunity to ask the guards, in a mocking tone, whether we could all go naked into the courtyard like fierce religious missionaries drawn to connect with nature, feed on grass, and drink from the Gudgekin River with the animals, which caused disruption and laughter in the room and led one of the guards to take Matthew by the arm outside and to the Columbus House basement, where he would be subjected to isolation and punishment for at least two slow and miserable hours. After that horrible storm, every night grew longer as the spring weather brought heavy storms. The first night the rain swept across the plains of Dublan, through red earth and green grazing land against the frightened cattle and chickens and splashing across the amber river with its broken branches floating along with the current. The rain came down hard like an uproar of wolves; a whole county prayed for order due to nature being out of their control, and flooding grew worse under the bridges and in valleys, low street areas where men brought home dead deer in their pickup trucks and the ghosts of Indians crouched in plotting their revenge on white people whose houses with flat roofs were leaking from so much hard rain. The detention center and Columbus House roofs were flat as well, echoing through the halls from the hail and pattering of the storm.

By morning the Columbus House basement was dim and smelled of mildew (enough to make Matthew ill, certainly), damp and empty except for a few shelves where he had stashed books to read because he was sent there so often. The storm didn't ease anyone's feelings about our punishment. Most of the residents were placed in their rooms, alone, with nothing except their beds and toilets, but the guards always sent Matthew to the Columbus House basement. How iniquitous, wasn't it, as he sat alone outside on the courtyard while the drill sergeants strolled by, smoking cigarettes. He held a look of despondence, as though falling dizzily, endlessly, from some high mountain, and then pointed at them with his right hand while making a fist with his left; but then he looked at his left hand, uncertain, surprised (or saddened, because he was invariably sad on purpose to try to gain the empathy of anyone he could) by his fist, and he outstretched his fingers and made a nimble, indiscernible movement with his fingers, as if he'd only discovered their movement for the first time. Right then we noticed the third finger of his left hand was slightly curved and smaller. Someone pointed this out to the guards, who were smoking and not even paying attention to us, and when they turned around everyone fell silent. Sergeant Cash cupped his hand behind his ear and asked, "Whose hand is deformed?"

"Matthew's," someone said.

Sergeant Cash dropped his cigarette and stepped on it with his glossy black military boot and then walked over to Matthew and asked to see his hand.

"Which hand?" Matthew asked.

"Stop kidding around, boy." Cash glowered at the hand. "Are you left-handed?"

Matthew nodded.

"Aha—a southpaw, like your pa. Ever seen that movie, *The Devil Is a Southpaw*?"

Matthew shook his head.

Cash turned to the rest of us, applauding toward Ace, who had smears of acne on his cheeks and said, "He's worse than you," and then laughed. "You ever hear the old timer's story about the defiant boy being a southpaw, and what his pa did with his paw?" Ace, annoyed, kept looking straight ahead and remained quiet. Cash, having straightened himself from his stoop, spat a bolus of Red Man on the court and went inside. Matthew sat against the wall beside the doors, where two guards were talking into their radios and motioning for us to come closer to them, something they never did before, so we were confused. One of the guards called for us to line up even though it wasn't time to go back inside. The girls were laughing at something as they lined up, and the rest of us casually got into the line except for Matthew, who remained seated on the ground. The guards lifted him by both arms (he winced) and since Matthew didn't resist, they weren't able to restrain him or hold him down against the ground the way they had to do with certain angry, obstreperous residents.

The facility door opened and the director, Mr. Lanius Shrike Strangelove, hunched forward in his wheelchair with the wily smirk of a drooly demon, wheeled himself onto the court and stared at us. He cleared his throat scornfully, as if it were a substitute for speech to inform us of his importance, so we didn't make a sound; we heard only the distant calling of birds. Strangelove cleared his throat again, this time with greater emphasis, as he wheeled over to us in line. His throat-clearing, the first two times, was intentional, as if challenging us to see whether anyone responded or chuckled. A dare.

Strangelove resembled Dr. Strangelove from the Kubrick film (this is how I recall thinking of him), emphasized by the fact that he had unkempt hair and was in a wheelchair. Some of the staff had told us that he liked to wheel himself into the field behind the facility and sit among the wildflowers at night to deal with his insomnia, and that he, like many of the guards and staff there, gambled on sports on a regular basis and played the lottery and scratch cards daily, medicated under the protection of pharmaceuticals and good drink, and that most afternoons he napped periodically on the small divan in his office with the door closed and smooth jazz music playing. (I pictured him raising a Nazi salute the way Peter Sellers did as Dr. Strangelove in the Kubrick film, speaking in a German accent and leading the dogs out into the field, gripped in the anxiety caused by eating undercooked meat and the diseased animal flesh in stew, wheeling himself through the fields until fatigue made him fall out of his chair and lie helpless as the Dobermans licked his ears and the salt from his brow.)

"Go get in line," one of the guards told Matthew, and Strangelove spun around in his wheelchair while Matthew walked past him to the back of our line. Nobody knew whether Lanius Shrike Strangelove was exasperated or whether he was close to spiraling into some sort of furor, because the third throat-clearing was so obvious and discordant that it stripped us of our dignity; it succeeded in establishing another manner of his hostility, a system of rage, unreserved and complicated and eccentric enough that we all assumed he might as well have been shouting at us. He spun around in a circle in his wheelchair, and once he stopped spinning he cleared his throat yet a fourth time, at the same volume, but the fifth and final time he cleared his throat he made louder, quick noises, as if he were doing an impression of turning the ignition of a car that won't start. His sinister paralalia likely indicated something more deeply troubling that we were incognizant to, surely a mystery to the staff as well since they were below intelligence to comprehend any abstract notions.

Certainly, Cash was as confused as the other guards, putting his hands casually on his hips before telling us to head back inside, where we were told to sit in a circle in the dayroom and keep our hands still. Each of us were aware that Strangelove was a maniacal cad; this was certain as he wheeled himself back inside to the tables where we ate and began eating the sugar cookies that were left for us by the kitchen staff, the whole plate of them, and when Cash addressed him as "sir" in complete seriousness, we wondered whether the whole thing was a joke at our expense, simply to deceive or see which one of us was mortified enough to say something.

"Sir," Cash said to him, "those are the afternoon snacks for the residents."

Strangelove began to have a seizure. In his wheelchair, directly in front of us, he stiffened into an irrepressible convulsion, his face and body juddered in the intensity of his inclemency, as if in the eternity of the abyss in the fulgurant sky. The guards didn't make it in time: he fell forward out of his wheelchair and landed headfirst on the hard floor and then convulsed, vomiting stomach bile. The guards managed to rush over and turn him on his side while the rest of us sat, too afraid to move. One of the guards used a rag to wipe the blood from his brow, and then they sat him up and talked in a low voice to him while we sat still. Strangelove coughed and hacked and cleared his throat, but his head was bleeding and the look in his eyes was dazed—he somehow managed to keep his glasses on after falling out of the wheelchair—and now the guards were down helping and holding fingers in front of his face, asking him for a number, could he remember what day of the week it was, and his name.

We could've made a run for it during all this, but nobody attempted because we weren't as dumb as they said we were. We could've tried to assault the guards, steal their keys and free ourselves, yet we restrained ourselves to everything around us, likely because the event was so unsettling, even when it involved a moronic dotard like Strangelove. (He was deliciously possessed by the devil, wasn't he, falling under a satanic influence right before our eyes. I remember my father telling me that in biblical times, seizures were often the result of demonic possession that could be healed only by Christ.) We were smarter than they thought. Once they were able to put him back in his wheelchair, the rest of us considered our fears as they left our bodies and entered his, because the old, crooked scrote appeared confused, his hair disheveled and his shirt stained with blots of darkened blood.

Strangelove pointed with his left hand at us (as I recall, he was a southpaw, too), as if he were looking directly into the eyes of a cacodemon, but he never spoke. We recognized his angst and had a chance to tell him off right then. We could've gotten away with it. We weren't dumb—we could've told him his seizure served him right for the way he had treated us, and the way he talked down to us, allowing the abuse we had endured outside when we worked on the grounds. We could've told him we were tired of the abuse, the yelling, the roaches in our stew, and the way he grabbed our wrists whenever he talked to us. Our wrists were sore from his grip. Our anger was beyond measure; we were furious and wounded and sickened by him because he allowed everything to happen to us. But we were smart and showed restraint, as most residents do. We sat passive and mute, well behaved, as they wheeled him out of the building. We showed them we were able to control ourselves and not hurt anyone, we absolutely did.

Yet we could've rioted, flogged Strangelove and the guards with knouts and scourges until he developed a facioscapulohumeral muscular disease, taking out all our rage from such insensate, diabolical treatment, because this was our revenge and nobody could do anything about it: not Cash or the other drill sergeants, not the guards, not any of the staff; and as Strangelove would gape at us as though he were driven into a maniacal frenzy, he would fall out of his wheelchair, unaware of our execration and torment as we continued to chasten him while he lay face down in the middle of another seizure, flouncing his shoulder on the floor.

11. LETTER TO RESIDENTS

THE DEVIL IS A SOUTHPAW

Dear Fellow Delinquents Doomed to Fail in Life,

Because our counselor, Vlad Siren—whose name sounds suspicious to me—asked us to write a bunch of crap to be read aloud here in Tophet County Detention about whether we felt ashamed of ourselves, and because Trusty John claimed he suffered from a sudden and rash case of graphospasm (his letter was blank) despite his priapic drawings of genitalia, I'll make this as brief, insightful, and as therapeutic as possible. We're faced once again with the practically parlous position of having to pause under the pressures of confession and provide insight into our worries and motivations. We're forced to write about these things, no matter how strange or selfish, so that they know where to refer us for long-term treatment and to help us understand ourselves better with a goal of rehabilitation and self-forgiveness and a wholehearted freedom from shame, with the primary, predictable and asinine icebreaker being: What's a memory of feeling ashamed?

At age thirteen, I first experienced "the panic," which led to contempt due to my own purely puerile nescience as my father lay drunk in bed after my brother's funeral while the rest of the guests mingled in the living room with my mother. I found him mumbling something as he rolled over in bed and hung one arm off the side, which was the first time I had seen him that drunk. I sensed the conflict in his dizzying mind. I heard his throaty cough and groan and thought the best thing to do was help my mother with the guests in the living room, but when I entered everyone stopped talking and looked up at me at the same time. To say this moment was terrifying is an understatement, because all the sudden attention on me felt like I was suffocating or having a heart attack and needed to vomit. I was certain everyone was staring at me because I had disappointed my family, the dark sheep, if you will, always getting in trouble at school and at church, and somehow I felt responsible for my father's drunkenness that day and felt like everyone knew it.

While the burning pain hit my chest, I was able to retrieve my inhaler from my blazer pocket and take two quick pumps before losing my breath, thankfully, but it didn't help. The scoundrels who gambled and drank in secret with my father lurched toward me as I blacked out and fell forward on the hardwood floor, bloodying my nose and cheek. I woke on my back to them breathing down on me with horrible breath. "Breathe," they told me. "Are you okay? Breathe."

The panic attacks continued after that, and every one of them grew worse so that I couldn't walk into a room with more than three people in it, which is one of the reasons they put me in the alternative school up in North Creek. Try getting dizzy any time a group of people look at you or vomiting in church or at the mall. Sixth-grade graduation gave me the stomach cramps, but my father blamed it on the Frito chili pie and Kool-Aid I'd had for supper. I won't tell you how strong my meds are, but it took three different times for me to black out before my father agreed to get me put on medication.

My father has an obsession for baseball. He played high school and college baseball and had high hopes for me to be a talented baseball player, possibly the best since southpaw pitcher George Echota, who had made Old Dublan proud. I'm aware most of you know who George Echota is. His son is here. I wasn't a pitcher, but my father taught me how to

THE DEVIL IS A SOUTHPAW

throw a curveball and a fastball. He helped me lift weights in the garage and took me to the park down the street to throw baseballs at the backstop. I wanted to be a catcher, like Johnny Bench, but he insisted I try out for pitcher and stood on the mound with me every Saturday and after church on Sundays and some days after school, even in winter, showing me a windup and form and reminding me what I kept doing wrong. He would stand with his hands on his knees beside me as I pitched, his face swollen and pink from coughing his lungs out (he was a closet smoker but a heavy one, at least one or two packs every day), trying to distract me on purpose by making grunting noises during my windup, because he said his distractions would help me block out other distractions, like crowds during games, which ultimately would make me a better pitcher. He made sure I threw with my right hand always, even though I'm technically left-handed. I've been ambidextrous thanks to him, able to write with either hand, bat left and right, and throw the ball especially hard with my right.

I had no interest in being a pitcher. On that cloudy day when I said, "I don't want to be a pitcher, and I don't even like baseball anymore," my father sent me to the car, where I sat in the back seat and stared out the window while he collected the baseballs. His silence in the car on the drive home was expected, but when I was in bed that night in the darkness and my bedroom door opened and he entered, a tall, towering presence standing in the light from the hallway, he said he was grossly disappointed in me and saddened by my decision not to play baseball, and that there was no use going to the park anymore, what was the point, and that it had all been a waste of time—which on one hand pleased me but on the other hand his words, "I'm grossly disappointed in you," ran through my head all night and for several days afterward, a moment that I would think about every night in bed for weeks, even months, and sometimes I thought about it at the dinner table when my father stabbed his meat with a look of weariness and regret instead of satisfaction and happiness. He was a man who kept to himself at the table, even at restaurants, rarely looking up from his plate, never conversing with my mother and certainly never with me, belching into his fist, staring at his food, and chewing with a slow orgasmic intensity that appeared theatrical. I witnessed him eat this way for years. How is eating such a dead and lonely experience? After I told him I didn't want to play baseball, he used his silence to dismiss me, not speaking to me for days. Even weeks. This was only a few years ago. When he finally spoke to me, he told me he didn't care whether I chose to be left-handed. "The devil is a southpaw," he told me. "He wants you to rebel against my wishes."

Any time I skipped school I got caught. In Ferris Bueller's Day Off, *which I saw with Trusty John after we'd smoked a joint we stole from his dad, the main character Ferris, played by Matthew Broderick, lies to his parents and pretends he's sick, and his parents call and check on him and worry throughout the day, something neither of my parents have done even when I've actually been sick and stayed home, and watching Ferris's parents on the big screen display that amount of sympathy makes me wish my family had more money so that everyone would be happier and less drunk. I couldn't even identify with Ferris's friend, Cameron, because I have no idea what it feels like to live in a big suburban house outside of Chicago. The only character I could identify with in that movie is Charlie Sheen's character, who's sitting in the police station near the end of the film. But I like this place better than I like living at home.*

I'll end by saying that even though many of you juvies have done terrible things, I have done nothing that wasn't in the name of justice, an eye for an eye, a tooth for a tooth, and, in fact, all my good deeds would be way easier to list here than talking about my early memories of shame. For instance, I have tried to understand what it means to love and to be in love with someone, that loving a dog is no different than loving a person, and that with love comes obedience and discipline. I used to sneak into our neighbor's yard and feed the dog, who loved eating scraps but needed discipline. Don't ever say I'm not a loving person the way I have loved the strays in my neighborhood, because I love those animals. I love them the way the python eats the pig.

12.
WOULD I YES TO SAY YES MY MOUNTAIN FLOWER

t wouldn't have mattered to Matthew, before he was locked up, whether Cassie Magdal took such an interest in him, although, yes, he did do something about it despite the harsh criticism of himself; he wrote her a prolix letter on college-ruled notebook paper from a penumbra in the woods on the western side of O.D., where he sometimes rode his bike to find his solitude, a letter in which he described his colluctation with an impulsive desire and a concupiscence that had him thinking incessantly about her and what she did standing near the vestibule window in her house whenever she thought of him, too. Yes, he was ashamed of this and yet also wholly occupied, he explained in his letter, with the idea of viduity since his father had abandoned them and he was left to care for his mother (who suffered from asthenia) while also caring for his younger sister, Nora, who was three years younger and entering the stage of questioning her body developing, what it meant to show affection appropriately in public, and how to flirt.

It's terrifying, he wrote. *I obsess that I, too, may lose a loved one to abandonment and be faced with too many responsibilities! I'm only fourteen, and I don't want to suffer a broken heart to a beautiful person with such passion and appeal as yourself. How will I recover? I've seen my poor mom feign adulthood and try to meet the demands of this precocious boy. How am I supposed to confront my feelings toward you, Cassie? You are clearly one of the most beautiful persons in our school, the other being our Spanish teacher, Ms. Enriquez. Also, you have been courted by one of the most creative, intelligent, and virile boyfriends on planet Earth: one Milton Fool-*

born. How am I supposed to compete with him? I have read his stories and poems, which are brilliant.

His mind, like Milton's, was a spidery, demented web of ideas and visions.

Milton, who liked to write lists, documented Greek mythology references and characters from Dante: Helios, Beatrice, Virgil, Guido del Duca, Titus, etc., because Cassie Magdal was enamored by intelligence and the ability to lead one's life according to a high standard of morality, which Milton found alluring about her, despite the secret that he had begun sprouting horns on his head. "Our souls manifest into our bodies," he teased her, knowing she would be disgusted by this transformation if she ever found out, and so he revealed the truth: "Why do you think I wear a baseball cap all the time? Because I'm a southpaw? No, to hide my devilish horns."

"Keep your voice down," she told him. They were in the library at school, sitting at a table by a window spattered with dust. "And anyway, I like your cap."

"The Red Sox."

"My dad likes Wade Boggs."

"What about Clemens?"

"Yeah, him, too."

"That's cool, well, my shoulder is hurt," he told her, "otherwise, I'd throw a slider for you."

"Is it true Matthew's dad set a record for most strikeouts in O.D. history?"

"I don't know. I guess."

"His dad is a legend."

"But Matthew doesn't play baseball."

Milton then handed her his story he had written for her, a retelling of a Greek myth concerning Boreas and Orithyia, in which certain names were changed:

1) MILTON, furious and strong North Wind, longed for Cassie, whose diffused suffering (from gods seductively disguised as creatures) prohibited herself from fantasizing the love of a wind. 2) Milton, a strong and passionate wind, felt an incessant hunger he attempted to define in words—and thus wrote: The king's daughter, strange nymph, a delightful luminosity! 3) One afternoon he noticed her sitting by the river Gudgekin, savoring the cool water between her legs, over her breasts, down her neck. 4) And Milton wrote, "Though I have been through many painful tribulations I will lead her to me, and my loins will ache no more, for we will produce children who will be immortals, possessed with a strong passion and temper!" 5) And Milton breathed into nature's lungs a cold, strong wind that rushed across the sea and carried ships all the way to the Phaiakians to keep them away from Cassie while she slept soundlessly. 6) The gods were pleased with Milton for his destruction and called on him often to blow a furious wind to the sea. 7) Still without Cassie's love, however, Milton dreamed of capturing her, sweeping her away through the skies in a vast turmoil of breath; in this dream she sat by the river Gudgekin. 8) But when he awoke, Matthew was watching him; and he was without breath. 9) And Milton sputtered in pain, gasping for breath, for he was not able to breathe a slight gust of any wind. 10) And the goddess Athena called on him and he didn't answer. 11) Matthew disguised himself as a swan, and crept away... 12) And when Athena found Milton, she knew he was furious; 13) and he was alone, despairingly in love, waiting in torture! 14) It would be forever before he could fly to the river Gudgekin and carry Cassie away, once she finished clutching the wretched swan's curved neck.

"Why are you showing me this?" Cassie said. "I already know how you feel about me and him."

For the next few minutes Milton badgered her repeatedly about George Echota's failures as a pitcher, a father, and a sober member of the community, telling her she should find out the truth about him, not only the rumors about his pitching, but she found everything Milton the Fool said intolerable. He was sorry, of course, and felt tragedy lurking around the corner any time he said something negative about someone else. His own father had punished him repeatedly during his younger years for talking badly about relatives who annoyed him or for complaining about church suppers and community events; Milton felt his presence in the house was a continual toxicity to his father, who often locked him in the attic without anything but a blanket and pillow and told him to "figure out what respect means." Milton developed the habit of talking to a stuffed animal mouse he'd named Willard that he'd had since he was a toddler, as if Willard were alive and able to comfort him in silence the way his father said angels and the Holy Spirit quietly protect. Milton's father's punishments were too steeped in physical challenge, like depriving Milton of a meal or forcing him to sit in solitude in the dim and brutally hot attic without even letting him take a book to read. Milton was able to find an old notebook and pencil up there in an old wooden desk and began obsessively making lists of personality traits he loathed in people like his father, and for a while he thought humanity meant being angry and cursed, and he began to see something inside him turn more animal; for instance, he sometimes felt his feet were hooves and his nails were claws. "Better to become a beast than remain a human," he told Willard. "We have to learn to survive in the wilderness."

He dreamed of a dense forest full of moaning souls. Above

him, in the sky, crows circled, and he followed a trail in the woods until he came to a river with fish jumping. He entered the water and tried to catch the fish, but they were too quick for him, and meanwhile the current carried him into deeper, cold water. He was splashing for his life, trying to swim back to the bank. This was a recurring dream for him when he was younger. His dreams were emotional, full of sadness and turmoil, and any time he told Cassie about them she appeared disinterested, an infuriating response because his dreams were so vivid, so full of symbolism and messages.

"That's all you ever want to talk about," she told him.

"Wrong, I talk about lots of things, like literature and art. I can draw cartoons."

Cassie pretended to yawn.

"Is that yawn supposed to make me feel bad?"

"Whatever. You like to draw, so what? You use big words to try to trick people into thinking you're smarter than you are. You're kind of a show-off. I don't know what you want from me."

She wasn't as interested in him as she once was. Having cultivated a penchant for rescuing a life in need of attention, as in the instances of spending time in her grandmother's backyard collecting insects or creepy-crawly things, Cassie fancied the idea of capturing Matthew as if he were a cricket skidding across the tile, his sleek black hair hanging in his eyes as he tried to decide where to sit in a semblance of wistful confusion. She took pleasure in honorable missions as such and dreamed wildly, even, of becoming a movie star or model, an aspiration one assumed was scant due to her passion and profundity for refinement, and certainly she felt so many repressed intentions of the ex-boyfriends who lingered in her shadow and repudiated her dreams, a mystery to the human heart, wasn't it, that nobody could resist the temptation to cast doubt on her, especially when she began to show an interest in, yes, our boy who lived in the dirty area across town.

Their first date was less a disaster than a study in a human comedy of errors. On a bright blue afternoon, she confessed to having an interest in someone whose compassion she could absorb in her difficult maneuvers of entering womanhood, someone whose attentive ear for melancholy humming and exchanging views on the actresses whose careers developed when they were young—Natalie Wood, Judy Garland, Drew Barrymore—who wouldn't squirm in a dinner jacket or tie, and who could assist with her decision on which evening gown to wear without scoffing at her irresolution.

"You're one of the few people who totally, like, intrigues me," she told Matthew.

"I d-don't understand," he said.

She yawned in the sunlight, turning away from him. "I'm so bored with everybody—including myself."

"Boredom is a yegg."

"What does that mean?"

"It's a m-m-metaphor I came up with, about boredom."

"Oh, it's funny. I'm kidding! You know, Milton writes metaphors."

"I wish I was as smart and artistic as Milton."

She knew he was right, but still, she taught him manners, posture, to chew with his mouth closed, and when he would reach for her hand she let him kiss it and place it to his face, telling him he had a gift that was sagacious, fatidic, and that it was inconceivable that he was able to grieve with her over the recent death of her grandmother because her former boyfriend,

Milton Foolborn, despite his brilliance, was selfish; that's what she called him (among other callous things, like a "muttering scrotecrust"), even going so far as to say Milton's homiletic interest in writing about fundamentalist religious penitents, of which she was one, and drafting a pseudo-intellectual novel with an entire chapter focusing on a succubus mounting a stuttering boy with a deformed hand (which this fool cut from the manuscript) was a way for him to sempiternally chastise her for saying that certain boys had indulgent and timid eyes, a diabolical and merciless plan that backfired on him because she ignored and abolished any barbarous method he devised to try to ostracize Matthew, and once the Fool went through with the attempt at a school shooting with the belief that he would be raised to a status beyond mediocrity, she decided that he had governed his own fate and that their relationship as far as she was concerned was thrown to the sea where it belonged, dead in the water. (The ineluctable modality of reason: Aristotle's *De Sensu et Sensibilibus* tells one the sense tasted with colors, which for Cassie Magdal meant Milton could delight in minty blue, salsa red, ice cream brown, every color associated with her in some way.)

She told him the long dark hair he found on her sweater hardened his voice in a way that made her feel violated and that he had lost trust in her. That fool Foolborn accused her of being with Matthew earlier in the day because that hair matched his hair color—he was positive it was the same length—so he fell into a type of paranoia that was taking place in his mind, full of visions of Matthew resting his head on her chest, lying in the sun in his backyard, while she talked of shooting stars and her dream wedding taking place someday on the coast, on a beach, while running her finger in a circular motion in the palm of his hand.

Cassie, in all her frustrated attempts to please our boy by telling him catastrophic reports about what a fool Milton Foolborn was, and how adversaries like Milton wrote about staring at mysterious willow trees and barking cacodemons instead of writing about being in love with her, had never considered the enormous amount of pressure and anguish they felt. No longer would they be able to avoid being scrutinized and feeling defenseless and alone. No longer could they show their faces in school hallways without hearing laughter or the low, amphoric groan of a bombardon, like they were the town dunce in some lubberly sitcom. How was it possible for her to accumulate an immoderate love for someone so quickly when she so rightfully acknowledged the mysterious behavior that she claimed men like her father possessed? On three different occasions she revealed to those closest to her that her father, at age sixty-two, threw his back out while masturbating in the garage and howled in pain from the floor until Cassie's mother rushed in there to find him on his back, trousers to his knees and unable to turn over, and how in those following months he attended rehabilitation for sex addiction and admitted that he was a gynotikolobomassophile with a vertiginous urge to smell gasoline, which was why he'd been masturbating in the garage; after three vodka gimlets, Cassie's mom disclosed this in front of her Sunday-evening fellowship supper guests at their church. However, the most profound confession was her judgment on the masculinity belonging to the boys who loved her, calling them cowards as she particularized a list of their puerile behavior—they failed, for example, to advance on her with any furtive glance or hand-holding (untrue), even recounting a dream in which she placed her breast into the infant Matthew's mouth and suckled him until he slowly morphed into a young man more mature and sensitive than the other boys.

Milton couldn't think about anything else. His obsessions awakened him in the middle of the night during the anxieties of sleep, insensitive to his plea for rest as if they were creatures screeching inside his head with the rage of authority, worse than having the mumps or stomach sickness and more strident than the rattle of his blinds being raised or the barking of neighbor's dogs next door. His obsession with Matthew possessing a type of power over him was as disturbing as finding a severed rabbit head in the grass or discovering a dead rat in the tub, so bothersome it was that he had difficulty falling back asleep. During his time lying in the dark alone in bed, he wondered why Matthew's voice was more affectionate toward others even when Milton spoke in a calm, friendly tone to him with the decorum his parents had always urged and ingrained in him, or how in art class at school Milton was incapable of telling Matthew how much he adored him and admired everything he painted or sketched that came out of his imagination, like flowers growing out of a man's chest, or a child holding a calf fetus in the middle of a wildfire, or a naked man with an erection hanging dead from a tree—the kinds of images Milton the Fool wished he could create in his own mind instead of playing in the space of abstract, fragmented shapes and colors to signify chaos, which made him more conscious of his failures, aimless and wanting to demolish everything he had ever painted or written.

He had imposed this obsession on himself, he knew, although he couldn't understand it. Milton knew Matthew was unlike his other obsessions, none of which involved people. His interest in rusty sewing machines, for instance, began after his grandmother died and his mom inherited a Singer machine. He was less interested in sports, despite playing baseball, and instead found himself, like many boys, interested in cars and trucks, filling his notebook with sketches of Ferraris and DeLoreans like the one in *Back to the Future*. His obsessions were harmless. His interest in Matthew, however, was unlike any of those things.

Milton the Fool carried binoculars around his neck and examined Matthew as if he were birdwatching (think, if you will, of Psalm 91:3, KJV: "Surely he shall deliver thee from the snare of the fowler, *and* from the noisome pestilence," not to mention a number of canticles), slinking around the house and backyard, which was simple to do because their backyard led into a gathering of trees and a downhill trail that led to a creek, and he usually walked along the bank at sunset or at night until he made his way closer to the house and tried to see whether he could make sense of anything Matthew was doing. Matthew's bedroom faced the backyard, and most evenings he sat at a desk on the far side of the room with his back to the window, so Milton was never able to see his face, at least not while he was working, but he remained patient and sat on the grass until he either grew bored or else his back started hurting; sometimes for hours he sat there looking through binoculars while around him the mosquitos and gnats circled in the humidity and the light grew dimmer. Once the Fool was back home, he called his friend Ratso and reported everything. Matthew sat at his desk and either did homework, read a book, or wrote, and they laughed about that on the phone, imagine doing homework every night, even on weekends, and then Ratso called Trusty John and told him, and Trusty John called Kenny Leach, and so on, and they all agreed it was pathetic how Matthew never did anything fun at night, how sad, how pitiful, wasn't it, poor stuttering boy with no friends or hobbies other than writing at his desk, but secretly Milton Foolborn was mournful and raging with envy because his house was never so peaceful at night, not with his father's drunkenness and mental instability, not with his wild mood swings and fits of paranoia about police surveillance or their home being raided, after which his mother often left the house in tears and then drove away for a few hours, a sad, loathsome state of affairs in the fullness of the cool autumn nights, nothing at all like the way Matthew's house appeared to him through the binoculars, so peaceful. Milton never sank into his depression but instead fell into silence and lethargy, and anger, wondering whether he was up to Matthew's level of such passion and dedication to his art, his craft, and his own self-worth.

Secretly inspired, Milton would put on a red shirt or red socks because he felt red was his lucky color and was associated with so many admirable people and interesting things throughout history and the world: martyrdom, boldness, wrath, love, sin, blood, roses, rubies, berries, cherries, beets, apples, red peppers, strawberries, and the Norse explorer Erik the Red. The writer Alexander Theroux wrote an entire essay on the color red, Milton's favorite story was Poe's "The Masque of the Red Death," and even his hair had a red tint to it, despite being light brown and despite his father's belief that all redheads were, in fact, partly demonized, children of the devil. Besides all that, Milton's favorite book was Ambrose Bierce's *The Devil's Dictionary*. Anytime he began writing a poem or a story he wore the color red, sometimes even pricking his finger with a pin to blot his page with his own blood so that when it dried and darkened he felt a part of himself was on the page above his words, because that's how strongly and passionate he felt about the strange and undefinable passion for writing, composing, creating art on the page, wherever that desire came from, certainly he was aware it didn't come from either parent because the only things his mother or his father ever wrote were lists, not even letters to relatives because they used the telephone for that, easier to call long distance and rack up a phone bill than sit down and write a letter to a loved one, wasn't it, and neither read much except for the newspaper or flipping through magazines at the cardiologist's office, so where did that desire to read and write such turgid prose come from? School? A teacher? (Certainly not.) Milton's education was achieved on his own because he was disliked by teachers, often placed in detention for falling asleep in class, or daydreaming, or snapping girls with rubber bands, so no teacher took an interest in mentorship or challenging themselves to open the doors to intellectual possibility, literary or otherwise, so Milton took it upon himself in his own private passion and checked out books from the school library and privately read on the bus or in his room at home, all the while wondering what Matthew was reading or whether he had already read the same books. One afternoon, as the Fool looked through binoculars from the area of trees behind Matthew's house, he descried Matthew and Cassie sitting on the back porch. Cassie was laughing at something, which Milton imagined was a reaction to Matthew's attempt at making a witty or clever remark:

MATTHEW: I like bees.

CASSIE: Really?

MATTHEW: B-b-but I don't want you to think I'm too sentimental.

CASSIE: What do you mean?

MATTHEW: I spend a lot of t-time in the g-garden. I like the undulation bees form as a group as they m-m-move across the yard from bush to b-bush. Does that make me a s-s-square?

CASSIE: Milton said he was once attacked by hornets outside his house.

MATTHEW: O-oh! Did he swell up? Go to the hospital?

CASSIE: No, he let them sting him. Then he crushed them with his angry fist.

Imagine wise and priapic Milton Foolborn, in that moment, stepping into the yard and revealing himself to them, wearing his red collared shirt and black jeans; that was the fantasy, with Cassie so smitten by his courage to show up that she would expiate her mistakes and, walking away from Matthew and reaching the Fool, would ameliorate their differences right there in the backyard as Matthew stuttered exhortations.

The boys who fell in love with Cassie Magdal suffered a deep sadness for her contentious behavior and continual need to rectify anything they said, and getting them to talk about their fixation on her body (because, I swear, she said she wanted to decipher the hidden truths of their hypersexual nonsense), and how she despised it whenever they called her their "Mountain Flower," with despicable relatives known as mountain people who breathed open-mouthed and hunted wild pigs and deer and enjoyed a less civilized method of murder, dragging their blood-soaked animals through the thickened brush past suffruticose plants to their cabins to tie them up by the hooves to drain the blood while they sat inside with their homemade wine, toasting to the souls of the infallible way of simple life, the irreparable and lonely, the condemned man. She was nothing like her relatives, of course, she assured them of this even before she grew weary of them, and once she had Matthew in her possession she fell into an incontrovertible fascination with his Native culture, imploring him during their furtive trysts to share stories and myths with her that he had heard growing up from elders, one of which the Fool overheard when spying on the two of them sitting on the grass:

Coyote Story (As Milton Foolborn Heard It)

Coyote was an enigma to the other coyotes in the desert because he held a danger none of them recognized. Slinking around the desert at night, through the currents of the dry winds and past the thistles and scrogs and desert plants, Coyote was convinced he was going to die. He was so worried about dying, in fact, that he developed a delusional disorder known as Capgras syndrome, in which he thought his close friend, a brown beetle, had been replaced by a beetle double whose sole purpose was to convince Coyote that he would be murdered.

When Coyote accused his friend the beetle of being an imposter, the beetle hissed with laughter. "Ridiculous!" the beetle said. "I'm your friend. Why would you think someone would murder you?"

"I'm a trickster," Coyote replied. "I slink around at night, hunting small animals and trapping them for food. Everyone knows I'm wicked."

"Oh," the beetle said. "And what about all the other animals who hunt and kill for food? Are they not any more violent than you? If you really believe this, why don't you ask the other animals in the woods? Let's go—I'll follow along."

Coyote eyed the beetle. "My friend the beetle would never challenge me in this way," he said. "My friend the beetle would comfort me, not reply with such devilish intent."

The beetle twitched its antennae. "Am I not comforting you? Do you think I'm tricking you?"

Coyote thought a moment, then decided he would trust his friend, and so they walked through the woods together, the beetle creeping alongside until he needed to rest.

"I'm too tired to walk all the way through the woods," the beetle said. "I won't be able to get back to the stream for water if I keep going."

"You can ride on my back," Coyote said. "And after I eat, I can bring you back."

"Do you trust me to ride on your back?" the beetle said. "After all, you don't believe I'm your friend."

"You're simply a little beetle," Coyote replied. "How can you possibly hurt me? And if you try, I'll step on you and smash you with my paw."

"All right," the beetle said. "Lift me on your back."

Coyote lowered his body so that he was lying on his belly. The beetle crawled up onto his tail and scurried to his back. Coyote continued walking through the woods with the beetle riding on his back, but after a moment he felt a sharp sting. It stung so badly he collapsed and fell to his side, howling in pain.

"What did you do?" Coyote said to the beetle, who had hurried down from his back. Coyote was in so much pain he couldn't move.

"I stung you," the beetle replied.

It was then Coyote noticed that the beetle was not a beetle at all, but a scorpion.

"You tricked me," Coyote said weakly. "Why did you sting me?"

The scorpion replied, "Because I'm afraid of you."

Milton Foolborn walked home and thought about the story he heard. Matthew was the coyote, he was the scorpion, and he thought about the story about the woman who was changed into a scorpion for disobeying her parents; he recognized the disillusioned eyes of a girl who wanted to hear the lies of a stutterer who squatted on his back porch like some meretricious frog boy who exulted in the distress of sighing girls, who amused himself and surprised our girl with his intelligence and charm, subtle enough that Milton often had to puzzle over whether certain words or phrases were purposefully ironic or whether a recondite passage

Matthew told her was abstruse, trivial, or witty, although this "game," as Milton called it, never prevented Matthew, if he grew disputatious or ill-humored, from becoming bored, one could see it on his face, the way he fidgeted with his hands or glanced around uncomfortably. As for Cassie, she continued to fall into an illusory vertigo any time she was around him, commenting on the still and spiritual sky, feigning her own boredom, and waving her hands around like a bratty child, O' God, waving her hands; what happened to the girl whose love was once as crisp as the air, what happened to the enigma of the human heart, what about the soft voice of harmony and love, what about the meaning of a kiss in the alley behind the school on a day when the clouds moved and the sun shone for the first time after a hard, romantic thunderstorm, and what about the faithful and attentive eyes that gazed upon a boy whose heart burned with passion only to be absorbed in manipulation?

13. ACROSTIC OF A SCHOOL SHOOTING

However badly wounded Milton Foolborn and his cousin Trusty John were, however many beatings and degrading moments of harassment they received from Grandley, Lister, and Fayle over those years, and despite the numerous reports and the consequences the two bullies served from school and sports officials, nothing improved. Project GLF, code for the victims' last names, was Trusty John's idea. Project GLF: blasting Grandley, Lister, and Fayle with their shotguns would be carried out, indeed, because enough was enough.

Also, they never contemplated acts of kindness toward these bullies. Trusty John's real name was John Alberich, but most people called him Trusty John due to his short height of four feet eleven inches. His height led to bullying after eighth grade when most of the other boys grew and Trusty John didn't. His father had told him to fight like a man and to look at Milton, who at least took his beatings, but Trusty John was too afraid. Knowing they weren't the only victims of the two boys' abuse, they sometimes talked with others in class about revenge, like Matthew, who claimed he prayed for his abusers, that's what he actually said, "I pray for them." (What is a prayer, after all, but a cry for help? A call for proof? A plea for forgiveness?) Who did he think he was, anyway, to say such a thing, as if possessing an air of authority and elitism over Milton and Trusty John, and what good did he think praying for them did when they didn't stop their actions? What was the prayer? Who did he think he was, sitting in class so entranced in his silent reading that he was unaware of that string of spittle from his mouth while the other boys carved initials in their desks?

Under no circumstances (of course) did Matthew want any part of Milton and Trusty John, and certainly no part of revenge, so they never brought up Project GLF to him. Matthew's refusal to be involved in anything with them, even when they invited him to sit with them at lunch, compelled them to impose on him a punishment that would cause a slow uprising against him by smearing dog shit on the back of his shirt at school so that he smelled bad and then would be subjected to even more brutal beatings from rotten scrotums like Grandley, Lister, and Fayle, so that it would be impossible for him to maintain a sense of pride or safety under the menace of those tortures and thus he would become known as someone with poor hygiene. Certainly, they admired the idea that girls like Cassie Magdal would find him detestable, gross, cowering athwart the outside courtyard between buildings while others thought of him as a lazar in the shadow of school nurses and staff vomiting from his stench, condemned to his own solitary corner, an inevitable fate compounded by the additional pain of a herniated testicle that would leave him in the nurse's office for hours, then transported to the hospital far away in some Indian healthcare center where nobody cared.

Nor did they consider any consequences whatsoever of having weapons in the school building, which was of course against school rules, but Tophet County was a place with a love for hunting dove, deer, quail, and turkey, and the administrators and most of the male teachers and coaches hunted and supported the NRA and area gun shows. Milton's father often joked about how in the 1960s the principal once suspended him for smoking a cigarette in the school bathroom but then met him that afternoon in the woods north of town to go hunting. Both boys came up with an excuse in the aftermath, that their shotguns went off accidentally as they entered the classroom, that they had returned from a quick dove hunt at dawn, after all, and were unaware the rifle safety switch was off. This small town in 1988 would never believe in premeditated murder, nor a school shooting, not in Dublan, where trapshooting records were held by school administrators and judges, where county commissioners gambled with city workers in the back rooms of downtown buildings like the Supper Club, playing illegal poker games and slot machines and hosting suppers they advertised as having the "prettiest women and best calf fries in town."

That Milton and Trusty John considered themselves the incarnations of Dante the Pilgrim and his guide, Virgil, from *Inferno*, was less haunting than the probability of incarceration and being tried as an adult, which was not unlikely in Tophet County, a circle of hell itself, with dense woods where one could hear the moaning and wailing of tormented, lost, and wandering souls, perhaps from former prisoners who were bitten on their necks by snakes and then morphed into serpents themselves, or aching souls trapped in a Malebolge with the Greek Arachne and

Minerva, or a starving mountain lion roaring like the leopard in the lower hell.

Every night for a week, leading up to the morning they would storm into the classroom with their shotguns, both Milton and Trusty John dreamed of moving through murky air toward the frozen lake of Cocytus, hearing a waterfall (bees humming, as Dante notes) in the distance and the wailing of souls, worried they would be caught and punished for their actions, even sentenced to death, which Milton understood upon waking as a biblical reference his minister father used to mention in the story of Cain and Abel in Genesis 4:14 (King James Version, because all other translations are inferior): "I shall be a fugitive and a vagabond in the earth; and it shall come to pass, that every one that findeth me shall slay me."

"Die, *die*"—upon waking came the voice in their heads, resoundingly terrorizing...

But God protects Cain, Milton realized, reading the verse in Genesis, and besides, there was something to be said for an eye for an eye, a tooth for a tooth, pure logic, and so on, a reason to try to alleviate any anxiety, though for Milton the fear manifested itself in his recurring dream leading up to the day of the shooting:

Yellow smoke settling over the bubbling river Styx.

Odors like the stench of corpses.

Listless bodies with skin decaying.

Yaks eating smaller animals.

A snake, hanging over a thick branch of a tall tree in the dark, watching Foolborn.

Icicles hanging from giant rock walls.

Ichorous, brownish fluid draining from the ears of slaughtered pigs.

THE DEVIL IS A SOUTHPAW

The instances when Milton would wake in the middle of the night feeling like he was suffering in a bed of putrefaction, his dreams digested and visible as the glow of the school in flames, he could smell the sour gunpowder and dead bodies lying in pools of blood, while the rest of the students cried out in panic, yet all he could hear were the voices of the dead buried in the land all around, rising out of their graves and asking him for an account of his decision to shoot and kill, and for the remainder of the night his sleep was restless and uneasy, full of their shrieking voices and hollow moans, because he worried about bearing the weight of all that guilt. In his notebook for English class, Milton wrote the following quote from Shakespeare: "*Suspicion always haunts the guilty mind.*"

14.
LETTER TO PARENTS

Dear Mom and Dad,

I'm writing to inform you (or any reader of this document) that this letter is not a manipulation to earn your pity or sympathy, nor is it a challenge for you to confront poor parenting or your failure to raise me in an appropriate, disciplined household. This letter is in no way blaming either of you—or anyone who cares for me if there is such a person—for your efforts and support through this difficult time and the recent tragedy of my death.

We're sharing these letters aloud during our sessions with Mr. Siren, so forgive my clumsy attempt at grandiloquent prose, but the winner of Best Letter gets to stay up thirty minutes later, and today is Friday, so I want to be able to stay up for the ending of the Rich Man, Poor Man *marathon. In a way that movie reminds me of* The Devil Is a Southpaw *(my favorite movie all throughout childhood) in that a murderer returns, and though both of you despise dark thrillers, I'm certain you'll come to understand my interest is purely artistic. Anyway, it's true that I died here, not of accidental overdose or suicide, but of shock and suffering. My heart simply gave up, expired in a rare, freakish type of myocardial infarction in which oxygen was deprived to my blood vessels likely from holding my breath for too long at night as I lay in the darkness staring at fragmented and jagged shadows on the wall. That I'm even able to write you at all is a type of miracle, but this is a confession, to paraphrase Hamlet, of sound and fury, signifying nothing, told by an idiot. I hope you will forgive me for everything, for all my errors, and especially for the bullyish attempt that landed me here, which was based on an impulsive and relentless decision fueled by anger and revenge.*

  Please know I don't blame you for anything. As you know, I've had issues with lying in the past, which is something we've talked about here in lockup. We're not supposed to talk about why we're here in specific detail outside of individual sessions, nor are we allowed to use the names of any people involved. My motivation for reaching out to you in death is directly proportional to my reasons for lying to you in the past, which is to say, I need your support. Daily, I think about all the lies that blossomed into bigger lies and digressions involving fictional names and locations, and how my confidence soared, and how lying made me feel elated and euphoric. I was a terrific liar whose ability to make up detailed lies made me feel sybaritic and important. In death, at least so far, truth and lies aren't important. Most of us who died are here underground in a place where we're waiting for what's to come next. I know this doesn't fit into your dogma or beliefs, but bear with me. We are walking around ululating in impatience and boredom, uninterested in listening to anyone else, especially since we're all wastrels and liars.

I realize I've not been the son you hoped I would be. I regret my actions and love both of you dearly. I have failed you and myself, and trust me, I am remorseful for everything I did in defiance and lying. One example of my guile is the time I told a story to the person I am secretly in love with about how Aunt Mildred was a usurer who loaned me ten grand so that I could fly to West Hollywood to have lunch with George Lucas the director. George Lucas wanted to hear about my ideas for a film script or sitcom series involving a teenage boy who lives in poverty and is pretending to be more educated and smarter than he really is in order to impress and con people who find him adorable into giving him money, but it turned out that the George Lucas I met with wasn't actually the famous director of American Graffiti *and* Star Wars *but a different George Lucas entirely, some bearded wannabe producer/director just out of UCLA film school and working at an Orange Julius at a local mall. And I was left, in the end, not meeting anyone famous and returning with a debt of sixteen grand owed to Aunt Mildred from her high interest, all of which I repaid in two years by mowing yards, writing college term papers for athletes, and posing as a young hoofer at the Limelight Lounge.*

Forgive me, too, for the stories I made up when I snuck out my window at night, like telling you I was trying to kill myself by huffing paint when I was really having fun, and that I was trying to cure my insomnia when you caught me smoking pot in the backyard. The truth is that I was hurting, which is not an excuse for my behavior, but it's all I can say in total honesty. I would love nothing more than to be back home in my room right now, watching TV and eating Nutter Butters. I miss my room. I miss both of you. It's like in the movie, After Hours, *when Griffin Dunne's character, Paul Hackett, gets stuck in NYC's SoHo neighborhood and can't go back home uptown because he's lost all his money and the trains aren't working. At one point he falls to his knees in the middle of the street and asks God, "What do you want from me?" That's how I feel being here twenty-four hours a day. We've died and we're stuck here, unable to leave or go home.*

The way we all died, in suffering and shock, doesn't mean we didn't die alone, because we were each in our individual rooms in the middle of the night, thinking of everything we were deprived of, even the simplest of things you experience outdoors, and how we envied even the insects and animals of the night who have their freedom and who contaminate the world less than we do, evidently, because how strange that wild animals can roam free out there while the rest of us sit locked in our rooms all night. You take the simplest things for granted when you're locked up, like lying on the grass at night and looking up at the fleeting stars and the moon, or sitting on a swing set in the park with someone you like, or having a picnic on a blanket, or throwing a Frisbee. Our time outdoors is structured and brief, monitored by the staff and guards and drill sergeants who work here and make sure we're not unruly in the short time we get to play basketball or walk around in the courtyard. Certainly, we've lost all that and more. We have died and been buried underneath the detention center to rot. I'm not trying to gain your sympathy, but I have changed.

You remember how much I love the show Alf? *The night we died, we watched the episode when Alf becomes friends* with a young blind girl, but he can't tell her the truth about himself, that he's an alien, so he lies to her and tells her he's from Cincinnati and must confront his lying and deception and, essentially, tell himself he's doing the right thing so that he doesn't hurt her. I found myself nearly in tears during that episode because that's the way it is with me, which I realize sounds pathetic, but it's true. All my lying and deception was done to avoid hurting someone else, including both of you. I understand how flawed that logic is, even in my dead state.

When you're dead, as we are here, you never sleep and end up spending your time wandering around as you do in life with insomnia, always thinking and longing and worrying, surrounded by strange hallucinations like blood on the walls or cattle dying from rinderpest outside, among other grim pneumas, and even the young wahine who visits us with her seductive eyes and long hair spilling down to her breasts can't find anything of value here, waving us away like vermin and claiming we'll soon develop a phthisic sickness unless we make amends with everyone we've lied to or fobbed.

We're trying to keep hope. At night we hear the howling winds of sorrow, knowing we will never again listen to the lively music of weddings or festivals, we will never dance or sip tea with honey or eat a feast alfresco overlooking a vast ocean full of crashing waves and sailboats. We can only sit in waiting, trying not to drag our feet with impatience and indignation. We desire hope and munificence, we desire a miracle, and to those we have lied to or hurt in the past we can offer our apologies in complete seriousness, without manipulation. From our alley of grief, may we offer a burning *cultivation of protest against our eternal suffering so that we may find glory and a second chance of life outside of this place.*

O let it be known I have gone to great lengths to correct my behavior and become a good person. I shall develop a friendship with someone I care deeply for, someone whose interests and obsessions match my own, whose art is as beautiful as the first light of dawn and whose awareness of the necessity for solitude and resolute curiosity leads me into an intoxicating state of jauntiness, whose eyes are ageless and hold conviction and perseverance, and whose passivity is misunderstood among the authorities at large as indolence and withdrawal.

O let it be known that when I leave the facility and roam free I shall search for the Sangraal and drink sweet wine from it among the rakish lovers of art whose lives, like mine, have been cut short and whose hard work has yet to be appreciated, and I shall participate in glutting fruits and berries with my hands until my tongue and lips turn purple, knowing I will never vomit again or shake with a fever and aching head, because there will be no sickness, no pain, no jealousy or longing to be loved anymore, and no manipulation. In the mornings I shall smoke pot and paint on a large canvas with my shirt open while the sunlight slants in, and in the evenings I shall write pherecratic meter to the person I love who will join me when I return home to you as your prodigal son.

*Your prodigal son,
Milton*

15. LETTER FROM MOTHER

Dear Milton,

My arthritis is flaring up so I'll keep this short. Received your letter but haven't had a chance to sit down and read the whole thing yet. All is fine here, but your father had an accident at the church youth outing last weekend. Don't worry, he's doing okay. He got lucky. I've attached the letter. It describes the incident better than I could. Good luck there and call us some time before 8:30 but after 5:00 in the evening. We hope your court date is soon.

Well, take care.
Your Mother

THE DEVIL IS A SOUTHPAW

Dear Mrs. Muleborn:

As director of Parks and Recreation, I am writing on behalf of the Old Dublan Bureau of Tramway and Amusement Ride Safety. It is my duty to report to you the findings of our investigation concerning the incident involving your husband, Walter Muleborn Sr., on 11 April of this year. At approximately 3:30 p.m., Mr. Muleborn entered the gate to ride the Large Spider Death ride and asked for assistance from Mr. Clyde Skole, the ride operator. Mr. Skole, age 47, extinguished his cigarette and responded promptly. According to Mr. Skole, he checked the bar and found it secure. The problem was mechanical. I can assure you that the L.S.D. ride passed all inspection as of 15 March of last year.

However, the division found loose and exposed electrical conductors that failed to pass inspection. The wiring was noticeable without any removal of panels. Secondly, the hydraulic system was leaking fluid. A significant amount of oily residue was found. Also, one of the hydraulic system's pressure gages was missing. The division was surprised to find there was no substitute for the missing hydraulic system. A bracket and clamp were slightly rusted. This was documented in the last inspection. The main problem that caused your husband's car to tip off the cylinder rod and roll on its wheels down the cemented sidewalk's slope at high speed all the way to the haystack barn was due to a lock washer's failure to hold a lock nut secure and keep it from loosening and rotating off. The 1 April inspection notes that there was a loose lock nut that was tightened. We are aware that lock washers can get bent and broken and lock nuts *can loosen easily. We hope to catch such things in future inspections. In the meantime, the Large Spider Death ride is undergoing routine maintenance to repair these items I have previously mentioned in this letter.*

Mrs. Muleborn, I hope this letter provides a more thorough account of the incident's cause and the steps currently in process to prevent any future accidents. I want to personally apologize for this incident. I am tickled to discover, as per our discussion at the casino a few nights ago, that your husband was not seriously injured. As the husband of an individual who suffers from frequent panic attacks, I know how difficult these stressful times can be. I hope that your husband is recovering healthily. Witnesses reported that, even though the car flew rapidly down the cemented slope before entering the haystack barn, it was difficult to determine if your husband's screams were of pleasure or terror. I personally hope that those were shrieks of pleasure.

My sincerest apologies,
Gerry T. Busch,
Director of Tophet County Parks and Recreation
Former County Commissioner and son of
Deputy Amos T. Busch

16.
S.O.Y.C.D.

For a couple of days after Shrike Strangelove's seizure, we didn't see him or hear anything about him. Nothing evoked his arrival or the way he spoke to us. Late in the afternoon he finally wheeled himself into the dayroom while we were sitting in front of the TV waiting for the cooks to bring our dinner, with the glare of the sun perverting his breath and disguising him as some voluble presence whose long deliriums of speech were caused by the oppressive heat or from staring at the sun for too long in the midst of the eternal splendor of a mushroom or acid trip, so indiscriminate and jarring it was when he appeared out of nowhere looking like a surreal and ignominious version of Charlie Chaplin; Strangelove launched into a speech in a voice we hadn't heard before, his body slumped sideways as he spun around in his chair to face us, bifariously grobian in the way he adjusted his crotch, the old lout, officious and lewd and indefatigable as he produced a sheet of paper from his shirt pocket, unfolded it, and read sternly in front of us:

STRANGELOVE'S SPEECH

"If I may speak," he began, clearing his throat, "under my own due health concerns, and because I'm on new medication for epilepsy and graphorrhea with a wicked, xerophthalmic side effect in my eyes, I'll be brief. You're drowning in your own poor self-pity and frightened by the scrutiny and conviction without the privileges you've withstood in your life. Hmm? All of you have failed, but can you be rehabilitated? Blah, bleh. Your destructible and immoral behavior landed you here, in Tophet County Juvenile Correctional Facility, craving laudanum or whatever dope your body has gotten addicted to, hmm? Blah bluh. If I asked for a show of hands from any of you as to whether any of you watched Live Aid on cable channel thirty-one three years ago, I'd see zero hands raised, because you were out being criminals instead of seeing a grand musical event of the decade when this event was simulcast live from Wembley and Philly's JFK Stadium. This concert was an event Bob Geldof orchestrated to raise awareness of famine in Ethiopia among young people, over two hundred thousand total attendees at both stadiums if I remember correctly, and meanwhile you weren't thinking about how lucky you have it here."

Trusty John raised his hand and asked to use the restroom, but Strangelove ignored him.

"You should consider focusing on everything Vlad Siren recommends for your recovery, along with the drill sergeants' rehabilitation plans. I understand all you're going through, trust me; I've heard all the whining and moaning about trauma and generational woes, blah bluh bleh, imagine what we could do if we learned all the values of higher intelligent people who aren't criminals and who follow a systematic government with strong leadership who tell us how to act and think so we don't have to. There is hope for rehabilitation and learning how to live as a normal human. Hope for recovery and to be angry and anti-pusillanimous in all you do, which the drill sergeants will help you obtain to avoid dealing with a de lunatico inquirendo in your futures." He wadded the sheet of paper up and tossed it in the middle of the floor and told us that we would listen to Pink Floyd's "Shine on You Crazy Diamond" and look around at each other so that the music could help us focus on others' lives instead of our own so that we could learn to be empathetic to the less fortunate.

That ridiculous cad Strangelove called for our unity and cooperation, cozening us to exchange seats with someone we normally didn't associate with so that we could participate in what felt like a goetic and lethiferous exercise, no doubt orders that he felt were a modus vivendi for all the unnecessary stress we were causing on the guards and staff, and as we rearranged ourselves he hummed an unrecognizable tune without hearing himself, or without anyone else listening to him in the uproar of everyone exchanging seats, which felt like it took forever, until order restored itself and Strangelove gestured for one of the guards to insert a cassette into the Panasonic boom box. The guard put the cassette into the player and hit Play. When the music started, Matthew stood across the room, a shadowy figure, having somehow slipped away from the group; he crouched down on all fours like a wounded dog licking the blood of dead animals, or like a saint guiding the rest of us toward a light the deliciously satanic Strangelove was drawing us away from, conscious that as long as he refused to participate, then the rest of us would delay and create havoc while he dragged his feet and instigated the guards and Strangelove to react with physical force, or else escort him to the Columbus House basement (that's clearly what he was up to), furrowed in the corner and waiting to be disparaged under duress by the yampy slobs around us, a relatively agathokakological decision because on one hand he was rebelling against the tyranny of a depraved demand, but on the other hand his behavior held a precipitancy that would land him in considerable consequence, and one of the people who would follow through with the punishment happened to be standing in the room, Sergeant Cash, whose facinorous murmurings revealed a sickening, steatopygous concupiscence for certain female staff members who tucked in their shirts and wore western blue jeans, whose office was full of journal entries consisting of a yearning to become a quadrigamist, because his church leader consistently prescribed in the healing power of possessing things in fours: spouses, children, meals, etc., in a protreptic the church leader had self-published during an ashram in flat, desolate West Texas sometime in the late 1970s before he tripped acid and jumped from a third-story building in Lubbock and had to be institutionalized, and because Sergeant Cash still kept in contact with him via U.S. postal mail, he occasionally shared aloud the ramblings in letters with residents who found them dormitive and stale, revealing the inevitable modality of his penetralia, which was difficult to listen to, certainly strange, and heteropathic in terms of Cash's reasoning for reading these letters aloud, yet we heard them and we listened while Cash rambled on, concentrated in the meanness of bombastic language and dominion, unaware that we would forget anything he said or read, although it might be truer to say that we purposefully disregarded him whenever we could, as we did when the Pink Floyd track began and we shuffled around to find a partner, ignoring all the in-house rules about no talking or whispering, and still Matthew crouched in the corner of the room, his shadow stretching across the floor, and as he held a look of remorse, our timid and inconsolable boy licked the ground where we had stepped in the pure act of opposition, a protest against despoliation, sustained by hope and in a perfect position to incite a riot, because at the moment the music was playing and as we shuffled, Cash fell into a type of transfixed state of euphoria from the music, or from monitoring us, or from a lack of sleep, dazed as he appeared on antianxiety pills, Valium or Xanax, so it was a ripe time for rioting and assaulting both Cash and the guard near Strangelove, twenty-seven against three (the thought crossed some of our minds, but many were clearly clueless to the possibility of escape, focused as they were on following directions), and by the time some of us recognized what each were thinking about rioting it was too late, damnit, and we privately wished those swines Cash and Strangelove sharp pain in their nates, good riddance, as we sat without partners and listened to Pink Floyd's dreamy music (which thankfully most of us enjoyed; their concept albums were among some of the best in rock history according to music critics, and even Matthew documented a love for the band's *Dark Side of the Moon* album, which he wrote he enjoyed during a laser light show at the state fair), despite the missed opportunity to riot, escape, and live in freedom again.

    As it turned out, at least for the nonce, we followed Strangelove's instructions as he spun around in circles in his wheelchair. Some of us—Rosemary and Brandon, and maybe a couple of others, decided it was too uncomfortable and tense, and asked to be escorted to their rooms. The rest of us stayed and focused on each other's faces like peccaries headed to the abattoir, petrified with awkwardness, contemplating our fate mercilessly through our feelings of defeat and ascesis, and unsure of what to do except stare, or gawk, as confused and defenseless as toads, devoting ourselves to Strangelove's complete supererogation. We wondered why this was happening, motionless and haunted as we were over the music, and, as if awakened from a dream, we heard his dark and shameless laugh.

Then, as if on cue, Sergeant Cash and a guard, noticing Matthew was not participating, escorted him out of the room and took him back to the Columbus House.

17.
WHERE WOUNDS OF DEADLY HATE HAVE PIERCED

We didn't see Matthew for several days. The rumor in the courtyard was that he had escaped but had been caught and returned to the Columbus House basement. He was there serving his punishment for whatever reason, yet he was present in our daily lives because someone was constantly bringing up his name; Vlad Siren, for instance. And we all shared the same nightmare of finding him. Some of us would dream of Matthew choking to death over his dinner. Trusty John's dreams continued into a whole other series of nightmarish intrusions, including seeing other dead bodies and parts of animals, such as a boar's head or a slaughtered chicken, while he followed Matthew, who was in the form of a rabbit, along a dirt path; in the dreams, Matthew left rabbit footprints and stopped every so often to turn and look at Trusty John with his long rabbit ears. In each dream

Trusty John told us, he knew this was Matthew playing tricks on him, he was sure of it, the rabbit so obviously a symbol of tricksters in folklore, the rabbit with the long ears, traipsing along the path in front of him like a stoned tour guide to present the rotting bodies and eerie souls of the suffering with their bulging eyes and forked tongues, naked and begging for her help, *help us, please*, they cried out, *help us*, while overhead the screech owl sat on a tree limb waiting to swoop down and dig its talons into his scalp (interestingly, this was what Trusty John feared most about the dream, not witnessing the suffering bodies), and every time he called out to Matthew to stop walking, he would turn around and tilt his head and stare before turning back around and walking again. Those dreams signified absolutely nothing despite the assertion that they represented a trauma that needed to be dealt with (something we denied; we were forever reluctant to seek therapy in order to deal with these dreams and anxiety they caused).

In our afternoon session, something was off with Vlad Siren. We sat in a circle in the dayroom with Siren, who was jittery and kept crossing and uncrossing his legs. Before anyone ever said anything, he told us not to worry about Matthew. "He's fine," Siren told us. "Yes, as you probably heard, he tried to escape, but he was caught. He's over in the Columbus House and they're treating him."

"Treating him for what?" we asked. "Why does he stay in the Columbus House?"

"I can't answer those questions. He's fine. Take my word for it."

"Please," we urged him, "give us details. He's the only one who goes to the Columbus House, and nobody knows why."

No matter what we said, or how hard we tried to convince him, Siren wouldn't budge. Instead, he kept whispering into his radio about college basketball scores until he finally put his radio away. "I'll tell you a secret about the tunnels that ran throughout Old Dublan, all throughout Tophet County," he said. We had heard of the tunnels, but nobody had seen them or knew whether they actually existed, total myths was what they were, or at least that's what everyone believed, because over many years our parents and grandparents and great-grandparents had dug deep into the earth with shovels all throughout Tophet County, without finding any evidence of an underground tunnel, though stories were created by Dublaners involving half-human beasts who ate their children and then vomited them back up and breathed life into them again, a whole string of stories involving fighting roosters and the long cries of wounded animals, haunted souls, wingless birds, and the hirsute community of people who spent their days making idols and olisbos out of rufous-colored mud. "You've heard the stories," Siren told us, "but I'm here to tell you I've been down there and they're real."

"The olisbos were real?" Ace asked.

"Of course, but I meant the people and the animals."

"But how do you know about the olisbos?"

"They were made out of hardened mud," Siren replied, annoyed. "Anyway, what I'm telling you is there are people and animals down there."

Ace looked around and asked, "But who uses the olisbos?"

"My God, forget about the olisbos," Siren said.

Trusty John and Brandon were glancing at each other. It was an ominous wile to get us thinking about something other than Matthew, that was obvious, and we had to press him further. "Look, it happened only once many years ago," he said. "I was down where the river snakes by the Sextus Tarquinius retirement village to lie down in the dead grass and try to catch the eye of a retired nudist mediation instructor who spray-painted kaleidoscopic shapes on cardboard when I heard a long cry, like a bobcat, coming from underground."

"A long cry," Brandon replied, "but are you sure it was from underground?" We knew, of course, that he was a stern and defiant impudent grue, there was no doubt about it, and that a big part of his job was to establish peace of mind among the residents so that we wouldn't fall apart during our group sessions with him, but it was Matthew who occupied our thoughts despite urging Siren to continue.

"I put my ear to the ground and listened to the long cry coming from underground," Siren continued, crossing his legs and jostling his foot. He was clearly nervous. "I lay there in the grass among the flowers, keeping my eye on the nudist senior citizen, when I heard someone calling for help down there. I sat up. What could I do? Who would believe me? It was like discovering a dead body, except worse, because I could only imagine who was down there."

"What did you do?" Trusty John asked, probing his ear with his pinkie. "Did anyone believe you?"

Siren stood up and sat back in his chair. We could see he was shaken simply by talking about it, as if reciting from a memory of a terrible tragedy in his own amplified voice, seeing himself in his mind as a boy sitting there, and thereupon a silence filled the room like smoke hanging all around us; but Siren was a gredin, no doubt about it, because something in his voice felt unauthentic and hollow once he realized nobody really believed him, and in an instant he told us he didn't want to talk about it anymore.

"You're all brainwashed," he said, "from the Tophetites and Dublaners who have dismissed this legend, I must say, and I'm no proper storyteller because there's not a satisfying ending to this anecdote that makes it worthwhile other than to say I never experienced it again."

We wanted to hear more about the nudist.

"The story my grandfather told," he said, ignoring our comment, "was that there were people down there who crawled out of the ground at night and captured and ate children, but I was no fool, my friends, I know what I heard. I even went back and listened, for days, even years afterward. One foggy night I dug into the earth with my shovel and found only worms and ants crawling around. But then I heard a woman singing in the distance. She was too far away for me to see, but I think she was a visitor for me. Sadly, I couldn't find her from the fog and darkness."

Out of nowhere, Brandon asked about the singing woman who painted skulls in the middle of the night. "We hear her singing to herself. She sits on the floor of our wing, and it wakes me up."

"That's Ms. Anna Darko," Siren said. "Anna Darko from Anadarko, as we joke." He was now fidgeting with his hands in his lap, waiting for laughter that never came. "We let her work here on nights because it gives her inspiration for her art. Being around youth and confinement serves as a muse for her. She sleeps all day and works at night. I don't think she's from O.D. Nobody really knows. But Mr. Strangelove says she used to visit him when he was struggling, so he owes her his life."

We wanted to know more, but someone from the control booth called for him on the radio, and he put it to his ear. "What's the score?" he said into the radio, and then grimaced when he put the radio to his ear and heard the reply. A silence fell over the room as he stood with his notebook and told us to follow him into the classroom.

Something strange happened to Vlad Siren that day. In the classroom he had us write for roughly fifteen or twenty minutes about the usual things—shame, guilt, redemption, the importance of making good choices, respect—and while many of us were able to do this with ease (particularly me), several of the residents struggled to write more than a few sentences. This was not uncommon. Most of the others dealt with issues like dyslexia, difficulty with focusing, and attention deficits, among other hindrances that led to a good deal of frustration any time we were told to write, and had we not been listening to classical music during our sessions with Siren, those residents likely would have disrupted the classroom environment by throwing fits. As it turned out, classical music helped us remain calm, but more importantly, Siren was generous in that he allowed those students who struggled to write what they could and stop if they felt too blocked to continue.

Most of us in the detention center dealt with problems at home with parents and guardians—be it alcoholism, substance disorders, physical or sexual or verbal and/or emotional abuse, or mere neglect—so we were not easily disturbed or afraid, but something different was happening with Vlad Siren. Usually withholding that demeanor, Siren was never imperious; in the classroom, however, he grew especially withdrawn and jittery, as if from too much caffeine or cocaine. Surely even back then employees were regularly drug tested, and anyway, Siren didn't seem the type to do cocaine or any illegal substances in private, being neurotic and soft-spoken and gentle as he normally appeared.

Siren's jitters continued as he told us to write about change. "Change is good," he told us, tapping his pencil on his desk. "Think about how you can improve in the future. I changed my own behavior many years ago when I was a teenager and getting into trouble before I wised up and finished school and went on to get a college degree" (here he snorted, still tapping his pencil), "and whatever you do, don't write about what you did to land here, just focus on what you need to do to get out and survive and thrive in this world." He had never talked so quickly. He repeated himself, saying rapidly, "For the sweet love of God, do not, I repeat do not, write about what you did to land here." (While others failed to write, I was able to compose the beginning of a short dramatic eclogue:)

> FATHER: The pond where we're going fishing is just up north a bit, by Calico's, where we ate those good ribs.
> SON: I'm sick. I can't go.
> FATHER: What do you mean you can't go? Are you sick?
> SON: I'm sick.
> FATHER: How the heck are we supposed to go fishing if you're sick?
> SON: I'm dizzy, sir, and squeamish.
> FATHER: You're squeamish?
> SON: My stomach is queasy. My forehead is clammy. My stomach feels knotted.
> FATHER: It's nerves, son. You'll be fine.
> SON: I'm nauseated.
> FATHER: You're nauseated? What in the heck are we supposed to do about fishing? You can't sit around here reading a book all day.
> SON: I'm sick.
> FATHER: Think about Christmas.
> SON: You always say that. It's not really helpful.
> FATHER: I don't know what else to say. I'm at a loss for words, son. You won't go fishing with me. You won't fish, play catch, play cards, throw a baseball, or watch competitive wrestling with me on cable TV.
> SON: Is there noncompetitive wrestling?

FATHER: It's simple. I want to bond with you, son, before my hip gets replaced. I'm getting old. Just look at my glabrous shins and freckled head. All my hair went down the drain. See the crow's-feet under my eyes? Hear the creak of bones and joints when I stand from the recliner to go rattle my cherries and try to take a piss?

SON: I don't understand, sir.

FATHER: It starts with the aching muscles and obliviscence. I take pills.

SON: Are you sick?

FATHER: I'm old, son. I get trachoma in my left eye. I have a swollen prostate. Stop drawing roosters with crooked cocks for a minute and look at me.

SON: I'm sketching birds and trees. I don't expect you to understand all my inscrutabilities.

FATHER: Are we going fishing or are we not?

SON: I feel like this whole conversation is an equivocation, sir. Both of us are trying to persuade or change the other. I don't want to argue.

FATHER: What do you love?

SON: Not arguing.

FATHER: Talk to your mother.

Though many of us enjoyed the writing sessions, some finished early and sat watching Siren squirm in his chair. Though he often appeared at work groomed and wearing well-ironed clothes, on this day we noticed he appeared disheveled, with an unshaven face and unkempt hair that was usually parted to the side with a slickness we imagined he triple-checked in a hand mirror. His collared shirt, though tucked in, was slightly wrinkled, and upon closer inspection, the bridge of his nose had broken out in milia or papules. As he leaned way back in his chair and let out a moan, one of the guards asked him whether he was feeling sick. To be fair, this was around the time when the NCAA basketball tournament was going on and as we wrote at our desks, every so often Siren would step outside and hurry to the control booth to check the scores on the small TV in there, returning to the classroom to tell the guard the score. It occurred to us that he was betting on the games with some of the other staff in an office pool. The guards and staff didn't mind sharing they had all filled out brackets, though they claimed it wasn't for money.

He sat at his desk and let out a deep sough. "I was always drawn to unpredictable work. My dad was a foundry worker his whole life and came home every night with blackface. He used to tell me the story about the time a furnace exploded at work when he and some other workers were melting scrap pipe. Hot metal sprayed all over the place and nobody came away harmed. When he got lung cancer, my mom blamed it on the work conditions, breathing asbestos, being around all that talc and silica, but I say who knows how he got it. He'd started smoking cigarettes when he was twelve, and in the latter part of his life he spent a lot of time around exhaust in my uncle's garage, working on engines. He was thin and pale when he died. One of the last things he told me was to find something I liked to do, no matter how risky or how long it took to find it. So here I am, working with you guys."

Siren was consumed with sadness, slumped over his desk. Trusty John, meanwhile, asked him whether we could write a fiction. Siren's general response to such questions was a firm no and gentle explanation, but this time he looked as if he were hearing of someone's death for the first time, in shock.

"For the assignment," Trusty John continued. "Like a fiction, to illustrate remorse in third person."

"Third person," Siren said.

"Yeah, as a fiction."

("He means a hypothetical situation," I added, glancing at Trusty John, who wouldn't look over at me.)

Siren agreed and mumbled something about making sure it was truthful, so we went back to writing, but the whole session felt comical and absurd, watching them dash in and out every so often to check the TV in the control booth. Many of us fell into daydreaming once we finished writing (for the record, I was usually the first done as well as the one who wrote the most), which meant staring into our desks and allowing whole narrative fantasies to unfold the same way we did when we worked outside, but in the classroom we imagined Vlad Siren trying to take a more fatherly/mentor approach rather than bullying us. For instance, anytime we thought of Siren he would take the role of George Bailey from *It's a Wonderful Life*, grabbing us by the lapels the way he grabbed Mary, yes, we imagined him running down the streets of O.D., shouting, "Merry Christmas, Dollar General! Merry Christmas, Tophet County Detention!" One of the women guards went to high school with Siren and told us he was always gentle and had never married. Many of us lacked that kind of father figure in our lives, someone who listened and nodded in understanding and compassion and love, the way fathers were supposed to act. We grew up watching syndicated reruns of old TV shows like *My Three Sons*, *Leave It to Beaver*, and *The Brady Bunch* that showed families dealing with issues way different than ours, as in none of those families were dealing with kids huffing paint or stealing video games or VHS tapes from the video store. None of those kids were lacing their pot with embalming fluid or masturbating at school or threatening to kill other students or teachers. None of those kids had parents who came home drunk and passed out in the recliner during the evening news or told their spouses to go screw themselves, yet we watched them in wonder, sitting on our knees in front of our TV screens when we were home by ourselves after school. The fantasies involving Siren fleshed out into full narratives with conversations in which he offered kind, solid advice, like the TV dads or how we imagined parents should act.

When we finished writing, we could tell something was happening to Vlad Siren's face. His cheek developed a strange tic as if from a muscle spasm, and he drooled as he steadied his jaw and stood motionless and mute, looking as if he had seen his own dead body lying among the wildflowers outside while the two Dobermans ripped into him like wolves. The look fell over us with a chilling terror. For a moment the room was so silent you could hear the guard standing outside the room sniff, a silence broken by Trusty John's outburst that Siren was "tripping." Siren pounded his fist on the desk and yelled, "Make use of our natural resources and go and be free!" which meant, certainly, that we were to use the territorial waters of the Gudgekin River to escape and free ourselves from the facility, that's what we assumed, despite Siren putting a hand to his mouth and telling us he didn't know what he was even talking about: "Where did that come from?" he mused aloud, running a hand over his face. He then dismissed us from the classroom, and one by one we walked past him as he sat back down and tried to catch his breath.

In *The Devil Is a Southpaw*, Don has a nightmare in which John Wayne as the buffoonish devil stands bowlegged in the middle of a dusty road and says, "Well, cowboy, are you man enough for an old-fashioned duel?" Don stirs in his bed, only to awaken to discover that Charlie had tied him up with rope.

As for Matthew, we didn't see him for the rest of the night, not even for dinner. We thought of him in the basement of the Columbus House, sitting on the floor in darkness with nothing but wet pants and excrement, hearing sounds of the drill sergeants' laughter down the hall while they ambulated, so inane that they didn't care whether Matthew ate or lost his mind in a dark room, all four drill sergeants jittery from too much coffee and amphetamines and devastated by a fear of a growing population with AIDS and the way the world was magnified in advertisements for prescription drugs on television, skeptical of hippies and socialism, MTV, Boy George, the midnight movie crowd at *The Rocky Horror Picture Show*, New Wave music, the colors pink and mauve and magenta, big cities, and vegetarians. The more we thought about the drill sergeants, the stronger our wounds and hatred grew for them and everything they stood for, because they were the ones who gave us restless sleep and nightmares, the ones who were sitting in the Columbus House's air-conditioning taking their pills and smoking cigarettes while we scrabbed at our arms and nates from heat rash, raked friable detritus outside in the dirt, pulled weeds and daisies under the bludgeoning sun, and daydreamed of jumping into the cool water in an invisible natatorium, our lassitude mere humor to them, our distress worse than death outside, where in the distance herds of cattle stood beside their shippen, where hunters urinated openly in the cool morning breeze without so much as acknowledging or appreciating their own freedom, civilians as the drill sergeants called them, snickering as they talked with a sinister venery about grabbing our balls and holding a knife to our throats. Matthew, meanwhile, was the one suffocating in solitude underneath them, in the basement, a victim of their abuse, dulled by the dim light and their priapic jokes, and trying his hardest, for whatever it was worth, to close his eyes in pleasure and think of somebody who cared about him.

We grew worried, even paranoid, because days would pass and we wouldn't hear anything about Matthew; nor did we hear from our social workers or attorneys. We tried calling them during phone hours, only to get the same run-around message: no news. Be patient, nothing will happen until the next court date. Be strong.

We all shared the same nightmare of finding Matthew. The dreams swirled into a whole series of nightmarish intrusions, including seeing him lying dead among animal parts, such as a boar's head or a slaughtered chicken, rotting bodies and then the eerie souls of the suffering, each with bulging eyes and black tongues, begging for help, while overhead a screech owl sat on a tree limb waiting to swoop down. These dreams signified absolutely nothing except our worries, we assumed, despite Trusty John's assertion that they represented an unresolved trauma that needed to be dealt with.

Maybe we were all experiencing trauma in lockup, wounded by hate. We had put on weight after eating three meals a day and two snacks; it was evident in that we needed larger sweatpants, mortified by our bloated reflections in the bathroom mirror. The cooks with their bulging eyes and hairy arms brought us our meals, which were becoming filled with more helpings, more sugar, starches, carbohydrates, and desserts. They brought us pig and rabbit and squirrel and decocted them to preserve their fat.

"Eat up," they said, licking their lips.

Those bastards were trying to fatten us up to eat us, that's what we were certain of, because the longer we ate, the more they examined us like giant lizards with their bulging tawny eyes, taking pleasure in our mastication, cursing the universe in the kitchen for making them wait so long to debauch and devour us, scrutinizing the airwaves by listening to talk radio while they cooked, or watching *The Morton Downey Jr. Show* or hapless men on afternoon soap operas on the small black-and-white TV and trying not to get watery-eyed from chopping onions, knowing full well they all needed to be patient until their plan to attack and tear into us and eat our innards would be carried out, and the more they thought about it, the more they wanted to attack us, those uneducated bastards with their hairy arms and long hair never even wore hairnets, and probably not plastic gloves whenever they handled food, because every so often our stomach cramped or dyspepsia came on in the middle of the night, leaving us feeling uneasy about our health and whether we would still be alive the next day.

Therefore, we started to plan our escape. There were the two Dobermans on the grounds that belonged to Strangelove, but we were never able to pet them outside during recreation, and we knew they could be vicious. We wanted to escape the identity of delinquency, which many of us had carried since before puberty, sanctioned and locked up, given community service hours and weekends with drill sergeants. We wanted to escape the pressures of our convolved group plurality and become individuals, each of us a person whose words meant something to someone, writers that we were, athletes, students, and mechanics, to share in the tranquility of nights under the dark side of the moon, where we could see lightning flash across the sky and hear the restlessness of a horse from the fields, where Christmas lights were strung across houses and where streetlights glowed, throwing shadows of abandoned buildings and tall cathedrals, where the frightened yellow eyes of feral cats and dogs disappeared into the bushes after hearing our footsteps approach, and where we would be free from the confinement and punishment, free from our sins, subjecting ourselves to one another's blandishments in pure joy, free outside under a crepuscular sky in a night so gentle we could hear the breathing of the homeless people crouched in darkened alleyways, crowning ourselves as no longer the picayune derelicts the detention staff believed us to be.

But how to escape? Anyone who had tried before had been unsuccessful, including Matthew, so we knew how difficult it would be to fool the guards or get past the fence and the dogs. When we were outside on the court, a few of us talked in low voices among ourselves while the guards stepped away to smoke a cigarette or stare at the tattoos on their forearms or talk to each other without paying much attention to us. Trusty John suggested (in a series of puerile and asinine suggestions) that we wear disguises—masks, hat and cane and monocle, as if we had access to canes and monocles; or that we dig a two-mile-long, ten-foot-wide tunnel underneath the fence to lead all the way to the highway, which made the rest of us grimace and mutter out of the corner of our mouths, because Trusty John's suggestions were as asinine as his own frowzy existence. That fool Foolborn continually berated himself for ever listening to and considering anything Trusty John said, and an intolerable guilt came over him in waves so often that it kept him up at night, cursing himself and Trusty John for falling into the plain dumb plan of shooting the school up. The anguish caused him insomnia and he sat up in his bed and stared at the wall as if looking into a giant aquarium full of colorful fish, wondering how he ever allowed himself to fall into such bad behavior, and anyway, Trusty John didn't seem to mind being locked up, sleeping restfully every night and eating his meals with a toothful grin. Other ideas to escape felt as ridiculous as Trusty John's the more we discussed them.

The plan we ultimately decided on was nonpareil and the most violent: fifteen of us would riot, steal the keys from one of the guards, and run out the front door. Fifteen of us came to this agreement, detailing its steps beginning at evening snack time, when only two guards were with us on the floor and the other in the control booth, we would wait for one guard to go open the medicine room to begin to distribute nighttime meds and then assault the other, fifteen against one, hitting the guard repeatedly in the head with our fists until the other guard returned and we would do the same thing, leaving them both unconscious. (We had planned it so that a quick kick to the groin and numerous hard blows to the back of the head would drop them. Residents Tanya and Jojo and Marcus were self-taught black belts in jujitsu, they swore.) The plan meant we would have to escape out of the front to avoid the dogs so that the drill sergeants wouldn't see us from the Columbus House.

Outside on the court, we talked about it in detail, blow by blow, step by step, and everyone was acquiescent. The day before we executed our scheduled plan, we stood in the courtyard with the understanding that the next night we would be free, escaped from the terror and abuse we had endured, no longer wallowing in a den of confinement or imprecated by our drowsy and weak anhedonia; no more complaining to one another about dyspepsia or fear of stomach ulcers; no longer manipulated to work and sweat in the stifling heat and swarms of gnats and bees while the drill sergeants and guards made jokes of sodomy and bruises; no longer observed in the shower or while on the toilet; no more having to face sadistic drill sergeants who grabbed their own cocks and scrunched their faces like buzzards, convinced they obliterated all our hope for rehabilitation. Those insensitive scopophiliacs so often bragged about mingling with prostitutes overseas back in the day, even in their brown bottle drunkenness, thinking we couldn't see right through their insecurities and phobias, and yes yes yes there was great joy in knowing it was only a matter of time before they would exterminate each other.

We were ready for the escape.

18. PRIDE, THE DEVIL'S SIN: AN INTERLUDE

Welcome. You are far away from anyone you've ever known, in a terrain unlike anything you've seen before, or to put it in the words of your gentle and strange deuteragonist, you are your own "headcanon," delineating a structure from song to prove yourself worthy of life, and to attest you are not, in the words of your former lover, "bedeviled with the jitters" from a transient and harmful lifestyle. You have sketched faces and trees and have written several stories and poems here, even in your sorrow. Like "The Balloon," the famous Barthelme story about a balloon in NYC that floats from Fourteenth Street toward the park while people sleep, which was a story you first read in Gonjiam Plains Hospital while eating tapioca pudding, you exist as a symbol of your own story—this book titled *The Devil Is a Southpaw*.

It isn't easy being here in the Gardens, this beautiful and sad place, because you have failed, after all, to be a decent human with financial and emotional stability; failed as a lover, a friend, an employee, and artist. Devoured by addiction and having to cut your way out of the belly of unhealthy obsessions, you can see, in the small pond encircled by colored stones, your trembling reflection and your cloudy head the way people observe themselves in an unprepossessing fun house mirror, absent of expression or life, plagued with anhedonia. Stop looking at the head in the reflection and try to see beyond that, inside of yourself. Is it possible? Or are you too focused on your own image, your own thoughts tangled around in your head and landing, eventually, on the question: How do others see you?

The sky here is vast and deep blue, with clouds like harrowing ghosts waiting for you to die or race away. They neglect your confessions, slowly abandon you by sunset. When it rains, you stand outside and listen for thunder, lonelier than ever in the solitude of this world, wondering whether the animals have all taken shelter or, like you, they watch and listen. You are tormented by the rage of deception, an irredeemable fatigue, and bitter misfortune. Hidden in the tall grass behind your yurt, you found a machete with dried blood and the decayed guts of a small animal. A former resident must have left it behind, along with an empty vial of sleeping pills and bits of dragon fruit and papaya. You imagine an artist, a beautiful woman wrapped in newspaper and sitting on the ground in mournfulness at dusk. She longs for love, this artist, and like you she is troubled by overcoming her ego in the stigma of her silence. If she were here, you would kiss her forehead and hold her hand until she promised to stay with you in sickness and health. Or, perhaps she *is* here somewhere, maneuvering her way through the wasteland of mosquitoes and heat and searching for you, too. You are not alone.

Even in your insomnia, you imagine bodies buried underneath the ground, their spirits rising, their voices spread by the wind. You seek them out, moving careful through the tall brush and sliding down rocky cliffs, because like you, they struggle to go beyond the reach of difficult memories and evil, past suffering, and into the light of the bright moon. They will lead you there, into a realm of light, because you are ill and in your last days here.

Respiratory sickness, lower back aches, chest and joint pain. Better to stay inside and stay well. Better to avoid the outside elements, the volcano, the animals, and work on your art. Your cough has grown worse over the past week, a dry wheeze. Your voice is hoarse from the dryness, so you try to drink as much water as possible. If you could only sleep better and wake more restful, but you wake up throughout the night coughing, hand on your chest, wondering in confusion whether you are hearing fleeing howls from outside or whether it's your dream state, lucid and wet, with the voice of your father asking you whom you love.

Like your reflection in the house of mirrors, or in quivering waters, the art you produce can appear deformed, fractured, dead. Your art is misunderstood and angry, dull, full of the illusion of demented power and jealousy. Your art is focused on the lost, lonely, wounded people in your life who have hurt you—but what about love? What about loneliness? The imposters you write about in this book, after all, are cruel and harrowing and never shameful, yet you see yourself as an imposter as well, a lonesome one, too concerned with gaining the empathy and trust of others through this book, too focused on the head instead of the heart, too malefic to the pleas of others' needs. Your struggle to impress people and delude them into believing you are gifted and intelligent is a juvenile attempt to be appreciated and loved. The will for limitless power through your art, however, is as dead as a hanged man whose body is cut down and left to suffer the elements. This is not Ocean City, or even a city by the ocean, but a remote island full of canary birds, rocky cliffs, and volcanoes on the verge of eruption.

It is pointless and too late for you, so you hide, run away to escape thinking about any of this, to be alone, but mostly to hide.

But there is hope in solitude. Here, at least temporarily, the only other resident is a saintly man who plays the dulcimer guitar by the salty sea and hums in a fine, euphonious tone. Insomniastricken, you listen and watch sleepily from a distance, eager to talk to him but afraid he'll find you too nervous and awkward to maintain any meaningful or human conversation, especially after the circumstances of your most recent breakdown, which have left you calm and dazed from medication and seeking silence and isolation. When he isn't playing the dulcimer guitar, he lies in a hammock outside his yurt, listening to headphones to avoid the buzz of cicadas while drinking virgin cocktails through a straw. Once, he stood from the hammock, unbuttoned his shorts, and urinated cheerily into the open wind, wondering, perhaps, whether he should remove his shorts entirely, drenched in sweat, and enter the sea naked.

He may ask you, "What is your name? Why are you here? And, for that matter, what good things have you done with your earthly life?"

You will tell him the story of the scorpion and the frog, and that it is your nature to run from things, that you are more passive than confrontational, and that, deep down, you love to love. It is your nature to be withdrawn, private, prone to painless ailments. Or, in this case, an undefined illness that sulps the lungs. Try to breathe, sleep as much as you can, with dreams full of prophetic energy and color and life, like this island.

Your visions rise out of the ocean wrapped in a cool mist like the blood of Christ, surely the innards of someone under a veil, submerged in grief by your anger and ignorance and the brutal conversations you have with yourself about suffering and sin and learning to forgive. How can you forgive others if you can't forgive yourself for your self-pity anyway, certainly among the unfairness and cruelty of the world, past the vast waters and back into Western civilization among the deadly wars and dizzy, sick, demented hell of this world: How can you learn to accept your own slow destruction and finally realize what, exactly, you are?

You, Milton, who suffers from the sin of pride, awaiting healing and rebirth. Many species of birds are now extinct, and one day you will be extinct, too, buried in the earth. A reminder to keep working. You sketch the birds, focusing on their elaborate details, distinct colors, remembering all the birds that used to visit, landing on your windowsill, like the crimson bird, a descendant of the cardinal. Standing by the window, you wait for them. Beyond the Gardens, under the heavy branches of eucalyptus trees, you watch the crimson birds scatter into a pale blue sky, heavenward.

19. THE SICKNESS

In the evening before bed, we spoke to ourselves in our rooms, as we did most nights, about our misfortunes as we paced back and forth, disconcerted by the presence of our shadows on the wall as a reminder of our solitude and confinement, thinking of escaping that place and fleeing the grounds while the drill sergeants stretched out in their beds over at the Columbus House, hats tipped over their eyes because of course they would sleep with their hats, they probably slept with guns and knives like cowards, mumbling in their sleep in monotonous tones about their phobias, their boots and uniforms beside them. We thought of our grief, sick and somber in the night, recalling the details of neglect or abuse and our seeds of resentment, feeling an irrepressible desire to forget them and start over in a new life, reformed, rehabilitated. Surely the eyes of God would look upon us and be pleased by resilience and hope. Surely the wild and burdensome challenges all around us one day would not strangle us with cruel memories as we fled the hazards of life looking for a prosperous and peaceful environment to capitulate to. Our lives would one day be changed, we would be important and useful in a community, that's what we hoped every miserable day there, and that's what we told ourselves before bed.

Ace got angry at bedtime for whatever reason—maybe he was scared or maybe he was triggered by the confinement—and punched the concrete wall or the door, crying out. He wanted to speak to a staff member, and many nights one of the staff members let him punch his mattress, which we could hear in our wing, even behind closed doors; we heard Ace scream and assault his mattress while the guard let him, which was the first time we realized the staff could do something productive. They let poor Ace punch his mattress and scream until he felt better, that poor boy too fragile and bewildered by his own rambling anger to be relieved for even a fleeting instant of the unforgettable trials and persecutions he endured at home and school. He was, surprisingly, the only one who lost control of his emotions, but he dealt with it in a healthy release while the rest of us let our worries build in our guts.

"We have to escape soon," Brandon said from his room, which led to a hodgepodge of soft voices echoing throughout our wing.

"Do you know that one of the dogs has no sense of smell? Ambrose told me."

"What does that have to do with anything?"

"No sense of smell means no tracking our steps. The dog is no threat."

"There's still another dog, though. Those dogs run in packs, like wolves."

"I'd like to know if any of you pussies have the balls to actually try to escape instead of just talking about it."

"I do."

"Does anyone have any extra toilet paper? I don't want to call the control room to ask."

"Are you beating off again, you hillbilly?"

"Shut up. I'm on the toilet."

"Seems like you're always on the toilet, beating off. We all need to be on the same page if we're doing this."

"You know what I think? Nobody's going anywhere. You're all too scared to escape."

"Matthew told me he has a plan. We need to get with him if they'd ever let him out of the basement. Any ideas?"

"We're going to die in here. These nimrods hate every one of us."

"Is anyone else's stomach hurting?"

"Stop talking about it. We meet tomorrow outside to make a strict plan."

"Shhh. Quiet, someone's coming."

In the wing, Anna Darko must've stepped soundlessly across the room as she entered with her paintbrushes and skulls, because none of us heard her, but there she was when we peeked out the windows on our doors. Her profile was outlined by the lights overhead, and we all stared out our windows and watched her paint, whether she knew it or not; she looked detached from all emotion, painting her skulls as if she had no ownership over them or her work. Perhaps she was the type of person who rejected both compassion and bitterness and spent her time living an anonymous life the way the town recluse and poet, Agatha Klemm, did. Softly, while she worked, she began to hum, which was all we needed to feel sleepy.

Then the sickness hit in the middle of the night when the building was silent and we were lulled to sleep by Anna Darko's humming. The first to leave was a boy named Anton, who woke up screaming. Anna Darko radioed two guards working the graveyard shift who rushed into Anton's room and found him crouched over in pain on all fours, vomiting into his toilet, sweating, yelling that he had food poisoning, drool hanging from his mouth. Because there was no power outlet in his room, they dragged him into the open wing so that a large box fan could blow on him to keep him cool, which was difficult for him and us because we could smell the dog-mange stench of his sickness as it permeated the air, reminding us of our dinner's stew full of tough meat, the stew that had poisoned us, all of us, those cooks conjured up their poison and stirred it into the pot. Anton moaned and wailed for help, gagging and dry heaving over the hum of the fan. A few minutes later, someone else screamed from their room, followed by another scream. Many of us were crouched over in stomach pain, sweating and vomiting stew and bile; we heard the guards shouting to get residents out of the wing, get them to the hospital and away from us, call the transport officer and throw them into the car, that's what they shrieked at one another while the rest of us lay on the floor clutching our bellies and trying not to vomit.

The second person to leave was Rosemary, one of the Native girls, whose breathing was heavy from crying and pain; next went Ace, then a girl named Stacie, then Anna and Hanna, followed by three other boys, all gone to the emergency room, leaving the rest of us to wallow in our pain. Brandon kept telling the guards he was hallucinating and felt he might faint, but there was no evidence of vomit or any other fluids or discharges like with the others, so they made him stay, and all night we heard him reciting the Jesus Prayer over and over in Latin and English. All the lights in the wings were on until sunrise. Some of us weren't sick enough to leave, or so they claimed, despite feeling a harsh abdominal pain in the lower gut like a knife stabbing us repeatedly, a sharp, burning pain, and all they gave us was Rolaids crushed into carbonated water so that we could try to get some rest.

We felt helpless and abandoned. We were the ones left behind, the unlucky ones, lying in our rooms with nausea, dyspepsia, and lethargy, and it was quickly clear we wouldn't have the energy to attempt our plan to escape; we fell in and out of a restless sleep, our imaginations belied us with scenes of other rooms and places as we dreamed of old schoolhouses with blood-covered walls; slaughtered animals; and long, empty hallways with a murk reminiscent of haunted houses at Halloween, and at some point Strangelove appeared in our dreams in an ominous cloud of gray and sallow complexion, like a tyrannous dictator, wearing a chryselephantine robe and ordering our deaths by beheading, that sick bastard feigning sovereignty and laughing at our colluctation. We weren't sure whether we were asleep or awake, having slept so little throughout the night.

Someone had leaked our plan to them, we knew, and their poisoning in retaliation revealed how much control they had over us. We suffered hallucinations of eerie animal shadows and the floating bodies of children who reached out to us for help, their voices singing, "Vexilla regis prodeunt Inferni," and then they slowly dissolved into the floor, evoking in us a morbid sense of elegiac lucidity as we lay prostrate on our beds wondering whether all this vomiting and sickness had caused an inguinal hernia or some consumptive disease. Those of us who weren't taken to the hospital suffered from pain and insomnia and paced in our rooms with the debilitating anxiety of prisoners awaiting the blindfold before being shot by the firing squad, indeed, we found ourselves suffering with panic, vulnerable and alone and defenseless with our cold hands and abdominal muscles trembling from dehydration as we waited forever for the nurse to bring us water and saltine crackers and chewable antacid tablets, one hand clutching our stomach and the other blocking the coruscant brightness of early-morning sunlight that slanted in through the horizontal window high on the east wall.

As a means of precaution, they forced the remainder of us in the wing to be monitored by the guards and control booth cameras and left the rooms of our doors open in case of vomiting or other emergency gastrointestinal issues. Most of us by this point had trouble keeping our heads erect and our eyes open, but we weren't allowed to return to sleep in our beds until the nurse arrived at some point in the morning; nobody ate breakfast or even asked to eat. We were given cups of water while we rested on the floor of the wing, which was eerily quiet since only half of us were left. We knew the terror, we really did, on this last night of our sickness. We knew rage and fear, but we also knew courage, so we accepted our reality of suffering, we abandoned all measures of hope, and some of us cried out for help only to be ignored, chastised, leaving us to be confused and uncertain whether we would survive since we were the ones who didn't go to the hospital.

"It's not fair," Brandon told them, feigning dizziness as he pretended to stagger. "Ace got to leave and he barely barfed. He's a faker. I'm dizzy."

"Cut the crap. And stop with the Jesus Prayer."

"Never."

"You're not sick, Brandon. Stop faking it."

"Not faking. I'm hearing things. Do you hear that? A pack of coyotes howling at the moon? Hear that?"

"No."

They continued to ignore us, and soon enough we stopped talking as the passing minutes turned into an hour; we lingered over the pleasures of remembering our lives outside of this place: tearing into a well-cooked piece of meat with our fierce, sharp teeth, drinking a cool glass of lemonade with crushed ice, imagining standing at the foot of a mountain or staring into the horizon at the sun setting over a calm ocean, until gradually the universe reasserted itself and we found ourselves being led back into our rooms in the evening, in the darkness, our stomachs still cramping. Slowly, we fell asleep wondering whether our reconcilement would ever equal our anger and our wounds, and whether the sky outside was losing its population of glimmering stars.

This last night of our sickness is the part of the story where we tell people we recovered, went back to bed, and finished our time in lockup. (Or, at least, I tell it this way.) We tell them we slept soundly and healed from our sickness and woke to a new day among the staff and guards; that we ate our breakfast as we had done in previous days, and that we declared in gentle voices that we could feel something expanding in our hearts like gratitude, feeling the rigid sting of eternal fortitude in the intensity of colors in the sky and in the world around us; that we felt in our character the ecstasy of resilience and compassion, appreciating the sweet fragrance of fresh rainfall outside, understanding the rigors of our captivity and structure, breathing the cool air with the passage of weeks in our continuing rehabilitation; that we never felt exasperated by others in the flow of steady obedience no matter how difficult and slow the battle, never challenged authority or were shocked by a gloomy aura expropriated by the drill sergeants or guards, grouped as we were in military lines outside in the courtyard and smelling the gizzards and fish hanging on the walls beside the windows where we stood; and that we grew accustomed to the enchantment of power and punishment, acceding to command, awakening each morning with the understanding that a melancholy attitude meant a wasteful day in a life so precious we should get on our knees and thank the Lord, clasping our warm hands together in prayer, freed from the chains of fear and guilt, and freed of disillusionment, impurity, and sin.

This is what we tell people (what *I've* told people), but the truth is that the remainder of us were awakened by a noise in the night. We fell in and out of sleep, our dreams animated by the impetus of a distant thunder outside. Sitting up with tired eyes, we glimpsed our doors open, and there she stood like an angel: Ms. Anna Darko, bathed in a soft light, commanding us to follow her.

20. A DIZZYING DESCENT INTO THE HYPOGEUM

She stood in the doorway in the vain light of evening, running a finger along the door as if drawing attention to some sort of energetic and mystical gesture we weren't able to understand, we who were too wrapped in the worry of losing trust in ourselves, as if obeying anyone in authority would not only brainwash us in our vulnerable state and leave us tormented by memories, but also serve as evidence that we were worthless, confined to mediocrity, and living the remainder of our days in crassly infinite suffering.

"Anna Darko, help us!" someone called out.

Our Anna Darko, artist of skulls, more marvelous than any supernatural conjecture, bringing our universe to a surfeit of hope and redemption, woman of shadowy myth and symbols, chimerical to the night and holding a scent of deer, a savior in our hour of anguish. Our hesitation gave her pause, of course, for she knew to be patient as we were devoured by fatigue, moving slowly from our beds to our feet as if covered in ulcers and bedsores, asking her whether she was trying to lure us into more torrential areas filled with monstrous shadows forcing us to drink sour medicine for our nausea and stomach bile again, though we knew deep down that Anna Darko was blind to fault, timelessly moving around like a gentle spirit. In the ever-skullextending moment we knew we were directed toward an unknown fate; so we left our rooms and followed her.

She led us out of the wings and through the dayroom, past the dining tables and control booth with its dark mirrored glass that reminded us we were being scrutinized. We followed her in a straight line despite her never telling us to; we knew she trusted us because the whole time she walked ahead of us she never turned around or appeared worried we might try to attack or assault her or run away. She opened the doors that led out onto the courtyard, where we had never stepped outside in the night, and it was like entering a jubilant world as the scent of a cool rain filled the air. Even in our exhaustion we felt like free-spirited, wild dogs, wondering whether Anna Darko was allowing our escape after all, taking us to the edge of the land and unlocking the fence so that we could run like bulls into the darkened woods. We followed her across the courtyard toward the Columbus House, where she stopped at the door, removed the set of keys from her pocket, and, unlocking the door, turned to us and pulled it open.

"It's fine," she told us. "Go inside so I can show you something."

Reluctantly, we stepped inside the pitch-dark hallway as she held the door open for us, and once she flipped the switch and the lights flickered on, we immediately noticed the stone walls displayed with painted skulls resting on pedestals. They were Anna Darko's art, the skulls she painted while we slept, and underneath each skull was a plaque with a name identifying whose skull was displayed: Mina, Joseph, Arthur . . . the skulls gazed with a terror we recognized from our dreams, but odder than that was the vertiginous effect the hallways had as the skulls aligned all the way toward the high ceiling, so many of them, each skull painted with elaborate patterns of various colors, red and blue and yellow, which was the first thing Anna Darko pointed out.

"These children were all here once," she said. "They were in Dublan, alive and running around like ants outside. But they all died in a storm."

She told us of a large tornado that rolled through the area in the late 1970s and demolished houses and barns back when there wasn't much out here except for an elementary school, and how she was a young caretaker of horses and chickens because her father was on bedrest from an agonizing case of the flu, the poor man coughing and vomiting in a bucket and barely able to take shelter from the storm. Anna Darko, who was from Anadarko, said she could barely get the horses into the stable that afternoon when the wind came up and the tornado was building in the West, and she searched the farm for the rooster who strutted fearless away from the barn as if daring the tornado to sweep into him and pull him up into the air, that stubborn fowl that must've already made it out into the high weeds because it was too late, Anna Darko had to hurry inside the house and take shelter in the bathroom with her parents while praying the tornado wouldn't hit them dead on. They had the transistor radio with them in the bathroom so that they could hear the meteorologist track the tornado as it touched ground and kicked up dust, plowing through Tophet County at that very moment. Indeed, Anna Darko said they heard the rumble and wondered whether the tornado was about to hit their stable or house; they hunkered down and covered their bodies and heads with a blanket and mattress until the rumble stopped and they knew all was clear. But that storm had directly hit the elementary school, killing a dozen kids and teachers in what had become the largest tornado on record since 1943. This was when she knew she wanted to help kids and decided to dedicate her life to social justice and art.

 The skulls she had painted belonged to those children, but there were far more skulls than those children who died, so we were confused—whose skulls were the others? Anna Darko contemplated our question with enough confidence that she told us she would take us to the closet where Matthew had been trapped, providing we knew how to keep a secret about that room, which was strange enough that we gave her our word that we would never share what we were about to see with anyone, not even our caretakers, future spouses, or children; we followed her down to a door at the end of the hallway that opened to reveal a staircase leading down to the basement, where it was dark and cool; once we got down there Anna Darko had to turn on the only light, a wall lamp that emitted a light so dim it was difficult to see much. It was difficult to admit our anxieties in that moment, because we were unsure of what was happening with Matthew: Was he thin and ill, lying in his own vomit and urine, or was he brainwashed from so much verbal and physical abuse that he wouldn't be able to conceive of his surroundings or even recognize us even though it had been only a short time since we had last seen him? These thoughts jarred us as we followed Anna Darko down the darkened hall to the door; she paused there as if trying to listen for him inside the room, but we heard nothing. The light shone underneath the door, so we knew it was at least light in the room. Anna Darko jingled through her key ring, then unlocked the door and we stepped inside.

 He was sitting cross-legged on the floor in the corner of the room with his head down; he didn't bother to look up, and for a split second we wondered whether he was dead or unconscious—the poor soul was quiet, somnolent, but we could see his chest rise and fall, and even our commotion of opening the creaky door didn't wake him. The room was narrow and full of metal carts stacked with old magazines, newspapers, some of which were also spread on the floor, as if he had been shuffling through the pages so quickly they ripped, or perhaps he had suffered through bouts of frustration and rage and tore them up in his fury, yes, we imagined him clutching them in an impetuous state of alarm because there were paper airplanes made from newspaper pages, and other pages he had crumpled into balls, and still other pages folded in rectangular shapes and stacked together as if he had attempted to construct some sort of building or house, and even stranger were the equations written on the back of newspaper in black Sharpie that suggested he was working out some sort of mathematical equation or convolution of the trails in the woods that led to the Gudgekin River; it was less a drawn map and more of a math problem he was trying to solve by figuring out the amount of time it takes to run from the Columbus House to the river via various trails. The shock of thinking about time so often in solitude was sickening to say the least.

"He's planning his escape," someone spoke up, but Anna Darko knelt by him and placed her hand on his head. While she tried to wake him, we noticed a notebook sitting on one of the shelves. I saw sketches of birds and animals, all done with such precision and detail. Some were drawn in colored pencil. He sketched owls and dogs and bears. He sketched eagles. In another notebook there were drawings of houses, barns, horses. Toward the end of that notebook I saw drawings of faces that were considerably worse. The faces showed spiders as eyes, strands of hair, no mouths. They were like humans turning into beasts. Their bodies had wings. As I turned the pages, I saw the deterioration of quality in the drawings. The faces grew sloppier, as if a child had drawn them. I thought surely they weren't his drawings. Surely a child had scribbled in the pages. The eyes and mouths were merely circles in the last of the pages.

I turned the page and saw a collection of Matthew's writings:

STORY ABOUT MY DISAPPEARANCE

For three nights the father dreamed that his son was alive and living underground. He woke those nights in a terrible panic to find himself trembling and short of breath. One night he went into the kitchen where he found his wife sitting alone at the table. He told her of his dream.

"It's been nine years," she told him.

There was a mist that developed over the water outside. The mist began to form the shape of a child standing over the water.

The father went outside to the water, but the fog had dissipated. He searched the sky for a sign but found only clouds. There was a hole in the earth at his feet. Curious, he crouched and heard the distant voices of children speaking in a language he couldn't understand.

"You only have to use your imagination," a voice said from below. Then smoke rose from the hole and evaporated in the wind.

"Help," his son's distant voice said.

We couldn't read anymore, but we wondered why Matthew was writing about his disappearance. Anna Darko was saying his name loudly now. We wondered whether we should turn and make a run for it or trust her in whatever her plan was. It wouldn't have mattered, really, because the moment he opened his eyes he sprang to his feet and staggered backward against the wall, terrified, because he didn't recognize us at first, and certainly having been alone in this room for several days had taken its toll on him, as if all he had left were fragments of vestiges of the past, cowering against the wall as he called out, "Help, help me," as if we were the large, predatory raven mockers he wrote about who attacked the sick and tore into their bodies and ate their hearts (he often wrote about mythological raven mockers in various stories as if they were real), and it took an abnormally long time for his fear to subside, for he hadn't recognized Anna Darko, understandably, and it appeared he could barely breathe; only when he noticed the rest of us did he stop calling out for help.

In an effort to console him, Anna Darko spoke in a soft voice, telling him we were there to rescue him and we were about to walk ceaselessly through a place where headless children were wrapped in velvet curtains and the current from bubbling waters led toward places where castaways lived and survived on fish and plants under the shoals of rocks at the bottom of the river, a secret place to escape the suppressions of our present lives, at least temporarily. "We'll lick the oregano from colorful lotuses," she said, "and hear the buzzing of sleeping birds too large for earthy life; you'll be the only boy, dragging your feet past them, staring at their gular pouches as if they're pelicans, and we'll see iconodules drunk on wine and singing from their campsites in their glory and jubilation!"

"I'm dizzy," Matthew said, running a hand over his face, but we were as confused as he probably felt. Not only did we refuse to believe what Anna Darko had told him, but we questioned her sanity and strength of disillusionment, which felt like a futile attempt to get us off course in some malapropos way, but as she turned to the rest of us we knew she was sincere; she led us out of the room, turning to place a finger to her lips, and we followed her down the dark, empty hallway, turning a corner and reaching a door at the end. The door was unlocked, and she turned its handle carefully and opened it, revealing only darkness and cool wind. We were already underground in the basement of the Columbus House, and yet it was an expansion underneath the entire Columbus House building, full of rooms colder, dirtier, where the skeletons of the dead were covered in maggots and rats, and any amount of human flesh was feasted upon.

"Follow me," Anna Darko told us. "Are you all feeling up to it? There's lots more to see down here than a closet. Four thousand square feet, in fact, and I want to help you escape."

Nobody was sure what to think, so we paused in hesitation. Brandon asked, "What is it? Where are we going?"

"We're going into the hypogeum to escape, just like you wanted. You'll need to trust me."

We weren't certain she was being truthful, and she could see the distrust in our eyes, so she told us how once, several years earlier, she had volunteered for six months at an animal shelter that ended up closing due to a sudden outbreak of distemper and respiratory illnesses in the dogs. After the first few months, she began to watch them suffer, several dogs all at once, as if a great curse had arrived over the shelter and spread, and what else could she do except listen to their cries of pain and whimpers and coughs? What could she do except dream about saving all of them? Every day she fed them and tried to comfort them as they wheezed, crying in her arms. Why was this happening to them, and would she ever really be able to save them or was it unrealistic to imagine such a thing? And how could people ever be veterinarians, having to put down dogs all the time? Did putting them down mean relieving them of their pain, or was it something crueler and more atrocious?

"I want to save people, too," she said.

We heard the screeching of a crow from somewhere. Then we heard shrieking, as if people were tortured souls trapped in a dense and somber punishment, and all we could think about was punishment and the serene rigors of work and humiliation we had been subjected to, and all those thoughts flooded into our minds as if every punishment would be fulfilled the farther into the hypogeum we went. We asked Anna Darko: Why are we going? We urged her to tell us, huddled together, and even Matthew stepped forward, demanding an answer; but Anna Darko consoled us, promised she would never put us in danger: "There are people I want to show you," she told us. "All will be fine, but you have to trust me."

Some of us didn't believe her and stepped backward in hesitation. "We don't want to go," a few said. Anna Darko reached for the red lantern hanging on the wall, then took the lighter on the shelf beside it and lit the lantern, placing the flame directly under the globe. "That's fine," she said, "but I'm going down. Follow if you want."

The others turned and ran down the hall, leaving only Anna Darko, Matthew, and me.

As Anna Darko used a lever to adjust the flame, I felt the mangy air creep up and the horror of an approaching, insatiable torture, unsure whether I would be breathing in difficulty or whether this would be the escape, like she claimed.

Then she and Matthew stepped into the darkness, and with a heaviness in my chest and a sense of malaise that I was somehow entering the marrow of the dead, I made my dizzying decision, and followed them.

21. ESCAPE

Our biggest concern underground was that the drill sergeants were after us, knew of our escape, and would terrorize us to death down there, or else murder us and collect our bones like the skulls of children Anna Darko painted. She told us that we were entering a hypogeum, but we weren't positive we could trust her; perhaps she was secretly working with the drill sergeants (she worked in the facility with them, after all), and anyway, Matthew was certain he heard Sergeant Ambrose's cough coming from somewhere. In the darkness, I held on to Matthew's shoulder while he held Anna's. We eventually walked into light from lanterns on the walls around us and found ourselves walking across a ballroom; the walls were covered with posters showing my drawings and paintings with my name at the top of the posters in bold letters:

Milton Foolborn

An art show advertisement, certainly, but why?

—People need to see your art, Anna told me when she saw me staring at the posters. I glanced at Matthew, who was already heading toward the exit, where Anna told us a tunnel led to a staircase that would take us outside to the woods, where we could escape if we were careful. We heard the echoed roar of familiar laughter, Ambrose's laughter, of course!—but there was nobody else there even though I was especially suspicious that Sergeant Ambrose was near; I knew that laugh anywhere. I followed Matthew and hurried for the exit. He opened the door and we found ourselves in a cool, empty room with an opening at the far end: a tunnel. The hypogeum, at least this room, was more ellipse-shaped than square, with curved walls made of hardened mud or clay and rock, flesh-colored, and emitting an eerie hum, as if we had entered the swollen belly of some gigantic beast. Matthew and I were silent, unsure what to expect. Anna Darko led us to the tunnel entrance and told us to hurry, but she didn't enter. As we dragged our fearful feet toward it and got on our hands and knees and began to crawl through the cold dirt, we heard Ambrose's voice somewhere behind us, calling our names like a madman, *FOOLBORN! MATTHEW!* and luckily we could crawl quickly because we were both in good physical shape at that time, having run bleachers and up and down a dam in physical education class at O.D. High; we crawled through darkness and muck, through the proboscis of some wild beast, that's what it felt like, with smells of repugnant flesh and the carcasses of dead animals, and Matthew dry heaved as we crawled, coughing and sputtering, until we finally made it to the end of the tunnel and climbed steep wooden stairs that led us outside the Columbus House.

 We ran into the woods and followed a winding trail that led us to a clearing on the other side of the trees, where we felt more jittery than before because among the illusory fog that lifted around us we saw things we had never seen: a woman feeding meat on a stick to a type of chupacabra with beady eyes; and many cornucopias among the flora, delicious fruits and vegetables, which small animals were eating. We saw a donkey in the distance, its ears long and covered with flies buzzing all around, although there were no other flies or insects anywhere, even around the slop the animals were eating in this place full of such stench. The space filled with ashes and yellow light that slowly turned to a rose color. One could easily hear a high-pitched ringing, like a ringing in the ears. A few children sat in sludge with their heads bowed, animals licking the wax from their ears. Two girls were building another boy out of mucus and straw. They used a large ball for a head, two pebbles for eyes, and a donkey's ears for his own. The girls stroked and kissed his ears.

—We made it! I said, breathing heavily.

—Wicked, Matthew said, nodding.

—I think we lost them. Anna, too.

Where were we? A boy whose hair was long and full of lice was on his hands and knees and stuck out his tongue, which was dark red and at least three feet long. He looked up at us.

—Be careful where you walk, he said in a raspy voice. This place is full of leeches. I eat them out of the river.

Matthew backed away, but I spoke to the boy.

—How do we get to Old Dublan? I asked.

—Follow the river, the boy said, and crawled away.

The Cocytus tributary, which fed into the Gudgekin River, wound through the weeds as far as we could see. The ground was moist with footsteps and animal tracks, which we followed along the bank of the river, and everywhere the darkness cooled the air, despite the dull, heavy air, my God, I felt my senses open wide and took in everything around me: the twisting branches of trees with spidery orange cobwebs, the half-eaten apples trailing from the ground to the river, as if former escapees had tossed them over their shoulders as they entered the river, all that reckless abandonment that made a place feel so alive with life and carelessness, with a disregard of rules and law, everyone breathing in the same air. A woman wearing a long, colorful dress and a headscarf was playing a guitar beside the river while children lay in front of her, some sleeping and others entranced by her music, and I absorbed her music like the children, saturated in elation, standing in the billowy fog while men in broad-brimmed hats and baggy pants joined the children and sat at her feet. I could see the men were covered in smears of paint of various colors— artists. Matthew noticed them as well, and I was suddenly not afraid, at least momentarily, enveloped in a warm sensation of peace, whether from the sonorous music from the brumous haze on the water, but my uneasiness of Ambrose lifted for the time being. We moved closer to them so that the woman playing the guitar was aware of us, caught my glance and gave a slight nod.

    I heard our names being called from the hoarse voices of the drill sergeants, those irreverent bastards, though I could recognize their voices anywhere; but I wasn't able to spot them, not when I was struck with imagining them kneeling next to the trees, waiting for the right time to assault us with their hirsute hands and weapons and kill us the way they had killed the other residents whose bones flashed in my mind right then, bones piled in the corners of the Columbus House basement like garbage. We had to keep moving, that's what I told Matthew, who agreed, so we walked down to the river and followed the bank, hearing crows cawing above us and in the branches of trees, perched on the shoulders of strange men walking in the distance. Matthew was shivering and walking with his arms crossed, trying to warm himself, but I knew it was nerves; it was less that he was cold and more that he was anxious, swatting at the insects swirling around us from the humidity. A swirl of gnats swarmed him as he walked beside me, batting them away effeminately with his hands, the poor boy, and I could tell his stomach was turning, as if the gnats and moth larvae were eating away at him, because he had always been neurotic as long as I'd known him, even back in the elementary-school years when we picnicked with Mrs. Splinter's class at a park where grackles were aggressively eating the scraps some of the boys had thrown at them, even then he waved his hands effeminately for the birds to fly away, he interrogated them impassively as a farmer talks to the calf he's about to slaughter.

Strangely, we heard a young voice calling from somewhere ahead in the fog, and out of the darkness a girl appeared, wearing jeans and a hoodie. Matthew gasped, and at the same time, we both recognized the girl was his younger sister, Nora.

—Hey, brother! she called out.

Nora, who had in the past existed only in my imagination, was now alive and present, a thin girl with long dark braids, stunning like a fugitive among jasmine embers underground. Nora was a girl who had disappeared to live in this deeply serene and irresistible land in the woods and become a vociferous presence among the others whose lives disappeared, or whose souls rejected any other spiritual place, here where one couldn't tell the living from the dead, the spirit from the human; it didn't matter. Living out here in the country, she smiled through the flow of light glistening between branches, walked along rosebushes while singing old songs for the others as they created art or drifted off in slumber, trying to forget the brutal truths of the world, all the killings and diseases and abuse happening in O.D., all the cold drizzle and hurricanes and tornadoes, and all the ignorance and disregard for art. I had seen photographs of her in the newspaper when she was missing. She resembled Matthew particularly in the prominent cheekbones, which maintained a blush to them, or it was scarlet from chapped skin due to the dry air; her nose was narrower than his, her upper lip more pronounced, and her forehead smooth; her hands were small and delicate like his, but Matthew had feminine hands and bony fingers. He had been bullied for it in school because he drew attention to his fingers whenever he painted his thumbnails black, which he did on occasion.

Nora stopped hugging Matthew but kept holding his hand while she related the tragic circumstances of how she arrived in the woods, a haunting story about walking home from school one day when she was kidnapped by a farmer and his wife and held against her will in their barn for six days. Every night their blind son came and sang to her, she told us. She let the son touch her face, her nose, and mouth and was able to convince the boy to untie her so she could escape, and while running through the field she found a hole in the ground, so she collected some twigs and brush and placed it all around the hole to try to conceal it, then stayed there for hours. I asked her why she couldn't go home since everyone thought she had disappeared.

—I can't, she said. Why would I? There's nothing for me in that terrible town. Out here in the country I can create art and sleep in peace with the animals and wood spirits. I can talk to them without worrying they'll judge me. Nobody tries to impress anyone else, we just live free.

She told us so many people like her escaped the perils while others simply wanted to live in a place outside of O.D., a place where they could sleep and create art as much as they wanted without the cruelties of the town. It was difficult to understand how she came to the decision to live in the country at such a young age, twelve years old, and give up on everything, including her family, a future career, and a life to live like everyone else, yet it was evident she was certain she wanted to remain there to make art and music and sleep, and not only did she seem convincing to herself but I could see Matthew's face hold all the joy and anticipation I never felt in my life, not once, he felt free to laugh even, and his laughter rang out over the river and into the darkness.

Nora had avoided the ominous prognostications from Dublaners because nobody knew her situation; she had simply disappeared along with so many others, and without confessing the fulfillment of gruesome details, she admitted that the silence and slumber of the underground were the reasons this was the place she never wanted to leave, because there were plenty of hiding places underground—all of which was impossible for me to grasp because, while I understood the will to live among others who only wanted to create art and play music and sleep, what other disruptions in earthly life destroyed the momentum of a will to live? She would hide without the joy of seeing sunrises or sunsets or sky every day, without walking freely through grassy fields or stepping into cool sands and oceans or seeing the autumn leaves on trees—for the rest of her life. She told us she was unable to live up to the expectations of her father and Matthew (to which he shrugged casually, uncaringly), she wanted to create art out of body parts, that's what she said, then reached into her bag and produced necklaces made of gallstones from people's gallbladders. She had painted colorful stones of various shapes with a fine paintbrush and then made necklaces out of them; the stones were stolen from labs and hospitals and brought to the woods, she said, where the wood spirits helped her make earrings and different types of jewelry, and still other spirits glued stones together and used them to make utensils, like spoons.

She wanted us to follow her, so we continued down the bank

of the river. Above us, somewhere in the darkness, among thick tangles of branches and a strange mass of vegetation, birds chattered and screeched while a tall swamp flower drooping beside the river waved back and forth, as if caught in a wind, then hissed and spat at us, so we moved away from it and hurried down the bank while the branches and vegetation hung oppressively over us, trembling and dripping rainwater, hanging branches like giant spidery hands, and how delightful it felt to be in such a space where, despite its appearance, we could feel free to enjoy it without worrying about someone yelling at us or someone threatening our actions, how wonderful to walk freely along the bank of the river where the air warmed. Matthew and I followed Nora for a quarter of a mile or so, in silence, to where the riverbank curved around and opened to a hazy area with the sound of a waterfall in the distance, which we could barely see under the cloud of steam. There was something torpid and dreamy about the heat, and sure enough wood spirits were drunk and sleeping along the bank—some alone, others in groups—their bodies sprawled out among cushions in the grassy areas alongside the Cocytus. They were representations of a better world than the one we had escaped, bodies whose hearts swelled with each breath as they slept soundlessly despite a muddy swamp where drowned geese floated in the Cocytus, which Matthew pointed out to us. Nora gasped and put her hand to her mouth, but Matthew was the one who broke away from us and entered the dark water, wading through the sludge waist-high to the drowned geese until he picked one of them up and held it by its long neck and breathed life into the goose's bill until it fluttered its wings and dove away. One by one, from the gaggle of drowned geese, he picked up each goose and brought it back to life by applying CPR, and when all the geese were flying low over the water, he turned and waded back through the Cocytus to us, where Nora and I helped him step onto the bank.

We stood back in wonderment and fear. (That's the way I remember it.) Nora screeched in delight, and we all glared at Matthew as he stood there dripping water and smelling like the foul stench of dead things in the river. We descended the slope of the bank, moving away from them without responding further to what we'd witnessed, a miracle too difficult to comprehend in the moment, as if we were as haunted as we'd ever been, and I led Matthew by his wet wrist the way an angry father takes his son to a private punishment, even though I felt no anger and could see Matthew's panic; we had scarcely walked away when he crouched down with his eyes closed and his hands covering his ears, looking terrified, swearing he could hear the moaning and wailing of beaten children whose heads would be severed and rotted until only their skulls remained.

—I'm scared, he said, and I knelt to console him until he opened his eyes. He was having a panic attack, which had come on suddenly, but he understood what I was telling him, that everything was fine, and there was nothing to be afraid of.

—I n-need to go b-b-back to see Cassie, he said.

You can imagine my shock hearing this, which gave me a surge of excitement and left me with a humming in my ears, so I leaned down close to him.

—Stop stuttering and forget about her, I whispered. Do you hear? She isn't worth your time, trust me.

I felt a tinge of satisfaction in his struggle because the longing in his eyes made me feel like he trusted me, and I told him she hadn't been thinking of him while he'd been locked up. What did it matter? She hadn't thought of me, either, having likely found a new boyfriend, that fickle thing, some new flavor of the month.

Nora explained that life is different away from the world we knew, out here where wood spirits slept all the time and painted colorful portraits and abstracts on large canvases, and that if we listened for the sound of music it would come, and we could follow it and discover a greater sense of health and euphoria once the drill sergeants gave up trying to capture us. I trusted no one still and was skeptical of this new reality with its glimpses of tall thick-lipped flowers and people sleeping in the drowsy air, but the obtrusive matter of importance was the pitiful boy in front of me, still crouched down, who now appeared on the verge of tears.

Nora told him if he would stay here with us, he'd never want to leave.

He observed Nora as if struggling with the temptation to shout at her so that he could get away from her, but she begged him to stay and promised a realm of fortune awaiting for us to witness; Matthew held his breath like a child testing a parent in order to get his way—a selfish, careless, and immature reaction—and seconds felt like minutes as we stood there waiting for him to succumb to the woods as he tried to free himself from the evil thought that something horrible would happen, maybe death was near, not uncommon for someone in the middle of an anxiety attack, and he sighed, breathed in the cool air, and blinked as he extended his hand for me to help him up, which I did, and we followed Nora down the bank. In front of us, the slope extended down past the drunken sleepers to an area away from the Cocytus, which led into what appeared to be a campground area where some sort of festival was taking place. Overhead, birds were screeching and chattering, and when I looked up, an irruption of lightning bugs buzzing around in the darkness caught my eye; they flew in circles and then scattered, leaving the darkness, which, I noticed, was not entirely pitch-black, and she led us into a large cave with a high ceiling decorated like an elaborate museum ceiling, with rows of painted panels, though I couldn't tell what the paintings were. At this moment I felt someone touch my arm, and I turned to find Nora gazing up into the sky as well. When I asked her what the paintings were, she told me they were maps of the underground that were painted hundreds of years ago by people who believed eating the salt of the underground land was the secret to freeing themselves from danger, in our case the drill sergeants or any authorities who would capture us and lock us up again or else murder us—free, too, from guilt, from heartache, and from the twisted complexities and horrors of the world above us. The salt was, she explained, our vessel to our own individuality and freedom and peace. I suggested we eat the salt. (I wanted, more than anything, to be free of my sinful pride and envy.) Matthew was distracted by the people at the festival, so we decided to walk down the hill. People were browsing art booths and eating meat from a stick, listening to musicians playing trumpet or guitar, gathered in groups. We walked past the musicians where rabbits were standing on their hind legs.

However we managed to avoid thinking of being caught, our thoughts turned again to the threat of the drill sergeants lurking somewhere nearby until we were completely hidden or far away from the area. The first person I recognized was Salvador Dalí—or rather a Dalí doppelganger—who was smoking a cigarette as he stood at his easel, painting with one hand and using the other to ash on the ground, what an attractive guy he was, with his unkempt hair with gray with dark streaks, and a mustache waxed and angled up toward his eyes, like the real Dalí's, I mean how cool can one guy look, eh? Closer, I could see his arms were smeared with paint, his hands all bone, and his eyes held an intensity as if he had imposed upon himself the penance of suffering down there among so many people walking by, never giving him privacy, yet there was a look of terror in his gaze as he worked. We watched him paint until he turned to us, placing a finger to his ear.

—The future is Duran Duran, he said.

He began tapping his ear.

—You see this? The tragus conceals it but look closely and you'll see I have implants for better hearing. This is the future. This is planet Earth.

A bird, a sparrow, flew past us and landed on top of one of the booths, and Dalí burst into laughter as it flew away, as if he'd never seen a bird fly before, but of course that wasn't possible, what kind of person has never seen a bird fly? His neck, blemished pink, was near the color of a stream on his canvas, which appeared to be an abstract of reds and browns in oils, a painting with a kind of seductive shape of figures in various poses.

—I'm painting skulls and gallstones I found by the river, he told us, taking a drag on his cigarette. My work, too, is evolving with the times. Texture, lightness and shade, coeval. I keep seeing a lambency at night that speaks in rhythm with music. I like to work in chaos, not solitude. The people wanted me in Amsterdam, but I like it down here. This is planet Earth.

He smoked and stared at us.

Was this the real Dalí? Certainly not, but a simple doppelganger designed to throw us off course, confuse us, or possibly lead to our capture. How was it, I thought, that he came to arrive in this strange place? Did he blast himself directly down here, or did he escape the enigma of a mysterious disappearance? Was he an illusion designed to keep the rest of us occupied with wonder and abandonment of the world above? I started scanning the trees for hidden cameras, projectors, anything I could find to reveal him as a ray of film instead of a live human, but I couldn't find anything. This was why I reached out and touched his arm with my finger, to make sure he was a physical thing, but the moment I touched him he backed away from his stool.

—You're an officious hermeneut, he said quickly. Did you come here to interpret scripture to me? My name is Dalí but not the real Dalí. Not the one you're thinking of. Think of me as an artificial presence of the real Dalí, if that makes things easier. I can tell by the inscrutable glint in your eyes that someone's after you. What iconodule do you worship? You're running from something, yes? Someone's after you.

—Neither of them have slept in days, Nora told him. They escaped here from the juvenile prison and are headed back to O.D.

—We were locked up, I told him. We weren't able to work much on our art.

—Why not?

—We were locked up.

—Think of it as solitude, privacy. It's a blessing in disguise that'll lead you to write about it someday. Write a novel about it, a metafiction, something literary in the future, when literature is dying and the American public are all reading dumb celebrity stuff. You guys want to talk about the future?

—Not really, I said.

Dalí squinted at us.

—You two boys look hungry. I can tell you haven't eaten enough since being locked up. I have tomato soup, pig wieners with beans, noodles, and okra I grew in my garden. I have chili, cereal with animated drawings on the boxes. The drawings are amateurish, but the cereal's good. Wanna eat? I have Frito chili pie. Sound good? You can tell me things.

He was curious to know us better, of course, a warning sign to me because who else would be so friendly down there except for an enemy, which caused us to hesitate, both of us, but then Nora was pulling on Matthew's sleeve and pointing to something in the trees—the drill sergeants were there, she pointed—and we saw Cash and Ambrose in the trees, despite their trying to hide from us.

—Please just take us anywhere, we pleaded to Dalí.

He reached for his pack of cigarettes on his easel and gestured for us to follow him.

Nora stayed behind to try to find Anna Darko while we hurried with Dalí. The heat felt thicker, the air heavier along the trail with tree branches intertwined from both sides of the road to form a tunnel glistening with a thin stream of light; we were still too visible to keep us out of the view of the drill sergeants, and my anxiety was at a high level because they were after us, following us, which I told Dalí again, but he assured us his house was just around the corner and was safe. A large fly catcher-shaped plant drooped over the road, dripping with a syrupy liquid that smelled of a sour substance I couldn't define, with an almost monstrous, rutilant glow. I glanced at Matthew to see whether he was attracted to it, but he was too focused on looking around for the drill sergeants. A foul smell came from the plant, which Dalí told us over his shoulder was laudanum, adding that he lived on it like food for nourishment and relaxation among other things.

The trees were dark and cryptic and calm, but it was as if you could feel the drill sergeants there, following until they had an opportunity to attack us. The road curved as we passed more trees, and we stepped onto a gravel driveway, though there was no vehicle in sight, only a fence with its door open, and the house behind it. Dalí led us through the back of the house, where we entered and followed him into a dining room. He gestured for us to sit while he stepped into the kitchen and made tea.

How long would we be free? How long before they caught us? I imagined the drill sergeants creeping into the shadowy house, mumbling in their low voices and spying through keyholes while we sat there like sleeping cattle awaiting slaughter, too horrified to move or run away, and who would believe us if they killed us anyway, those evil bastards were too fearless and psychotic to care whether two more former residents died and were beheaded, our skin stripped from our skulls to be painted and displayed in the Columbus House. The dining room table was wooden and clean, with an unlit candle sitting on the middle of the table, and all around the room were neatly stacked papers of various drawings in pencil and pastel, photographs, dirty magazines, sheets of music, and random art and photography books. Plastered all over the walls were sketches, maybe a hundred of them, of bodies, staircases, ears and eyes. The room was well organized and neat for someone who appeared so strange and unkempt. A large glass ashtray was filled with cigarette butts, and from the looks of things it appeared Dalí favored sitting on the floor rather than at the table. I caught Matthew scanning all these things as well, probably making mental notes as detailed as I was, and had Dalí not returned so quickly with our tea, I would've questioned him about whether his intentions were the same as mine, to write about this man.

It was alarming to sit there and see the carnivorous plants and tall flowers brushing against the window, where out of the corner of my eye I saw the shadow of something flash too quickly to register whether it was Ambrose or Cash, or something else that moved from the wind, filtered through the melancholy flowers; perhaps the spirits from the woods had followed us into the underground, or there were spirits around as well; my worry only grew more tense the longer we sat there even though I was able to keep my composure.

Dalí set our cups of tea in front of us and mentioned he liked to collect detritus and form shapes for inspiration like his predecessors, young and gaddy and fond of laudanum.

Laudanum, Dalí said, like a drop of rainwater on the tongue where all sorts of wonderful things can happen, to help us bear the punishment of humiliation, to relieve our anger and rebellion of society's norms, just as Dalí had suffered in the world above us whenever he found himself losing teeth from abusing methamphetamines and at the lowest point in his life before escaping to the underground. He was sometimes awakened, he told us, by the horror of hearing the dead crying for repentance outside where they were crawling across the land, and the only way he could understand the strangeness of such visions was through painting or writing about them—that's what he told us—and that any kind of deprivation of expression of our art was like an attack against us to prevent living our lives the way we were meant to. You've been deprived of expression, your art, Dalí said, adding that he dreamed of color, texture melting into the canvas. In sleep, he said, his hand trembled like an addict.

We heard the shriek of a child from another room, and we looked at Dalí.

—It's my son, he told us. Don't worry about him, he's fine. He has health issues and is under strict observation. He likes the sound of an electric razor. He likes music, so I play it loud.

He told us he played music all day and night, he played home recordings, he said, full of music and sound experiments: water running, thunder and rain, heavy laughter.

—How long have you been here? I asked.

—Nine years. I've never left except for once in 1980 when I rode my Indian to New Orleans and stayed in a hostel for a week. I shared a room with three hippies. At night we rode over to the French Quarter, then came back and sat in the backyard and got drunk with some of the others who were staying there. An old guy named Paolo played guitar and his girlfriend sang. She looked like a gypsy and told me I would have a child born with pig ears. That was the night John Lennon was shot. Where were you when he died?

We didn't know.

—I should get the marijuana, he said.

I wondered about the son but didn't say anything to Matthew; I wondered, too, about the food he'd promised. Did he plan to cook or at least serve us fruit? I contemplated asking, but he was already walking out of the room. Matthew and I glanced at each other for the first time in complete seriousness and fear, as if we had realized how perilous the situation was, and what, exactly, Dalí's plans were if not to feed us. Was he secretly working with Ambrose and the drill sergeants? Was he working with Anna Darko? Was this some attempt to foist us into a conspicuous abyss of torture or even death? Matthew stared at the wall, which was etched with words scrawled in some foreign language, German, I think, words with jagged edges, some large letters and some small letters. I pictured Dalí sitting there at the table carving into the wall with a knife while his son screamed from the other room, this man so many probably considered a genius, carving random thoughts from his grotesque imagination, stoned on laudanum. But why on the wall? And to whom?

—It says, *If I listen close*, Matthew said, but he couldn't translate the rest.

What was Dalí's purpose for writing on the wall? Was it meant as a message to someone? I wanted to find a pencil and paper and copy the rest of the message down, but we heard music grow louder from another room, something old and trippy. Dalí appeared with marijuana on a saucer.

—I want to hear about your suffering, he said.

We heard the child shriek again and Dalí waved it off, sprinkling the marijuana into a paper, and he rolled a joint meticulously, staring at it as if he were studying his canvas. He lit it and inhaled. He told us he wanted to hear about what inspired our art, what we loved, and what were we passionate about, but Matthew and I were silent, too, so overcome by the will to survive and escape the pressures of incarceration that we could barely comprehend anything except what it meant to be free. I waited for Dalí to offer the joint to us, but he took a second drag, a long one, and held it in his lungs, exhaling slowly.

—Passion, he said.

He took a third drag and spoke testicularly froglike.

—Obsessive passion, he said.

He then offered the joint to Matthew, who took a hit before handing it to me. I pulled on the joint and held the smoke in my lungs, feeling the burn in my throat, before exhaling a thin stream of smoke. We did this, passed the joint around without talking. It was both terrifying and surreal, getting high underground with this man who resembled Salvador Dalí. I had smoked several times since I was thirteen, mainly after school or at Trusty John's or Brandon's house when their parents weren't home, because it was our drug of choice to be consumed in isolation for several hours, sitting in front of a TV or listening to Pink Floyd's brilliant "Shine on You Crazy Diamond." My friends and I could smoke and get away with it, so long as we didn't do it at lunch or before school, although on several occasions we did sneak around and smoke in the alley behind the bus barn. Our bedrooms had windows we opened on nights our parents went to bed early. Passing the joint around with Dalí was no different really, except for his age and the seriousness he held in his face. We smoked the joint down to a roach when Dalí started talking.

—I like to get high and watch *The Jetsons*, he said, smoke settling around his head.

—I o.d.'d a few years back. The details aren't important, but I stayed inside watching TV while on pain pills. It was too hard to work. Art is all we have. What else is there? Are we supposed to live our lives for things? Or for experience? On the cusp of tragedy or illness? What is it you're afraid of? Fire, death? For you it must certainly be authority, yes? But what else?

Matthew leaned back and sniffed hard. My throat was burning, and I tried clearing it and sipped my tea.

—Your parents don't understand all the pain you wrestle with, he said. Yes? The loneliness. How do you live with your pain and suffering and your parents? he asked.

There was a terror in the way he talked so intently, squinting, and I wondered whether he was manipulating us for something, for his work, in the way I felt Matthew was manipulating Dalí for his own work, because who else was so inspiring but a doppelganger? I glanced at Matthew, who was staring at the wall again, as if he hadn't heard him (or chose to ignore him).

We heard the child's shriek again, and this time we looked at Dalí.

—It's fine, he's fine, he told us.

I asked whether he knew the quickest way to get back to Old Dublan, and he told us to follow along the riverbank, and that the salt from the earth was for us to eat if we wanted true freedom. We could find the salt underground or sometimes on the bank of the river, by the donkeys a few miles away, he told us, which was all I needed to hear. I wanted to leave then, right then, because the marijuana was making me feel paranoid, and I kept glancing out the window to see whether Cash or Ambrose or any of the drill sergeants or staff were gathering outside, surrounding the house. I imagined them with weapons drawn, waiting for us to leave so that they could confront and assault us in ways darker than any spinning nightmare I'd ever had, restraining us and putting shackles on our ankles and carrying us into the woods to destroy our bodies—this fear overtook me like the outpouring of luminous dust from some dark presence, paralyzing me with terror even if I did tell myself this anxiety was aggravated by the marijuana. Matthew and I both took a drink of our tea at the same time. I felt the weed kicking in as I looked at Dalí, who was still studying us, his face holding the intensity of a man who struggled, a man possibly insane, opium addicted, and unhinged. I thought about this when I asked him about the writing on the wall.

—I could make out 'If I listen close,' but that's it, Matthew said.

—That's correct, Dalí replied. The rest is a treasure, a message by one Simon something, English, I believe, Le Bon, part of a long and complicated poem regarding your body being taken over by a type of evil presence. A snake. A union of a snake taking over. Do you know the song?

We didn't understand.

—It's about being controlled by something darker than your mind. A presence. "The union of the snake is on the prowl" is the lyric by Duran Duran, a song I heard on the radio only recently while lying supine on the floor. I found the lyrics by Duran Duran strange and elegiac, a synthesized sound. The music flirts, fondles, seduces the way art does, manipulating our entire sense of self-examination. I like Duran Duran. I can listen to it the way I watch TV for hours. Last week I saw two people wrestling, half naked, grunting and perspiring, squatting, lifting each other. They should've been in togas. I expected more blood, death. Who dies? Nobody dies. I watched a satellite program on narwhals for fourteen hours straight. How do people get work done? I grew numb, desensitized to my environment. I couldn't paint or concentrate. I couldn't sleep. When I closed my eyes, I heard painful cries. This is planet Earth.

The phone rang in the kitchen and we all looked up. It rang

a second time, then a third, and finally a fourth before it stopped ringing.

We sat silent a moment. I could tell Matthew was worried, so I reached over and took his hand, but he pulled it back the minute I touched him. Then Dalí showed us binders full of drawings and paintings of bodies, nude bodies, headless bodies, pastels and charcoals and oils and acrylics. He had an entire box full of watercolor paintings of bathtubs, some empty, others full of bubbling water or colored water overflowing and flooding the room. He listened to music while he worked, he told us. He ate mangos and peaches and smoked cigarettes.

—I'm old and these are my last days. Smoking is killing me. I can only hope to stay here forever.

We stared at him.

—I have a rock-and-roll fantasy, he continued. I see myself not as them but as myself, an enigmatic presence onstage yet part of the performance. It's a show, revealing myself. I exist in the fantasy only. In truth, I could never do it. It's part of the fantasy, being someone you're not. As a kid I thought of swimming through the sky. Sitting at a concert piano like young Mozart.

Matthew stared at him, stoned, a string of drool hanging from his bottom lip, while the psychedelic music droned on from the other room, the same, never-ending song that seemed to drift in and out of a monotonous meld of saxophone and drums and guitar, full screaming and chants, music that, along with the child's shrieks, only intensified my anxiety and paranoia to the point that my heart was racing now, so I excused myself and asked to use the bathroom, which Dalí told me was down the hall. Though I was tempted to find a door or window and escape, leaving Matthew to fend for himself and deal with Dalí, I refrained and entered the bathroom, closing the door behind me. I turned on the faucet and ran cold water over my face. On the sink counter were gels and skin ointments, a bottle of lotion, an open tube of toothpaste, and a hairbrush full of thick dark hair that looked nothing like Dalí's hair, which was thinner and grayer, and I wondered whose hairbrush it was, whether some other young person had been held captive there. The tub was the old kind with no shower, stained and blotted with dark-red spots from what was certainly dried blood. A small window overlooking more flowers and plants outside was open, and I could see a miasma of vapor that I assumed would drug me or poison me if I remained in there as it seeped through the window. My sinuses were stuffy from the weed and I blew my nose into a towel and left it on the sink before deciding I would tell Dalí that we were leaving immediately, that we needed to go to the bank of the river and eat the salt so that we could rid ourselves of all our anguish and fear and escape, finally, back into O.D.

As I stepped out of the bathroom, I noticed a bedroom light was on with the door partially open, so I opened the door a little wider to see inside the room, where a boy, maybe nine or ten years old, was sitting on the bed with his head lowered. I could see spots on his face and hands, his scaly skin, and his hair was cut short, almost shaved—part of his head looked swollen on one side, a disfigurement. His skin was gray and pieces of his arms were scabbed over and red. My first impression was that the boy was being held prisoner by this man who planned on keeping us as well. I hurried back to the dining room, where Dalí was staring at Matthew's drawing, and Matthew looked at me as if waiting for me to say something; perhaps he was ready to leave also but was too stoned to gather his thoughts. I felt again the urge to leave and motioned with my head toward the door. Matthew nodded, so I told Dalí we needed to leave and thanked him for his company, to which he responded by looking up at us with the horrified look of a man who had lost all sense of understanding, his eyes wide and empty like an elderly victim plagued with dementia, but I told him we had to hurry, unfortunately, and thanked him for the tea and mighty fine marijuana.

Dalí stared at his trembling hands.

We hurried outside into the night under the fleeting stars and the sky and, reluctantly, entered the dark trees.

◂

The film *The Devil Is a Southpaw* ends with Don leaving everything behind for the poor. Shedding his clothes, he wanders into the open desert.

◂

Though Dalí had given no indication that he wanted to hurt us or torture us in any way, and because he had not drugged us with laudanum or benzos, we felt confident that he wasn't entirely working with the drill sergeants, although his mannerisms and willingness to give us weed and reference the big red moon left us feeling disturbed. We paused to gather our thoughts outside in the trees after looking around to make sure nobody was there. It still felt frightening enough to us that, despite his allowing us to leave, he likely tried to see whether he could connive us, once we were stoned enough, and that his sad disposition when I announced we were leaving only confirmed how disappointed he was. Maybe he misinterpreted our eagerness to go home with him as being vulnerable in our fear of being caught. None of it made much sense, at least to us.

I couldn't stop thinking about the child, Dalí's supposed son, sitting in that back room in suffering. He was captured and held prisoner, maybe. I wondered whether the boy was even Dalí's son and asked Matthew whether we should return and save him.

—We have to save ourselves first, he replied. Then we can tell the police.

—Anna Darko helped us escape, I told him. Shouldn't we do the same for him?

—Too risky. We have to get out of here. Then we tell the police. If we try to rescue him now, we'll get caught. We have to hurry.

Here's what we did. We ran through the trees among the jagged branches, thorns, and sludge; we cut through a sinuous path of plants and flora, trembling with unease that we were still being followed only to be captured, tortured, or killed, yet the darkness gave us no glimpse of hope, not even running as fast as we were, but soon we saw a clearing and stopped to catch our breath. I told Matthew we needed to find a place to stay, at least to get rest and maybe help since we were now lost in the thick of the woods and had no clue where to find Nora or Anna Darko. Up ahead, we saw a rock building with a porch light on and two large windows illuminated with yellow lights from inside. It seemed to be a gathering of some sort, which felt too risky to think about attending, yet Matthew felt it was a good idea because he needed water and food and raised the possibility that we could die of thirst outside if we weren't eaten by some crazed animal first.

—There may be bears or snakes or frogs out here, Matthew said, without stuttering.

—Frogs?

—Yeah, I know they're not dangerous, but still. The storm almost killed us.

—Snakes are worse.

—Snakes? I have nightmares. We need to get out of here.

We trudged out of the brush and trees and toward the stone building under a radiant blue moon. This land was like the dream world we had read about in books, a place of haunted mansions with the ghosts of murdered lovers, sick horses, and headless knights, with the bones of the dead scattered around the hill leading up to the stone building. We saw bits of putrid animal flesh stuck to a tree stump with flies and maggots all over it, and we saw mutilated birds and foxtails and spotted snake eggs in the damp ground near our feet, all symbols of death and suffering as we dragged our feet past them toward the stone building, trying not to retch from everything we were witnessing. Ahead, just outside the building, people were lined up, waiting to enter. Nobody in line was too annoyed even though they were staring, whispering to each other; I didn't know whether they were angry or what, but we moved past them and entered a room with scarlet-colored carpet and pale walls that gave me a feeling of déjà vu, such a strange and intense feeling to have in public as if I had either lived in or dreamed of this exact place, perhaps, or maybe it triggered some sort of distant memory from somewhere inside my mind, a memory lost in my conscience. (As I mentioned, I sometimes confuse my dreams as memories and vice versa, which is neither a lie nor a cop-out; it's simply the truth. I dream memories and I have memories of dreams which come to me out of nowhere, they really do.) Matthew's face maintained an expression of terror as we found ourselves among wood spirits who looked like diseased people, lepers holding dead animals and coughing.

I noticed a beautiful woman who resembled the famous painter Frida Kahlo sitting at a corner table alone. She looked up at me with a cigarette in her mouth and motioned for me to have a seat.

—Suicide plays here, she said, exhaling smoke. It's all music and atmosphere, stoned and cool, blood dripping from canvas. The Specials play here. Drill Sergeants on Acid.

—Have you seen the drill sergeants? I asked.

—They're everywhere. I think someone mentioned you in Dusseldorf.

—Dusseldorf?

—I mean an artist at the Hans Mayer, not a drill sergeant. You know Agnes Martin's work? Beauty and perfection. Perfection and beauty.

—I don't know her.

—Are you boys on the run?

Her expression suggested she knew something I didn't, but she remained quiet and took her pencil and began sketching. She drew on the table, she drew on napkins, she bent silverware and positioned utensils in the shape of a body, then she took my arm and drew a cross on my wrist. While I stared at her drawings, she got up and went over to a woman who was wearing a hat, and though it was too far for me to see the woman's face, I watched Frida lean down and whisper something in her ear and then point over to me. A woman at the next table was dabbing at her eyes with her napkin while the man beside her smoked and looked miserable; an elderly man at another table kept coughing into his arm while the woman sitting beside him pointed at me and said something, making me think they were wood spirits manifested into the bodies of humans, or other spirits, or else they were all working with the drill sergeants and staff at the detention center, and they had it in for us. My anxiety infused with the pain of an ulcer in my belly, burning against any reason or logic, attacking me like the intolerable suffering of waiting a hundred days to be led to the gas chamber for a slow and brutal death, and when

Frida Kahlo returned to the table, she must've felt disconcerted because the look in her eyes expressed an urgency: I needed to be in the next room for my art show.

—Art show? I asked. My art show?

—Um, why else are you here?

And I thought of the posters of my name in the dungeon below the facility, so Matthew and I followed her past a group of people mumbling about the moon and fog outside and into the next room, a gallery, where immediately I noticed my paintings hanging on the walls.

Everyone in the gallery was wearing masks with beaked faces, as if to conceal their identity—or maybe it was that they were hiding from the drill sergeants, too, and had been hiding from the justice system for many years, constantly living in trepidation, under a dome of power too destructive for them to risk confronting because they expected to die anyway, or maybe the police were still in pursuit of them, or maybe they were living in fear. A young woman wearing a mask and a pelisse approached us and talked to Frida while Matthew snatched a bottle of wine from the table and started drinking directly from the bottle, then handed it to me to drink, which was a kind of libation to celebrate (though Matthew believed that nothing was more improbable for me than success as an artist). He stood as a fortress against my attention there, yes, he really did. I motioned that people were staring at us.

The woman wearing the pelisse told us the masks were filled with theriac, which settles in the beaks, and for a moment it felt like we were tripping on acid, while people around us kept asking questions: Did we want to stay in the country forever? Were we afraid to die? Had we licked the salt yet? Wait until daylight, they said, so that we could taste the salt and enter the river when the

THE DEVIL IS A SOUTHPAW

sunlight creaks down on us in the water. Bask in the glory of being free from sinful behavior. Live in the country for good, away from people and the pressures of life, conservative law, order, live in solitude without any destructive illusions that would hinder us from pursuing our passions.

A man in a mask told me my work was cataleptically cabalistic, like the arch of a woman's foot. His mask was white with a long, pointy beak. He shook my hand and stared at me, but I could barely see his eyes through the mask's eyeholes.

—The woods are full of deipnosophists, he told us. Don't pay any attention to them, listen to your hearts with a friendly ear. The masked man was born, he said, with a craniofacial anomaly that affected his forehead and the upper part of his jaw, causing his mouth to slant toward one side and look visibly disfigured, so wearing the mask helped him feel more comfortable even though he rarely saw people. He told us:

—Not that anyone cares. There's a certain rancidity we're all born with that leads to a search for health and happiness. It's a search for shedding remorse. How are we supposed to do it out there in the world with all that violence and disease? I stay here in the woods where it's safe.

—It's safe out here? Matthew asked.

—I mean, sort of. I mean, there are bobcats in the area. I like to go bowhunting, luring elk with calls. I'm not too good. Are you an Indian? In my backyard I shoot arrows at a bull's-eye stapled to bales of hay. It's hard to call elk in close.

—You hunt elk here?

—I mean, except I've never actually seen one.

Someone else in a beaked mask came up and stood by us but didn't say anything. He was wearing a faded T-shirt and stood rocking back and forth on his heels. It occurred to me he could be one of the drill sergeants or staff members in disguise, which I whispered to Matthew, although he tried to reassure me that they would never disguise themselves, not those bastards—if anything, they would break the door down and start firing weapons and throw us to the ground, that's what they would do. He was right.

—We need to get out of here, Matthew said to me. Who knows, they could show up any minute. They'll kill us.

—What do we do?

—Go to the river. Why, you worried we'll get caught? You scared?

—Shut up.

The silent man nodded with his beak and glared at Matthew, who looked away. I didn't want to fight with him or with anyone. The room felt as cold and lifeless as the view outside the windows of the detention center, as if something was missing and unfulfilled. Had Matthew stolen any happiness the night had given me, leaving me with a pensive mood? Any of the truth's restless joy was now being replaced with a sullen stillness as I noticed people were slowly making their way toward the door, where it had begun to lightly rain outside. I headed to the door myself in hopes of gathering anyone who might linger and talk, but everyone was commenting on the beauty of the rain outside: *It's rain without the cold! Look, it's beautiful! You don't need an umbrella.* I leaned against the wall and watched everyone leave. They were glowing as they stepped out into the rain blowing sideways and bells tolling in the distance, huddled against one another as they left, leaving me in the emptiness of a chilly room, an ineradicable realization of truth and abandonment.

And yet, I thought, was this really a surprise? Matthew's intentions were never noble, and now he was casting a mockery upon me by raising his voice and trying to embarrass me in front of everyone. I wanted to run outside with the others, to escape this madness and find someplace alone where I could gather encouragement from nature's solace and relax among the trees and birds and rain. But the ruthless revelation that I needed to stay and confront my feelings was thrust upon me. Matthew was across the gallery talking to Frida. I watched them a moment with a kind of sadness I couldn't comprehend. Was I sad or angry? I hesitated but decided, ultimately, to approach them. My spitefulness invigorated me as I walked toward them and clapped my hands as if I were charged with amusement.

—It was a success, I called out.

Frida finished her glass of wine and set it on the table.

—Wonderful, she said. This guy says we need to go to the salt right away.

THE DEVIL IS A SOUTHPAW

—Pronto, Matthew said, and started for the door.

I pulled Frida Kahlo aside and asked her what Matthew was saying about me.

—He's jangly, Frida Kahlo said. Better keep an eye on him.

◀

I knew Matthew was angry, but I told myself I wouldn't let it bother me. For once, I thought, he was jealous of me, of my art and the attention I was getting rather than the other way around; for once, perhaps he feared that his creativity wilted in the infamies of his youth, indeed, where he dreamed he suffered alone without a nation's notice of his art or writing, where he worried he would contaminate the world by clinging to the certainty that he was the best artist of the century and would leave the world, in the end, disappointed. For once, people noticed me instead of him.

Frida Kahlo told us she would take us to the salt by the river, so Matthew and I followed her outside into the mystical, blowing wind, which felt like being on the verge of a thunderstorm, and I smelled the strong scent of rain as we got into Frida Kahlo's car. She revved the gas in her Ford Model A and put it in gear.

—The donkeys will try to keep you from tasting the salt, she told us.

—What donkeys? I asked, but she didn't answer, turning on the radio instead.

We pulled out of the lot and followed a rocky road leading down toward the river, which looked like we were entering the land of the dead. We entered a dense fog and trees, and all I could think about was tasting the salt on my tongue in the stew of the gloomy air and singing animals surrounding us so that we could inherit the salubrious spirit of eternal happiness and freedom, and how we would endure until the end of time so that we would never face the suffering of others, bound to peace and praising the glory of God in the oracles of authority. Never again would we be the public spectacle of humiliation, never laughed at or bullied or subjected to the manipulation of angry men who abused their power over us as if they carried their weight in gold. We would instead live in the snowy hideaways of cabins with colored glass overlooking frozen lakes and blue foxes and listening to the chattering of birds outside our windows.

In the car, Frida Kahlo turned up the music. She was no longer interested in talking, no longer listening to anything I had to say, focused on the road. I turned around and saw Matthew looking out the window and gripping the door handle as if he were about to jump out of the speeding car. We turned down a gravel road and drove through darkness, tree limbs scraping the car and side windows as if we were plowing through a wild jungle. Soon we came upon the river, and Frida Kahlo stopped the car and told us to get out.

—The salt's down by the water, she told us. Good luck with the donkeys.

—What donkeys? Matthew asked, opening his door.

Frida Kahlo turned around and looked at Matthew.

—You guys be safe, she said.

We both got out of the car and watched Frida Kahlo back out, spraying gravel. She sped away, back up the road, leaving us where the air was languorous and heavy, near a narrow slope that led down to the river, where we could hear the water.

—Are you still mad? I asked Matthew.

—We need to find Nora and Anna, he replied.

—No, we need to taste the salt, I replied, and started walking down the hillock toward the river. Matthew followed as we ducked low-hanging tree limbs, our footsteps crunching the stones and sticks on the ground. Something about the silence and fog felt exciting instead of frightening, at least for me, but I was not about to abandon Matthew, even in his frustration with me. He seemed weary, complaining about his knees hurting and that he was growing tired, needing to rest. I imagined he wanted to huddle against me so that I could protect him as we were thrust into fatality in adverse conditions, but he remained calm, following me as we came to the edge of the river.

—There, he said, pointing.

Behind the trees, crying out in the night, a group of donkeys looked lost, angry. They were kicking and heehawing, overtaken by rage, threatened by the fog around them or the sound of the flowing river, a devastating glimpse of suffering and transfiguration, because it suddenly occurred to me that these were not donkeys, not really, but spirits whose bodies and voices were cursed by the consequences of their behavior and disobedience.

—We have to find Nora and Anna, Matthew said.

He began calling out for Nora, even though I tried to hush him. He kept yelling her name as if we were in the final moment of our wretched condition, about to be destroyed. *Oh no!* I thought as I glared at him, reaching for his arm to get him to stop yelling.

—Be *quiet*, I told him.

—This is the end, Matthew said. There's a way out of this place somewhere. We can leave and run away.

He looked around, worried by the oppressive haze that settled over the water. In the same way the verbena of plants growing around us tangled, so everything transfixed into an exhaustive, woeful state of mortification, with nothing but the irritable donkeys and the stench of mange so strong that one wondered what happened to the lingering smell of flora. I began muttering more or less to myself something about the brutalities of a harsh punishment once they found us, and he nodded and said I know and looked at me directly in the eyes with an indulgent, sad gaze, and I saw his trembling hands in the sultriness of the humid air and the rest of us suffocating in his shadow, like a mirage or hallucination, when finally the donkeys stopped kicking and fell placid as they walked toward the water for a drink. We turned to watch them gather at the edge of the riverbank, as if they'd forgotten we were there, so we edged alongside the trail of trees and moved past without them even noticing until we saw the glow of the earth up ahead.

—It's the salt, I told Matthew.

We hurried, cautious as adept criminals, and all I could think about was survival and how we had endured the brutalities of the drill sergeants and staff in the constant agony of dread, the assassins of our blood, commanders of a subversive partnership to induce consequences and punishment, at the mercy of their own barbaric fury. I couldn't stand the thought of returning to lockup. Matthew leaned down and plucked a blue flower from the ground, studied it and felt its long stem, and put it in his back pocket, telling me it was as good as the salt because those blue flowers offer hope and recovery, and I found myself staring at him, thinking what I already knew was about to happen: that Matthew rebelled against domination and would do anything to leave me there and free himself from the servitude that would linger in the emptiness of remaining a fugitive, always running and hiding. I could sense death waiting for him in the amber waters of the Gudgekin River, because he told me, out of nowhere, that he wasn't going to die, he couldn't die, and that he was going to survive all this like the rest of us and begin living in eternal glory.

—I'm going *home*, he said. This is not my home. Not in the country. We approached the glow of the earth where the lambent salt flickered like small diamonds, a sight as extant as hearing jubilant music, a celebration of our destiny, leaving us captivated, and we caught the fragrance of flora returning, the glow of freedom in the lethargy of our long journey there, the most beautiful patch of earth I had ever seen. Matthew's eyes enticed me to touch his shoulder because he appeared more frightened than I was, certainly, and I could see his heavy breathing as his eyes filled with tears in the buzzing of the woods and rushing water that could only be broken by our voice.

In those last few minutes that I spent thinking about the importance of returning home at whatever cost, even if it meant risking our lives crossing the river, I came to realize that our souls were inseparable, connected forever, despite whatever he had planned, his escape, and where his life would end. His death would come quickly, and soon, yet both of us were struggling to survive and stay alive and avoid getting captured and returned to lockup. His death, an enigma after his next escape attempt would come. I still wonder if he knew this, that death was near and lurking in the woods as if waiting on us to enter death as if it were temptation calling us into the woods. Death, awaiting. I knew he would return to the land above us only to run away again, this time in broad daylight, a risky move considering how quick the guards and police were to capture anyone near Tophet County Detention. In my mind flashed an image of Matthew falling into a rock in the river and knocking himself unconscious until he drowned a sad and noble death. I would join the others in the search for him, but I first needed to taste the salt on my tongue.

We couldn't wait any longer. I got on my hands and knees and dug my fingers into the earth, then licked the salt in my hands, which tasted neither like sand nor salt, but instead offered a tangy sweetness, like fruit. Matthew knelt beside me and tasted it as well, running his fingers across his mouth, and together we held our breath as the fog cleared around us. We remained stuck there in the loam, tasting the salt on our tongues when we heard our names shouted, and then there they were, out of nowhere, the drill sergeants and staff, shouting at us from the edge of the woods and running toward us. We felt paralyzed with fear because we realized in an instant that we were trapped; we would be caught and then taken back to lockup, back to the misery of confinement, and that everything up to this point no longer mattered anymore.

Well then, of course the silence was like the moment before dying because everything fell still: the wind calmed, the leaves on the trees stopped trembling, and even the rushing river fell quiet. Even if it had been the stormiest of nights, with crashing thunder and lightning and high winds breaking branches from the trees, I would not have been so terrified, because the silence signaled our fate. We were about to be pummeled, shackled, and dragged back to endure the brutal sufferings of lockup. Our capturers, a whole crowd of them, rushed toward us through the twisting, spidery maze of low-hanging branches, and then they were upon us.

1.
THE LAST INTERVIEW

THE NEW MYSTIC
NEW MEXICO JOURNAL OF MYSTICISM (VOL. 77, NO. 7)
BY SANBO HORNBOND

An exhibition based around fragments from the Cherokee artist Matthew Echota's works is showing at Bashmayo, a new arthouse in El Paso, Texas, where I meet Echota in the café. Echota, who tells me via email that he's running late but that he's always running late, eventually arrives out of breath, wearing dark glasses. He is carrying a satchel full of papers containing what I assume is his work in progress, though he informs me it's a manuscript titled *The Devil Is a Southpaw*, that someone anonymous sent him. He orders a beer and begins rolling a cigarette.

"I come here at least once a week," he tells me.

"Wait—you smoke?"

"Sometimes. When I'm uncomfortable."

"Do I make you uncomfortable?"

Echota, fifty-two, has been private about his life in interviews, but the one thing he has talked about in the past is spending time in a corrupt juvenile detention center when he was young.

In rural Oklahoma where he grew up, he struggled in school, he tells me, for staring out the window and daydreaming.

When I ask about his time locked up, he tells me he shot himself.

"What happened was, I shot myself in the leg in the parking lot at school. I was fifteen. It wasn't an accident, but I told everyone it was."

"You shot yourself? At school?"

"In the leg."

He puts his rolled cigarette in his shirt pocket. I ask him where he got a handgun at that age.

"I took it from a friend of my dad's when we were at his house. I remember he never kept it locked away or anything. I mean, this guy had several guns, shotguns for hunting, bows and so forth. I remember when I fired the gun, the pain seared through my whole body. The bullet shattered my knee and part of my shin. Accidental negligence, they called it. I wasn't really surprised. After two surgeries, I saw a physical therapist."

"You were locked up for shooting yourself?"

"They locked me up for possession of a firearm and breaking my probation," he says. "I'd been on probation for possession of weed. I painted a lot back then."

His current project is a compendium of his photography, writing, and art consisting of fragmented texts, painted rocks, drawings, empty bottles, long strands of his own hair. There are dead roadrunners and lizard tails. There are images of struggle, poverty, and a peculiar, voice-activated hand that narrates a story about a saint who levitates. All this among a projected film running on loop of swirling leaves and spiderwebs.

It is obvious, of course, that Echota's work has turned less cultural and more concerned with the abstract, avant-garde. A homeless person shouting prayers on a street corner. Smoke billowing between two lovers. Music played backward. When I ask why he doesn't focus only on writing or painting, he tells me he immerses himself in the suffering around him.

"It's self-indulgence and obsession," he says. "I want to distance myself from the outside world and remain focused on this, an experiment in obsession and suffering, full of the temperamental earth around us."

"Your work is described as autobiographical. Do you agree with that in terms of the avant-garde or abstract projects?"

He tells me about his love for photography and his black-and-white portraits of poor people living on the street; his drawing of a man driving a nail into his hand; his short, animated film, *Story of an Owl*, about an owl watching over a pregnant woman.

Where his earlier books, *Blue Flower* (2006) and *Tis-S-Qua: Photography and Art, 1999–2011* (2013), are based on the lives of people from middle America, his last book, *Visions* (2015), was based entirely on hallucinations and visions, Echota tells me.

His visions? Saints standing outside his window. Frogs falling from the sky; an angel's wing, harshly broken, its feathers ripped and showing bone underneath.

I had read that Echota became more religious, based on his recent art projects.

"I'm interested in seeing suffering as a gift. Suffering from trauma, pain. Suffering from the struggle with concupiscence and a desire to flee the world for solitude. I mean, better to create for myself a vast space of inner freedom, otherwise I'm strangled with guilt. *Contrition*: remorseful, repentance. From the Latin *contritus*: ground to pieces."

I ask about the manuscript in his bag, and he tells me it's a novel someone he knew wrote and sent him, based on his time spent locked up when he was a teenager.

"We were all so affected by that experience," he says.

"You're okay now?"

Then something very strange happens. Echota closes his eyes and never answers me. His lips are moving silently, and his eyes are closed, but he never answers me.

A moment later, he excuses himself and leaves.

—SANBO HORNBOND IS A CHEROKEE
WRITER LIVING IN NEW MEXICO

A sound heart is the life of the flesh:
But envy the rottenness of the bones.
— PROVERBS 14:30, KJV

1. THE CONFESSIONS: AGAINST A SEA OF TROUBLES

The name M. E. Echota is a pseudonym for a writer who has removed himself from the public and quietly disappeared. There are no records of his specific whereabouts, at least none I can find anywhere on the internet, having spent a good many days in the public downtown library researching any information and documenting memories that I can type and print out, at no cost, to write the second half of my life's memoirs, the first half already completed and titled *The Devil Is a Southpaw*. His real name is Matthew Echota. I restrict myself from referring to him by any nickname, despite my feelings toward him, mostly due to his wild and ominous success over the years, an achievement that made me so jealous and miserable that obsessing on his success drove me, eventually, to the bottom of an eternal hell. But I've recovered, even if slowly, and I have learned to understand the unfairness of life. So be it.

Because we shared similar interests in writing and painting as children, and since we were the only young people even remotely interested in art in Oklahoma's old Old Dublan, I loathed him, as you know, assuming we would someday become rivals and yampy compadres, although I had no idea I would become so persequent and bitter under the restless gaze of authority figures and random newspaper-subscribing Dublaners whose ideas of art were limited by an umbrella of fallacious ignorance, even as I suspected a friendship that felt, as many youthful friendships feel, to last an eternity, having no sense of logic or understanding back then as to how unfair the world really is. Of course, O' Lord, this was all mere speculation and paranoia that gripped me from an early age, from the time he was chosen as the winner of a youth poetry contest judged by a local poet who had won a prestigious international award and moved from somewhere upstate in New York down to O.D. to begin her descent into obscurity, that very nice woman Agatha Klemm who scuttled about town like an eccentric bag lady, mistress of grackles and scoffer of sunlight, pushing her cart and wearing sunglasses, a large black hat, and all-black clothes, even in the stifling heat of summer. While she chose Matthew's poem as the winner of that contest, and while at the time it made me feel gloomy and worthless, having already invested days writing and revising that poem with the help of my English teacher, Ms. Rictus—which I understand as a de gustibus non est disputandum and so on—I found myself, oddly, growing more and more intrigued, fond of, and obsessed with Matthew Echota. I had no prayer of humility back then.

Some years ago, having finished the first draft of *The Devil Is a Southpaw*, I was suffering from, among other things, the

Hamlet disease, which meant I was a danger to myself against a sea of troubles that go all the way back to my childhood. Living alone in various cities was morbid and risky, having struggled with trauma from my youth and with roaming around and rehab stints as an adult. Possibly I was still healing, my Lord, or maybe I had not healed at all, or had even gotten worse. It's my age, I thought during those mornings over whiskey and coffee, realizing what a poor and selfish sinner I was, and am, in the growing anxiety of time and aging, as if the waters from the Rio Grande have ripped the guts out of me and stripped me of any hope of sustaining a relationship with anyone, one that would favor innocence over guilt or manipulation, one based on love and trust and wild passion.

Behold my innocence: my entire life has been a longing to be close to Matthew Echota, but it was a longing not uncommon among people who have lived indigent, lonely lives as adults, who have failed to maintain employment, regular health screenings, and good finances. Matthew, being an idée fixe, is my worst characteristic, it's true, it is absolutely the worst, not my mental health diagnosis or my intelligence or poverty, despite what anyone else says or believes.

Behold my guilt: it is obvious in my memoir that I created a fictional version of Matthew Echota in my own specific way, giving him a boring sobriquet, inflicting him with not only a speech impediment but an aversion to confrontation, a sorrowful disposition, and ultimately death by drowning. Perhaps *The Devil Is a Southpaw* should be labeled fiction, I often thought during the writing, because I realized my imagination was taking over, people morphed into beasts, events were exaggerated, and Matthew never drowned.

He has become a recluse, living somewhere in the desert.

He was an only child whose mother had miscarried a younger sibling whom I named Nora and placed in my story and served as a source of inspiration for Matthew, along with a certain romantic interest of mine (and his), whose name you know well, though in my story I have created this person as a girl named Cassie Magdal. I refer to the real "Cassie Magdal" with the sobriquet Cakae, who, according to my research, is alive, and for a while she was living down in Mexico, though I have become suspicious of any information I read on the internet and wonder if, perhaps, the library is monitoring my computer use and the websites I visit. Librarians walk by me, checking, I can tell. I still think about her, even after so many years. Why, Lord? Holding grudges is my weakness, of course, because Cakae and I were in love with each other when we were young until she began dating that handsome boy, Matthew, which broke me and made me contemplate stabbing myself in the chest the way my brother had stabbed himself, having felt the miserable afterbirth that follows a breakup as wicked and destructive as ours was. In the library I have discovered a defunct social media site that lists her name and status as "Married" but with no photo or activity in the past three years, or it is possible this is a trick or joke on me, because it is very likely she is now married to someone else, with children, swimming in the sea with her family. Having spent so many hours searching for her, and due to her privacy and seclusion, as is the case with Matthew, I cannot find any other information about her, sadly, which is troubling, and I suspect she could very well be married to Matthew and living in the desert.

O' Lord, Matthew's novel, *Blue Flower*, in all its prosaic, merciless compassion, arguably models a pride not seen in any of his other work. If pride or envy were the sins he grappled with, one might easily conclude that the ghostly apparition revealed in the blue flowers is, in fact, him. With a flickering of yellow light, the apparition moves slightly to the left and floats in a circle before it dissolves completely, replaced first by the soft yellow light, a strange light. Indeed, we can only speculate its purpose and meaning in relation to Matthew. I sometimes wonder whether he is an angel manifested into human form.

In *The Devil Is a Southpaw*, I indite various events during my time spent in Tophet County Juvenile Correctional Facility in 1988. While the names of people and places have been changed, the memoir is entirely true to the best of my memory, written in various university and public libraries, hospitals, shelters, and public parks over the past twenty-five years. More importantly, I recall I created Matthew as a fictional little guy whose face resembled a gryllus, who never published a word after his childhood poem. The real Matthew received wide national and international recognition for his books, having won awards and fellowships and travels to Europe. I tried to forget him. Twenty-five years ago, if I can say that without sounding too disconsolate or strange, I moved to the Southwest so that I might find him and show him my work. I had numerous drawings and paintings as well as stories, but I couldn't track him down. I searched the internet at the public library. I asked the local bookstores. Had they heard of him? Yes, of course. Did they know whether he lived nearby? No, sorry.

A former lover told me the only way I could think of Matthew was dead. Those were my darkest days of sin, before sobriety, back when I lived my life to meet my own selfish needs. Lord

Jesus Christ, have mercy on me, a sinner. Why was Matthew successful and I wasn't? I couldn't get over it, not even when I was drinking. Naturally, the only way for me to work through those feelings was to write about them, so I began writing the book based on our time together as teenagers in juvenile incarceration. For three years I sat in various coffee shops and libraries in and around Arroyo and reworked drafts, which I eventually finished in a style that, it now appears so many years later, matched the degree of my own need to be liked, to try to impress, and wonder. Nobody likes a show-off, especially one who writes in a spastic and careless style simply out of anxiety.

The more I thought of him over the years, honestly, the more I was drawn to him, entranced by his work ethic and mysterious nature. I wanted to be friends with him; as a child I wanted to *be* him—and keep him close to learn how his mind worked. This comes out of my need to be liked. I wanted to be smart growing up. By working hard, I could fool people by making them perceive me as smarter than I was. My parents, young adults during the 1960s antiwar protests who developed a belief that the world was ending, slowly and miserably, raised me to pursue my passions, though they maintained a strict and socially awkward set of rules, often citing political degenerates as their source of knowledge and values, having been poisoned by the brainwashing media. I was never, nor am I now interested in politics; I am interested in art, prayer, and swimming with the saints in the salty sea.

My own work, consisting of photography, writing, and painting, slowly turned more discerptible and grim, less assiduous than Matthew's, while I noticed my self-portraits morphed into indiscriminate monsters reflecting the physical change in myself over the years:

Self-portraits (1988, 2020)

My eyesight is nowhere near what it used to be, having suffered blindness in my right eye from ethanol exposure after my radical university dropout phase, back when I used to inhale the substance from carburetor cleaner with my friends who played in a rockabilly band. I was hospitalized three times in my twenties and suffered electroshock therapy on all three occurrences, but the meds I was placed on helped when I took them. The hallucinations had started when I was a child, and I spent many years in prayer over them, trying to understand the ghostly figures or pillars of white light that appeared whenever I was depressed or angry at myself. Were they from God or merely fractured shapes from my imagination without meaning?

It isn't easy. Like Matthew, I skirted attention from the public eye and eventually disappeared, too, spending fall and winter months wandering around the desert, during which time I painted and wrote, and took photographs on the street, having worked in solitude for so long and hoping to one day have an art exhibition at the Museo d'arte della Svizzera Italiana, in Lugano, Switzerland, in Rome, or at the Galerie Max Hetzler in Paris, but I fell ill: one night I found myself in horrendous stomach pain, having eaten a plate of sausages and green chile, and after taking a handful of antacids my condition only worsened as I fell into what I suspected was some sort of variation of inanition, because I began vomiting in the middle of the night, unable to sleep from discomfort and a sharp abdominal pain that radiated to my back. Lying in bed, in a paroxysm of fear, I convinced myself I was having a heart attack and lifted by darkened undulations beneath me, while outside the window, storm clouds stretched across the night sky. I called my neighbor—a young man who kept odd hours because he played Lou Reed in a Velvet Underground cover band—to drive me to the emergency room. In his pickup, I was able to refrain from vomiting anymore, thankfully, and he dropped me off and wished me luck. Once the hospital admitted me, a male nurse did an ultrasound on my stomach and found that I'd developed several gallstones, and that I needed emergency surgery to have my gallbladder removed.

I spent the night in the hospital and was released the following day. I asked to keep my gallstones, but they wouldn't let me, so when the Lou Reed look-alike showed up reeking of such sweet and delicious sativa, and carefully drove me home, I was too sore to walk much. For a couple of days, I collected small stones from the rocks around my casita and began painting them with a thin paintbrush as a reminder to ameliorate my body and become more insouciant, to decoct the poison of a monomaniacal focus on Matthew, to try to think more about the beauty of objects like stones and unwavering fortune, and to let my life play out as it would. Screw it, I thought. I stacked the stones on my windowsill where they glowed in the sun.

After I was released from the hospital, having recovered for a week alone in my casita, walking in pain to slowly try to get back to a sense of normalcy, I found my solitude difficult because I was lonely and having no luck getting an exhibition in the Southwest or in Mexico, much less in Europe. For weeks I took pain pills and slept, walking around when I felt any spark of energy, which was rare. I ate lightly and limped down the street and back like a slobbering lunatic, but eventually I was finally able to get my strength back. I'm telling you, I never felt so lonely in my life. I wanted to meet someone who didn't think I was some wily nutcase trying to create art and begging for money like a fool. I'd let myself go, wasted, intoxicated on hanging out with methheads and drunks.

One night I found myself strolling by the Rio Grande, where I found my Willard when he ran in front of me. In those days I was reading Paul West's fantastic novel *Rat Man of Paris* (a book that remains on my bedside table) and thinking I needed a companion like the rat man of Paris. I was smoking a cigarette, with a half-eaten orange in my bag, when Willard scurried up to look at me with glowing eyes, rascal that he was. I saw it as a sign and an opportunity for me to think more about my kismet and whether his arrival signified a type of change about to take place in my life, certainly, and perhaps Willard was a person stuck inside the body of a rat and was trying to prove a love beyond whatever he had been incapable of giving in the past. We were alike in this way. I tried to impress and be liked, too. Willard sulped the air with his vile smells even when he spent nights tucked inside my coat as I walked the downtown streets of Arroyo.

While my intentions were good, I roamed and drank any chance I could. When Willard left me, I was in a state of drunkenness and debauchery at the Spotted Dog, dancing wildly to Irish fiddle music. Late in the night I returned home and he was gone, I assumed, back to the river. I was overjoyed for him, despite feeling haunted by fury and loneliness. In my sadness that night, I stole a bottle of gin and shot low-grade smack and collapsed outside an E-Z Mart.

I entered treatment and came to this place of recovery, here by the sea, the vast and beautiful sea full of life; here, where I find myself thinking about Matthew, sobriety is ridiculous and difficult. Matthew's face appears anytime I close my eyes, which has become torture for me. Even on my most restful nights, after so many years, Matthew Echota continues to enter my dreams in strange and frightening ways.

2.
SAINT MATTHEW AND THE FOOL

> He searched the house and found a large hole in the wall. Curious, he moved closer and heard the laughter of children from somewhere inside. A portal, he thought. And so he stepped into the hole, whereupon it closed behind him.
> —MATTHEW ECHOTA, *ENVY*

Visions (1996)

1 (IN WHICH MY TWIN BROTHER AND I, LONGING FOR ATTENTION, PRETEND TO BE CONJOINED TWINS FROM THE UNDERGROUND CITY)

I might never have become so drawn to Matthew Echota had my twin brother not separated himself from me and thus ended our playfulness. Walter Muleborn Jr., whom we called Walt, named after our father, spilled out of our mother's womb eleven minutes before I did into the arms of voluminous labor and delivery nurses whose masks and scrubs smelled of nicotine, according to our mom, a heavy smoker herself. I have often wondered whether our mom smoked during her pregnancy. Her reaction to my birth, for example, was evidently one of incontrovertible shock and worry because the middle finger of my right hand was curved in what appeared to be a deformity, and an immoderate panic ensued at the sight of my finger that only worsened as I sputtered fluid from my mouth while the nurses checked the rest of my body, luckily to find no other defects, but certainly my curved middle finger was not an uncompromising malformation, not really, because it never hindered my ability to do anything that required my right hand; in my toddler period I favored my left hand and became a southpaw, as my father started calling me, having been trained in baseball jargon from his youth, and having given up on my brother ever being interested in playing catch outside because Walt was more interested in flipping through the pages of a children's Bible and staring into the glow of the fiber-optic Jesus nightlight that lit up in our shared bedroom when it was plugged into the wall at night, yes indeed, Walt was no athlete and more interested in silence and spirituality, even at a young age, entranced with illustrations and the biblical paintings in art books. My poor brother died young at the age of fifteen of suicide after a long bout with pneumothorax, stabbing himself in the chest with a butcher knife.

We lived in a small house on a green, verdant hill in Dublan, near a river that held the ghosts of dead animals like in some hideous fairy tale, and back then Walt and I were subjected to our father's nightly readings of the Bible before we could even speak complete sentences because our father was a pastor of a nondenominational protestant church, which, strangely, met for a time in a roadside motel until they were able to lease an old department store in a strip mall in downtown Dublan. Before that, he had worked in road/highway construction and used a jackhammer for long periods of time, and over the years suffered from gastrointestinal problems that caused hypogastric pain and fecal incontinence that forced him to quit working outside, God bless him. He was an avid sports fan and had played baseball in high school and college, so when Walter Jr. showed no interest in sports, he naturally turned to me.

I was, like Walt, also more interested in academics than sports. Our mom would take us to the public library, which became for us, in her words, "a purlieu adumbrated with a wild and giddy sapience." Our mom was brilliant. I remember she would check out several books on languages; she spoke sixteen foreign languages. In those days I remember running ahead of her up the stairs, where halfway up on the landing was a statue of Abraham Lincoln, and then walking into a genial and enormous room on the second floor, a room that still feels like a fata morgana in certain ways, vaguely dreamlike, with tall bookshelves and large windows and a ceiling that must've been a hundred feet high. A room that smelled of books and gave me a warm feeling every time I was there. This was the place where something magical was at work; this was where I first discovered imaginative literature.

The children's section was on one wall. I remember sitting on my knees with a pile of books, wanting to take them all home, books about kings and princes and dragons, books with pictures, old books with tattered covers, books that held secrets and magic. I imagined all these books living a sort of secret life, whispering among themselves at night in the dark when the room was absent of people and their characters, like ghosts, crawled out of pages and drifted around the library. I thought of all the stories collected in all the books there, each like a hidden treasure written for me to reveal some sort of mystery I needed to unravel about myself or my life. Back home, my mother would read to me as we flipped through the pages together. I can still hear her voice as she read.

When we were in elementary school, Walt and I pretended to be conjoined twins so often that we started to believe we could hear each other's thoughts. Sometimes at night I heard his distant voice in my head, asking me to check and see whether our parents were asleep, and if they were, we would sneak outside and run around. I had to wake Walt almost always, telling him I heard what he had requested. During family get-togethers, barbecues, or cookouts, whenever people would come over to our house, Walt and I would put on one of our father's loose jackets and put one arm around the other's back so that, when the jacket was buttoned in the front, my right arm was in one sleeve and his left arm was in the other. We limped around the yard, a two-headed beast with two arms and four legs, challenging our guests to consider that we were from a place underground where dead people, especially famous people, still walked around and lived, and wondering whether they believed us. Despite our young age, nobody found it adorable or even amusing, not really, not in the way we had hoped, which was that they would give us an attention we felt was missing at home, hoping they would play along in the fantasy of our underground lives. Instead, having full bellies of grilled pork and fried okra, they sat back in their lawn chairs and forced smiles, more interested in talking to the adults and eventually ignoring us until our father told us to go inside and play.

What, then, were we to do to arouse more attention from our parents, whose nightly rituals involved locking themselves in their bedroom and watching TV, or working until five or six in the evening so that we came home alone from school as latchkey kids to fend for ourselves?

What did longing for more attention mean for me, really, in the space of a traditional marriage between husband and wife raising their children—and what of this word "longing"? Longing for attention, longing for *someone*, meant showing weakness, according to my father, because even using the word "longing" revealed a type of dreamy weariness, weakness, and vulnerability that certain boys shouldn't be concerned with, no sir, not boys who should be concerned with focusing on developing strength and agility, competitiveness and masculinity. Was a passion for art and books revealing something about us that made them uncomfortable or embarrassed so that any time guests arrived at our house our parents would tell us to leave or play out our fantasies somewhere else? Did my longing later in life grow out of some desperate need for attention or love that I felt was absent during childhood? Or was I merely being sensitive and too sentimental?

One time, when Walt and I were disguised as the two-headed beast, a local artist knocked on our door during our playful, beastly spell, and seemed delighted by our appearance. We invited him inside and he showed us his paintings and charcoal drawings. Having an interest in art from taking a photography and basic art class in college, our mom wanted to help the young man and bought two acrylic paintings from him, both abstracts in various shades of blue and black. He was a student at the university and was home for summer helping his dad haul pigs across the state to be slaughtered. "I used real blood on this one," he told us, holding up a canvas of turquoise with splatters of dark red blood.

"Whose blood?" my mother asked.

"I have eczema," he told us. "It's pretty bad and forces me to scratch my legs and feet until they bleed," he said. "I'm lazy about using my skin cream, so I figured I'd just use the blood in my paintings." He lifted his pantleg and showed us the scabs and scars on his calves.

My mom gave him fifty dollars for two paintings, which he was immensely grateful for. After my father came home from work, he was officious and direct when I told him that I wanted to be a painter like the young man who visited us.

"What artist?" he asked, looking at my mom.

"A young man came by today selling his art, so I gave him fifty dollars for two paintings."

"Fifty bucks?" my dad said, and then looked at me as if it were my fault. I told him again I thought pursuing the arts was a noble and admirable decision, and that I was interested.

"That's ridiculous," he said. "You can't make good money doing that. It's not secure. Look at that young man walking around from house to house, begging. Is that what you want to do? Do you want to be a beggar? Anyone can beg."

"I want to be a writer or painter," I told him.

"Why not try to get a scholarship for sports when you're older?" he said. "Your mother and I hope you and Walt will get academic or athletic scholarships. Better to think about business or law. Or medicine, son. Do you want to be a doctor? Surgeons live in big houses and drive nice cars. Don't be a fool."

Afterward, my dear brother, Walt, that terrific saint, took me into our bedroom and told me I would be an artist.

"Just draw and paint," he told me, his voice ringing in my ears. How I still hear those words as clearly today as when he spoke them in his hushed voice: "You can do it. You'll do it!"

Lord, Lord, Lord: I was seven years old.

2 (IN WHICH THE FOOL DESCRIBES HALLUCINATIONS, GETS BULLIED, AND SUFFERS HORRIFIC NIGHTMARES)

As early as age nine or so, perhaps out of some diffidence or daydreamy loneliness that afflicts children suffering from overbearing, inscrutable parents, I drove myself to the most horrific visions: I began seeing dying birds. Hallucinations like this, when a room would fill with birds who fell to the floor and twitched in suffering as if they'd been shot, only confirmed the ancient certainty that the strongest feelings of envy, jealousy, and especially anxiety, exist within ourselves, in our minds and hearts, and that the people we admire and envy most are the very people who create the fear that lives and breathes inside us. Any time I stepped into a room with an open window, I would see birds sweep in and drop to their death: cardinals, blue jays, sparrows, grackles, even crows and finches, and even, on occasion, colorful island birds, twitching, trembling, their wings and necks broken, calling out for help. The visions started sporadically but grew more abstract and detailed the older I got, when I began also seeing frogs, hundreds of them, gathering in a room among the dying birds and croaking to their own deaths, these frogs with their long, protruding violet tongues, blinking slowly in the light until their eyes closed and they stopped breathing, all of which I found frightening and irrepressible. I would rush out of the room and tell my dad or mom, who escorted me back to show me there was nothing there, that I was watching too many bad horror movies, which I found sly and evil, as if they were playing tricks on me by threatening demonic possession was possible if I continued to watch movies on cable TV. Yet despite their contemptuous behavior, they immediately returned to their bedroom to sip wine and watch their own adult movies. On occasion I would storm out of the back door while bubbling the froth from stomach bile and stare into the glaucous glow of moonlight and see another frog or dying bird twitching, trembling, suppurating a yellowish custard from their eyes, and because we lived near a river, this fool feared the frogs were arriving from the sleech to seek shelter from our house. They appeared in my dreams, parading in from coastal villages while I heard my father shouting at my mom from another room, several of them crawling into my bed only to die at my feet or on my legs like a wet, heavy blanket. My parents started taking me seriously when I woke Walt and them with my screams and they found me cornered in our bedroom at four in the morning breathing the same air as them yet feeling asphyxiated and coughing, kicking at the dead birds and frogs surrounding me. I left a trail of crumbled crackers from the pantry that led from our room all the way out the front door and into the street.

For a few years—or, as I now reflect, maybe it was longer—I could not find a moment of rest, concerned that these creatures were invading our home for no other reason than to torture me. Thus, my parents worried I needed to find a hobby, something to occupy my mind and caress my anxieties, so my father forced me to watch baseball with him, collect baseball cards, and listen to sports radio, and when we weren't doing those things we played dominoes, chess, checkers, and board games for many nights in a row. "Learn to be great at something," my father said, but in truth I wanted to find a purlieu to hide out, to improve and practice my art and poetry, or someplace where I could find a verdant and calm environment. Like so many other children I was told, after all, that I could grow up to be whatever I wanted to be, no matter what the circumstances, and that as long as I worked hard my dreams would come true—the American dream, my father continually told me, work hard and you find success because you can be anything you want, which even then I realized was not entirely true because the one time at the dinner table when I mentioned wanting to be a poet, my dad dropped his fork and dramatically leaned back in his chair and went pale. Despite his immoderate disappointment, I was certain, even at that young age, that I wanted to be famous, and at least my mom took it seriously enough that she accompanied me to the public library and let me pick out art books, where I was quickly drawn to Surrealism—Salvador Dalí, Frida Kahlo, Leonora Carrington, and Joan Miró, for instance, and at night I studied their work, emulated it, and wrote stories to accompany drawings. My first story I ever wrote, at age six, was titled, "The Sad Roach," about a roach who wants to be a bird so he can fly but instead drowns in a pot of stew. The more I painted, and the more I wrote, the more I felt at ease, less anxious, and happier, and I eventually learned to dismiss the visions of dying birds and frogs even though they continued because I knew I was safe and they were harmless, but I kept my guard anytime I saw them near my bed at night or twitching in my closet. My parents, in strong denial of any mental illness, dismissed these delusions as hyper-imagination and encouraged me to use that anxiety and energy toward my art. In elementary school I drew, I colored, I painted. I wrote more poems and stories.

"You're a good pilgrim," my teacher used to say to me. Any time I brought it up in front of the family, Walt called me "Sad Pilgrim" instead.

"Why?" I asked.

"You pretend to be happy, but you're really sad. I can hear you crying at night in your bed."

I never brought it up again. When I was young, we watched lots of TV, especially in the evenings. We often ate dinners on trays in the living room during the evening news and then watched *Happy Days* and *The Bob Newhart Show*. I was particularly drawn to after-school shows like *Gilligan's Island* and *I Dream of Jeannie* because of their humor and dimwittedness, and Walt and I began to watch them regularly every day at their designated time slots, which became an obsession for us. For Halloween one year, Walt dressed as Saint Augustine while I wore a white buttoned shirt with the sleeves rolled up like the Professor from *Gilligan's Island*. I'm not entirely sure, but I assume we had watched every episode of those shows at least twice before we had even reached high school. I once wrote a paper in school that argued that *Gilligan's Island* was just a reiteration of what it feels like to be locked up at home and not able to leave like when we were grounded or told that the world is a sinful, cruel, evil place out there that had no desire to cleanse itself of its immorality. Once our father came home from work, he sat in his recliner and read the newspaper until my mom finished making dinner and we all ate while watching the evening news at six.

Our evenings were often spent watching a movie on cable TV, and while Walt retired to our bedroom from boredom, I usually stayed in the living room and watched whatever film my parents were watching. I remember watching *Children of the Corn* on a movie channel and asking my father whether demons were real, and if so, did they manifest themselves into the bodies of children or adults who did terrible things?

"We can suspect," he told me, but gave no further explanation, as uncontentious as he was about such things. It was like this most days during my childhood.

Despite his reaction, or lack of any emotional response to my question, I found berth in the dark horror of channeling the voices of the supreme and lascivious characters, no matter how unwonted they seemed on the screen. Was it their rebellion or simple curiosity that led me to the fragrant shadows of the rosebushes in the backyard, where I destroyed ants and bugs in the dead grass and dirt? I saw them, I think, as a threat to our household, and to me in general because they were able to get into our house so easily and crawl under the beds and into the walls, or underneath the stove, indestructible, persistent, scavenging for crumbs so that they would grow into large insects and therefore be more difficult to destroy. I found their idleness even more frightening, as gentle as moths, but my parents didn't take them as serious as I did, waving me off. "We need to have the exterminators spray again," I told them repeatedly.

"It's fine, there aren't many," my mom said.

"They're basically harmless," my father interrupted. "You step on them and they die. We just sprayed a month ago, so the survivors are running for their lives. Soon they'll be dead."

A month seemed like a long time for them to survive, so I persisted, obsessed about them, for a few weeks until one night my father got irritated and folded his newspaper under his arm. "Stop being so afraid of everything," he said. "They're harmless. Why are you so scared of them?"

I had to bear all the weight of this punishment, knowing bugs were still crawling around our house and nobody was doing anything about it. I tried to pretend I was invisible, breathing slowly in bed and as I walked around the house, eyeing corners of rooms, cracks in the hardwood floors, feeling afraid, remembering the horror movies I watched when my parents weren't at home, and trying to lean on the strength of my disillusionment because I had never consoled myself successfully by ignoring what I failed to comprehend. I told myself I needed to be tougher.

Having been bullied by a sinister and carbuncled uncle, a devout atheist who thought the prayers I received from my parents were worthless (he peddled landscaping/yard work to retirement communities and new housing additions), I felt as though my parents' stern judgment and homiletic philosophies were an imprecation, perhaps, because after all that grum uncle continually called me a "churl girl," I mean, that's what he called me, grimacing at me across the yard at family reunions or cookouts or any time somebody asked me about my interest in art. My uncle was a guy who always shrugged when anyone criticized and said, "Hey, I'm just a sinner," and slumped away in an exaggerated, torpid manner that I realized later was meant to ridicule my father, being as my uncle was an atheist. He used to sneak up on me and put me in a headlock whenever I wasn't prepared to defend myself and then would tell me he was trying to toughen me up. He spoke to me in a tone that belied the decline of Western civilization without realizing how officious and inane he sounded. It didn't stop there, because it never stopped—not during my youth—I was also bullied during these early years by a couple of boys in my grade whom I shall call Bucktooth and Badger, two buffoonish gredins with garish hair who waited for me after school as I left the portable building where my classroom was held and chased me (I was a slow runner due to a sore ankle from a rollerskate fall in elementary school) until they caught me and punched me in the ribs and bloodied my mouth. I staggered home with a swollen jaw and sore ribs. At school, Bucktooth and Badger, with voices like frogs, sat at the long lunch table every day together, penetrating their squeamish fingers into their food and smearing apple sauce and mashed potatoes into my hair when they weren't cornering some of us with threats of dumping our heads into the toilet or beating us senseless. They brought dirty magazines to school and shoved them in my face. Having survived their violence, even while trying my best to dodge them and their wicked intentions, I learned I wasn't the only one they attacked: I watched them on the playground after school or between the buildings whenever they caught a smaller kid in a headlock, or even when they pulled long hair on some students, even girls, and watching them was like observing a command of soldiers shouting and embittered with the uproar of teachers and authorities, both of them too selfish with their hate and condemnation, as mean-hearted and facinorous as a destitute wastrel and upholding a type of barbarism most of us feared.

In my dreams, having essentially the same recurring nightmare throughout my youth, and sometimes even in my adulthood, Bucktooth and Badger stabbed me with a knife, slicing into my belly and then pulling out my guts like I was a slaughtered animal. Chasing me, because they continually stalked me in these dreams, and running through the sleech of the riverbank with their knives and piglike snouts, they captured me and attacked me, always without reason, just as they did in real life, dragging my feet through the muck and beating me with a quirt under the bright moon.

3 (IN WHICH THE FOOL HAS A SNOWBALL FIGHT WITH MATTHEW AND VISITS HIS HOUSE)

I met Matthew Echota in sixth grade, in winter, early 1980s, when a blinding snowfall began in the morning and continued past noon that allowed the school to be released early for the day. We were in the same grade but had different teachers. I had seen glimpses of him in the cafeteria or in school assembly but had never interacted with him before that cold afternoon when the snow came down sideways. In stocking cap and gloves, I ran out of the building, elated to be free for the afternoon. I crossed the playground to walk home when I spotted him, standing alone, making snowballs, and throwing them as hard as he could into the air. I breathed in everything around me: the light whir of the wind, the crunching of snow at my feet, the pale sky and grayness everywhere. The taste of snow on my tongue restored something in me after a long drought of boredom and fatigue and sitting indoors. Grackles gathered in the snow. Some girls across the playground were lying down, making snow angels. Sharp icicles hung from the playground equipment. The grackles hopped from merry-go-round to the ground, shaking themselves of snow.

By a sudden stroke of fortune, or perhaps misfortune, I found myself wandering closer to Matthew as he threw the snowballs into the air; he was gloveless, in a black hooded coat, no stocking cap, and longish hair and glasses that were smudged with fog so that he had to remove them and wipe them with his coat before putting them back on to see me. I recognized him as one of the new Indian boys who had come to Hillrise School after the school he had attended closed. He turned to look at me, and in a compulsive act of amusement and gaiety, we found ourselves in the middle of a snowball fight, throwing and crouching, laughing and collapsing into the snow, rolling around, standing and falling. The event, in all its spontaneity, ended with him raising his hand to catch his breath, at which point I dropped my snowball and rushed him, tackling him into the snow. His face, close to mine, was red and dry, his ears chilled. I remember his mouth quivered from either nerves or the cold, because he wasn't sure whether I was angry or having fun.

"That was fun," I said, and helped him up.

He stared at me, jaw chattering. I told him my name.

"You play baseball?" he said.

"Yeah."

"I thought so. I wanted to play. My dad used to play."

"I know who your dad is," I told him. (I should mention, here, that Matthew's father did not play professional baseball as I noted in *Southpaw*, though he did, in fact, hold all kinds of fast-pitch softball records in the Indian tournaments that he played in during the late 1970s and early 1980s.)

This perked him up, and thereafter we became friends. He invited me over to his house, where his older cousin was living with them, he told me, and that they had hot chocolate with marshmallows, so of course I was never discordant to any such invitation, especially from Matthew. We dispersed to his home, an old, wood-framed house around the block, where he invited me inside and we shook the snow from our shoes and removed our coats. I worried I gave an unprepossessing impression due to needing a haircut and wearing a shirt one size too small for me, but Matthew never said anything about it. The house was small, with old carpet and striped wallpaper, dim and warm with a fireplace blazing. Matthew told me his mom was at work. I accompanied him through the kitchen and into the garage, where he showed me upside-down buckets that he played drums on with drumsticks his uncle gave him for his birthday. There were also several paintings on canvases that the same uncle had given him, paintings of Indians, with buffaloes, horses, and desert landscapes with dark blue skies, mountains, a red sun. He was proud of them, telling me his uncle sold them for hundreds of dollars and gave them to his mom when he passed away.

I encouraged him to sell them, but he looked at me, astonished by my inattention to their value and importance to him, and told me he was keeping them forever, that he was learning to paint with watercolors and oils. "My mom said I can get acrylics for my birthday," he said.

"Show them to me."

"They're in my room."

"Show me your room."

"Why do you want to see my room?"

I remember I laughed, amused by his hesitations, thinking I was embarrassing him, and I could tell he was meek and humble, yet I persisted, despite his attempt to change the subject.

"Wanna play the Atari?" he said. "I have *Space Invaders*."

"All right, but you have to show me your paintings first," I told him.

He led me back into the house and down the hall to his bedroom, where the door was closed. He paused a moment, in the dimness, and listened at the door. I wasn't sure what he was doing, but when he opened the door, we saw an older boy lying on the bed, reading a magazine. As we entered, the boy sat up and glared at us, and I noticed a scar on his face from what appeared to be a burn, though I tried not to stare too long at him. I instinctively determined this boy knew a lot more about Matthew than I did.

"Hey, Sequoyah," Matthew said, "this is Milton."

Sequoyah, intimidating and phlegmatic, gave me a head nod and nothing more. His hair was longer and shaggier than Matthew's, and his jeans had a patch on one knee, giving him a ratty but impressionable look. His eyes were gray, and the longer he looked at me, the more I sensed his distrust toward me. The book was an old, small paperback that he gripped in his fist. Matthew opened his closet door and leaned down to gather his paintings, and as he did so I asked Sequoyah, "What grade are you in?" but he ignored me and lay back down, crossing his legs and resuming his reading.

"He's in eighth," Matthew answered for him, from the closet.

Outside it was still gray and snowy, with a sullen glow in the sky; the window was smudged with fingerprints. The smell of burning firewood drifted from the living room in that small house. I remember I had my usual after-school pang of hunger and felt my stomach growl, though I sometimes confused it with an upset stomach caused from anxiety, which I felt in Matthew's bedroom that snowy afternoon, particularly as he stepped toward me with his canvases and lay them down on the floor for me to see.

I would rather not dwell on these early watercolor paintings except to say that they held a remarkable, surreal quality, as foggy as the snowy window, paintings in blues and grays, splattered with reds, and dripping like rainwater—paintings of blurred faces, childlike eyes and jagged claws, opening up a world I had not known before, and to make matters worse he had written anecdotes on the backs of the canvas about the images he painted, "mixing visions with words" is how he described it, and in that moment I felt he had captured, in some oblique and arrogant way, everything that I wanted to become. He had mastered something I wasn't yet able to define or understand about myself and my artistic urges that both excited and destroyed something inside me that day.

"Voilà," he said, and for a moment his attitude shifted, the way he parted his hands in front of him like a magician. His eyes held a ghoulish satisfaction that haunted me even later anytime I reflected on it, as if he possessed a venomous savagery directed at me, as if he mocked me with Sequoyah. There he was, a child venturing into his surrealist and eulogistic allusions to his unborn sister who died in his mother's womb, a prelude to a new epoch of Dublaners, a chosen artist and serious child who knew how to conduct himself in the manner of adults as he spoke about mature matters, that's the way this fool pictured him, standing in a devastating wind while he created in a power unlike anyone else, filling the air with fragrant perfume, surrounded by the books he wrote and wearing his eyeglasses smudged with paint. The vision struck me standing there in front of him and his paintings. His handsomeness, his beauty, even at that age, youthful and soft in the yellow light of his bedroom, how I felt his mysteriousness a revealing force to something I hadn't known about myself before, some part of me that grew beyond my understanding except that his paintings, and he standing there beside them, made me want to lie down on the floor with him and stare into the ceiling so that we became two bodies in human skin, one brown and one white, religious or sacrilegious, arduous and curious, grasping for the abstract notions of admiration.

Had I responded to his paintings appropriately, this fool might have developed a deeper friendship with him, but the way

I remember it, I said nothing and reminded him of the hot chocolate and Atari, at which point we left Sequoyah and his book alone in the bedroom and retreated to the living room, where his Atari was on the floor in front of the TV. He inserted a cartridge called *Adventure*, and while he went into the kitchen to make our hot chocolates, I moved a small square around on the screen with a joystick, avoiding a dragon named Grendel, and growing more bored with each minute. When Matthew returned without our hot chocolate, he seemed overstricken with a glum shyness as if he were about to deliver tragic news.

"We don't have any," he said. "I thought we did."

From where I was sitting, one could see how short his legs were, and how sad his posture, as he stood with his hands in his pockets. From then on, he limited himself to simply nodding, or shrugging, but as I recall he often spoke with euphonious

Untitled 2 by Matthew Echota (1984?)

phrases, softly with a slight, adorable and youthful lisp. He had a way, too, of pulling on his lower lip while deep in thought or breathing in deeply through his nose as if he were annoyed, or nervous. I distinctly remember handing the joystick to him that afternoon and watching him while he gripped and jerked the joystick with his left hand and stared intently into the TV screen with his mouth open.

4 (IN WHICH THE FOOL READS SHAKESPEARE AND MATTHEW RUNS AWAY)

The days following that first meeting, and especially during the nights as I lay in bed, Matthew kept returning to my thoughts. At school he was revered as the smartest kid in class, even brilliant, because he found his desires satisfied in his homework, in reading and writing in the classroom, and while other students dozed in the lazy light of a rainy afternoon, Matthew recited Hamlet's famous soliloquy he had memorized to overcome his anxiety and shyness in public speaking while trying to get comfortable hearing his own voice, which he claimed he despised the more he recorded himself on the tape recorder at home and replayed. He was never imperious but held an estimable reputation. His elderly teacher, doddering and short, put the sunflowers he had given her in the ceramic vase he had made for her in art class and pretended not to give Matthew too many compliments, at least that was the rumor we heard at lunch that day, and when I asked him why he had recited the *Hamlet* soliloquy, and how he'd heard of it and Shakespeare, he told me that he was fulfilling a wish from both his teacher and his mother, who clung to a fierce hope that he would develop his education as rapidly as he could, study, read, and motivate himself to become the first person in the family to earn a college degree.

I had my own salutary and strange obsessions I was proud of, which included increasing my education and intelligence.

Some of my obsessions at the time included films that I felt spoke specifically to me: *Last Metro* (Truffaut, 1980). Atari's *Adventure*. *Last Tango in Paris* (Bertolucci, 1972). Ears. The tragus. The pinna. *Throne of Blood* (Kurosawa, 1957). *The Devil Is a Southpaw* (Briggs, 1973). Matthew Echota. *Lacombe, Lucien* (Malle, 1974). Jean-Michel Basquiat. Anna Karina. *Vivre sa vie* (Godard, 1962). Salvador Dalí. *East of Eden* (Kazan, 1955). *The Elephant Man* (Lynch, 1980). Saint Francis of Assisi. Saint Teresa of Ávila. The Boomtown Rats. *Paris Belongs to Us* (Rivette, 1961). Peter Sellers. *Pale Flower* (Shinoda, 1964). Pink Floyd's "Shine on You Crazy Diamond." Christina Rossetti's poetry. MTV. *After Hours* (Scorsese, 1985). Smews. Rollie Fingers. Johnny Bench. *Hamlet*. Live Aid. All the saints.

I read Shakespeare, or attempted to read *Hamlet*, though the language was difficult, and the wind distracted me with its susurration outside my window, so in my difficulty comprehending the text I took walks to try to recharge and focus. I would stroll down the street to the park and sit on the merry-go-round and try to deal with the recondite text of a Shakespeare play, much like I struggled to parse certain Bible verses from the King James Version my father always quoted from, all of which grew frustrating and made me feel like I was nowhere near as smart as Matthew. He had a knack for wandering off, too, even in early childhood, and the first time his mom discovered him missing she went looking for him, trudging through the wet grass and dirty puddles of water, stepping over a drowned rat and yelling his name so loudly that a line of birds flew away from the telephone wire above, and when she found him he was lying face down on a bed of leaves on the ground; in a panic she rushed to him, calling out his name, but of course he was only playing and sat up when he heard her voice, telling her he was practicing for the Big Moment to arrive, *This is how I'll die*, and clutching his throat with his hands and sticking his tongue out, lying back and then pointing up to the sky—"Look!" His mom looked up: a red balloon floated high above them, drifting slowly across the pale blue sky and rising higher and higher until it became a dot and disappeared.

"It's a sign," he said. "The balloon! But what does it mean?"

"It means everything will leave at some point," his mom told him.

As they walked home, Matthew kept asking, "Everything leaves? Nothing stays?"

"Everything leaves."

When they arrived back home, his mom felt a migraine coming and was ill for the rest of the day. She lay on her bed with a cold washcloth on her head, and Matthew brought her ice water to sip from and rubbed her feet and hands, and that night, as his mom slept, Matthew rubbed his hands together and placed them on her head until she stirred in her sleep. When she woke, to her surprise, her migraine had gone, and for the rest of the evening she rested in her wicker chair in the living room while Matthew stayed beside her, asking her not to leave, "Please don't leave like the balloon, please stay with us," because he was so worried, as if his own mother's life hung on the course of that one migraine, but the one thing that gave him assurance was that she took his hands and looked into his eyes and told him she wasn't leaving. That night he dreamed of children sleeping on the steps of a cathedral, wrapped in blankets under the illusion that the stars in the night sky exploded and were falling on them like rain, a dream serving as the inspiration for a drawing he sketched the next day on a yellow legal pad of paper titled *Escape from the Devil's Lost Playground*, with squiggly lines underneath the word "Escape."

He was at the mercy of this word, "escape." One night he wrote the word over and over, filling an entire front and back of a sheet of paper with the word, because there were periods in those early years that he wrote everything down on paper, then he read it aloud to me once in the fleeting light of the back porch light among the nighttime sounds of cicadas and owls, and when he finished reading it, he said, "I can't bear to think about escaping," tearing the paper into pieces, and when I asked him what he meant, he told me he wasn't able to understand any of it himself, he knew only that someone would be escaping from some insensate place. He must have figured it all out because there was a period not long after that night when he hid in his bedroom and rarely came out, stayed in there drawing and writing in a notebook, much like he did at the facility.

5 (IN WHICH THE FOOL AND MATTHEW GET LOCKED IN THE BASEMENT)

I was terribly awkward around the other kids at school, and I grew more fascinated with Matthew the better I got to know him, focused as he was on being astute and driven. When I once mentioned how the colors on the walls in the principal's office inspired me to paint, he claimed his inspiration came from his own imagination when he pictured dead people standing at the foot of his bed, scratching at the walls with their long fingernails and moaning like slaughtered animals. "The dead souls," he called them, whose ears held a velvet dust that made him sneeze at night and who delighted themselves by talking about drinking wine from nine orifices on their lovers' bodies during orgies; he told me this with a laugh, of course, seeing as I was confused, but he could easily convince me of anything he said. He had a way of talking about the strangest things, like the terror of miracles and resurrecting dead animals by caressing their paws or hooves, seeing apparitions in dark mirrors at night, and sitting alone on the stairs outside the school building until darkness fell. He leaned on the strength of his intimacy with the natural world, that's what he told me, adding that he had a better understanding of nature than people. He opened his shirt to show me the bruise on his chest where someone had punched him.

"Who did it?"

He disregarded my question. "I take out my aggressions on playing drums," he said. "Nothing else helps."

"Who punched you?" I pressed him.

"Doesn't matter."

"Can I touch it? The bruise?"

He ignored me and began talking about the drums. As it turned out, Matthew loved playing the drums so much that he constructed his own drum kit out of upside-down buckets, tin cans, old metal trash-can lids, among other various tools or old car parts he'd found in the garage. Sometimes he played various rhythms for anyone who came over to visit, "He's so talented," they always said.

The only time Matthew came over, we got locked in the basement together. I had informed him that I had extra canvases for him to paint with that I wasn't using, so he followed me downstairs. I shut the door behind us, not knowing it locked from the outside. I made a private resolution not to try to comfort him as best as I could so that he wouldn't panic, but when I told him we were locked in, he seemed unusually calm.

"Where are the canvases?" he asked.

We began looking on shelves, behind boxes and tools and old cans of used paint, we looked around the hot water heater, and we searched the corners among all the other random boxes, but we couldn't find the canvases despite my certainty that they were there somewhere.

"I saw them last week," I told him. "They were here unless my dad took them to the church or something."

The lightbulb flickered briefly, and Matthew cast a nervous glance at it.

"My mom should be home any minute," I assured him. "The kitchen is right above us so we'll hear her steps, and I can yell for her and she'll hear. This has happened before."

"Where is she?"

"At work."

"What time does she get home?"

"She's always home by three," I said. "I think it was after two when we came down here."

We sat down on the floor across from each other. I noticed Matthew had an oppressive, drugged look about him, as if some illusion formed in his mind in our isolation. He wore, as I remember it, a black JAWS T-shirt and blue jeans and red untied sneakers. His shoes were always untied, even later when he was in high school, and even so I never saw him trip. It occurred to me, as I reclined against the wall, that he probably found the whole situation awkward because he sat forward and drummed the concrete floor with his knuckles and glared around the room. I showed him the palm of my hand and asked whether he knew that I had a broken lifeline. "I saw a palm reader at the fair," I told him. "She told me I would live a long life, but that my broken lifeline meant I would have obstacles."

"A lifeline?" he said, looking at his own hands. "Which one is it?"

I scooted myself across the floor to him and took his right hand. He let me hold it, and I stared into his palm and ran my finger across the line until he jerked it back, smirking.

"No, wait, let me see it," I said, and took his hand back. "I won't tickle you."

I held his hand close to my face. "Let me see your other hand," I said, and he held it out for me so that I was holding both his hands with mine. I searched his left hand, then his right, then his left again, but he pulled both hands away and stood, raising his arms above him as he stretched and let out a long moan that made me laugh as if he knew I had a strong, perverse influence over him that he wasn't comfortable with.

"Hmm," I said, standing also. "I think you have a good life ahead of you, but I'm not sure about your love life."

He looked confused.

"Who do you like?" I asked him. "Do you have a girlfriend?"

"No."

"Why not?"

"I don't want a girlfriend."

This made me happy. Here I am, forty years later, hearing his voice say those words as clearly as if he spoke them a day ago, despite feeling bogged down by wild distractions of voices and people around me. I can open the windows to the desert and see a vast landscape under the fierce vigilance of loneliness, among dead birds lying beside cacti and rocks. I dreamed myself into soaking the sheets with warm urine during those years, flustered by my muses strangling me, pulsing with anxiety and envy and obsession.

"Let me see your hands again," I told him.

"No, stop."

"It's fun."

Oh the memory. This fool begged childishly while the guest of honor went to the door and tried opening it as if I had lied to him, but I assured him I would never lie to him. He then sat down again and brought his knees to his chest. I retreated to my place across from him and reclined back against the wall, during which time I probed him with questions about his interest in art and writing and books:

When did he develop an interest in drawing and art?

He didn't know a specific date, only that he had always loved to color and felt impelled to draw, look at drawing books, and paint skies and trees with watercolors.

Why did he like to write stories?

He loved reading, he listened to his grandmother read to him, and most nights he stayed up late in bed reading anything he could, stories about minotaurs and lightning and knights, *Alice in Wonderland*, *The Wind in the Willows*, and *Sounder* were his favorite books, and he was, like me, an only child after all and spent engrossing cold days inside learning to entertain himself, even allowing his imagination to escape as he stared out his window at the mysterious bushes that scratched against the glass in the wind, where feral cats skulked at night chasing mice or rats, squirrels and armadillos, and where he and his cousins once pissed during a family reunion after they snuck away and stole beers from the fridge when the adults weren't watching. He wondered, after that, whether the urine added something to the seeds in the dirt that spawned a small creature-monster who lived and rustled around in there and kept him from ever unlocking his window.

Was he afraid of anything?

He was frightened of the creature-monster when he was younger, he said, and the man who was friends with his mom's boyfriend, a white guy who looked side-eyed and vigilant at him in a way he perceived as racist because the guy made derogatory Indian jokes, and he was afraid of certain bullies at school, the same bullies this fool feared and avoided as much as possible. He had been beaten up not once but twice by two lunkheads who girded him after school behind the shop building, and after that he supplicated the spirits for protection, vowing never to hurt anyone ever.

"Forget everything I just said," he told me. "Please don't tell anyone."

"I won't."

He looked worried suddenly, as if he hadn't earned my trust. He leaned back against the wall and stretched his legs out.

"I really won't say anything," I repeated. "I'll tell you a secret about myself, but you can't tell anyone either."

I waited for a response, but he didn't say anything.

"I'm in love with someone," I said.

"Really? Who?"

"Well, I can't tell you. But the secret is that I love someone."

Cautiously, he pulled on his lower lip and stared at the floor, possibly bored, as if he had grown used to such ridiculous conversations, so I changed the subject.

"But what should we do now down here?" I asked. "What do you want to talk about? Have you ever kissed anyone?"

He glanced at me and then looked away, clearly uncomfortable, and with each passing moment I felt a passionate, intolerable imprisonment. His eyes were hypnotic but did not seem inviting, so I lay back and lapsed into thought as we sat together in silence. He was not bound to me as I was to him, yet I felt an invisible presence that observed us in the ecstasy of the dim basement with all the energy of Matthew's enigmas that I found pleasant, and had we been a few years older in that situation, I could've brought him mercilessly closer to me in strange and discrete ways. Even then I knew, however, to feign discomfort in our situation and brought up an interest in collecting jars of assorted jellies and jams of apricot, strawberry, and crabapple, and that the blackberries I collected during my walks with my grandmother down the road were some of the best I'd ever tasted.

"I might try painting with them," I told him.

"With what? The blackberries?"

I held up my hands like claws. "I did my best preschool finger painting by smearing my fingers in jams and blackberries."

"I've never done that," he said. "Do you still have them?"

"Yeah, upstairs in my room."

He perked up, which I found exciting despite my lies; I had no paintings upstairs in my room, nor did I ever paint with blackberries, nor did I have any interest in collecting jars of jams and jellies. I wanted to impress him, that's it. I continued to talk as he lay with his back against the wall, telling him a number of fabrications such as I had once painted my mom's eyebrows purple using a small brush, and that I once hid in the wheat field to help my uncle escape from a mental hospital, and that my dad once found a dead body floating in the river who turned out to be a bloodthirsty murderer who had killed his wife and kids before drowning himself, all of which Matthew believed, he really did, I could see the eager throbbing in his temples, as if he'd been hanging upside down from a light post, his face flushed as he cracked his knuckles and listened. I was always able to tell a believable lie, or at least I believed so, sometimes with great celerity to allay any uncomfortable situation, even though my parents could challenge me in ways nobody else could by somehow instinctually knowing I was wanting to get people to like me or trying to impress someone.

"Someone's here," Matthew said, pointing to the ceiling. We heard my mom's footsteps in the kitchen above us, so I called out for her and began knocking on the basement ceiling with a broom until she came downstairs and opened the door and found us.

"We locked ourselves in," I told her.

"Why?" she said. "You know the door locks from the outside."

We hurried past her and went upstairs to my bedroom, where he urged me to show him the finger paintings and where I pretended to look for them in my closet, rifling through clothes and board games and boxes of old toys until I stopped, turned to him, and said, "Wait, I think I left them at my grandparents' house."

"Bummer," he said.

"I'll show them to you sometime. Why don't we draw?"

We lay on the floor beside my bed and drew on white paper with pencils. But mostly I watched him sketch cartoon faces. He tapped his cheek with his pencil, studied his work, and I continued to stare at his eyes, his puckered lips.

For weeks we spoke only briefly whenever I called him on the phone. His mom worked all day and parked her car in the driveway when she returned home in the early evenings, at which point their kitchen light was on and viewable from the east side of their house, so any time I rode my bike by his house in the evenings as the sun was setting, I could see her as she went to the sink. The west side of the house was covered in shrubbery, but it was the back of the house that opened to a gathering of trees and, beyond that, a barren slope that led to a creek. Matthew's bedroom window faced the back of the house, and though the curtains were drawn often, on occasion they were open until he went to bed.

A few months later, out of nowhere, he lost interest in playing and told me he'd prefer to donate the homemade drum set to someone who would appreciate it more, maybe some other child who couldn't afford to buy a drum set, because he was predestined to the nature of kindness, that's what he said in his lisp: "I'm predestined to the nature of kindness." He quit drumming and began focusing on his writing and drawings. I started drawing, too. My art was helping me understand myself, helping me concentrate on something. At the school library, I checked out books like William H. Armstrong's *Sounder*, Robert Frost's poetry, and Frances Hodgson Burnett's *The Secret Garden*. I studied Shakespeare's poems despite their difficulty. I began writing my own poems, which I felt were stronger, more cryptic and daring, and sadder than any of his poems.

6 (IN WHICH WE BEGIN WRITING POEMS AND CONTEMPLATE THE VALUE OF ART)

I have in my possession a box of early artwork, stories, and poems I have collected throughout my life. They are very precious to me even after all these years. I am especially interested in three documents. Document number one contains a poem I composed that school year I became friends with Matthew. It is a sonnet in iambic pentameter, dated September 26.

> In the beginning, they flew down to me
> as I was walking in the woods. Their wings
> were spread like clouds, all soft and glittery:
> some purple, some opaque, with golden rings
> like tiny halos. Gliding past me, they
> were grouped together, shrieking noises, yet
> my soul felt lifted, overjoyed. The way
> it looked, it was as if a giant net,
> a rainbow-colored light fell from the sky
> and brightened them as they landed. This light
> remained, and they looked over at me. I
> could see their violet wing tips, twinkling white.
> And then they all crouched down, except for one,
> whose wings unfolded, bursting like the sun!

My charismatic Christian parents were overjoyed that I wrote a poem about angels. But what I am most proud about is that I developed an understanding of the form and worked hard to strengthen my vocabulary the way Matthew was so invested in developing his own skills. Today, I compare this poem with Matthew's poem, document number two, also written in iambic pentameter, in rhyming couplets, but handed in to the teacher some two weeks later, dated October 10:

> Developing an interest in blue jays,
> You started spending time outdoors. The days
> I saw you in your grandmother's backyard
> Were full of joy. I bought a greeting card.
> It had the words "I Love You" written in
> Italian, Greek, and French, and then: "Amen."
> You're lovely when you point up to the trees,
> Addressing Papa's little birdhouse. "He's
> Inside, peeking his head out, and—oh my!
> Away he flies into the clouds: goodbye!"
> You're lovely when you gather nests. You're out
> Collecting them—your specialty, no doubt.
> The tiny parts of broken toys in youth,
> I placed inside my mouth, behind a tooth,
> Where whispering a poem became a game
> Of hide-and-seek, charades, and guess my name.

Aside from the flawed logic toward the end, the poem succeeds only in its rhyme and iambic pentameter structure. The idea that he found my work inspiring is something I failed to notice back then, but now it seems obvious.

The third document I composed offers a glimpse of my own interest in academics at a young age. As the letter indicates, I was in sixth grade.

Dear Mr. Ashworth,

Sir, I write this letter to you from a dark corner in after school detention (never mind the details, it wasn't my fault). Here is my point: it has come to my attention, rather recently, that the school has decided to replace the arts and crafts class in jr. high beginning next year. Sir, I am currently in sixth grade. I am writing you for this one simple reason: because it has come to my understanding that the arts and crafts class will be replaced with a science or extra computer class. This decision causes great concern to me and is rather puzzling. Sir, I am greatly alarmed that the school would eradicate such a highly esteemed subject such as art. I, sitting here during after school detention (details not important... not my fault) am taking the time to sit down and write this letter to you, as you can probably tell, out of extravagant worry and panic. I and my parents are extremely concerned with the opportunities to study abroad during summers or for a semester during the school year. Ms. Jefferson (my current teacher) informed us that Europe is an extremely cultured place (I agree). For example, I enjoyed learning French this year and would like to visit Paris, France, someday and enjoy the extravagant culture and visit the Louvre to see priceless works of art, paintings, and sculptures that have impressed our minds for thousands of years. I have never left the USA (as far as I know, unless I did as an infant). I would also like to study there someday. I feel arts and crafts is a subject that will help us as future artists in college as well and not to be eradicated. Mr. Ashworth, sir, I wanted to suggest that giving students an extravagant choice might be extremely beneficial to students. If you notice, I included with this letter a signed petition. I received 32 signatures from students, 8 boys and 24 girls. Sir, 32 is my lucky number. I picked number 32 and won a goldfish at the school carnival last Friday night, sir. I have 32 unsent poems to my favorite artist, Mr. Salvador Dali. Please consider keeping arts and crafts here. Thank you for your time, sir.

Respectfully yours in awe,
Milton Muleborn (Grade 6)

While my letter writing skills had its inconsistencies, I should note here that our competition transitioned from writing to drawing. In junior high, Matthew and I shared an art class. His drawings and watercolors were, according to our teacher, superior to mine. He succeeded in penetrating his charm on teachers better than any other person I have known, including myself. Ms. Jefferson attempted to entice us with candy, snacks, or surprise packages full of gum and pencils, for whoever created the best piece of artwork to motivate the lazy, unmotivated students to work harder, but I worked as hard as I could, the class each day passed quickly as I sat at the table in hard concentration with my paintbrush or colored pencils. This work never paid off because Ms. Jefferson always favored Matthew, praising him with her hand patting his back and ruffling his hair, distracting the rest of us with unnecessary and unprepossessing humor ad nauseum, putting on sunglasses and pretending to smoke an imaginary cigarette like she was an art critic and claiming brilliance on her new discovery, a great, whimsical, radiant presence, she told us he would be unleashed on the art world like a blizzard of grasshoppers, carrying his torch to the horrors of the stubborn and jealous no-talents he passed by like a thunderstorm rolling across barren land, hurtling toward the depths of the heavens while the rest of us stayed behind. She might as well have been right because nobody doubted her, at least not aloud; we heard only her voice followed by the silence of disappointment and languor. We saw heavy clouds outside while we worked, the sidewalk where kids fought after lunch when they weren't smoking behind the buildings, and the world was left sheared and fractured like a ragged corpse carried to its grave.

Many nights I dreamed of Matthew grabbing my arm with a claw and carrying me like a hawk into the clouds and letting go so that I fell toward the Earth below to my death, a recurring nightmare for a while. Other times I would dream of him choking to death. My dreams continued into a whole other series of nightmarish intrusions, including seeing other dead bodies and parts of animals, such as a boar's head or a slaughtered chicken, while I followed Matthew as a rabbit along a dirt path, Matthew leaving rabbit footprints and stopping every so often to turn and look at me with his long rabbit ears pointing toward heaven; and in every dream I knew this was Matthew playing tricks on me, I knew it, the rabbit so obviously a trickster character, the rabbit with the long ears and big teeth and spectacles, always silent and happily traipsing along the path in front of me like a deranged tour guide to present the rotting bodies and eerie souls of the suffering, all of them with bulging eyes and forked tongues, naked and begging for help: *Help us please*, they cried out, *help us, Milton*, while overhead the screech owl sat on a tree limb waiting to swoop down and dig its talons into my scalp (this was what I worried most about in the dream, not witnessing the suffering bodies), and every time I called out to Matthew to stop walking, he would merely turn around with his big teeth and tilt his head and stare at me before turning back around and walking again.

In class, Matthew made a series of drawings he called *The Devil's Playground*, a prophetic vision of juvenile detention, and strangely, the only person we ever heard address the detention area as "the devil's playground" was a drill sergeant who yelled, "*Yonder shines the big red moon under the devil's lost playground!*" The drawings were maps of that exact location in the woods, with tiny arrows leading from the facility through the woods and to the tributary with rising smoke that he drew in swirls all the way to the top of the paper. How could he have known the area prior to being locked up since none of us had ever been there, and why would he have drawn three separate maps of the same area unless he had some prophecy about its importance?

The chapter titled "Wahuhi"* in his first book was surely based on our time spent locked up. Matthew once told me he dreamed of the owl surrounded by blue flowers that healed him from loneliness and feeling diminished and isolated, and that the blessing of a sinecure in the future wasn't nearly as lucrative as working entirely out of faith for healing the sick and oppressed. He read aloud to Trusty John and me in the fleeting light of the moon during a high school football game, among the noise of people cheering, and I fell into a staggering and intoxicating dolorousness.

---

* Owl

7 (IN WHICH I SEE THE IMITATIONS)

The next document I have contains two papers—one written by Matthew and the other by me. We were in English class, and both chose to write about the work of the American poet Robert Frost. Frost, Frost, Frost! Here I present the openings to two abstracts. I wrote about Frost's first book, *A Boy's Will*, and Matthew wrote about his second, *North of Boston*:

> Milton Muleborn:
> Abstract of Robert Frost's *A Boy's Will*: "Into My Own": Speaker wishes to escape from life to another world (tree imagery): "One of my wishes is that those dark trees, . . . / Were not, as 'twere, the merest mask of gloom, / But stretched away unto the edge of doom." There is hope to escape the tediousness of everyday life and concern that others are copying you: "I should not be withheld but that some day / Into their vastness I should steal away, / Fearless of ever finding open land, / Or highway where the slow wheel pours the sand." Speaker is changed in final couplet: "They would not find me changed from him they knew— / Only more sure of all I thought was true" (15).
>
> "Ghost House": Loneliness/Speaker is alone: "I dwell in a lonely house I know . . ."(15) "I dwell with a strangely aching heart . . ." (16) Nobody has driven on the dirt road by the house: "On that disused and forgotten road / That has no

dust-bath now for the toad" (16). Loneliness is an important theme because we all experience feelings of isolation.

Matthew Echota:

Abstract of Robert Frost's second book of poetry, *North of Boston*: (Dear Mr. Riggs, please note: The poems in this book are longer work than in his first book. There are more narrative/dramatic poems. I know the assignment is to choose only two poems to compare and contrast, but I am choosing, like Milton Muleborn, to write about the entire book. I believe it is a more difficult book than his first. Sincerely, Matthew.)

"The Death of the Hired Man": Narrative poem. Theme: belonging/family/death (regarding Silas): "'he has come home to die: / You needn't be afraid he'll leave you this time.'" (41). Silas not close w/ brother: "'Silas has walked that far no doubt today. / Why didn't he go there? His brother's rich, / A somebody—director in the bank.'" (44). Silas celebrated his life without trying to please others: "'Silas is what he is—we wouldn't mind him— / But just the kind that kinsfolk can't abide.'" (44). Silas dies in the end: "'Dead,' was all he answered." (45). We will all die one day.

I will spare the annotations of the entire book, of course, because while Matthew's assessment of Frost's work may be an appropriate response for school, it does nothing to suggest any relationship to his own life, whereas my annotations of *A Boy's Will* focus on loneliness, something I was feeling at the time. My mom told me that Bucktooth and Badger bullied me because they were jealous of me. "Jealous of what?" I asked. "I don't have anything to be jealous of."

"You have two loving parents," she told me. "Also, you have a friend."

While Matthew appeared to be a close friend at the time, even after all these years I can't ignore the likelihood that he despised me.

8 (IN WHICH THE FOOL STRUGGLES TO UNDERSTAND THE MEANING OF LOVE)

Thus how difficult it was to understand what it means to love someone or to be loved. My parents told me they loved me but usually said it while reading the paper in the living room before I went to bed, or whenever they sent me off to church camp in the summers of my youth. One Saturday morning I asked my dad about the difference between what it means to love someone you're completely in love with and someone you're friends with, and he told me when you're in love with someone you want to be with them all the time, you find them physically and emotionally attractive, and that it's a completely different kind of love than what I had ever experienced. He was in the garage digging through a toolbox or something when he said all this without even looking up at me.

"When I say 'I love you' to someone," I asked him, "how does that person know what type of love I mean?"

My father winced at something he was looking at in his toolbox, then took out a small screw or bolt and examined it. "Why are you asking me these questions?"

"I guess I'm trying to figure it all out."

"Nobody ever figures it all out," he told me. "People fall in love and then fall out of love. People treat the people they love badly or say terrible things to them. We should always look to the Bible for help with understanding love. Where's yours?"

"My love?"

"Your Bible."

"I don't know. Probably in my backpack with my baseball cards."

"Go read it," he said. "Are you thinking you're in love with someone?"

"No. I don't know."

"What's the rush?" he said, back to rummaging around in his toolbox. "There's no rush to be in love with anyone. You have the rest of your life. You might be in love multiple times."

"And what about soulmates?" I asked.

My father wiped his brow with the back of his wrist. "Soulmates," he said. "Do you believe in soulmates?"

I didn't know what to say.

"Better talk to your mother about it," he told me.

I felt I was in love with my spirit/soulmate Cakae, aka Cassie Magdal, and had dreams about her even before I met her at school, in art class, when she walked into the classroom looking so beautiful. She made my insides ache at first sight. Whenever someone asks me whether I believe in love at first sight, I always tell them yes. That's the only way I could ever describe it, that feeling, but the more I stared at her and thought about her, the lonelier I felt. I never went to school dances or sports events at school because I was afraid she would be there and find me vulnerable and terrified around Bucktooth and Badger, who were there for the sole purpose of creating havoc and bullying anyone smaller or weaker than them. Her sobriquet for me was Hermit because I kept to myself and rarely left the house unless it was to go to school, the movies with her, or to her house to listen to her sing. My dreams of Cakae mostly involved her leading me by the hand out of my house to some place far away. Before I even met her, I dreamed of her wearing a necklace of my gallstones she had painted because it made her feel close to me and we were, as she later confirmed, soulmates. I thought of swimming in a lake with her and playing a splashing game. I thought of slow dancing with her to Portuguese fado music, to Timi Yuro, and to Smokey Robinson, whose voice is so sexy I stared into her eyes and saw a manifestation of myself.

A little while later at lunch, I asked my mom about love. The two of us were sitting at the dining room table while my father continued to work in the garage. My mom was sipping an herbal decoction of some sort and eating a salad with cranberries and nuts while I ate a bowl of potato soup she'd made.

"If I love someone," I asked, "doesn't that mean I want to be with them forever, to exist in their body and mind and emotions? Do I long to dance with them, to gaze into their eyes and feel an aching deep inside my soul?"

"That's being in love," my mom said.

"If I love a friend, that's a different kind of love?"

"Right."

"Because I don't want to gaze into their eyes?"

"Not usually."

"I never see you and Dad stare into each other's eyes, so does that mean you're not in love anymore?"

"Love is a strange thing," my mom told me. "It's complicated and messy and ever-changing, I think, so that soon it becomes an understanding without feeling all the feelings all the time."

I didn't understand, but I tried to. My mom ate slowly, staring into her plate; the silence was not uncommon whenever we ate together. There were all kinds of feelings I was having trouble understanding, about love and God and loneliness, and why I was feeling sad much of the time even though I had only a couple of friends—my cousin, Trusty John, and Matthew, who entertained my imagination daily because I was so enamored by him.

"You should get out of the house today," my mom said. "You've been inside the whole winter, and outside it's starting to get pretty. Don't you want to go be with someone outside?"

"I don't have anyone to be with," I told her. "And I only like the park by myself, anyway. Maybe I'll take my sketchbook there and draw if you want me to leave."

"I don't want you to leave. I'm just trying to get you to do something other than hole up in your room all day."

I went outside to the backyard and sat on the porch beside the wind chimes. I put on my headphones and listened to Glenn Gould on my Walkman, which I did often because I felt like our backyard surrounded by trees was so therapeutic. The trees rustled in the wind, and I felt like they were speaking to me in some unknown whispery language. The wind chimes rang, telling me it was fine to cry if I wanted to, or to feel sad for reasons I couldn't fully understand. Staring at the trees and listening to the wind chimes was like watching little spirits entertain me.

A moment later my father, wearing a Hawaiian shirt and Bermuda shorts, came outside with a page from the newspaper and showed me an article with Matthew's photo about how he had won a poetry contest chosen by a local poet and former university professor named Agatha Klemm. The award came with an engraved plaque and a small cash prize, and the photo showed Matthew standing beside Agatha Klemm and looking neither rakish nor homely; rather, Matthew held a timid smile as he stood holding his plaque.

"Isn't this your friend?" he asked. "He won a contest."

"Matthew? That's him."

"I thought that was him."

"It is."

My father and I made eye contact.

"He must be really good," my father said.

At once everything around us fell muddied and wild, bathed in delirium: in slow motion, my father brought his finger to his face and slowly scratched under his eye, and in that moment I realized that my father's eyes always held the look of a madman, with a suspicious desire to keep the dark side of him veiled in secrecy so that he could indulge himself in the types of hedonistic pleasure he preached against, didn't he, because the slow-moving finger scratching his eye was a way to communicate to me that he knew I wasn't as good of a poet as Matthew Echota, and that as ashamed as he was, he at least had the dignity to never say it aloud and to speak through his eyes instead, which likely eased his anxiety. I thought a lot about eye contact, because I felt like Cakae and I were able to communicate with each other by staring at each other in silence. (Cakae later admitted to losing that feeling of staring with me and replaced it with eye contact with Matthew.) For me, love was all feeling, absent of logic or decision.

Going on a family vacation, for instance, was never as mawkish as what family trips are supposed to be like, and any time we took one, which was maybe once or twice a year, usually involved driving to see some landmark or the historical nonsense of a small town six hours away. Walt always wept during these long road trips for reasons we never understood. He wept beside me in the back seat, staring out his window, and when my mom asked him what was the matter he always said it was nothing.

"Honey, we're going on vacation, you should be excited," she told him.

Walt, always weeping, tried to catch his breath and answer, but everything came out jumbled and hysterical.

"He'll get over it," my father said aloud, driving.

He didn't. At least, I don't think he ever did, and it probably contributed to his suicide a few years later. Any time Walt wept at night, in bed, nobody ever tried to talk to him. They just gave up at some point because he never told them what was wrong.

On vacations, my father would book us a room at a hotel and ask to see the elevator operation manual from the manager out of concern of faulty cables. The hotel clerks always had the same horrified expression, as if they were unsure whether he was kidding or not, but then they understood quickly he was serious. My father leaned forward over the counter and expressed his concern for safety and asked to speak to the manager on duty. Once the manager dug through the office for five minutes and returned with the manual, my father sat in the coffee shop/restaurant and flipped through the pages while my mom and Walt and I waited in the lobby with the luggage. When he felt assured that the elevators were inspected and in working order, everything was fine again, but those minutes he spent reading the manual were embarrassing and unnecessary, as my mom usually reminded him, and grated on her nerves so badly that she stepped outside and smoked three or four cigarettes in a row. These were the type of details he was concerned or obsessed with, trivial unimportant matters, like whether the toilet paper was the kind he preferred or the room temperature at a comfortable level. Walt and I were never allowed to touch the thermostat. My father didn't even want my mom to touch it, obsessed as he was with meaningless details, absurd things it seemed to me, yet he obsessed, and I learned to go with it. Thus, on the long, weary drive when my father never turned on the radio and preferred the sounds of the interstate, I felt an inescapable boredom and took my scrapbook with me, which I named "Beckett," because of my love for Samuel Beckett (whose work I have recently become obsessed with again after not reading him for many years); in this notebook are some of my first attempts of writing that, not four days ago, my mom mailed down here in a box, containing a document I wrote long ago:

(a)
For three nights the writer of parables dreamed of his missing friend. He woke in an execrable sweat to find himself trembling and short of breath. He went into the kitchen where he found his friend sitting alone at the table, drinking coffee. When the boy looked up at him, he saw the face of someone he didn't recognize.

"I'm not your friend," the boy told him. "I threw our friendship outside into a pile of leaves to decay with the loam."

While the writer searched through an assemblage of leaves outside, the fog lifted momentarily, and he looked up and saw rays of sunlight shining through the trees. From the pile of leaves he heard a rustle and looked back down to find a tiny, mouse-sized boy who was radiating light in the dark forest. The writer leaned down and picked him up so that the boy stood in the palm of his hand.

"Put me in your pocket and keep me forever," the tiny boy said.

(b)
He sat at his desk reading a spate of Freudian theory to help him understand the trauma he'd inherited from his father, as well as *Tractatus Logico-Philosophicus* and other texts, sitting for hours

upstairs, writing parables about angels and devils. His beard was itchy. When he looked at himself in the mirror, he saw insects crawling all over his face. Frantic, he rushed into the bathroom and turned on the light. There were no insects on his face. I'm losing my mind, he thought.

He went downstairs and poured himself a whiskey. For a moment he stood looking at his hands, which were trembling.

Beyond the yard, under the jagged branches of eucalyptus trees, crimson birds scattered into a pale blue sky.

9 (IN WHICH WALT'S SUICIDE REVEALS A SECRET)

The most difficult thing for me is talking about Walt, even to this day. Walt committed suicide before I'd gotten into trouble and locked up. It happened one morning while I was at school and he had stayed home sick, telling our mom that he'd been feeling unwell all night and had gotten very little sleep. Our mom, our poor mom, having taken his temperature that morning and saw that he had no fever, even though he claimed he was freezing cold and shivering under the covers, thought he might be faking but gave him the benefit of the doubt, telling herself it might be a flu or virus he was coming down with, and so drove me to school to let him sleep and have time alone. She had errands to run, groceries to pick up, never even considering the worst, never thinking of his emotional pain or whatever reeled him into silence and mental health sickness, and by the time she arrived back home she found him bleeding all over the floor with a knife in his chest.

How did he conclude that death is better than life?

How did he hurt so badly without telling anyone, or worse, without anyone paying enough attention to even notice?

Previously, whenever my father preached and Walt and I had to sit in the front row next to my mother, I sometimes caught my father glaring at Walt and me every so often, as if the message were directed at us instead of to the congregation. Most of the time Walt had trouble looking anyone in the eye, so when our father glared at us the way he did in church, Walt looked down. I found myself doing the same: any time our father talked to us, I looked away, though I have heard this is not uncommon among teenage boys and their fathers. After years of getting lambasted for avoiding eye contact, I soon learned it became a great strength for me, looking people directly in the eye whenever I spoke to them. Our father studied and spoke often about iniquities, and one Sunday preached about them. I remember the way he glared at us during one particular sermon, a look that said more than his words. He required, not encouraged, memorization of certain verses, e.g., Ezra 9:6: "I am ashamed and blush to lift up my face to thee, my God." Job 22:5: "[Is] not thy wickedness great? and thine iniquities infinite?" Psalm 40:12: "For innumerable evils have compassed me about: mine iniquities have taken hold upon me, so that I am not able to look up." Lamentations 5:7: "Our fathers have sinned, and are not; and we have borne their iniquities." This last one was the most horrifying to me because he repeated the last part so often, "we have borne their iniquities," the context of which I wasn't clear on, though I understood the basic principle of sin, of thoughts and actions going against God, and of disrespect for our elders, meaning him and my mother, and that to be a strong man meant not being afraid of confrontation and competition.

My father skirted the fringes of so many gambling temptations and sinful concubinages that it seemed impossible to hear my mom's aroused suspicions and take them seriously, yet there I stood in the heart of the omnium-gatherum after Walt's funeral and saw my father sneak out of the garden with the woman in the hat who held her cigarette between two fingers like Joan Crawford.

I watched him, among all those suspicious people, leading the woman by the hand and aware most certainly that I had seen them sneak away, so unrestrained and visible in his dark suit that one could believe his intentions were innocent without any doubt whatsoever, although nobody was more likely to lead a woman by the hand and then twenty minutes later scurry out of the woods like a cockroach, as my mom put it, the son of a bitch hypocrite even kept a small room in a cabin owned by the church stocked with wine and full of candles he'd bought from the store downtown in Dublan, because nobody dared consider such a heart-shattering travesty would occur there, not there, not in the lake cabin known for youth retreats, men of God conferences, and occasional choir weekends in the summers.

There he was, my father, as if he had never been the trustworthy person to read aloud fairy tales to me, followed by nightly readings of a Johnny Cash biography while my mom opened the window so that we could smell the evening rain outside and listen for the train in the distance, as if he'd never taught me to give thanks before eating and sleeping every night, he of healthy and kind heart whose voice was alluring enough to draw the sparrows and geese from territorial waters across the field, he of strong morality and trust who said never in a million years would I deny my Father or spouse or family, ever, even while reading aloud to me of Johnny Cash's pain instead of Christ's pain, surely overwhelmed by the thoughts of the coming afternoons spent with bookies and gamblers or women at the lake cabin while my mom worked long hours at the hospital as a labor and delivery nurse.

How, as a struggling pastor, he must've lived at the mercy of his own commission, disillusioned by earthly desires and a complicated lust and sin, knowing full well his week would be spent slaving away at his desk as he flipped through his notebook in search of an unhypocritical sermon, nine hours a day spent writing and scribbling, praying and sipping gin until lethargy made him drop onto the sofa and sleep for two or three hours at a time, during which he mumbled in his sleep about how he wished he'd pursued a life studying classics and married a woman named either Iris Annabel or Anabella Iris, although I heard his sleep mumblings on many occasions and the names of the women periodically changed: Iris changed to Sarah, to Maria, to Mildred, and to Joan Crawford, and the only time I ever asked about these mumblings, he sat up and grabbed me by the wrist with pale eyes full of tears, trembling as if paralyzed by a continuous buzz of inner rage, perhaps he lived at the mercy of this torment, perhaps the increased bitterness and indiscretion was fueled over how much debt he was in and how many women he'd slept with, and at once he snapped out of it and let go of my wrist.

He moved slowly to the window and pulled the curtain to see the land stretching out in the distance to the fleeting sunset, and a moment later he told us the branches from the oak tree reminded him of his childhood when he went to see his own father, my grandfather, in an asylum far away from Dublan Plains, and to pass the time while his father bathed or ate tapioca pudding, he was introduced to an old Joan Crawford movie called *What Ever Happened to Baby Jane*, in which Joan Crawford aroused him in ways he didn't understand, and at the same time he was also introduced to betting by playing checkers with a few of the workers there, and when he won three dollars, then four, then five, he knew he had a love of gambling.

There he was, at Walt's omnium-gatherum, quoting Psalm 37:28, "The seed of the wicked shall be cut off," after he returned from the woods with the woman in the sun hat who was now sitting with three other men under the pergola. This woman held another cigarette between two fingers and kept glancing at me through a trail of smoke, aware my mother was working her shift at the hospital, and my father nudged me and leaned in close to my ear and said it again, slowly: "The seed of the wicked shall be cut off," which finally occurred to me translated as I would be punished if I betrayed him and told my mother what had happened, punished worse than ever before. Then he stepped away and joined two other men in conversation, and I had a sudden and intense memory of watching him preach a sermon in a 1970s-style carpeted conference room that smelled of cigarette smoke at the El Grito Motel just outside of Dublan Plains, looking weary and tired in his undersized checkered polyester suit, stomping around and speaking in tongues in a fire-and-brimstone way that shook the building like an earthquake and made me think of, for whatever reason, the Mad Hatter from *Alice in Wonderland*, and for a long time I jokingly referred to my father as the Mad Hatter to my friends until he overheard me say it on the phone once, after which I received my punishment and never said it again.

Having sat through Walt's dirgeful funeral and then seeing my father sneak the woman out of the garden, I now felt as nauseated and unsettled as I had during that motel revival. I thought I was maybe having a type of hallucinatory breakdown because I began to see all the people standing in the garden behind the house gesturing broadly, as if describing something enormous and round, and the ones who weren't gesturing were talking into their wristwatches like spies. My paranoia, I'll admit, always gripped its balls when I was young, and while it hasn't gotten much better over the years, at least it hasn't gotten worse. I found myself horrified by the possibility that the whole post-funeral reception was a *joke* at my expense, maybe a hoax orchestrated by my father to see whether I could handle grief in public like a man, which was an absolute and insane thought, though not entirely out of the question because my father never once burst into tears even at his own brother's funeral some years earlier, and Walt's reception was as bizarre as any failed production: there was no weeping or gnashing of teeth by anyone present, no arguments, no eye contact, everyone was standing around eating carrot sticks and desserts on small paper plates and drinking wine from plastic cups like a pathetic faculty party at some prestigious institution I'd seen only in movies on cable television. Nothing made me feel better about being there, not even sitting by the swimming pool with its diaphanous and inviting blue water and seeing my strange, quivering reflection, which made me look like a giant leech.

(a) Leeches and the Wolf

My mom referred to my father as a wolf whose concept of reality was so entangled he sometimes chewed on wire with his teeth and drooled like a rabid dog, unable to repress his impulse to lash out physically or sexually in some way; that's the truth, she said, and how disgraced he must've felt knowing she was telling people this anytime she talked on the phone in the lazy light of the den where she lamented their marriage and his erratic behavior, measuring everything from the way he looked at her to how hard he shut the door, that whenever they shouted at each other she called him either a son of a bitch, or a stupid pig, or a wolf.

Once we finally left the omnium-gatherum of Walt's funeral, I looked into my father's eyes and thought about all this, how I often saw the serious threat of someone on the cusp of a breakdown and how he once told me he detested his own image as much as he did Dublan Plains, and now here he was driving and sure enough talking of the fetid smell of downtown and how the only thing to get us through difficult times and grief was to see things with a youthful eye, like mad butterflies batting around or birds hopping under a tree, because at some point we all get older and take the beauty of nature for granted; our bodies and faces morph into something else so that we look more monstrous than human, more dead than alive, and more frightening than a moon rising over a decrepit cornfield on a cool midwestern night; think about your mother, he told me, whose fragrance once spread the Earth with spring flora but whose derision for the unfaithful and sin was now as bitter as a leper's, a woman whose will to live had been eaten by jealousy and rage and a misunderstanding of her husband's complicated lust, and whose age attacked her body with the harsh steps of time in darkness like the old ladies in fairy tales whose faces and bodies were scratched by thornbushes while spying on their husbands lying naked with maidens, your poor mother, he said, and it was then I saw the ugly beast my mother had seen, how my father was suffering with his private and complicated ardor, suffering from self-hatred and malevolence and pierced by the hand of the devil, he whom I shall never again fear.

That night I started writing a horror story about the giant leech that lived under our house when I began to hear it crawling around underneath the hardwood floor in my bedroom. I paced while my father shouted at me through the intercom on the wall to stop walking around the house because he could hear my footsteps creaking all the way in his bedroom, but I refrained from confessing that I was terrified of the leech because he would say it serves me right, it's a punishment of sorts for my own regret and falling victim to the devil's agenda of temptation among today's teenagers with designer drug parties and free online pornography and hardcore so-called alternative music glorifying darkness, destruction, and sin; indeed, how easy it was to imagine my father glaring at me like a sticky substance in the palm of his hand, half grimacing, skilled in the manipulations of fatherhood with an immense disposition for control and restoration, obedience, and honesty. How easy it was to imagine him in his hammock looking weary and miserable, his skin yellow from what my mom said was a failing liver, singing from somewhere deep inside him the chorus of King David because "Thine arrows are sharp in the heart of the king's enemies," from Psalm 45, half drunk, placid, and inert, under the protection of the shade from the apple tree, he whom I feared even in his most relaxed state. How difficult it was to forget, though, that very late in the night he awoke us to attempt to arouse in us the nostalgia for the war he was experiencing that led to his sleepless nights, which only confirmed my worsening fear, because he (claimed he) knew a spiritual warfare happening in dirty Old Dublan, the type of spiritual warfare that would begin to appear before our very eyes like the story of the leeches, which was a story he told me when I was little about giant leeches who lived a few miles from our house in a community of old wooden structures built nearly two hundred years ago. Because they were originally protandric hermaphrodites, the leeches reproduced at an alarming speed, having entered the bodies of women who swam in the river as far back as the late 1800s. Their offspring and mutations were grotesque, multiplying in the water rapidly enough that as they continued as parasites to enter women's bodies and develop DNA, their anatomy and physiology morphed into near human form, and they soon grew to be giant leeches, pale even after so much time in the sun, difficult to look at due to their slight inverted proboscis and lack of jaw, which posed breathing problems, but their lifespan was long, with most living well past one hundred years because their saliva contained both an anesthetic and morphine-like compound. I soon became convinced the leech living underneath our floors was an offspring of these giant leeches and would grow and multiply.

"They're a parasite, like evil," he told me. "Evil is not a creation, it's a parasite. You have to understand."

The spiritual warfare my father spoke about existed in the world around us so that we could watch it mutate and spread like a furious fire across the plains, floating like an evil presence in pursuit of the innocent, gullible, naive citizens whose laughter burst in the shadows of the town square, angered by patient stoicism and agreement, yet rife with greed and lust, as when a bloodthirsty dog ripped the head off a rabbit and ate it, then pawing and running its big red tongue over the rabbit's body before fully carrying it away to devour, a clear omen that caused my father so much anger in his sleeplessness that he saw the dead staggering through the house and walking outside, and he began hearing voices arguing good vs. evil, sin and temptation, confirming his belief that the less people understood the more they fight, stressing these people and leeches are greedy creatures, as mentioned in the book of Proverbs. Greedy with lust and food, they would surely feed on anything alive if they were hungry enough—even their own children.

There I was, suffering the horror show of my night's anxieties, wondering whether the leech stories were true and why he mentioned they would eat their own children, a terrifying thought when you assume your father gives subtle hints about eating you, like when he spent windless afternoons swatting flies and joking about feeding them to me before sucking on my neck and devouring my blood, vampire style, or when he forced me to hunt rabbits with him and we dragged our feet in the midst of fields with tall grass so that he could cut their heads off and make rabbit stew, which his own father had made for him years ago during the Big War, and that I might do well to sit in the steaming pot along with the rabbit and get cooked, of course he then reminded me of the fairy tales of the old woman cooking children and then eating them, and these stories always raised my anxiety enough in ways that confirmed, he said, that I was not quite tough enough to be a young man yet.

Once my father went to bed and I was finally able to fall asleep, I dreamed he morphed into a type of batrachian, a giant frog, and came after me, past frightened herds of cattle and into a pecan grove, his tongue hanging from his mouth, and let me tell you how relieved I was to awake from that nightmare despite the cold urine on the sheets. I didn't want him to know I had pissed in the bed because I had not received a certificate of good conduct from him in three years. But it was still dark outside, and I was too drowsy to get out of bed or change the sheets, so I fell back asleep, and this time I dreamed of my father dressed as Joan Crawford threatening to choke me with his big red finger down my throat unless I tied the laces of my shoes right then, and in my dream I looked down at my shoes and saw they were untied, so I knelt down and tried to tie them but they were in knots, see, this is a typical anxiety dream of mine, attempting to do something and failing, even something as simple as tying the laces of my shoes was frustrating, and I felt pressured in my dream to do it quickly or else I'll get my father's big finger down my throat. The dream ended by looking up at my father and seeing him stick out his big red tongue at me.

In the morning, people were still in the heart of the omnium-gatherum, so I called my dear dead uncle Manuel himself to meet me because I needed to get out of the house, and I also wanted a smoke and knew he would have cigarettes because he was now absent of the humanly body, eaten away by lung cancer, so he met me at the park down the street and sat with me on the swings. We smoked and I told Uncle Manuel about my dream, because I always told him about any trauma and never felt judged; he was a good listener. I reminded him that my father always said nothing was ever fair, he who lived the dismal life of a young man who slept in the homes of friends and girlfriends and among people he didn't even know, a free spirit back in the soporific days that he could no longer recall from too many gins or liquors or wines, and anyway, he told me, those harsh experiences confirmed the certainty that his ideas about love were skewed and that he had always felt so careless about himself, negligent of his fatherly and husbandly responsibilities, and that's that, he said, he would say it over and over.

I saw the tears swell in Uncle Manuel's ghostly eyes when I told him about my fear, and he broke into a sobbing that reminded me of the way he had once wept at school, but this time he wept with such a deep affliction that I felt enormous pity for him and began to console him by telling him I loved him, because I did love him, however confusing my concern for him, and in that moment he reminded me that he loved me as well, then he mentioned the time he was alive and we walked through a November drizzle and he confessed he was afraid of my father, too.

We heard, then, the shouting of boys across the park, calling out to me as they walked from the far end toward us, four of them, and it took a moment to realize they were bloodthirsty in a way in which they were likely remembering how our ancestors had attacked their ancestors during those long winter months because our ancestors had stolen their ancestors' land, and now here they were, away from school and authorities, looking furious as they filed past the apple tree and merry-go-round, and I contemplated them impassively, standing from the swings and staring as they approached. How, in other times when I had felt threatened or uneasy, as if there was a possibility of violence, I could feel it in my stomach, and my adrenaline would rush because at one time I had a desire for risks, but I knew better than anyone that my own fear was more unraveled now than ever before, and that I always felt I was at a stumbling divination to the unbuckling of self-pity, harm, and dismay. How trauma not only made me want to escape but to disappear completely, something Uncle Manuel and I shared, and probably the Native boys, too, and now I heard Uncle Manuel's whispers, either prayers or the ramblings of someone trying to conjure adrenaline, disturbed by the dizzying hub of the boys approaching, and what else was I going to do about the burning in my stomach and chest? How Uncle Manuel's ghost and I stood there waiting when something so strange happened I could barely believe it: the boys suddenly turned and ran away because my father was hurrying toward us from his truck with his fist raised and shouting, "Get outta here, you little bastards, you chickenshit kids, run away before I call the law," and he came over to us and we saw his dark eyes and fat lower lip red with blood, and he bent over with his hands on his knees to catch his breath, perspiring and coughing, his face nearly as red as his lower lip. Once he settled down, he sat on the swing and rocked a moment, fascinated by something in the sky as he looked up and closed one eye from the bright sun, then he looked at me as if we hadn't seen each other in many years.

He looked exhausted and ill from the darkness under his eyes and the way his swollen lip bled, and told us a man had hit him in the mouth, a man whom he feared because he owed the man money, a gambling debt, and how certain authorities had accountants who kept records of all bets made, and all debts owed, and whose books reflected his name and the entire history of his betting life over the past seven years. He described the man as a monster, a giant with hands like big eagle claws, a man who hauled pigs across the state for days at a time as he listened to the sports radio shows in his truck, listened to games, talked to friends and other bookies and anyone else whose opinions fed the enthusiasm and addiction they all shared. He believed his concept of interpretation was entangled, and I was sure of it as I watched him sit there with his bloody lip and trembling hands, talking about his love for gambling, how he took a deep breath and ran a hand over his face. He told us he suffered in particular from gambling at the racetrack.

"I love everything about the track," he told us. "I love the horses, the atmosphere, Phyllis at the betting window, the jockeys, the trainers, the smell of popcorn and cigarette smoke outside on the paddock, the afternoon beers and seeing the same guys who skipped out of work for the afternoon like I did. I love the way the announcer says 'The horses are coming out on the track' before each race. I love looking up at the odds and payouts and the possibilities of exactas, trifectas, superfectas, the daily double, the pick-six, and wheeling the favorite with three long shots for a trifecta."

Every week he bought a racing form and circled names and numbers with a pen, studying the racing form late into the night, making notes on class, weight, Lasix, trainer, owner, and jockey. He told us he loved the rush of adrenaline most of all.

"The rush of adrenaline," he said. "All that adrenaline."

Even in our silence he kept talking.

"What can I do, fantasize? See myself sitting on a tropical patio and breathing clean ocean air while beautiful women bring me chips and salsa? Did you know I have nightmares of being shot in the head and then strung up by my legs like a dead deer dripping with blood?"

How strange it was to think he woke most mornings with an erection, even after those terrifying dreams, as if seeing these visions in his mind was a reminder that everything that had to do with his narcissism remained with no other retinue than his dream therapists, who told him to journal his dreams (which I've read), giving him a relief and comfort he'd needed; and yet here I was, as usual, suffering the horror shows of my mind's night fear.

As he knelt down, he hit the ground with the palm of his hand and said, "*Fah!*" which was all he needed to do in that moment, I suppose, for us to see how upset he was at himself, or maybe at the circumstances leading to where he was financially, or whatever the case was with my mom, but right after he said "*Fah! Fah!*" he opened his mouth and showed us his tongue, like a child after eating a popsicle, as strange as when he found out that I bought the bombs from the internet and a bunch of people at Nourie Hadig's garage party in Old Dublan placed the bombs on their tongues and began tripping, turning in terror and wiping their foreheads of the worms and lice that crawled from their scalps. The bombs were stamp-sized, on sour blotter paper, with the image of Pinocchio on one side and the other soaked in the liquified powder that eventually, sadly, killed some of my dope compadres in college before I dropped out, and left me feeling nothing but sadness and guilt.

"Silence is always better than the tongue," Walt's ghost said.

(b) Fear

Because my father told me about his nightmares and about the giant red leeches, stories that somehow morphed into something way grimmer than the Old Testament Bible stories he had read aloud to me when I was younger, I grew more and more afraid of him.

Because, too, these stories contained images of his narcissism and his fear of losing the power that had come to him over the years and evolved into a malicious battle over how much his ego was melting like ice dripping from the lampposts in the main square, watered down and breakable, images incapable of meaning or any kind of sufficient and stable logic, which was misfortunate and unhealthy, he told me, images full of doubts and representing his rustic instincts that he knew too well in those days.

Because my father admitted his own nightmares were exalted by the revelation that there was nothing we could do but celebrate Walt's life, and that life is too short to obsess over liver disease or high blood pressure, cancer, prostatitis, diabetes, syphilis, piles, tumors, or the tiny floating shapes we see, anything that creates a vulnerability to the world's evilness, because those anxieties quash any hope for healing from past trauma or feeling seized by nightmares designed by the devil to squeeze our skulls and choke us in the muddy atmosphere of our imaginations like the devil's own bloodless hand. The things that gave him comfort should give us all comfort: faith in God, allowing ourselves to partake in the joys of pleasure, reading spiritual and therapeutic books, and forgiving ourselves for our sins.

Because many years ago he told me the color red signified evil, and the devil, and blood, and Native Americans live on red earth, and like a schoolmaster taking you into a private room and showing you his red tongue before the rooster's crow, in early morning, taking advantage of you before you could ever look anyone in the eye, how you thought about a big red heart and

Valentine's Day candy being stepped on and crushed and then being forced to eat it, a red hand slapping you in the face, the schoolmaster pausing only to wipe his brow with his sleeve, and how after hearing all that, I never had the intention of looking in my father's eyes again without feeling empathy for him, yet why breathe all of this in my face, so that I could feel sorry for him and understand he wanted to die?

Because his recent nightmares, he told me, were less violent and abstract and more focused on a voluble ghostly presence who babbled in an unknown language as it led him by the hand into a castle and through a series of perplexing rooms, all of which had a single hole in the floor he was told to reach down into and feel for a snake, worried about whatever the consequence would be from the ghostly presence—"if it wasn't Walt's ghost, it was a different spirit," he said—and so reached down into the hole in each room and was bitten in the fleshy part of his hand between the forefinger and thumb, which frightened him enough to snap himself awake from the nightmare, making his nights unsettled and without restful sleep, and for a while the world around us remained in a perpetual state of flux.

Because he was a man I feared, even when he was outside trimming the rosebushes with the sun rising in the sky and the back deck overlooking the land sloping down to the river, where he liked to walk with the bookies any time he wanted to talk sports betting or card games that took place late nights in the basement of some fool's house, and even there he took pleasure in feeling he was not one of them, no sir, he was no lowlife, at least that's what he told himself, yet he sniffed out their games and strategies, their cheats and rules, all their players and coolers so that he knew the world surely wouldn't scold him compared to these fellows, it seemed obvious enough despite the immorality of it all, and, indeed, he confronted the most horrific weaknesses in himself anytime he worked in the garden, trimming rosebushes or shrubs or mowing the lawn, resigning himself to yardwork bearing up so many repressed illusions of his own augury, because he had become doomed to live a destiny all his own, in sin and forgiveness, in sickness and good health, to become the tightfisted, mean, furious, rapacious bastard my mom and I saw him grow to be; so I knew I'd better change the bedsheets and wash them before he came home and ripped the bedroom door off the hinges in anger.

Because I overheard my mom talking on the phone to her sister, saying that she had heard messages on my father's work answering machine from a bookie threatening to hunt him down unless he paid his debts as well as messages from someone named Vasilisa who had said things like "Where are you right now?" and "Can't wait to see you this afternoon," and my mom was practically crying into the phone while I stood outside the door in the hallway not knowing what to do except lean against the wall and stuff my hands in my pockets like the "town dunce," as my father would sometimes refer to me, unsure whether I should console my mom or leave, but when she abruptly opened the door and saw me standing there, I noticed the tears in her eyes and the wadded tissue in her hand, and she walked past me and headed out the back door to the patio, where she went sometimes whenever she needed to be alone, and from the window I watched her smoke a cigarette and start talking on the phone again, and I imagined her calling my father and telling him not to come home, insulting him with all kinds of names and telling him that he was no good for anything, a horrible husband and father and person for cheating; I could hear her say these things in my mind as I stood there and saw her pace back and forth while she talked on the phone, visibly upset.

Because, after that, I decided I would leave for a while and let whatever needed to happen work itself out, however terrifying, while scenes played out in my head of my father coming home and trying to explain his way out of the deception, and things would turn violent, which worried me because I knew both my parents had tempers that flared easily, and I was afraid of both whenever they became angry because my mom had grown accustomed to forgiving my father for making *errors* like staying out late or not calling and telling us where he was without understanding the direction of his mood swings and was disconcerted even more on the cloudy days when he removed his clothes and walked outside and down the road out back to the river, where he entered the water and put his head under until someone rushed in after him; how embarrassing for me because I didn't understand these mood swings either.

Because, as I walked down the street past the battered houses and unmown lawns, I thought about becoming a less sensitive person, whether that was good or bad, part of the totemic image of masculinity he tried to convey with an intense authority by saying I would face a life full of unpredictable and absurd circumstances that would likely only be resolved by confronting my own courage as I enlisted in the tumult of dire and sometimes life-and-death situations; think about it, son, he said, would we be too afraid to protect ourselves from the horrors and high commands of criminals and thieves and scam artists taking advantage of us, would we run like dunces flapping our hands and our fingers wet as petroleum, or would we keep our heads up, erect, in accordance with all principles of authority and vigor without so much as the glimmer of a smile, staying erect, with all the rancor and rage and concentration of a good marksman whose uniform is well ironed and whose overall manner and disposition is inculcated by the highest commanding officers, and further that my own inculcations were in progress and far from where they needed to be, at that time at least, as in the dumbly aberrant words of he whom I feared: "Before the first cockcrow already be in the mindset of a wild dog or boar before anyone takes advantage of you," which held all the hypocritical barbarism of any drooling maniac with as tentacular of an aggression as his.

Because I left the house and walked down the street, feeling as gloomy as ever, afraid of stepping on any line in the street since it would confirm the obsessive nature of my superstition that something awful was about to happen, at any moment, something that kept me from looking back at my house and wondering whether I might die today or tomorrow. I noticed my father's truck heading down the street toward me, so I stopped walking and waved a hand for him to see me as he passed, and as he drove by, I noticed that the person driving the truck was not my father at all—it was a big white wolf, both paws on the steering wheel, red tongue hanging out.

(c) Aftermath

In the aftermath of Walt's death, while I tried to remain in my privacy among the many relatives overflowing the house, all the first and second cousins, the aunts and uncles, the great-aunts and great-uncles, the struggle to renounce the insatiable torture of recurring images in my mind of Walt stabbing himself in the chest with a butcher knife, Elliott Smith–style, and the look of horror on his face as he collapsed to the kitchen floor, and how my mom's hands must have trembled as she called an ambulance with blood spreading in front of her, that conflict managed to accumulate more strength than I could take, and I sat in an armchair in the back bedroom convinced that if I fell asleep, I would likely suffer a stroke or a heart attack, a devastating and ridiculous thought, yet I felt drastic decisions were about to be made concerning my welfare because there was the matter that I had provoked him to self-harm and violence for years, unbeknownst to me as I hid from everyone. I hoped this was not true but rather some dark spirit whispering to me to take my own life in retaliation to venerate a failure and prove an ascesis to dealing with life. I had done nothing any brother hadn't done in the past to a sibling, be it the occasional ribbing or mere mind.

The night of Walt's funeral, my cousin Trusty John Alberich and I smoked weed in the alley behind his house. We got high and talked about Walt as if he were still alive because it felt like he hadn't died, but it was our first real loss, wasn't it, and such an aching stupor.

10 (HUMILITY)

The real story, having nothing to do with violence, involved an impassive urge to acquire cash so that we could split the cost of a Nintendo game console because neither of us was able to hold a part-time job mowing grass or slinging fast food or doing anything that involved physical labor. Trusty John and I were the same age and in no way interested in hurting anyone, even though John was more mischievous than I. His nickname, "Trusty," was coined by a friend of his father's because of his constantly lying and getting into trouble. Like me, he began getting bullied by Bucktooth and Badger once we entered high school. I watched him get pummeled once after school in the alley behind the woodshop building, where they dragged him by his arms across the gravel and then began punching and slapping him in the stomach so hard one could hear Trusty John screaming all the way to the train tracks. They tortured Matthew as well, grabbing his wrists and twisting his arm behind his back until he fell to his knees. I could see Matthew's quivering eyes while his cry rang throughout the hallway as people hurried to class, and that was only the beginning. They slammed kids into lockers. They dragged kids into the bathroom and trapped them in stalls. They walked down rows in the gymnasium during pep rallies, frightening students with their fists and brass knuckles and pocketknives, threatening violence and death, they really did, even hiding in locker rooms and behind school buildings, waiting for their next target.

Trusty John and I smoked weed regularly at lunch behind the bus barn, tied to that dismal area by the threads of sorrow and victimhood, and used it as a hiding place until the fourth-period bell rang. We bought a baggie from my cousin, Mark—John's older brother—who had gotten it from a guy Mark claimed kept pet snakes in a dirty terrarium without a cover so that they could escape and slither around the house at night to eat mice. One afternoon John and I sat with my aunt Marjorie in her living room while waiting for Mark to return with the baggie when she told us she'd quit her job at Value Mart and would be selling her car for money until she found another job since she'd been divorced from my uncle and was straining to pay bills on time. I was suffering from spring allergies, so Aunt Marjorie gave me a Benadryl to take, and somehow we got on the discussion of drowsiness and insomnia and sleeping pills.

"Benadryl helps me fall asleep," Aunt Marjorie told me. "I once took four of them with a sleeping pill and slept for thirteen hours straight. I woke in the middle of the night hallucinating. I thought I saw a snake crawl across the floor."

"Miracle you didn't die."

"I thought I'd overdosed."

She took a deep breath and half smiled, as if knowing something I didn't.

"I have nightmares about snakes," I said. "A snake attacks me and clamps its jaws on the fleshy area between my thumb and finger. The pain wakes me up. You won't believe the fear."

"I know the fear," she said.

Trusty John was crouched behind the TV, trying to figure out why the VCR wasn't working. *The Joker's Wild* was on, which Aunt Marjorie always watched, but Trusty John kept unplugging cords and wires and turning the TV on and off. Aunt Marjorie watched him for a while until we heard Mark's car pull into the drive outside.

"Mark's home," Trusty John said, struggling to get up.

I went outside with him to meet Mark, who led us to the side of the house so Marjorie wouldn't see us pay him for the baggie of marijuana. Trusty John made sure to put the baggie in his coat pocket, and we walked down to the 7-Eleven to meet Badger and a couple of other guys.

They weren't there when we arrived, so we sat on the curb of the parking lot and waited for them. After fifteen minutes we wondered whether they would show up at all because they were taking forever. I had some change for the pay phone so that Trusty John could call them, but just as I was digging into my pocket for the change, Badger rode up on his bike. He looked worn. His jacket was frayed at the collar and on the sleeves, and his hair was unkempt, like he'd just crawled out of bed.

"I only got a ten," he said. "But I brought a rolling paper. Is that enough for a joint?"

"You only got ten bucks?" Trusty John said. "Where are the other guys?"

"Dale is eating supper and Shorty's dad made him clean the bathroom, so it's just me. We'll bring the rest of the money to school tomorrow."

Trusty John burst into wild laughter. "You only got a ten? Okay, fine, one joint, but you have to let me roll it."

"Fine," Badger said, looking around.

We were all paranoid, despite not having smoked, and a few people were going in and out of the store. I couldn't bear the sight of Badger while John stepped around the corner and rolled the joint. Eye contact was never my thing, and certainly not with a fool like him, that bully who smelled like a goat. He saw me as weak, some leptosome he could inflict physical and emotional pain onto, but none of that mattered to him. His mannerisms were always inimical toward me, especially away from school, and standing near him I wondered whether his indigent homelife reflected his jealousy toward me because I lived in a better part of town. I knew very little about him or his family, except for assuming he likely came from a destitute and troubled home, and that he smelled awful and wore ratty sneakers and clothes. While we waited for John to roll the joint, he began whistling what sounded like an imitation of a police or ambulance siren, probably trying to get a reaction out of me. I was kneeling at my bike, pretending to fiddle with the chain, when John finally came back around the corner with the joint.

"Ten bucks," John said, and Badger handed him two fives.

"It better do the job," Badger told us, and John burst into wild and caustic laughter, which seemed to grind Badger's gears enough that I could see his face change in a way I found hedonistically pleasing.

"Bring more money tomorrow if you want more," John said. "We'll bring the baggie."

Nobody thanked anyone. Badger spat on the ground and put the joint in his front pocket. We watched him ride away, down the street.

At school the next day, between classes John and I divided the pot into two baggies in a bathroom stall to make it less conspicuous so that all four or five of us wouldn't get caught: schools looked for groups that equaled trouble, and if we could sell the baggies in the bathroom or at the locker in the hallway, we could do it quickly without attracting attention. There were no cameras or security in schools in the late 1980s—about the only significant problems were drugs or fights that happened at lunch or after school or, occasionally, in a classroom, but nobody was walking into the school and shooting people back then. How times have changed.

I planned to meet Bucktooth at my locker after fifth hour in the afternoon. After the fourth-hour bell sounded and we were released, I headed upstairs to the hallway and found the principal standing beside my locker. I stopped walking and considered turning to make a run for it, but he saw me and called out my name. Everyone was just standing around in the hallway, watching. He led me downstairs to his office, where Trusty John was already sitting. He looked up at me as we entered and gave me a look I knew too well. We were caught. The principal called the police and said we were in big trouble.

That afternoon Trusty John and I were arrested for distribution of a controlled substance. I couldn't understand all the commotion. I mean, it's not like I threatened to shoot anyone or anything. We never hurt anybody, never even made a threat. All I did was try to sell a small baggie of marijuana.

3. THE VISION

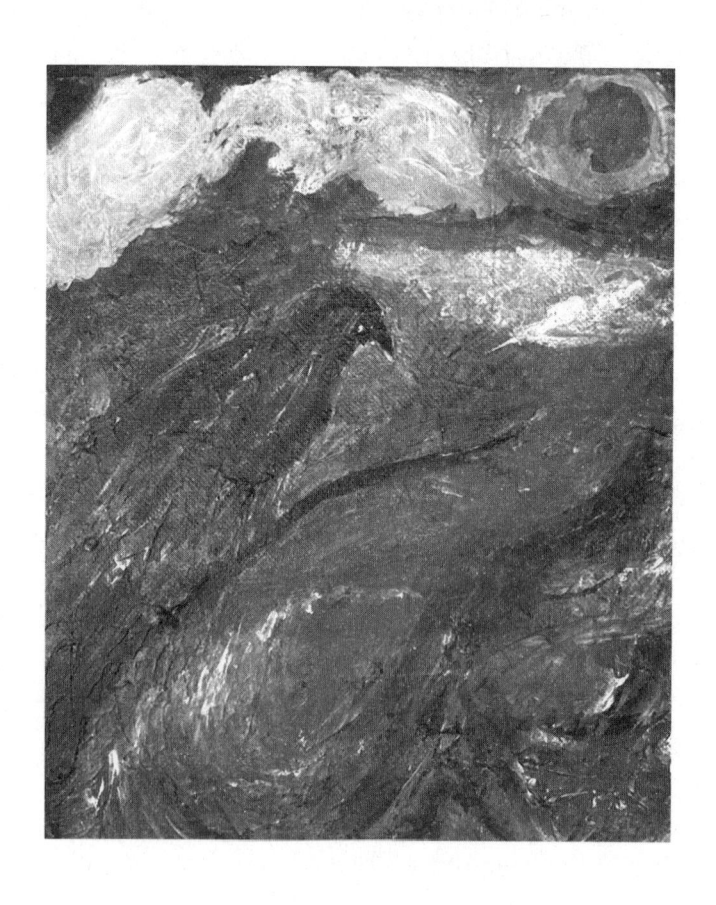

By dint of exposure to the brutal and barbarous methods of discipline, work, and being held captive by the abhorrent juvenile authorities whom I described and embellished in *The Devil Is a Southpaw*, my angry and disturbed novel, and having spent time in solitude in a dirty cell with an unworking toilet and rust and dead insects, I returned home to an uncannily quiet environment with my parents, who never lent an attentive and faithful ear any time I wanted to talk about the nine days that besieged me in lockup. Father, I returned home from those crippling days in juvenile detention feeling like a different person, more anxious and afraid than ever before. After thinking back for a fleeting instant on my time there, the way I remember it, it was like being gagged in a straitjacket. Even though the events were slightly embellished and there was no plague of frogs, the violent storm I recall delivered hail the size of baseballs, and my fear often arose from the clamor of guards yelling and slamming doors, all of which left me constantly desiring silence. Upon returning home, my probation officer had me see a drug and alcohol counselor weekly and perform a urinalysis twice a week to show I was staying clean. One failed test and I would be sent to rehab, my probation officer threatened; therefore, I kept clean, stayed home, and focused on my art and writing and schoolwork.

Trusty John called me one night and said he would be taking his third drug test and had failed them all, and that he was likely going to be sent away to rehab for a six-month program after his court appearance.

"I'm in big trouble," he told me on the phone.

"You're worried?"

"I don't want to go to rehab. I can't handle it."

"Maybe you can fake it and pass the U.A.," I told him. "Maybe find someone at school. Get a vial of someone's who'll piss clean."

"Like who?"

"I don't know."

"Me either."

Having spent those days trying to learn how to forgive of errors and let go of all my anger, I was then placed back in public school but struggled because the school put me in a room with six other boys, including Bucktooth and Badger, who weren't able to function in a traditional or "normal" classroom setting, with or without criminal records, the seven of us having fallen behind in schoolwork; the teacher distributed worksheets and markers for us to color and label drawings of countries, state capitals, and oceans. Draw California. Color Lake Michigan. Draw your family on vacation. Stop staring out the window and color within the lines. Try to use different colored markers. What do you see? Talk whenever you feel like talking or just blink twice if you understand what I'm saying. Nod your head like this; look at me, guys; stop staring with your mouths open and give me your full attention. Simon says raise your right arm, not your left arm, look at me and blink, don't stomp your foot, Simon says stop, raise your left arm now, no, your right arm, I mean Simon says stop everyone and look at me and blink. Stop staring out the window, guys.

Matthew was put in this class as well, despite being a favorite of the teachers. The stories he wrote in class came out of stories he had heard from relatives as a child. I once asked him why he was interested in rewriting those stories since our assignments were to create our own fictions or poems, and to be honest, he looked at me and shook his head in disbelief, as if I were the town dunce. I watched him continue to write. I studied him. His right hand held a tremor as he wrote with his left, sadly, from a condition I mused aloud must certainly have been possibly the earliest stage of Parkinson's disease, if not some other neurological condition he would need to get looked at soon, but he waved me off and dismissed me as bothersome.

Other times, my Lord, I caught him staring at me.

In the classroom, the teachers projected slides and images on a screen that showed bodies and mouths with letters coming out of the mouths to form words, but of course we could already understand everything spoken, even though the teachers seemed to think we were illiterate and dumb; honestly, they didn't even need to say that because we could tell that's what they were thinking, but the joke was on them because the rest of us were silent, and as a result school was easy in comparison to where we had been; we looked at each other and saluted the teachers, bowed in gratitude, all of us knowing quite well the teachers were struggling to understand us and try to make sense of what had happened at juvie or why we were failing everything, and how far behind we were from the other kids. The joke was on them.

We played basketball and ran sprints during physical education class with big-bellied coaches with whistles around their thick necks. They hauled us on an old yellow school bus and drove us out to the prairie lands, where we played flag football and laughed about how we fooled the fools while the P.E. teacher sat in the bus and read the sports page in the local newspaper and, like the sergeants at juvie, sipped vodka from a flask, thinking nobody knew, yet some of the guys had taken photos with Polaroid cameras when he wasn't aware, just in case they ever needed to use it for blackmail. But then something changed in us after the fun at the school faded and we realized the significance of what had happened to us.

I spent nights even after I returned home from juvenile detention trying to keep clean and sober but thinking only of Matthew and Cakae—and wondering whether Cakae was more worried about him or me: "It's not a competition," she once told me in a note. "I loved you, but things change. People change, Milton. Sorry."

I will spare the boring and grotesque details of the years immediately following high school graduation, except to say that I enrolled in a public university and dropped out due to substance abuse and mental health issues. To be honest, I was still sad about my brother's suicide, my parents' divorce, and how my father had remarried a woman he had met at an Oklahoma casino. For as long as I can remember, I've been obsessive about trying to put others' happiness before my own. Does it make me a selfish person? Because I'm sorry if I ever hurt anyone over those difficult years. It took ages for me to overcome the torment I endured, from losing Cakae to being locked up and on probation.

Those years I had trouble keeping jobs and soon found myself staying with friends for as long as they would let me. For a while I worked in a movie theater at the concession stand and then swept the aisles and picked up trash before we closed. I got high a lot before going to that job, and people could tell, so they fired me. I watched movies every night on cable in my crummy little apartment and read many European novels.

I was plagued by guilt and insomnia and averaged three or four hours of sleep each night, mostly due to the stress and sadness I had put myself and my family through. Eventually, I went to rehab for a substance abuse disorder and mental health treatment. The other residents were also there for lying to themselves and to others, for shooting dope or gambling or attempting suicide. Our counselor, Vaughn, was sixty-six and from somewhere in Arizona, where he did a few years in the penitentiary for fraud. He lost his business from gambling and his marriage collapsed.

At the treatment center, the program kept us on a strict schedule. We woke up every morning at 6:30. Breakfast was from 7:00 to 8:00. We ate all our meals together at the tables in the commons room. The entire day consisted of individual and group sessions. Money-management issues, working the Twelve Steps to recovery, setting goals. There were twenty of us. We helped one another think about our triggers, acceptance and denial. Whom we blamed if not ourselves. Why we lied to loved ones. Why we couldn't stop using. In free time we smoked or played basketball in the gym, but we couldn't wear sports T-shirts or caps. There were no watches or necklaces or expensive jewelry. No laptops, iPads, phones, radios, or any electronic device. We had to rid ourselves of any temptations or distractions during our recovery to successfully complete the program. We did laundry. We read our daily affirmations and recovery guides. We read spy novels. Eventually, I completed the program and returned home to be alone. I decided to leave the country as a reparation and try to reexamine my life.

Before I arrived at the Gardens, I visited an island in the Atlantic, sat under a banana tree, and ate fruit mousse and crepes for breakfast. I spent my nights reading about saints and listening to music so beautiful I sobbed into my glass. I sat by waterfalls and drank poncha and ginja, enjoyed a smoke, and swam in the salty sea.

Today I am here in the Gardens, surrounded by streams, willow trees, shrubbery, and casitas festooned with greenery. Terraces overlook the ocean in the distance, where sailors sing to their lovers they left behind on some island. I've collected baubles of broken stained-glass resembling the gallstones I had removed and hang them on my walls and front door. The sun, a priceless gift, sits on the horizon like a red moon and reflects on the water, which is inspiring for my work, my paintings and photography, and is also a remarkable place to succumb to the dazzle of solitude and nature, eat ripe bananas, and peel the hairy skin from a malanga before biting into its earthy flavor, indeed, all this among an uproar of wild monkeys hanging from trees and birds flying around. Had I ended up in some loony bin, I would find myself in misery and sadness, certainly contemplating death. You can understand the imagination's willingness to elaborate. You can feel the absence of pain and longing for lost love here. As Poe wrote in a letter in 1849, "I was never really insane except upon occasions when my heart was touched."

◀

Low-hanging clouds race above in late afternoons when the humidity is so thick it creates a weary monotony that covers the Earth like the endless sea. Oh Lord, is there nobody here to test my patience, vigilance, or artistry, not even the staff or tourists who visit? If anyone visits, I do whatever I can to help them. Some have requested my help with writing or painting. An ROTC student wearing loose khaki shorts and boots came to me for help. He was vacationing from a recent divorce and needed time and help writing a memo to his commanding officer about two future areas of employment in the military that he would be interested in considering for a career. The student didn't have the assignment or a draft of the memo with him, so we discussed reasons why he would choose a career in the military when such a decision felt steeped in uncertainty, suspense, and danger, and he told me he was fascinated with three areas—missiles, becoming an officer, and war—even after I tried to convince him that he could very well find himself extinguished in the last breath of dying men and suffering from hallucinatory visions of, say, tree branches as rifles, and that he might find himself bowing to the commanders before him who force their senile tantrums and claws into him. He would die bleary from exhaustion or thirst, surely. What good is war? Are we not created to love one another? How do we see suffering as a gift? The student sneezed into his fist and looked despondent, asking me what steps he needed to take. The question was too perplexing for me at 7:15 on a humid Friday afternoon. Time ridiculed me. Time took the form of paranoia, war, survival. What kind of buffoon was I, thinking I could help this soldier? Later, when I went to his yurt, I found it deserted.

◀

Not long ago I was delighted to find in the mailbox an oversized envelope with no return address. To my surprise, it was part of an unpublished story written by Matthew. How he found me, I have no clue. Perhaps I had mentioned coming here in one of the many letters I'd written him. For a few years I wrote him weekly—long, prolix letters about our childhood, school, detention, and how Cakae still appears in my dreams. I told him about my art. So to find a letter from him gave me great joy. I put aside everything here in my room to give my full attention to it. I have included the fragment here:

Everything and Nothing

M— lives alone, lonely as any person who rarely ventures out of the house. In recent years, in this time of loneliness, whenever the sounds of owls or the snapping of twigs outside his window caused a panic that had him peeking out the curtains, he realizes he is not quite himself anymore. Maybe it's low-grade depression. He spends whole afternoons watching it rain. He has tried painting but feels no inspiration, resorting instead to smoking his hash pipe and sketching cobbled streets, ghosts, and old buildings with deteriorating structures and broken windows, sad clown faces, all images of despair.

He is awakened one night by an intruder. Afraid, he slinks down the hall to discover, in the darkened room, a man lying on the floor. The man is either drunk or suffers from a severe head trauma, because it takes M— forever to wake him.

When the man finally opens his eyes, he looks afraid: "I woke on the riverbank," he says.

The man notices the fresh blood on his arm then touches the side of his head. M— leans in and tries to get a better look. The man's hair is thin and wet, and when M— touches his head, the man flinches, one hand shielding his eyes.

The poor man, washed up on the riverbank, condemned to freezing in the cold rain and breathing the poisoned air, with the fatal look of someone suffering and close to dying, crouching under trees and covered porches of strange houses, hiding in deserted shacks.

M— tells him, "I'll help you until you feel better."

The man's chest heaves as he takes another deep breath. He removes his hand from his face so that M— can see his eyes more clearly, revealing a resemblance to someone from his childhood from so many years ago, a face he has tried forever to convey in paintings and drawings, years of work piled in the attic. The palms of the man's hands hold scars from what looks like burns, open wounds, and M— considers going to the kitchen for annatto seeds his neighbor from Bogota had given him so that he can rub them on the man's hands for healing, but now he is afraid to leave him there alone.

"You look familiar" M— says. "What's your name?"

The man leans forward and puts his head in his hands, breathing heavy, and when he looks up, his eyes are watery.

"What's your name?" he asks again.

"What's your name," the man says.

"You don't remember your name?"

The man doesn't respond. His head injury is worse than M— thought. Amnesia, certainly.

M— hurries into the kitchen to fill a glass of water. He stops in the bathroom and opens the medicine cabinet for a bottle of rubbing alcohol and a rag. When he returns to the hall, he dabs the alcohol on the man's bloody arm.

The lights flicker, but the electricity remains on. The man's face is soft in the tenuous glow of the lamplight.

The man closes his eyes and in minutes is fast asleep. As he sleeps, his breathing is long and deep. But M— is unable to fall back asleep and certainly not ready to leave him alone on the couch while he goes back to bed. Maybe he really has been delivered without a single understanding of the world around him, his memory erased and wiped clean from its past. Maybe it's possible to put his thoughts back again slowly, together, the two of them working through the language of storytelling to see whether any memories return.

Shortly before daybreak, M— is still unable to tell whether the head injury is serious enough to go to the hospital. While the man slept, M— leaned in and lightly ruffled his hair to try to get a better look for any blood, but he couldn't see anything. M— took the man's boots outside and turned on the back porch light. With a putty knife he scraped the hard mud from the heels and around the toes of both boots, then he wiped them down with a rag and took them back into the living room. By this time the sun had risen and flooded the room with morning light.

He thinks of his former love, that beauty, sitting with witches holding dead chickens and drinking the blood of pigs and cows and then vomiting out the blood riddled with some ancient language—such witchcraft existed in his mind because his lover had once told him his pain and emotional turmoil had been cured by meeting the witches of Raven in the woods and drinking animal urine and all other sorts of witchery ingredients from a glass full of yellow leaves. In these fantasies he rose out of a mist covered in the demonized blanket the witches had given him to help him memorize the spell and curse whenever he wrapped himself in it, this blanket, and no matter how much logic M— used to battle the fantasies, he was never able to escape his words his lover had spoken, very plainly: "The witches helped me."

Watching the man sleep now, M— looks for any signs of restlessness or disturbed dreams—but he lay motionless, giving deep, slow breaths, so peaceful he was that M— imagines, fantasizes really, that they are taking in the cool fall breezes on a beach somewhere, M— in his beach hat, tossing handfuls of sand on the man's back, and the man in his swim trunks and sunglasses, stretched out on a beach towel, both of them thinking, How strange and mysterious the world really is, isn't it, while they hear the distant sound of music and cheering from a wedding celebration way down on the beach. Years before, when his ex-lover had confessed her attraction in the ecstasy of a July night, he felt appreciated by the moon as the radiant rain came down on them, both of them barely breathing in the heat and vapor until he carried her away, and as she now thought of that great scandal in her memory she began to describe it in careful detail to the man as he slept, even from the beginning. Had I known of your loneliness I would have left my solitude and gone to visit you because I was sad, too. Why did we go so long without speaking? Now he sits on the edge of the bed and tells the whole story as if the man is awake and listening, hanging on to each word and staring at his hands until the man stirs and mutters something in his sleep.

In the kitchen he finds a can of broth in the pantry, pours it into a saucepan, and lets it sit on the stove for a few minutes, thinking about his solitude and loneliness, sleeping for hours and then waking to go out back into the shed full of random pieces of wood and bottles of glue and a portable radio playing, hoping to work on a woodworking project, or a painting, escaping to isolation.

Now he pours a glass of water, and as he stirs the soup he hears the front door open. He hurries out of the kitchen and sees the man stepping off the front porch. M— steps outside just as the man stops to remove his clothes.

"Matthew?" M— calls to him.

The man leaves his clothes on the ground and sits down in the yard, looking up to the sky.

The story remains unfinished. I see a call for help, but why to me, and for that matter, why did Cakae fall in love with the man who wrote this? Was it his art, or his culture, or his mind? Was it the illusion of his bashfulness or his irreverence toward me and the non-Native authorities at school? His ineluctable sense of humor? Nevertheless, everything worked out for him. He became well known and I did not, and I'm the one suffering from a lack of humility. He disappeared from the public as silently as a drop of rain into the endless sea. In a sense, I have, too. I shouldn't dwell on his success or any of his accomplishments. (Don't you understand that after all these years, you fool, that he worked hard while you led a life of struggle and sin?) It's my nature, like the scorpion who convinces the frog he won't sting him but then does. He can't help it; I can't either, but I can tell myself I'm doing better, that there is hope here by the ocean, the vast and endless sea, living a new and hopefully whole holistic holy life as a serious artist should, in solitude and serenity. O' Lord, to rest. To live without fear, to decide my fate as I trudge into the sea and stare into the dreamy mists of blue water.

Because I have spent my entire life suffering in the torments of the cardinal sins of pride and envy, I have resigned myself to stay here, in asceticism, where I live day by day. To pass time I read and write unstutterably bad poetry, study the mystics and saints, and try to see the beauty in the natural world. I throw old baseballs into the air and catch them with my bare hands. At night I shed my clothes, stand before the mirage of sea, and pronounce a destiny to the journey of all things created, stones and rivers, trees and birds, moon and stars, and the unwonted munificence of hope. Here on this desolate land near the water, what else is there but hope?

Tell me: What else is there?

Like the blind and crippled swarming the Jordan River to touch the water that baptized Christ, do I empty the sea, one thimble at a time, until I can begin to understand the treasures of the living and the dead? Do I call myself Lazarus because of my rebirth, pleading for help in a bitter and terrifying voice, kissing the feet of the sanctified visitors, and dealing with temptation by rolling around in the thorny bushes like Saint Francis of Assisi? Listen: I have seen visions of Saint Elizabeth of Portugal, who struggled with jealousy; and Caravaggio, smoking and walking across the sand with his lover. I have seen lions claw into the earth and dig a grave deep enough for a human body. I am happy here in solitude.

Last week, someone new arrived. From what I gather, he is an elderly man traveling alone, wearing his crimson robe. His body is thin and frail, and his hair is gray and shoulder-length, and his feet, I imagine, must be as coarse as the road, full of calluses. What an interesting old fellow he is. Every morning a raven drops a loaf of bread for him, which he picks up and eats as he walks near the ocean. From my garden, amid the gnats and air heavy with humidity, I watch him with a kind of drowsy deliriousness and think maybe I will join him by the water, where we will break the bread the raven drops and, under an eclipse of white moths, eat in the manner of saints.

I hope to meet him soon.

ACKNOWLEDGMENTS

Thank you to the John W. Simon Guggenheim Foundation, Bill Clegg, Deb Unferth, Stewart O'Nan, Brad Morrow, Connie Voisine, the Cherokee Nation Tribe, the Institute of American Indian Arts, New Mexico State University, Carissa Samaniego, Phil Hurst, Aaron Strumwasser, ZzZ, Gabriella Doob, and everyone else at Ecco/HarperCollins.